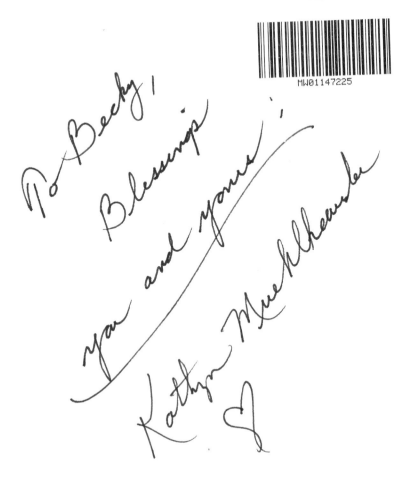

To Becky!
Blessings
you and yours

Kathryn Muehlbauer ♡

TRILOGY

of the

MAGI

KATHRYN MUEHLHEAUSLER

WESTBOW
PRESS®
A DIVISION OF THOMAS NELSON
& ZONDERVAN

WestBow Press books may be ordered through booksellers or by contacting:

WestBow Press
A Division of Thomas Nelson & Zondervan
1663 Liberty Drive
Bloomington, IN 47403
www.westbowpress.com
844-714-3454

Scripture quotations marked (JB) are taken from the JERUSALEM BIBLE Copyright© 1966, 1967, 1968 by Darton, Longmand & Todd LTD and Doubleday and Co. Inc. All rights reserved.

ISBN: 978-1-6642-8849-2 (sc)
ISBN: 978-1-6642-8851-5 (hc)
ISBN: 978-1-6642-8850-8 (e)

Library of Congress Control Number: 2023900191

Printed in United States of America.

WestBow Press rev. date: 02/23/2023

ACKNOWLEDGMENTS

How blest have I been during the writing and publishing efforts of this book. I thank my sons, Bret and Nick, for their expertise and support. I thank my sisters and friends for their editing, suggestions, and patience. I thank God that my prayers were answered—often in extraordinarily timely ways.

CONTENTS

Melchior's Book

Balthazar's Book

Gaspar's Book

MELCHIOR'S BOOK

A Prophecy

Near Rome, Italy, December 25,
circa 4–1 BCE

Augustus Caesar reined in his high-spirited mount as he approached the falls of the Aniene River, where he hoped to find and question the sibyl about what lay ahead for him. Waking even before the sun rose on this late December morning, he had decided that he would test his fate this day. On leaving his estate in the Roman Campagna, where he currently resided outside the city of Tibur, he had given orders that no one was to accompany him from his home. Those orders would be obeyed since he was indisputably the most important person in Rome, which meant that up to this day, he was the most important person in the world.

Gathering his red cloak closer around him, he withstood a brisk gust of wind off the river. Straightening in his saddle, he reflected on his life up to this unique point, which had brought him to his current pinnacle of success. This was the true purpose of his visit to the prophetess—what would be his final fate?

In a bit of reverie, he considered with a degree of satisfaction the mostly fortuitous events of his life that had changed dramatically when his powerful maternal great-uncle Julius Caesar had named him heir. Long ago, however, the Roman leader had vowed to avoid a similar destiny from his uncle's brutal assassination. He had no intention of his life ending in a pool of blood on the Senate floor. Hence, his purpose this day was to determine if he should accept the rumored honor the Republic's Senate seemed about to confer on him.

Nudging his white stallion forward, Augustus moved toward the Tiburtine Falls where the sibyl lived. Another gust of wind tore his cloak loose, and as it waved in the misty air from the waters of the falls, he laughed aloud. Feeling powerful and invincible, he cantered forward to embrace the future. Godlike was a term he deemed could easily be applied to him. No man on this earth could rival his achievements and the glory that was his—and would be his in the years to come, if he had read the signs correctly.

Through his mind flitted other times when prophets had been aware of his family's destiny. The prediction of the day of his Uncle Julius' death on the Ides of March was such an event. His own destiny had been marked out by the seer Nigidius Figulus, who had told his father that his son would be the master of the world—at least, in so many words. As a young man, when he was still known as Octavian, he had consulted the sage Theogenes, who had foretold his ascent to imperial power. Flames had burst forth in other predictions related to his future—flames such as were said to only have occurred over the destiny of Alexander the Great, three hundred years earlier.

Cresting a slight rise in the land, suddenly Augustus reined in his fidgeting steed, jerking his mount to a standstill. He gazed forward to a cave where a woman in wispy gray garments stood—as if awaiting him. Almost impossibly, a ripple of fear seized the emperor of Rome. In childlike obedience, with no word spoken, he dismounted and bowed to the oracle. She beckoned him forward with a slight hand movement. He threw off his momentary anxiety and moved toward the still, almost gaunt figure. As he was about to speak, she raised her hand to forestall his words.

"I knew you would come this day." Her raspy voice and tone of prophecy both chilled and excited Augustus.

At his raised eyebrow and look of inquiry, she stated, "You too feel the prophetic nature of this day."

Silence reigned as she said no more. Encouraged by her words that this would indeed be a day of destiny, he boldly asked the central questions he desired to have answered: "Is anyone greater than me? Will I take my place among the gods?"

The Tiburtine sibyl gazed at him at length. In a dispassionate voice, she proclaimed, "Until a virgin gives birth to a child and yet remains a virgin—"

Suddenly, the sibyl halted and peered eastward to the distant dawn sky, followed by Augustus Caesar's own look of awe as a magnificent starlike object shot across the heavens. She intoned, "Look! A sign of the future is revealed to you! One world is ending, and another is beginning. Ah—the king of future millennia, the true God of the world. His divinity is unrealized."

She paused but continued to stare upward, as if she too were mesmerized by her own enigmatic words of prophecy. Then she slowly and solemnly prophesied, "I see him victor in the end over death. He will reunite all nations."

In the years that followed, the greatest of all Caesars honored the sibyl's prophecy that he undeniably knew applied to him. Rejuvenated in spirit, he felt that, as before in his life when renamed Augustus, he had been born anew. Interpreting the prophetess's words to fit his circumstances, he erected a lasting legacy, calling it the *Ara Primogeniti Dei*—"Altar to the Firstborn of God." Deified by all of Rome, Augustus Caesar quite naturally interpreted the sibyl's fateful words favorably—for it was clearly impossible that a virgin could give birth to a child and yet still remain a virgin.

CHAPTER 1

The Rise of Herod

Rome, circa 40 BCE

Mark Antony speculatively peered at the two younger men seated near him. His new brother-in-law Octavian, at age twenty-three, was advising the thirty-three-year-old Idumean Herod that on the morrow, he should offer sacrifices to the Roman god Jupiter. A public ceremony was essential to give homage to this godhead for the honor the Senate was about to confer.

Antony had known Herod for almost two decades. He knew the younger man to be a crafty individual who always managed to wind up on the winning side in any political situation. Unfortunately—or fortunately—Rome's far-flung empire required just such men of vision and cunning to run the various client kingdoms. Men like Herod could be counted on to back the might of Rome and her policies that would, in turn, keep them on their thrones as well.

Between Octavian and him, they had engineered the bestowal of the crown of Judea, Galilee, and Perea on Herod, which would be conferred two days hence. Having the Eastern provinces in hand, with the king beholden to Rome for his title, would help ensure peace in that troublesome part of the world.

Taking a sip of wine, Antony wondered if Herod would turn a cold shoulder on his religious Judean heritage and embrace Jupiter as the all-powerful father of the legion of Roman gods. How would Herod reconcile what Antony, and most of the world, considered the total absurdity of honoring a single deity—as the Jews did—with the current need to show his allegiance to all things Roman? After all, the gods had to be thanked for every fortuitous event, much less placated for the calamitous ones. Watching Herod honor the Roman pantheon of gods was going to be a fascinating juggling act that Antony would be both interested and entertained to observe.

Octavian glanced at Mark Antony and, in his usual perception of events, seemed to mock his brother-in-law's thoughts. "Herod, through your father, Antipater, who was named a Roman citizen several years ago, you have not only inherited his mantle of leadership, but in your own right, you have held several titles, including your current one of being the Governor of Judea. Your father embraced Roman customs and accepted our ways. You would do well to follow in his footsteps."

Herod gazed briefly at Antony, who had been his mentor long before his father had been poisoned three years earlier. Obsequiously, he said, "Octavian, your words are wise. I thank you for this advice and will certainly follow your counsel. Because this is my first trip to Rome, what would be an appropriate sacrifice?"

Octavian noted the correct offering. "Jupiter is acceptably revered with the sacrifice of a fine young heifer when a high honor is received."

Antony threw in his own bit of irony, which also could be construed as a test of Herod's true loyalty—either to

Rome or to his Jewish God. "You should purchase at least three heifers in case the priests discover an ill omen in the intestines of the first—or even the second." As his foreign guest digested this news, Antony seemed to carelessly add, "It is best to have a pig on hand too, in case there is a problem with the first sacrifice. The priests will usually sacrifice the pig to atone for the heifer's ill-omened innards."

Disregarding the Jewish religion's well-known disavowal of pork, Octavian casually remarked, "All the meats can be used for the traditional feast held afterward. The temple priests will oversee the prayers and details of the rituals."

Herod swallowed hard, visualizing the cost of these traditions to ensure his kingship—not to mention the religious issues quickly cropping up, one after another. "Whatever needs to be done will be done."

Dismissing the rituals, Octavian blithely concluded, "These events usually go smoothly, though they are bloody affairs. However, there would be little sense in offending the gods who must be honored—trouble could follow. In your case, you do not want to offend mighty Jupiter himself."

Herod knew it would behoove him to respond to this masked order to honor Jupiter. Even more so, he needed to express his gratitude to both Mark Antony and Octavian for their support. "I am grateful to you, my earthly Roman protectors, as well as to the gods. Octavian, your help has been above and beyond what I hoped for when I left Jerusalem to plead my case. In escaping the perils of the war between mighty Rome and the Parthians, I hoped you would hear my pleas." Turning to the slightly older man, he both thanked and cajoled in the same calculated speech. "Mark Antony, you have my thanks for your current help.

In addition, it will be through your military might that I will be able to return to Jerusalem."

Antony inclined his head and raised his goblet to Herod. Before he could speak, however, Octavian took the lead again. "While you are here in Rome, Herod, I want you to make the acquaintance of the Assyrian trade contingent. Their purpose is to try to reestablish some of the past glory of their land. Historically, the decline of the Assyrian Empire, centuries ago, dovetails with the rise of your own Israelite leaders, David and his son, Solomon. But at this time, I would like to see cooperation between you diverse peoples. Commerce links our modern world; there is much to be gained through such relationships. Among your duties as the new Judean king and for your other Palestinian regions will be the task to generate alliances of this nature."

Octavian meant his comments to be as dictatorial as he hoped they sounded. Nonetheless, he threw in a question to Herod to ease his command. "Do you see the logic of such alliances?"

"I agree with you. I will make certain I meet with these Assyrians."

In a loquacious mood now, Octavian laughed. "Perhaps you should send them an invitation to the feast you are giving, which includes your offering to Jupiter."

Antony mockingly countered, "If I understand your thinking, you propose that the Jewish God be a bystander, along with the Assyrian godhead, Ashur, in this holy ceremony honoring our all-powerful Jupiter?"

Octavian took Antony's words as an insult to his leadership abilities. Although they were co-leaders, each in his own right in the Second Triumvirate—along with the absent Lepidus—this was another example of their not seeing eye to eye. Coldly, he addressed his sister's new husband, refusing to back down. "Political and trade alliances cross religious boundaries, as you would do well to remember." Piercing deeper, Octavian scathingly added, "You had no problems in Egypt allowing Cleopatra to be worshipped as a goddess herself!"

Antony raised his wine goblet toward Octavian in a salute to the successful thrust. Preferring not to rise to the bait and attempting to keep things peaceful, he acknowledged the hit. "All in the past—all in the past, dear brother-in-law."

"As are her newborn twins?"

"Not mine, I assure you."

"Seemingly, you have enough children to populate the Senate," Octavian jibed.

"Your sister will surely be my last wife." Wisely, Antony added, "My last love."

"Four wives—that ought to be enough for any man, but it is your mistresses who will be your downfall!"

"I have no *mistresses* at this time."

Octavian raged, "You quibble with words, but yes— presumably an Egyptian queen raises your woman above the title *mistress*."

Antony clenched his jaw and took a sip of wine, though his eyes shot daggers toward the younger man who was intent on defending his sister's honor.

Herod closely watched the byplay between the two powerful Romans. They were political and military allies, while now being related through what was apparently only a political marriage. Clearly, the two men were not the closest of friends. His own intelligence-gatherers had informed him that in all likelihood, the twins were

Antony's. At this time, however, the Roman leader had not admitted the patrimony, which would definitively prove his unfaithfulness to his new wife, Octavia. Herod himself, at the previous night's, well, orgy—to be blunt—had seen Octavian turning away from his own pregnant wife as he eyed a woman named Livia Drusilla. Herod had made it a point to be introduced to the aristocratic woman's father, as the relationship could well be worth cultivating.

Herod had always considered that women were both a pleasure and a burden, and now was no different. Briefly, he recalled his own first wife, Doris, whom he had banished two years ago in favor of the more politically-connected Mariamne. Use them and lose them was his own personal view of the weaker sex. And children, including those unclaimed twins and many if not most of his own offspring, could also be consigned to perdition, he arrogantly concluded to himself.

Two days later, with great pomp and circumstance, Herod slowly moved forward to mount the Senate dais. As he walked along the red carpet, he reflected that his journey to Rome, after escaping from the Parthian invasion of Palestine via Masada, would be well worth the many months of danger, travel, and expense. Passing close to Mark Antony, he slightly nodded his thanks and allegiance to the triumvirate leader, who had rejected those who had clamored for Herod's ouster from power. Putting down the current Jerusalem revolt would be an undertaking in the near future that would make him even more unpopular with the denizens of his lands, but he would never relinquish power. Once more he vowed to himself that his enemies would be made to pay for their denial of his authority. A thrill of unmitigated desire to return soon to Judea to wreak havoc on his enemies abruptly ended when he heard the leader of the Senate loudly proclaim his name. He counseled himself to focus on the all-important present.

"Herod, son of our faithful Roman servant and citizen Antipater, we greet you and honor you today." Having been told in advance of the ceremonial requirements, Herod knelt in deference as the Senate's leader continued. "For your exploits on behalf of Rome, the Senate today confers on you the kingship of Judea, Galilee, and Perea. As a military leader, you fought alongside our beloved but deceased leader Julius Caesar at Apamea and helped to hold that treasure city for the empire. You successfully settled disputes in Samaria during your time as our Roman-appointed governor of Coele-Syria. When Marion of Tyre invaded Galilee, you outmaneuvered him in battle and recaptured three strongholds. You displayed wisdom by garrisoning these sectors to preserve your victory. As Rome has always approved, in dealing with conquered cities and regions, you showed mercy to the rebellious citizens of Tyre. For these past actions and military victories, we salute you and give you honor. Rise, King Herod, and go forth to win honor and acclaim for yourself and for Rome. May your reign be long remembered throughout the world."

Later, at the banquet in his honor, Herod set about the task of further moving forward his future. As a young slave moved near with a tray of intoxicating beverages, Herod stopped him. Taking a fresh goblet, he approached and bowed to Octavian, while proffering a heady red wine.

Almost absentmindedly, Octavian accepted the drink but ignored Herod as he continued his conversation with an elite senator. Still, Herod hovered nearby, hoping to be acknowledged by the younger man. His astute assessment told him that, one day, this man would be the real power in Rome. Beginning to feel embarrassed by his own servility on his day of triumph, Herod began to edge away when Octavian finally deigned to speak to him.

"A fine day for you, Herod."

"Indeed, it is, my lord and benefactor. Once more I want to express my gratitude for your support."

"I am sure it will be repaid many times over as you capably serve in your new role. These continued uprisings in Judea must cease. We require you to exert your authority— Roman authority—to quell these frequent upheavals in your part of the world."

Fully aware of Octavian's use of the imperial plural— which proved Herod's judgment correct, that this man could aid in his own continued personal rise—Herod smoothly answered, "I plan to make it my first order of business upon my return."

"When do you and Antony leave?"

"The ships are being made ready as we speak, Consul."

Briefly smiling his approval of the title over the usual "Triumvir," Octavian continued. "Where specifically will you begin this campaign?"

"We plan to land in Ptolemais first and then proceed to Joppa. Immediately after that city is taken, we will move on Masada."

"A solid plan. Jerusalem must be retaken as soon as possible."

"As you command."

"War is thrilling, but it drains the coffers! It disrupts lives and trade."

"You are most wise."

"Common sense—any leader should prefer peace over disunity. Have you met the Assyrians as I recommended?"

"Not yet, but I intend to do so."

"I saw their group arrive earlier. The Assyrians realize what it is incumbent upon them to do—trade is the key to their successful revival. Trade will similarly see Rome remain in power long after her conquests have ended. Ah, there is young Melchior. His father is over there too. Come!"

As befitted his rank, the crowds dispersed as Octavian, with Herod slightly behind him, moved toward a group of obvious foreigners, distinguished by their many-hued woven attire and distinctive bearded faces. The youngest member of the group smiled a friendly greeting and advanced to meet them. He and Octavian grasped arms together, displaying their affinity for one another. Herod considered it was possibly because the two were among the youngest in attendance.

"Octavian!"

"Melchior. I am bringing our newest king, Herod here, to meet your father, King Aralius."

Melchior formally greeted Herod. Cordially, he invited them to accompany him to a nearby group of four envoys, dominated by a tall man with more silver in his beard than black. The lesser officials immediately made way for Octavian and Herod to be introduced by the eager son of King Aralius.

Speaking to the tallest man, Melchior began, "Father, Triumvir Octavian has brought with him King Herod, this evening's guest of honor."

After introductions were made all around and greetings exchanged, the true purpose of this impromptu meeting was moved forward by Octavian. "Once Herod has affairs well in hand in Jerusalem, I want to encourage a trade partnership." Addressing Herod, he commented further. "Mayhap some of the fertile crops from Assyrian lands can help feed your Judeans, as I understand your lands frequently experience drought followed by famine."

Herod nodded his agreement of this unfortunate cycle as the Assyrian leader spoke. "It is my purpose in coming to Rome not to grovel for assistance and recognition. Rather, my intent is to display the many current aspects of our heritage and resources, which do include agriculture, as Octavian has said. I am also proud to state that we are, as we have always been, a nation of builders and craftsmen. However, my own son, Melchior here, is far more interested in religion and the stars."

Lest his words be somehow misconstrued, the king showed his pride in his son by clapping him on the back. Deferentially, he added, "All praise to Ahura Mazda."

Herod ignored the younger Melchior and instead addressed the Assyrian leader. "Your mighty buildings of old are known to me. I too have an interest in building."

"We must discuss what our kingdoms can offer to each other."

CHAPTER 2

The Celestial Light

Assyria, circa 5 BCE

Newer books of astronomy and ancient tomes graced a long table amid measuring tools of varying sizes and complexity. To the untrained eye, it seemed that one strange apparatus after another was scattered among the papers. The gray-headed Melchior lay sleeping amid the manuscripts with his head resting on a paper with mysterious writings—as if his work was beyond him. When the streak of morning sunlight edged its way closer to his face, he blinked open his eyes. Slowly, it registered that once again he had fallen asleep over his nighttime studies of astronomy and the works of ancient writers—not to mention the newest published information. Yawning, he stretched and slowly worked out the kinks in his back. A lifetime of studying the skies had left him slightly hunched over and old, fulfilled and yet unfulfilled, and wondering anew at his recent research.

Melchior glanced up through the sky vent he had personally designed and had mounted in the ceiling of this work area several decades ago. Through this large glass window, which opened and closed as he chose, he could view the ever-changing spectacle of the night skies—and daylight events as well. In the early morning light, he could still see the star that had appeared in the skies for the last several sennights. Even in daylight, its glory was still evident. He had been delving into books since the star's appearance, but thus far was at a loss as to its origin, and why it had suddenly appeared out of nowhere. Its brilliance beckoned him even now. In all of his celestial sightings and studies, he had never witnessed such a spectacular object—that was at the same time so frustrating to identify.

As a student of the skies, he knew there had to be a rational explanation for this brilliant night and early morning visitor. Thus far, however, he could not identify it as one of the five known planets, which its size and steady light seemed to indicate it had to be. He had cross-referenced this phenomenon in Greek, Egyptian, and Babylonian texts, but it continued to defy descriptions written by the ancients that he had pored over for the last several days and nights.

From his own extensive knowledge, he knew that new stars appeared, and others disappeared, with some degree of regular visibility to the eye. Comets came and went and were said to predict changed fortunes of humans. The five planets appeared at intervals, with Venus and Mars detected through their consistency and color. Mighty Jupiter, at this time of the year, was the brightest object in the dawn hours, yet it paled in comparison to this new celestial visitor. Jupiter's present nighttime position was between the constellation Virgo, with its bright star Spica on the east, and Leo the lion to the nearby west, dominated by Regulus, the star of kingship. All these and more were as familiar to him as the patterns of his own lands. As each season marched forward, he could anticipate what the night sky would bring.

This new presence in the heavens, however, shone strong

and clear, more like a planet than a star's light, which would flicker and shine brighter or dimmer at different times. In addition, a unique aspect of Jupiter this year was that it had been joined in the constellation Leo by Venus, the mother planet. Her brightness added to the object's luster, and they almost appeared to merge as one. What was happening in the skies? What was being foretold? As an astrologer, he was certain that these extraordinary movements could be interpreted that some radical change was about to occur in the world.

As a new idea came to him, Melchior searched through his own private mountain of resources to find Hesiod's seven-hundred-year-old original text *Works and Days*. Maybe this ancient almanac-poem might reference the object shining through his celestial viewing window. Was it possible this spectacular body had not been seen for centuries and thus had been "lost" to the astronomical world?

Delightful hours of study passed in researching the old material.

Finally, he sighed at another unsuccessful attempt and accepted, as he often had to do, that the more he wanted to learn (and then did learn), the less he seemed to know. The distinct notion continued to lurk in the back of his mind that he was looking at a new planet—one previously unknown to man. This radical solution was part of the excitement he was feeling. Invigorated, it had kept him focused on his research to determine exactly what this new phenomenon in the skies could be.

Ignoring the rumblings of his stomach demanding to be fed, he reached across his worktable for the complex Babylonian device that had allowed him to calculate the position of this entity in relation to other bright objects in the sky. He would rework his earlier mathematical calculations in case he had made a mistake. Maybe this really was a previously known celestial star.

At times, as he had manipulated this mechanism, he had been concerned if it was as accurate as others believed it to be. The instrument had been a gift from his brother, the present king of Assyria, and had been presented in gratitude for his years of service as an adviser and prince of the realm. Thus, Melchior continued to use it. Only a few of the complicated devices had even been made. Its series of disks and levers opened up intricate methods to study the heavens. His ever-fertile thinking, however, had him considering the idea of experimenting with a new prototype, which he hoped might yield a more precise apparatus. After all, incorrect measurements would make a world of difference.

Giving another deep sigh, he considered how much there was to do and how little time there seemed to do it. As always, his decision years ago to turn from matters of state and his duties as the chief court magus/adviser was one he did not regret. The heavens pulled him as never before. More than ever, he knew his destiny was with them.

Two months later, Melchior's studies had him even more excited.

Quite by chance, he had discovered that the luminous sighting was constant in the skies above him, but that, strangely enough, whenever he traveled in a westerly direction, it moved westward also. In riding in other directions, it did not! He had come to this extraordinary conclusion based on data gathered from his own experiences during his travels. The first trip on which he had observed these unique movements—and even its disappearance— had been to speak to a group of like-minded seekers of truth in the western part of the realm. The star moved forward in the sky as if it were guiding him along.

Surprisingly, however, when he tried to share and talk about this phenomenal body with his fellow astronomers, he could not locate it in the sky. Astoundingly, none of his learned colleagues had even detected it! Thinking back over that humiliating experience, he would long remember feeling like a fool in front of them. When he was returning home and by preference traveling at night, like a vagrant puppy, the star had appeared once more and seemed to— *dare he use the word?*—"reluctantly" follow him home.

Since that strange trip, his prolonged research still had left him unable to account for the star's movement and its disappearances and reappearances.

Melchior continued to think back on the situation that had occurred six days later when he embarked on a visit to an ailing cousin who lived a far distance to the east of him. The star had not appeared at all on that venture until he was returning home. Then, inexplicably, it had again shone brightly as he was homeward bound, going west. His curiosity more than aroused, he had experimented with a number of trips, traveling in different directions. Heading toward the Tigris and Euphrates Rivers, the star had vanished! With any trip westward, it was gloriously present. From this personal experimentation, he felt he had evidence that suggested that only as he was heading west or to the south did the celestial visitor move brightly ahead. It completely vanished as he followed his compass north and east. He had to ask himself what was to the west or to the south?

Since the literature on the cosmos he had studied thus far had not given him the answers he sought, his rational brain pushed him to turn to other sources. Being open-minded, he had turned from all things related to his particular field of expertise and had begun to explore writings in other genres. During the course of his own brainstorming of where and what to research, he had begun exchanging the varied books on his worktable related to the universe for writings of a more religious nature. His years in the court as a Zoroastrian priest-adviser, before he chose to leave the court to pursue his studies of the stars, gave him a comfort level for these books as well.

In answering his own earlier question of what was to the west or to the south, he had resolved to forego additional studies on Rome, knowing, as he did, much of the empire's history and theology. His decision was also because it was an undisputed fact of life that the Roman Empire, under the leadership of his old acquaintance and infrequent correspondent Octavian, had already expanded north, south, east, and west anyway. Instead, after much deliberation and the systematic deletion of other areas to consider, he had finally opted to concentrate his studies on the once powerful nation of Israel. Rationally, this made the most sense—clearly, the remnants of the descendants of Abraham were mostly found in a southwesterly direction.

With his lifelong love of learning, researching in another area where he had insufficient knowledge was no great hardship. Indeed, it was a joy for him to expand his personal horizons. What was unique to this new phase of scholarly research was that he had begun to feel in his heart that he was bound to the star by more than mathematical equations. He could not begin to explain why he felt this way, but the star had become more than merely an object to be studied.

At this moment, his thinking was interrupted by the fairly unusual sound of horses clattering into the courtyard below him. He was hopeful that this newly arrived entourage might be the old friend and rabbinical scholar he had invited to come to his home. Abandoning his apparently fruitless studies, he hurried down the steps.

With great joy that the newcomer was indeed his friend, he addressed him by his religious title. "Welcome, Rabbi Seth. Your presence honors my home."

"Ah, Melchior, your invitation was most welcome. I am refreshed just seeing you, even though I have been in the saddle for most of this day. Why you live in this distant spot is beyond me." He grinned, embracing his host. "My friend, too much time has passed. We must not wait so long between visits."

Wholeheartedly returning the embrace, Melchior endured Seth's close scrutiny. He then clapped his hands, signaling that his servants should see to his guest's needs, as well as those who had accompanied him. Melchior was familiar with the Jewish prescription for washing, and he initially offered a bowl of water for his guest's ablutions. "Come! I ordered that your favorite refreshments be served upon your arrival, and I am most eager to catch up on what you have been doing. However, as you have traveled this distance for my benefit alone, I insist you rest, if that is your preference."

"Your note to me, Melchior, was so insistent that it is I who will be enlightened and thankful, I feel. For that reason alone, I left my beloved Sara-Ashta. By the way, she sends her affectionate regards to you, my friend."

"Your beautiful wife is a pearl among women. Long have I envied you."

"Well, Melchior, few would call you foolish, but in this one area of choosing a wife, I am your superior."

"No woman would put up with my desire to place searching for knowledge above her—to say nothing of this long gray beard of mine."

Later, with Seth refreshed and fed, they caught up on the affairs of old acquaintances and laughed about earlier times together. Eventually, Melchior's visitor suggested, "We have danced around the reason for my visit long enough. It is obvious that you invited me because of my religious background, as well as my studies at the library of Alexandria. What about the history of the Jews intrigues you?" With a twinkle in his eye, he asked, "Do you plan to convert?"

Regarding his friend steadfastly, Melchior stated, "I am interested in learning more about the person your religion calls the Messiah."

Melchior registered Seth's puzzled reaction. With sharpened eyes, his friend repeated the last words: "The Messiah?"

Silence hung between the two until Seth broke it, seeing that Melchior was all seriousness and was waiting for him to speak. Eventually, the rabbi began, "Moses, our great Hebrew leader who brought Israel out of slavery in Egypt and into the promised land, wrote our first five books, the Torah, sometimes simply called the Law. He proclaimed in Deuteronomy that a great prophet, a *messiah*, if you prefer that term, would be sent from among the people of Israel.[1] I'm not sure, but possibly this is the person about whom you are referring."

"This prophet is still awaited?"

"Yes."

"The word *messiah* is Aramaic in origin?"

"It is."

"Savior, liberator, the anointed one."

"You are correct. The extension has always been that the 'anointed one' will be a king—exactly as a king is 'anointed.'"

"Tell me more, Seth," Melchior quietly requested.

"Why this sudden—and, if I might add, seemingly urgent—interest in my people's long-awaited Messiah?"

"Call it a mere request for information that I do not have."

"I have known you too long, my friend. It is more than that. If you prefer to keep your secrets at this time, I will tell you what has been vaguely foretold. But there will be a price to pay, I assure you."

Melchior bowed his head in assent.

"In terms of the hope of this messianic figure, the longing is that he will deliver my people from dominion."

"He will be a warrior?"

"It is the promise that Israel will rise again and be dominant over the world that has sustained Jews from the days of our slavery in Babylon until later in Egypt—nay, to this very day."

Melchior felt dismay that the Messiah of Israel was to bring destruction, and he lowered his eyes feeling sorrow. Still, he remained focused on his need to know more. "Is there any specific awareness or indication of the time period he will come and from where?"

"No specific time was given, but he is to be descended from the line of David, our first king of Israel. Thus, he will be a king himself, arising from our royal family."

Melchior put his two hands together and thoughtfully tapped two fingers, taking in these words before asking, "How long has he been awaited?"

Quietly, Seth answered, "Almost 1,500 years have passed."

Registering the length of time, Melchior gently probed, "Do you still believe he will come?"

"We believe. We hope. We pray—as we have since the beginning."

Melchior said nothing because he knew little of this ancient religion or their early leader Moses.

"It is my turn now, my friend. Why this interest in our Messiah?"

Attempting to mask his initial disappointment, Melchior countered, "It apparently means nothing."

"Not a sufficient answer, Melchior. You have brought me here on a wild goose chase?"

Regretfully, Melchior responded, "It appears as if that is the situation. Forgive my wasting your time." Then he revived somewhat. "But wait! Since it is evening, let me show you something." He chuckled, "Or at least, let me try to show you something!"

"With this being the extent of the help that you wanted from me, I am glad that there is 'something' more—though your words are cryptic."

Melchior laughed ruefully at Seth's quizzical look. At this point he urged his guest, "Come—this is a clear night with only a crescent moon. Maybe I can show you a marvelous sight."

After walking up the five flights of stairs to the observatory level, Melchior held his breath as he cranked open the window that would let the heavens shine forth.

Catching sight of the luminous object, he asked, "What do you make of this sight?"

In amazement and awe, Seth gazed upward but did not mention the special star in the sky. Staring up and out, he eventually exclaimed, "What extraordinary marvels our God has made. Thank you, dear friend, for bringing me up here. In our busy lives, we often fail to see the many glories of our world. This window to the skies opens my eyes. I see why you love your studies so much."

Melchior hid his initial regret that Seth did not single out the special object as being above and beyond the other wonders in the sky. Dispassionately, he tried to consider it from the other's point of view. Yes, it was simply one of millions. He was trying to make something out of nothing.

In the days following Seth's departure, Melchior pondered why he could not accept what his brain told him he should. The spiritual strength expressed by his rabbinical friend that the Jews still hoped for their Messiah after centuries of waiting had at first amazed him, then almost immediately disheartened him. His later thinking confirmed this feeling of dismay. After fifteen centuries— for a conquering Messiah to arrive who in essence would be taking on the might of the Roman Empire—*bah, this was an impossibility* and would prove futile. No, this was *not* the time for the arrival of a Messiah.

Also, the fact was that Octavian—acclaimed as Augustus Caesar—had the world in a decades-long era of peace. And furthermore, the star must not be related to the Jews' future king because he himself was not Jewish, and he certainly did not worship their one singular God. Instead, his Assyrian religion was that of his fellow Zoroastrian astrologic priests. Along with them, he gave honor to their several gods, including the supreme being, Ahura Mazda, the wise lord of all.

Seth had not noted anything of significance about the special star. Nor, in his strong commentary on the long-awaited prophet, had he mentioned at any time any writings about a sign in the heavens to foreshadow the Jews' promised savior. Obviously, his own straw-in-the-wind effort to push his star into the ideology of the Israelite people was both pompous and superfluous.

In the days since Seth's departure, he had not felt the energy to push forward into other areas of research that might provide clues to the star's origin. If this luminous object was simply one in a million—then it was just that—no more, no less. Brighter than most—but this was true of any number of objects in the night skies. *Let it rest*, he counseled himself.

Pummeling his pillow for the umpteenth time on his fourth restless night, he tried to shut down his mind to the problem. However, much later in the night he determined that a lifetime of asking "Why?" and then seeking the answer could not be dismissed. Here he lay, basically wide awake and continuing to stare at the ceiling, which had slowly become discernible as the dawn hours approached. Still, he lay abed—an unnatural thing for him to do. He usually bounded up as soon as he awakened, caught up in the excitement of a new day of living and learning. The problem was, he was not merely waking up; he had not slept!

Trying to calm himself through a series of mental exercises he had developed over the years—and that had not worked on the previous four nights—he came to a decision. He must still investigate the star, but he needed to divorce himself from the almost preternatural effects the object had made on him. He was jumping to conclusions, which had never been a part of his methodology. Cautioning himself to back off and back away, he questioned himself if he could do that. He doubted if he could ever remember not pursuing a solution to a problem simply because he had come to a dead end in researching something new.

"So think, Melchior!" he chided himself.

As before, another new approach was needed. He must adopt a more disciplined method of studying this newly observed object. It was wholly unlike him to be so—well, what had he been? Cavalier? Biased? Spiritual? Undisciplined? All of these? Some of these?

He grimaced for a moment—still amazed at himself and his research. What would his past students think of him if they ever found out that this Gordian knot of a problem was rendering him almost useless? He must get past the issues of the celestial object that he was letting distract him. Maybe if he gave it a rest, the way of discovery would hit his consciousness out of the blue, as had often happened in the past for other difficult studies—not to mention for life in general.

Ah, he thought, *the solution is right in front of me!* He would pick up on other areas he had been studying and working on prior to the night he had first noticed the star, which was a good six months ago at this point. So, he would *not* be disciplined; he would simply drop this current conundrum and turn to a new area of study—at least for a while.

Determining this plan was easier said than done, he realized, as evening neared that same day. He had first cleared his work area of all remnants of the previous dead ends he had experienced. Restlessly, he then had left his workroom and interfered with his well-ordered household. Undoubtedly, his people were amazed—probably even offended—that he was interjecting himself into their affairs. Then he had headed to the stables, where he had his favorite steed, Pegasus, saddled, and he put the gelding through its paces until they ended by cantering back to the stable. Energized but still unfocused, he generally made a mess of the rest of the day. He wished mightily for the company of others who might help him move forward to new projects or—may the gods forgive him for his waywardness—return to the puzzle of the star, even though he had told himself to drop it for a time.

Five nights later—and mentally kicking himself for not finding other avenues to investigate or projects to start—he finally gave in to the inevitable. Possibly the star's glowing yet mute presence on a series of extremely clear nights had helped push him to resume studying the glimmering orb that refused to let him rest. During his assessment of this entire perplexing scenario, he recognized that he had absolutely gone astray when he had ventured away from his spheres of expertise in mathematics, astronomy, and astrology. He should never have tried to determine the *why* of the brilliant orb but should have instead focused entirely on the *what* of it.

What was this object in the sky? As he had pondered earlier, he again asked himself if it could be a yet-undetected planet. Its steady beacon of light undoubtedly put it into this category. Rationally, he reasoned to himself: This "object" does not flicker—ergo, it is a planet. The other planets moved, so why should not this one? *Aha! I will go down in history as the discoverer of a new planet!*

Here, as before, he hit a wall—it was a planet that no one else could see. His discovery would be an asterisk that an insane old man once claimed there was a new planet. If, several months previously, his colleagues had wondered at his claims of a new celestial object—which none of them could see—they would now have it confirmed that he had gone completely over the edge. Publishing his investigations would be futile—he would be ejected from all future gatherings of the various learned groups of which he was a member.

"Poor Melchior," they would whisper, "his age has finally caught up with him." They would begin to question his past achievements. He would be regarded as a sham. Facts—firm and incontrovertible—would be his shield and also his weapon to counteract their suspicions that he had lost his ability to think and to function.

CHAPTER 3

Yeshayah

Running his hand through his somewhat shaggy, shoulder-length gray hair, Melchior let out a small sigh. It had been months from the time he had first sighted *his* star—as he had begun to call it. As time marched along, his research had been deliberate and had intensified. This methodical approach had yielded data, but nothing that he could definitively say gave him the answers he was seeking. Ever-present in his studies was his previous awareness that mighty Jupiter and Venus, the mother planet, were closely united in the heavens. To his human eye, they seemed to have become one glowing orb. This event had to mean something!

Exhausted, he sought his bed, but once again a peaceful sleep eluded him as he tossed and turned. His last cogent thought was a prayer—almost a plea—to Ahura Mazda, the creator of the universe, to guide him to the truth about this one shining light of his creation. In his heart, he felt that there was only one thing left for him to do, but still he held back from making the final decision on the drastic course of action he was contemplating. By nature, he was not a frequent traveler—unlike the planets he observed that coursed through the skies above. As of late, his query to himself upon waking each morning was where his star intended to lead him. It was also his weary last consideration at night as he finally drifted off to sleep.

Rising with the sun, Melchior brought forth once more the daring plan he had been assessing for several sennights. Undoubtedly, he was becoming an addlepated old fool for not dismissing the idea as soon as it had entered his consciousness. Was he audacious enough to pursue it?

You *could* do it, one part of his brain told him.

You would be considered to have lost your mind his cautious side responded.

He had weighed and dissembled whether and how he could or should or might move forward his continued investigations into the star's strange yet brilliant appearance and movements. He felt that the consequences of his intended actions would be far-reaching. At this point in his thinking, he always had to chide himself. Would the consequences of inaction be equally far-reaching?

Lost in his convoluted theories—and, yes, inaction—he was brought out of his reverie by the sound of footsteps coming up the stairs to his rooms. Young Bijak's head appeared first, then eventually his lanky body as he took the final step up the last set of stairs. He appeared slightly winded as he lugged in a bulky package. When his breathing became more even, he finally spoke. "Forgive this interruption, Master, but I was told by Sarkev, immediately after the arrival of this parcel, that I should bring it to you immediately."

"Catch your breath, Bijak. Actually, I welcome your arrival." With his usual self-deprecating kindness, Melchior added, "I wish I could say you were interrupting some great, momentous finding, but I fear that is not the case. From your heavy breathing, I feel it is I who should apologize for the long climb you have had on my account. Let us see what you have brought."

Standing up, Melchior moved toward a semi-empty table and waved his hand for Bijak to join him. Grinning conspiratorially and almost like a young child opening a gift on his name day, Melchior took off the bindings of the package. As he had surmised from the general shape and weightiness of the parcel, it was books—one of his favorite gifts. After reading the extraordinary titles, he then gently put aside the carefully wrapped tomes, which had each been encased in separate animal hides for protection against the elements and possible traveling hazards. Melchior turned his attention to the accompanying letter from Seth.

> Greetings to my friend Melchior,
>
> Subsequent to our unusual meeting some time past, I am taking the liberty of sending you these books, which may be of some assistance to you. Your interest in the Messiah leads me to believe that the writings of Moses may assist your research. I feel I was vague with you about our long-awaited Messiah, and I must beg your forgiveness. However, the writings, too, are indefinite about this prophet, and I did not want to lead you astray, as has happened to others. Knowing your zeal for authenticity, I have been given special permission to send you early texts, along with modern translations. Not being aware of your precise interest in our long-awaited Messiah, I cannot direct you further.

I can sense, however, even as I write this missive to you, your delight in this bountiful collection of the heritage of my people Israel. With some caution, I also direct you to the words of our prophet Yeshayah, which may be of interest to you as well. On a personal basis, Melchior, Daniel is one of our latter-day prophets, and was a known magus, like you. His words have traditionally been considered to be a prophecy relating to the arrival of our Messiah.

Whatever further assistance I can give you is yours for the asking.

Your friend,
Seth

Pure joy spread from Melchior's eyes to his lips. Placing his right hand on the books, he nodded his head several times, as if knowing in advance that he would find the answers he had urgently requested from Ahura Mazda just last night. Inspired and still smiling, he looked at Bijak and spoke his thoughts, "God is good, Bijak. I asked—and he answered."

Bijak's confusion was evident. "Pardon, sire?"

"Answers, Bijak, answers are here. And just maybe the answers to questions I would gladly discover. Come, help me move these writings over here. Then leave me, and please tell Sarkev that I am not to be disturbed until I come downstairs."

After moving the assorted materials as directed, the young servant showed his love for Melchior by tentatively asking, "Have you eaten yet this morning, Master?"

"Yes—no—I mean, you are right. Bring me food in a bit, but no other interruptions. Understood?"

The youth bowed himself out, "As you command."

Melchior almost reverently opened the first book that Seth had sent. The rabbi had indicated that this was the start of Moses' inspired words and that he should begin here. He decided to commence with the translated book first, rather than the original Aramaic writings of their leader, Moses. The initial words astounded him, and he closed his eyes briefly. Experiencing a spiritually direct link to his own Ahura Mazda and to his decades-long study of the skies, he read again the first words: "In the beginning God created the heavens and the earth ..."[2]

Days and nights blurred together for Melchior as he immersed himself in the words of Moses, written fifteen centuries previous. Not being a member of the nation of Israel, his search for references to the Messiah was both hampered and helped by his general unawareness of these ancient people. Obviously, they were from a much earlier time than when Moses was writing. With no spiritual involvement, he could somewhat easily move forward to piece together the history of the Israelites and the pact—nay, covenant—they had with their one and only divine being. Strangely, they would not or could not name this supreme being, other than to call him by the words, "I am who I am."[3]

He read the texts as history books and discovered much from reading in this way. From the start, he had been transfixed by the words and verses of the first book of the Jew's Genesis reading. Additionally, he was later staggered that the first man and woman eventually had a third son they named Seth, who was conceived to replace Abel, who had been killed by another son, Cain.[4]

Such troubles to begin the existence of human beings for these Jews! However, it was the same as with his own Zoroastrian religion's Ahura Mazda, who created twin spirits that reflected choices between good and evil.

The Hebrew story continued that at age 105, Seth fathered Enosh, who was the first ever to "invoke the name of Yahweh."[5] He could not help but be amazed at the great ages of these early people. It was written that Seth lived for 912 years, and "then he died."[6] Like many others in those early times when people lived for many years, a man named Lamech survived a mere 777 years—and "then he died."[7]

Days later, having read over—not once but twice—the first five books that comprised the Pentateuch, Melchior was dismayed at his inability to perceive why his friend Seth said these five books spoke of the coming of the Messiah. In addition, his star search of the readings had similarly proven unfruitful. There were merely random times that a star or heavenly body was referred to by Moses. They were mentioned as part of the great creation of the world—which took place in six days!

During his first reading of this creation scene, he had realized that he should not take events to come as totally factual, but rather as a general telling or explanation to cover the history of humankind from a religious point of view. Because his purpose was only to try to gather information on this Messiah and the narrative of who he was and when he would come—if ever—and apparently not in the past one and a half millennia, he easily bypassed inconsistencies and astonishing statements, like the great ages of those they called the patriarchs.

Melchior was currently carefully studying both the original version and the translated version that Seth had generously supplied. Referring to his notes, he decided to reread what had been written about a star late in the book of Bamidbar, which translated as "In the Desert" and was also called the book of Numbers. Melchior had a keen appreciation of the naming of this part of the Israelite story in what was the fourth book, since the Hebrews had wandered for four decades in the Sinai Desert after Moses led them out of slavery. During those long forty years, the Israelite population had grown exponentially as they had extraordinarily multiplied and flourished, despite the nomadic and harsh life they were forced to live. In fact, their numbers had become as great as the sand on the seashore.

In this book, the prophet Balaam, *not* an Israelite and definitely on the side of their enemy King Balak of Moab, had a prophetic vision of times to come for the Hebrew people. The translated text indicated that Balaam had refused to curse the Israelites as the king had wanted him to do. Instead, he had prophesied, in a spiritual trance, "I see him—but not in the present, I behold him—but not close at hand: a star from Jacob takes the leadership; a scepter arises from Israel."[8]

It was Melchior's past experience that original texts should be studied, if at all possible. There was much here that could be misinterpreted and that would lead the reader—in this case, him—to false conclusions if a poor translation occurred. Clearly, analogies were being made with the references to a star and a scepter—as if they were meant to be people and not mere objects—if those were the correct translations. Therefore, this emphasized the importance of those words and underscored for him the need to go back to the original text. He felt that Hebrew scholars before him had to be correct, but his own expertise with stars in the heavens made it imperative that he leave nothing to chance. He decided that when he was fresh in the morning, he would tackle the original Aramaic texts. He had been familiar with this language from a young age because it was a Semitic family grouping that included his own Assyrian tongue, as well as those of Babylonians, Chaldeans, Arabs, and, of course, the Hebrews.

The next morning he awoke from a restless, dream-filled sleep and worried how fresh he was to tackle the translation. In what actually could be called a nightmare, he had vividly dreamed of myriad stars and a scepter and a baby who morphed into a bloodied man amid people clamoring for his death.

It was difficult for Melchior to shrug off the horrific memory of the bloodied person in his feverish dream. He almost experienced physical illness when he recalled the suffering human being. Mentally, he could not shake off the scenes of violence in the nightmare. His background had taught him that dreams, especially ones as strong as this had been, have meaning and must be regarded as omens for good or evil. Obviously, this man was a menace to others. The Hebrews? If so, he could not be their long-awaited Messiah who was to lead them to triumph. Was this nightmarish vision meant to be a warning to him to leave well enough alone? Was he to abandon this search for the origin and meaning of the star that had become almost a passion for him? The power of the lengthy and terrible nighttime event now caused him to reevaluate once again what he was doing.

Over a sennight later, as the gruesome images had faded, Melchior continued to question if he should have written down particulars of the powerful nightmare. His normal way of dealing with significant dreams would have been to detail the specifics of it, but he had not done so—though he could not fathom why. Maybe it was because of his being fully occupied with the books Seth had sent. And in the way of dreams, the specifics were hard to recollect unless written down almost immediately. Truthfully, he admitted to himself, he was grateful that with each passing day, it had become more difficult to remember the horrors of the nightmare.

Was he getting too old to remember things and events? He was certainly old—closer to seventy than sixty. Growing older, however, had never been a problem for him; he had simply never felt old. In wanting to always learn something new, and enjoying such experiences so thoroughly, he now reflected that he must have considered himself to be ageless.

Suddenly he laughed aloud, recalling the great ages of the Jewish patriarchs in the Genesis readings. *There, I have remembered something!* he exulted. Methuselah was said to have lived for 969 years[9]—almost a millennium. Noah was 500 and still fathering children[10]—egad! He was a mere child compared to them!

With that energizing notion, he returned to his

translations, scolding himself that he had wasted enough time.

Striding toward his desk, he opened the original Aramaic text of the pagan Balaam's prophecy. He would concentrate on what he knew best—stars—because he did remember that the word *star* was in that prophecy! Feeling more hopeful, he chuckled to himself as he prepared to tackle his work again.

Sometime later, he sat back in his chair pondering once more the possible meanings of that prophecy. *Star*, in this material, seemed to mean that a child of Jacob's would take on a leadership role. However, he had discovered that Jacob could boast of twelve sons, plus adopted sons, and at least one daughter!

The family tree he had carefully created showed that the pledge made to Abraham that he would be the father of a great nation apparently had been fulfilled through his grandson Jacob's many children. Those twelve sons had, in time, become the fathers of what today were known as the twelve tribes of Israel—the Israelites. The sons had been leaders in their day, some more than others, naturally. The problem was that all had taken their place in the history of the Hebrews and were honored—*as they well should be*, he thought.

Melchior speculated whether or not he had been enlightened further.

If this was the correct interpretation, then which of the sons of Jacob had taken the leadership role? The oldest son? The youngest? One in the middle, possibly? Was he making progress or not, he had to question himself?

According to Seth's note, these first books had references to the Messiah. Melchior had found very little in that regard, but with the writings being not merely historical but religious as well, the references had to be buried in the text in a more mystic sense. Maybe the Jews construed a meaning that certain words could relate to this personage. During Seth's visit, he had averred that his people believed emphatically that Israel, under the leadership of this messianic figure, would regain its lost dominance. In this context, the "star" could be related to the long-expected Messiah, who had yet to make his appearance. A promise had been made to Israel, it appeared, and was sealed by a covenant: Israel would rise again. Melchior reflected that this was certainly a point that he would do well to keep in mind.

To his knowledge, no particular star was more or less related to Jacob. That was further information to be gained at another time, he hoped. As of now, he had well over one thousand pages of the Hebrew Tanakh to read, along with his own personal effort to translate a similar number of pages from the original Aramaic. Again, he pondered if he should save time and only work with the original Aramaic. He did have confidence in his own rendering of the Balaam prophecy, and he reasoned that this would also be the case as he plunged deeper into the other old Hebraic writings.

Melchior, however, did have another major concern, which was possibly even more of an issue than the readings. The bright object he had become fixated on would not stay forever. He had to know and know soon. Therefore, reading all the books plus the translations was probably not his best course of action. Referring to Seth's letter, he decided to immediately begin reading the two prophets who had been recommended by the scholar, Yeshayah and Daniel. This meant that he would skip forward over a multitude of books, but with time such a factor, he felt he had no alternative. With that decision made, he dove first into Yeshayah, as it was written earlier than the Daniel text, even though the latter book was much smaller.

"Unbelievable!" he breathed aloud after translating the first few pages. The Hebrew God Yahweh was more than angry at both Judah and Jerusalem. Isaiah—the translation of Yeshayah—had written that the nation of Judah was to be punished "as a breed of wrongdoers, perverted sons."[11] The text seemed to have been written about a time approximately seven centuries earlier. Actually, Melchior's own Assyrian ancestor, King Sargon, had destroyed Judea about that same period. He calculated that this prophet was writing a few decades from the time that this destruction had occurred.

Excitedly, he discovered in the second chapter a mention of Jacob's name. This gave him a point of reference connecting the first writing in Genesis to Isaiah's much later book. Apparently, the Israelites' God was a forgiving one. Although the land had become full of soothsayers and idolaters, the House of Jacob was being invited to once again walk with Yahweh. However, the Israelites were also being warned that if they did not repent and humble themselves before their God, he would send earthquakes and would withhold his support. Their sinful ways ranged from the heinous, unforgivable idolatry to greed[12] to presumably the usual array of the sins of humankind, Melchior thought ruefully.

Apparently, no one in the tribe of Judah was willing to be a leader to stop the insolence, ruin, and collapse of this once-favored people. Recalling the words in the earlier text that a star from Jacob would take the leadership role,

Melchior sat back in his chair, musing aloud, "Well, I now know that from neither Judah nor anywhere in Jerusalem will the Messiah come." From his perspective, Melchior decided he could cross off Judah, the fourth son of Jacob and Leah, from figuring in the Messiah's lineage.

Only eleven more brothers to go! Should he not consider Jacob's daughters as well? There were those adopted sons that he probably should investigate too.

Suddenly, and probably because of his thinking about Jerusalem, he recalled the Idumean Herod, the current strong but erratic ruler of that Jewish city of faith. He clearly remembered his first meeting with Herod in Rome as a young man almost forty years ago. His own royal family's trade dealings with the Judaic king, over the years, had almost always ended with Herod gaining the upper hand and getting the most with the least offered.

Melchior also had not forgotten the probably true rumors of the king murdering his own wives and even several of his sons. One wife—whom he supposedly loved to excess—he had killed in a jealous rage. Politically, in Herod's self-serving effort to support Augustus Caesar, he had alienated Jerusalem's leading rabbis in the temple. Herod had brutally solved the resultant acrimony by methodically murdering the Jewish religious insurgents in numbers too horrifying to contemplate.

Linking these recollections of Herod with his present research, Melchior emphatically concluded that Jerusalem—while the ambitious Herod reigned—would not be a safe place for the promised Messiah, should he be born in these times.

After he had completed translating the first six chapters of Isaiah, the scholar decided to halt his day's work and start anew on the morrow, when he would be fresher. A swift invasion was coming once again from a well-prepared enemy equipped with chariots. Yahweh was still angry with his people for their infidelity. It almost seemed as if it was their God himself who was calling forth this powerful enemy to destroy Judah and its proud city of Jerusalem.

Rising at first light, Melchior hurried to his worktable where he began to translate the seventh chapter of Isaiah. The prophet had been told by Yahweh to warn King Ahaz of Judah that if he did not stand with Yahweh, he would "not stand at all."[13]

Melchior glumly wondered aloud, "Judah again—is that tribe back in the mix?" If it was, then that meant that much of his work of the previous day, when he had crossed off Judah from being a part of the Messianic story, had been for naught.

Historically, Melchior knew that the powerful Assyrian army, with its fleet of mighty chariots, had been a threat to other groups of people over time. He was aware that the Judean Ahaz had given his allegiance to Assyria to gain protection from the Jews' enemies, and thus Judah had become a vassal state under this new Assyrian Empire. However, Melchior could recall his childhood tutor instilling in him facts about the rise and fall of his nation, and that eventually Babylonia had conquered Assyria. He reasoned that probably this meant that Judah's land had also once more experienced a decline in fortunes as well.

Judah is out again, he reasoned, as he again methodically updated his notes.

By mid-morning he had learned that Isaiah had told King Ahaz that a virgin would soon give birth to a child, whom she would call Immanuel.[14] That child, presumably born about seven centuries earlier—the text did translate as "soon," after all—as he grew older, would again bring good times to Israel. *So maybe Judah did not experience long-term problems under Assyrian leadership*, he mused. At any rate, Melchior was looking forward to discovering in the next several hundred pages how this Immanuel had brought possible prosperity, good times, and maybe even independence for Judah, or Judea, as the land was known today to the Israelites.

At this point, he was forced to stop and take time for the refreshment and food that young Bijak brought to him. The youth said that he had strict orders from Sarkev to stay until the food was eaten. As he complied with the orders from below, Melchior chatted with the lad, glad to take a break from his strenuous intellectual labors. Noting Bijak's interest in what he was doing, Melchior shared some of what he was attempting to discover. Long ago, Melchior had taken Bijak under his wing when the lad was a mere child in the household. He had remained interested in Bijak's well-being, and as soon as the child had shown an aptitude for reading and writing, Melchior had personally helped in the schooling.

Aware that he was favored, Bijak requested, "While you eat, Master, may I read what you have written here? I will be very careful with your pages."

"Be my guest, Bijak. It has been some time since we have read and studied together. I was wanting another set of eyes and someone to talk to about my findings, and with you here—well, go ahead and read to yourself while I eat."

As Melchior spooned out the last of the rice stew that Sarkev had sent to him, and brushed away an errant crumb from the flattened wheat bread that had accompanied the dish, he almost smiled to himself when he saw a puzzled look appear on Bijak's face. He watched the lad reread the words, and when Bijak glanced at him inquisitively, Melchior found it hard to keep a straight face as he inquired, "Is something wrong?"

"No, sir."

"I can see where you are reading, my learned young scholar, and I assure you that I, too, read and reread and even doubted if I was reading what I thought I was reading. My main concern was if I was translating it correctly."

Quizzically but hesitantly, Bijak asked, "But how can this be? A child cannot be born to a virgin—can it?"

Now it was Melchior's turn to hesitate. Not wanting to have to make a detailed explanation of something he had little experience of himself, and having no children of his own, he instead asked, "How old are you, Son?"

"I am fifteen—actually, I will be sixteen years old next month."

Relieved that Bijak probably had a modicum of information about how children were conceived—which was obviously why he was curious about the written words—Melchior chose to answer as vaguely as possible. "I am not certain why my translation reads like this—it is probably not quite right. I have another book that I was planning to cross-check to see how that compares with my work."

Having confidence in Melchior, the youth countered, "You will figure it out, Master. You are surely correct in what you wrote, but it does seem strange to me."

Melchior smiled kindly. "I also am puzzled by the words. However, since it was supposed to have occurred 'soon,' according to the writer Isaiah, then it is over and done with—I would say about seven hundred years ago, and will be of little concern to my current studies."

Gathering up the dishes and other remnants of the meal he had brought, Bijak offered a last comment and a cheeky grin as he departed. "It would have had to be a miracle of some sort if it was true."

"You are impertinent, Bijak," the older man admonished, but he returned the grin with one of his own.

As he took up his work again, however, he could not help muttering to himself, "But these Israelites have had a long and strange history with this God of theirs."

Days later, as the dusky twilight faded into dark, Melchior found himself gazing outward to the brightness of his star, as he continued to call it. Through diligence, he had spent time translating the beginning of Isaiah's eleventh chapter. The words of the prophet could be references to the Israelite's Messiah. A strange hope and even a glimmer of excitement filled Melchior. The Israelite God promised to send a scion from the root of Jesse who would be full of righteousness, but who would also strike down the ruthless and bring death to the wicked. The powerful words from Isaiah about "integrity" and "faithfulness" flitted through Melchior's mind as he gazed upward. The prophet had written that animals which were naturally enemies would lie down together, like the wolf with the lamb, and the calf with the lion cub. This descendant of Jesse would have wisdom and insight along with power to strike at the wicked and ruthless. Yet somehow, in the midst of all this, he would also bring peace when he came.[15]

But the question the magus most wanted to have answered was the same one that the Israelites had seemingly asked forever: When? *When* would this Messiah come?

The past was done and over—no Messiah had come to save them in all these centuries although both Moses and Isaiah had foretold his coming. As an astrologer, he believed that the heavens held messages for mortals, if they could only be interpreted. For months, this bright object in the sky had gleamed. Above, in the evening sky, were both Jupiter and Venus, near Regulus, the star of kingship. Surely some great leader, some king, was being born or had already been born somewhere on this earth. Maybe he was born in Rome? Possibly in Britannia to the north? Maybe in Gaul or Greece? Could this king be a Parthian? A Mede?

But could not this bright object in the sky portend the birth of the Messiah? In truth, the heart of the Israelite history was in this part of the world, and here was this star, shining forth from the heavens above—here and now! The heavenly message was strong and true and must be heeded.

And if it was happening soon, or maybe had already happened— in his lifetime—he had to act!

He had to follow the shining orb that shifted among the stars as he moved and of which no one else, apparently, was even aware. He was not an Israelite, but he was a lifelong seeker of knowledge. If this just ruler was entering the world, then he simply had to know!

CHAPTER 4

The Journey Begins

Leaving had taken—well, was taking—a bit longer than Melchior would have liked.

Swept up in his enthusiasm for this journey—which, he acknowledged to himself, he had been contemplating for many months—he had rewrapped the Tanakh that Seth had sent him, told Sarkev to prepare camels for a journey that might take weeks or months to complete, and let Bijak know that he was to accompany him on this trip. Reluctantly, he had left behind the originals in Aramaic, fearing something might happen to those ancient writings as he journeyed into the unknown.

During Sarkev's several entreaties for more details about his destination, Melchior could not help but be vague. He himself was uncertain as to where the star might lead him. He was aware that Sarkev was unhappy about his vagueness and not merely because it left his manager in a quandary about how long a journey it would be. Melchior knew his household cared for him, and that this was at the heart of their concern about his sudden journey.

He had decided to take only Bijak with him for a number of reasons. First, the lad seemed to be a part of the books; after all, the youth had first carried them up the long flights of steps to him. Second, Qasim, the usual retainer who traveled with him, was laid up with a broken foot from a recent encounter with a recalcitrant ox. Accidentally, the animal had placed a weighty hoof accompanied by its even weightier body atop Qasim's left foot. The man's ankle had suffered damage, along with a multitude of broken bones in his foot. Third, Sarkev would never allow him to leave home without someone to accompany him. Therefore, he might as well have Bijak with whom he was comfortable as his companion. There was also the fact that the youth would not question why and how and where they traveled on what Melchior felt would be a meandering trip.

Bijak, of course, with so little time to prepare—due to Melchior's deciding that he wanted to leave within two days—had no time to probe where they would be going. It was not until just a few hours before their departure, when helping Melchior to clear up the work area in the study, that the youth was able to query his mentor about their travels. "Does this trip we are going on have anything to do with the Israelite books you were translating?"

"What makes you ask that?"

"The one large book you had on the table here, where you were working a few days ago, is missing. Then, over there, sticking out of your clothes bag, is a similar animal hide—if not the same—to the one that covered the books I brought up to your room that came from your friend. To me, it looks like its size is about the same as the book that is not here."

"Astute observations, young man. I can see I have made a wise decision to take you along. Yes, I am taking one of the books because there is still much for me to try to decipher, and there will be many hours to while away as we wait each day for nighttime to arrive."

Bijak ducked his head at the compliment but also smiled companionably with the older man. "I still do not understand why you plan to travel mostly at night."

"We are going to follow a star, Bijak!"

"I am sorry, Master, what did you say?"

"I am sure your young ears heard me correctly. We are going to follow a star that I have been observing for many months."

"But why?"

"I am not certain." As a look of distress crossed Bijak's face at these vague words, Melchior attempted to distract him, "Never mind what I said. Suffice it to say that we are going on a journey—an adventure—to an unknown place that will take us an indefinite amount of time to complete."

"I see, Master."

"Thank you for saying so, Bijak, but I doubt if you see at all."

"That is true, Master," Bijak responded with a lack of confidence in his voice that matched his demeanor.

"We will be safe—and I assured your mother this morning that I would bring you back home wiser than you left."

"She does wonder where we are going. I think she is concerned that this trip has come up out of nowhere." Reluctantly, he added, "I think too that she thinks I am not old enough to be helpful to you."

"I would imagine that others will think these things to be true as well. I realize this household seems to know my every move, even before I do, but this time, undoubtedly, I have surprised them." Melchior laughed softly as he gathered up a second stylus and wax tablet to add to the one he had packed earlier.

"I—we are all curious as to why you have suddenly decided to go on this extended trip to a place that you are not certain where it will end."

"You must not be so stodgy, Bijak. It worries me you are too set in your ways," Melchior returned jovially.

"It is just that—"

"Tell me your concern, Bijak. I will answer you, if I can."

Hesitantly, the youth spoke. "I am honored that you want me alone to accompany you, but I could never forgive myself if something happened to you on this 'adventure,' as you call it. I know little of the world. I have only traveled once or twice with you on short journeys. Am I really the best person to go with you?"

"Yes, you are. Your youth and my experience—we are a perfect pairing!"

"But—"

"Bijak, I would be clearer if I could, but I cannot tell you what I do not know. I will share with you that I am more excited than I have been in years. I believe that something is going to occur—or has occurred—that will change the lives and destiny of the entire world. So, do not worry that you do not grasp things of this world. If it changes, what will it matter anyway?" he asked Bijak—and himself—somewhat rhetorically.

"Your words are strange, Master. Almost as strange as the words that were written about the virgin giving birth to a child."

"I told you that was in the past. It was predicted by a Jewish prophet centuries ago and was to take place in their not-too-distant future."

"Did you read further and find out what happened?" Bijak inquired, as if he wanted to take Melchior's mind off the trip and to delay their departure.

"To be honest with you, I have not had time to read much more because I went to bed that very night with the resolve to follow the star. However, what I did read—well, never mind. Now, Bijak, I want you to quit looking so disturbed when I mention following the star. It will lead us, never fear."

"But to where?" the youth almost wailed.

For the first time, Melchior seemed distant as he gazed outward. "To a baby, I believe."

"You just said the virgin's child was born hundreds of years ago."

"Yes, so I did."

"Then who else is having a baby?" Bijak's voice rose upward in total surprise at Melchior's unexpected responses.

"I am not sure, but she must be somebody extraordinarily special."

"You say her baby will change the world?"

"He will."

"He? What if she has a girl?"

Melchior's quizzical look and stunned silence was too much for Bijak, who could not stop himself from laughing out loud as he added, "Women do have girls, Master!"

"For goodness sake, Bijak, the Messiah of the world has to be a boy."

"The who?"

"The Messiah—the hoped-for leader the Hebrew people have been waiting on for over 1,500 years."

"That is a very long time—and who are the Hebrews again?

"Enough, my young friend, we have many days and nights ahead of us, and you may question me at length as we travel. I will finish here. Go and reassure your mother—at least, as much as you can," he told the youth, who clearly still had many concerns. "On your way to her, please tell Sarkev to send someone up for my baggage and say that we will leave by sunset. Kiss your mother goodbye, and do tell her that you and I have talked and that all will be well."

Melchior smiled warmly at Bijak as he urged his reluctant co-traveler forward.

The velvet sky was a dark blanket of vastness pierced by the distant glow of myriad lustrous objects. The magus called to Bijak to move his camel closer, although the lad's animal was fairly near already.

"With the night being darker, can you tell the star we are following?"

"In truth, I cannot, my lord Melchior. Though I have been trying, I cannot figure out which one you say is guiding us. Quite a few of them are brighter than others. Yet no single one in particular seems to outshine the others...or to be leading us," he added deferentially in a low voice."

Melchior nodded his head, as if his young companion's words confirmed a personal theory of his—which, of course, was the case. "The one we are following has been close to the horizon for most of this night's journey, but it has now risen higher." Noting Bijak's puzzled look, Melchior commented, "The horizon is the distant place where the sky looks as if it meets the earth. So follow the line of my arm outward, as if it could go on forever." Melchior raised his right arm and with his finger pointed to where he wanted Bijak to

concentrate on detecting the star that for him blazoned out
the trail they were to follow.

"Ah—I see it! The bright almost blue-colored star?"

"No, that is Regulus in the lion constellation."

Melchior was about to redirect Bijak, but the youth
blurted out, "The lion constellation?"

Choosing to respond to the interest in the other's voice,
Melchior replied, "Yes. Since time began, we earthlings
have sought to chart the heavens by seeing patterns in the
night sky. The star you are looking at is where the heart
of a lion would be. Look up higher in the sky, and use the
brighter stars to see the head of a lion."

Patiently, Melchior waited in silence as Bijak dutifully
looked outward. His companion finally spoke. "I do not
really see a lion's shape, but as I look, I feel very small down
here."

"It is enough that you feel the power of the heavens,
Bijak. We are indeed tiny specks in this great and grand
universe. When we halt for a rest in a few more miles, and
you lie down in the sand and gaze up, you will begin to see
differences among our friends glowing high in the sky."

"I am glad to be here, Master. You have much to teach
me—as you always have. I would like to understand more
of what is truly another world to me. I guess I have misspent
my life, not paying any attention to the stars that are so
important to you. I think I really see them for the first time
ever."

Melchior's spirit sang at the enthusiasm in the youth's
words. He answered, however, with a calmness that belied
the joy he was experiencing. "The blue star you sighted
tonight was considered by our ancestors to be one of the
four royal stars—the guardians of the heavens."

"It is certainly wonderful to know we are guarded from above."

Thus, their first night of following the star was spent in a rambling lesson of lore and legend passed down from ages past. As they traveled, the youth and his mentor pointed out one glowing object after another for the other to see, discuss, and even to discover anew—as generations of stargazers had done for centuries before them. Their voices and the soft clop of their camels' pads on the sand were the only sounds that pierced the surrounding vastness.

Forty days and forty nights had passed since their journey began. On this night, Melchior and Bijak were huddled together for warmth under the canopy of stars. The camels rested nearby, and their warmth radiated out and provided some heat against the cold of the desert night. Melchior had decided not to travel this evening to test his theory once more about the star's movements and his own travels. Neither the youth nor the man had spoken for some time as they both gazed upward.

Suddenly, Bijak's excited voice cried out, "My lord, did you see that?"

"See what? Where?"

"Over to the left—it looked as if a star just shot across the sky."

Melchior smiled in the dark before responding. "It sounds as if you saw what is commonly called a falling star."

Unfortunately, his answer panicked the youth. "Are they all going to start falling? Will they hit us?"

"No, no, be calm, Bijak. There is no cause for alarm."

"But—"

"It looks like a falling star, as you said, but it is probably a meteorite."

"Is it a good sign or a bad sign?" Bijak completely ignored the scientific term as he expressed his continued fear.

"Let us say that it is a good sign."

"I like that, but are you only saying that for me?"

Melchior spoke without hesitation while blithely ignoring his own training. Bowing to traditions from childhood, the wise man suggested, "Make a wish upon it."

"What should I wish for?"

"You cannot tell me, or it will not come true. Wish for whatever you most want in the world. Close your eyes and make your wish."

Seconds later, Bijak seemed relieved as he stated triumphantly, "I did it!" Then, he could not contain his excitement. "Please, may I tell you what I wished for?"

"I told you that you cannot tell me—or anyone else."

Almost ready to burst, Bijak exclaimed, "I did not wish for something for myself."

"Excellent," Melchior responded dryly. "Your total unselfishness will help even more to make the wish come true."

"Do you really believe in wishing on a falling star?"

"What I do believe is that the stars tell us we are not alone."

Bijak's eyes grew round and definitely frightened. "What do you mean—that we are not alone?"

"There is no need to be scared, my dear young friend. Look at all that is happening above us. Surely someone or something controls that world up there—keeps it in order, if you will."

Bijak expressed a new and even scarier thought. "So that the whole thing will not fall on us?"

Chuckling slightly, Melchior encouraged his young companion. "Precisely. Bijak, you can take comfort in this—my life's work of studying the universe tells me that for thousands of years these same stars have eternally lit the night sky."

Bijak inched even closer to his mentor than he had earlier for warmth. Melchior had little experience with children or even youths as old as Bijak, but he recognized his young companion's need for comfort. Seeking to prepare Bijak, as well as to distract him, Melchior instructed, "At this time of year in the constellation of Leo the lion, which we have talked about, stars appear to shoot across the sky quite regularly. Usually you can spot them best closer to morning—this happens every year, with some years having more sightings than others. Bijak, I am certain they almost never reach earth, and indeed, I have never seen one do that. Maybe their speed causes them to flame out. Maybe they simply become less bright, and we cannot see where they settle in another part of the sky."

To further divert his young companion from his fears, Melchior redirected their conversation. "As a matter of fact, Bijak, a little over one thousand years ago, our own Mesopotamian scholars prepared a chart of the stars that showed how the constellations and planets move in distinct patterns. I tried to find our star, but it does not appear in any of the catalogs I have researched. Comets come and go, sometimes not returning for vast periods of time. But you might be more interested in hearing about a fairly recent comet that affected the life of Julius Caesar, a great Roman leader."

Bijak asked in a sleepy voice, "I thought you were telling me about meteors. What's a comet?"

Somewhat ignoring the question, in part because he was currently focused on the appearance of the Caesar comet, Melchior muttered, "Well, it was really a number of years ago. Time does fly."

"Like stars?"

"I see what you are getting at, and I do not know whether to tell you of meteors or comets or time or shooting stars."

Bijak mumbled, "I am getting awfully tired, Master."

"Well, we could wait for another time, with the many miles we have yet to travel ..."

But the sound of slow, even breathing beside him indicated that Bijak had fallen asleep. Melchior gently readjusted the blanket over the youth before looking to the skies again. Happily, he gazed out toward "his" star, which had remained in place this night—as he had known it would.

CHAPTER 5

And Then There Were Three

Melchior had decided that his young traveling companion should keep a log of their travels. Giving this task to Bijak was a way to encourage him to practice his writing skills. It also gave him an additional chore to help him to while away some of the hot daytime hours before they slept prior to continuing their travels at night. Each day's entry was made according to the fairly new Julian calendar, and the month had just turned to November. This was the time of the Romans, and these were Roman lands they were traveling through; therefore, it was best to teach the youth that powerful empire's calendar. Melchior long ago had given up pretending that his own birth kingdom of Assyria would rise again to the heights of its former glory. His friendship with Augustus Caesar had made it easier for him to accept that Rome ruled the world—which it indeed did.

This evening, Melchior had delayed their start. Awakening as the sun was near to its descent, he had begun to intensely read the book of Daniel. Heretofore, he had focused on the first texts of the Jewish writings, along with the book of Isaiah that had given him challenges with its blend of history and poetic writing. The two authors his friend Seth had recommended to him were Isaiah and the later prophet Daniel. Yet the virgin birth in Isaiah had still intrigued him, as it had Bijak. Therefore, he had changed course again and felt the best plan—at least until tonight—was for him to continue in an organized manner straight to the next book following Isaiah.

Thus far, the new book of Jeremiah had made no reference to a virgin giving birth. But gloom and doom seemed to be the message, which could affect a reader's mood—certainly his own! And Melchior had no use for negative thoughts on this cryptic mission. The length of the Jeremiah reading was daunting as well.

When he had awakened this evening, however, it suddenly had occurred to him that for his current purpose, he should simply revert back to his earlier plan of reading Daniel. Thus, he could leave Jeremiah's grimness for another time. Melchior felt more certain than ever that a child of destiny was soon to be born, as the alignment of stars in the Leo constellation seemed to portend. If that child could possibly be the Jews' promised Messiah, then the book of Daniel needed to be read sooner rather than later.

He recalled that Seth's letter had alluded to the status of this Judean writer as a magus similar to Melchior. The rabbi had stated that the Hebrew was said to have prophesied specific information about the Messiah. Melchior had briefly glanced at Daniel months ago. He also remembered that there had been a prophecy related to seventy weeks. He had not had time to delve into that prophecy earlier, but certainly, those weeks were ancient history since the words were centuries old. What else was in Daniel that Seth had wanted him to know?

Melchior chuckled to himself—skipping forward to Daniel would also let him avoid the next readings called *Lamentations*. According to that title, this would be more negative reading on top of Jeremiah's generally gloomy and lengthy message.

As Bijak was making his preparations for their evening travels, uncharacteristically, Melchior told him that they would not travel this night. The youth looked astounded at this remark. Previously speed, speed, speed had been Melchior's mantra—or at least the speed of their plodding camels, along with the old man's need to rest after each long night in the saddle.

"I know you wonder at my not wanting to travel, but something compels me to stay here this night. We will, instead, read the book of Daniel that my friend Seth urged me to do in his letter."

"As you wish, Master. Let me hobble the camels once more."

Soon, Bijak rejoined him, but the lad seemed restless. Because their normal activities would have had them mounted and moving forward, Melchior sought to divert him. "Would you like to lead us, Bijak, in this required reading?"

"What do you mean?"

"Here—you take the writings of Daniel and read to me. It will be good practice for you, and maybe it will give me a different perspective on what this less-ancient Israelite prophet had to say."

"I will do the best I can. I would not want to disappoint you or to hold back your own studies."

"Then please begin. I think you will enjoy reading this because I believe that Daniel was a youth about your age when he began to write."

As the story unfolded, Bijak was almost wiggling with excitement. Unconsciously, he was quickly reading the verses to see if Daniel was going to escape the terrible death planned for him by King Darius' satraps. As the youth began reading the lines where Daniel was actually thrown into the lions' den to be eaten alive,[16] he and Melchior exchanged looks of amazement.

Bijak fairly raced through the words about the sleepless king returning in the morning to see if Daniel was alive. He then unconsciously slowed as he read the portentous words: "Daniel, servant of the living God! Has your God, whom you serve so faithfully, been able to save you from the lions?"[17] In an awed voice, the lad then spoke Daniel's response: "My God sent his angel who sealed the lions' jaws, they did me no harm since in his sight I am blameless, and I have never done you any wrong either, O king."[18]

After reading how King Darius then proclaimed his newfound belief in the Israelite God,[19] Bijak questioned Melchior, "Daniel's God—is he all-powerful? Is this another god we should believe in too?"

Melchior considered how he should reply to the youth, who was obviously impressed with the God of Daniel. "These words and stories are in the Hebrew Tanakh, the collection of Israelite writings. It is their faith journey as they lived through the centuries, frequently in captivity."

Melchior sighed to himself, correctly predicting Bijak's next question. "Why were they often in captivity?"

Where will this end? the old man wondered. Patiently, he gave his opinion. "Sometimes, they sinned against their God, and he punished them."

"They only have *one* God?"

"Yes."

"And when they do something wrong, he throws them into captivity?"

"Not always—but, yes, several times."

"Well then, he's not the God for me!"

Feeling he had been let off easily, Melchior turned their conversation toward the skies since it was finally dark enough for the star's nightly appearance to be visible above the vast desert.

Later, Melchior wondered—much like Bijak, who seemed inclined to doubt the Israelite's Godhead—how the people of Abraham continued to have faith in the face of all of the oppressive troubles that their divine personage had thrown at them over the centuries. Doubt shook him as he questioned if this venture would turn out to be a monumental waste of time and effort.

Despite their great age difference, as well as the obvious knowledge gap, Melchior and Bijak always found something to discuss as they whiled away the hours. And this night was no different. Bijak's craving for information matched Melchior's willingness to patiently respond to the youth's curiosity about this, that, or the other subject—whether it was about the past, the present, or even the future. As they talked on the subject of why distant objects appeared to always recede as they moved toward them, suddenly the boy's better hearing alerted him to distant sounds in the desert. Their conversation immediately ceased. Shortly thereafter, Melchior felt the tremor of the earth. Glancing at each other, they both peered out into the distance trying to determine who or what was not far from their camp.

At no time during their weeks of travel had they

encountered any other human beings, outside of those in small villages along the way. Now, both experienced degrees of concern at the approach of strangers. Bijak superstitiously considered that their talk of far-off objects was somehow responsible for the dark mass of people on the distant horizon. His fear grew, as the group was definitely not receding from them.

In fact, the silhouetted group seemed to be moving in a straight line toward their campsite, which was almost a phenomenon in itself, considering there was a massive desert available for them to choose a different way. Bijak comforted himself that, most assuredly, the night travelers would soon steer away from their own small campsite. Additionally, he could not help but be concerned that he alone stood between the safety of his beloved mentor and these nomads. Images of Melchior being captured and himself being kidnapped and then sold into slavery suddenly flashed into his head. He peeked at Melchior who was alertly watching the group move their way.

As if preordained, the night travelers could now be distinguished as a band of separate camel riders unhurriedly moving toward them. Melchior seemed to be able to look outside of himself and to wonder that he was not more alarmed. He had never feared Bijak's and his traveling alone across the vastness of the desert, despite the situation that outlaw tribal groups frequently preyed on those unable to defend themselves. In a moment of clarity, he knew that these unknown wanderers brought no danger. Kindred spirits, perhaps, searching as he was? This trip with its undeniable element of spirituality also would be less than expected if events out of the ordinary did not occur. Was this such a time?

The camels' muted approach was matched by silence from all parties.

Aware that Bijak had bravely stationed himself slightly in front, Melchior quietly moved to his side and spoke to the five riders. "Will you join us?"

"Gladly," responded the taller of the two riders in the forefront.

Dismounting, the two leaders moved forward simultaneously as Melchior also closed the gap between them.

"I am Balthazar."

"Melchior—at your service."

"I am Gaspar."

"Welcome, welcome, welcome."

They clasped arms firmly with one another. Mutually they smiled, as if this meeting in the vast desert was not an extraordinary event in the sands of time.

Melchior looked to the other mounted men and called to them, "Come, be at peace. Refresh yourselves. My young companion Bijak and I welcome each of you."

The first of this group to speak was an eagle-eyed man who clearly was evaluating all aspects of their small camp. "I am Namon."

"Kateb, companion to Balthazar of Arabia."

Bowing slightly, the last man to introduce himself said, "Raheeb, servant to Gaspar."

Curiosity—at the least—weighed heavily on each of the men, but the laws of hospitality had to be fulfilled first. After Melchior's duties as host were carried out, the men became even more relaxed in each other's company, including Namon, who was eventually identified as Gaspar's tracker.

Melchior took the lead, not only as the obviously eldest

of the group, as was identified by his flowing grey hair and long beard, but in his role as host. Avoiding discourteous inquiries, he spoke in somewhat veiled language of their reason for traveling the broad desert. "Bijak and I are bound for the West and generally travel at night following the stars. However, this evening we decided to stay in this place and rest." Smiling, he ended with, "It was a good decision, for we might not have met up otherwise."

Glancing at Gaspar before moving his gaze to Melchior, Balthazar replied in a deep bass voice which rumbled pleasantly around the campfire, "We, too, follow the stars and have been guided to the West as well."

With a slight pause, Gaspar declared, "Perhaps it would behoove us to travel together for a time." Nodding to Melchior, he gently inquired, "With just you two together, possibly there would be greater safety in your joining us?"

Carefully, Melchior countered, "We would not want to inconvenience you. Perhaps our way is not your way, and we would not want to delay you." His answer was as much a question as a statement.

Balthazar added, "I, too, join in Gaspar's invitation. Let us seek our way together. Mayhap we were meant to meet under these desert stars."

The reference to stars was exactly the encouraging word that Melchior needed. He decided to be more open about their mission. "You noted the stars above, Balthazar. Would you think me an addlepated old man if I told you that we are following a particular star as we journey?"

Both Balthazar and Gaspar abandoned their lounging positions, and after looking briefly at one another, stared at Melchior—as did the others in the group. His steady look told them he spoke truth, and also compelled them to an awareness that all three of these wise men were on the same quest.

As mature men on this decisive journey of a lifetime, there seemed no need for any of them to blurt explanations. Having spoken last, Melchior left it to either of the other two to speak next.

Gaspar broke the silence. "Balthazar and I, traveling separately—and by night, of course—met mere days ago, and now it appears we will be stronger yet."

Balthazar began to speak directly of the star that apparently was the impetus and guiding light for each of them. "All my life I have studied the heavens. My existence has been driven by the answers I have found in the dark skies above. That bright light"—he gestured to the brilliant distant object at which the other two were unconsciously looking—"appeared out of nowhere many months ago. Searching for its origin, I found none. Seeking answers, I felt it calling me to do more than to study it from afar."

Gaspar easily told his own story to his enthralled host and the wide-eyed Bijak. His decision to leave his kingdom in the hands of others, and to journey with Raheeb to where the star would lead them, had not been easily made. But in the same manner that both Melchior and Balthazar had been drawn to the star, he too had been unable to resist the pull of the magnificent light in the sky for which he could find no explanation.

The floodgates of speech opened wide for the men, who had been strangers barely minutes ago. Sharing their separate discoveries over the past months, and even years, reinforced the new bonds they were forging. In their separate kingdoms, separated by hundreds of leagues, they each had tested and evaluated hypothesis after hypothesis about the unfamiliar object in the sky. Delving into ancient books, they had separately found no reference to such a light in the known universe ever before. As soon as one magus brought up a book he had used in his research, one or the other would nod in agreement that this was a familiar source—and that it too had failed to answer the need for knowledge of the celestial object.

Bijak's head was spinning as his master and the two other learned men exchanged ideas and paths they had turned to for clues. He was nodding off to sleep when Balthazar brought up a book he knew! No longer sleepy-eyed, Bijak gazed at the dark-skinned man, who was beginning to talk about the book of Daniel and of that prophet's visions.

"Turning to other sources, I found this Jewish prophet who holds much for us to ponder."

Melchior smiled knowingly at Bijak, who had edged closer to him as they listened to Balthazar speak of a past time that seemingly was important to their present and future.

"I am here on this quest for more than knowledge." Eloquently, he intoned, "In Daniel's seventh chapter, it is written:

I gazed into the visions of the night.
And I saw, coming on the clouds of heaven,
one like a son of man.
He came to the one of great age
and was led into his presence.
On him was conferred sovereignty,
glory and kingship,
and men of all peoples, nations,
and languages became his servants.

His sovereignty is an eternal sovereignty
which shall never pass away,
nor will his empire ever be destroyed."[20]

Balthazar's resonant voice slowed as he emphasized the last few lines, all of which he had committed to memory. No one was asleep, yet no one spoke—until Bijak's youthful voice tentatively questioned, "What does it mean?"

Again, silence reigned, until Balthazar apparently answered for each of the magi. "I do not know."

Melchior, who had been quiet for some time, spoke from his heart. "Before leaving my homeland, Bijak and I were studying another of the Jew's prophets—one they call Yeshayah. Bijak, do you remember what words we stumbled over and had difficulty understanding?"

The youth's eyes went wide, both at his recollection of the puzzling words and because he was being asked to speak to these distinguished men. Gathering a degree of confidence from Melchior's encouraging look, he still rather hesitantly responded, "You mean about the virgin having a baby?"

"Yes, that part." The quizzical looks from the newcomers spurred Melchior on, "As with your delving into Daniel, Balthazar, these ancient writers are difficult to interpret much less to comprehend. Is a particular passage to be taken literally, or is symbolism involved?"

Gaspar contributed his deliberations. "The multiple heavenly gatherings direct us to evidence that a powerful king is soon to be born or has already been born. Your Yeshayah writes of a birth. Balthazar's Daniel writes about one like a son of man who will eventually rule over all nations...I think we seek a child of destiny."

In the silence that followed Gaspar's statement, Balthazar calmly expressed his own reasoning. "The words of this Israelite prophet fill me with hope that men of all nations might join as one under an eternal king—and that this union of all will bring peace in an empire that will never be destroyed."

His words conveyed the unspoken assertion that he would give up his own kingdom, if necessary, to serve this unknown sovereign.

Melchior told the others of his friend Seth who had brought the Jewish writings to his attention. To Balthazar, he said, "Seth, a rabbinical scholar, particularly encouraged me to read Daniel, indicating I might find pertinent information there. As a matter of fact, tonight, Bijak and I were reading the beginning of his book. That is why you found us here."

Both Gaspar's and Balthazar's nods of agreement spoke volumes to the others, which served to confirm what all were thinking—this was no chance meeting of distant wayfarers. Awe and wonder continued to be central to this night's events.

Gaspar began to speak about Daniel's vision that they had all just heard Balthazar speak so eloquently. Haltingly at first, he put his theories into words. "I am not of the Jewish religion, but as I have stated, my studies of the skies reveal to me that a great leader of men will come among us."

Pausing a moment, he looked searchingly at the other two men. "In recent years, Jupiter and Saturn have aligned together. Then, the following year, Mars joined these other two planets. Three planets—Jupiter, the Romans' chief god; Saturn, standing for justice to the Latins; and mighty Mars, all unusually located in the constellation Pisces—have possibly joined together to form this 'star,' as we all are calling it. I have shared with Raheeb, here, my belief that the greatest ruler—*ever*—is alive even now.

"These words from Daniel proclaiming that in a vision it was made known to him that an eternal sovereign whose empire will never be destroyed would come from the heavens ..." Gaspar paused again at the enormity of his own words that seemed almost incomprehensible to understand.

Melchior broke the ensuing silence. "My studies indicate that for thousands of years, the Hebrews have waited for a great king to arise from their midst. They refer to him, not just as a messiah, but as *the* Messiah. This personage will lead them back to their former glory. Considering Daniel's words in their entirety, could not this vision refer to a future earthly leader—the Jews' long-expected Messiah?"

Balthazar ventured, "This prophetic vision occurred over five hundred years ago. And to this date, according to my research, no such eternal sovereign has appeared—unless we consider that someone from the Roman Empire, in existence for 750 years, should count?" His tone implied he was opening up this idea for debate.

"Yes, I can voice an objection." Gaspar eagerly took up the gambit, even as late as it was getting. "No single 'sovereign,' as such, has emerged among past Roman leaders. The name Romulus has lived for that long, but 750 years does not make an eternity."

Out of the darkness, Kateb entered their conversation for the first time. "Rome was founded on the tragedy of the twin brothers, Romulus and Remus. As I am sure you know, they were said to have been raised by a she-wolf. Considering these events, I do not feel that Daniel's words that this future leader, who was to come on clouds from heaven, could or should apply."

Balthazar spoke to his learned companion, who was sitting slightly outside their central ring of discussion. "Continue, Kateb. I know from past conversations that you have strong reservations about even considering Rome in this 'eternal sovereignty' discussion."

The others respectfully looked to this newcomer in their dialogue. Kateb began again. "Sires, forgive my intrusion. King Balthazar is too generous and should be the one you listen to..."

"No, speak!" Melchior and Gaspar exclaimed simultaneously.

"As you wish, wise ones. The Roman Empire was already in existence for over two centuries, I believe, before Daniel received his singular vision. This eliminates Roman leaders born until that time from being considered. I also object, however, because I do not believe that an earthly kingdom founded on the slaying of one's brother could be the one prophesied to endure forever."

Noting that Bijak was trying to follow Kateb's reasoning, Melchior put in, "Ah, yes, Romulus killed his twin brother, Remus." Downplaying his comment, he winked at Bijak. "Not to mention that both the boys were saved not just by a she-wolf, but by a woodpecker too."

Gaspar, the youngest of the magi, also smiled encouragingly at Bijak as he spoke his thoughts. "But, my lords, this does return us to Mars again. Legend has it that the parents of the twins were the god Mars and a vestal virgin named Rhea Silvia, who was the daughter of a king herself."

Melchior added, "A point to be considered, definitely— as well as that the Roman god Mars considered both the wolf and the woodpecker to be sacred and special. In addition, my dear new friends, we have talked the night away and a new dawn is rising. Let us sleep on all that has happened this night. My tired young friend Bijak and I will gladly accompany you to where this star of destiny chooses to lead us."

CHAPTER 6

Behold Jerusalem

In the days and weeks to come, the leagues of what was now the sands of the Hamad Desert passed underfoot for the Eastern travelers. The discussions, debates, and exchange of information had become a daily ritual. All grew comfortable in each other's company and felt their extraordinary finding of one another was meant to be. As Melchior and Bijak had done, they always traveled in the cool of night—obviously, it was much easier to follow the star as it blazed in the dark sky, rather than to try to discern it in bright sunshine. The nighttime ride was always pleasant, as the canopy of brilliance above them had a calming effect on all members of their small band, including even the camels, which were rarely cantankerous.

Of late, each day's march inevitably drew them closer to a once-distant mountain range, which Namon had identified as the Judean Mountains. He told them that the hilly region they would enter on the morrow was known as the Judean Hills, and that in these lands the earliest Jews had settled.

As they made camp and then the sun rose the next day, there appeared to be a general change in demeanor for the travelers. It was as if the difference in the land that would take them from what had seemed unending desert to a region of grass and trees, foreshadowed that the end of their quest might not be far off.

Bijak voiced his excitement. "Master Melchior, how close do you think we are?"

With a twinkle in his eye, the old man answered, "Our star has not stopped yet, nor has it told me our journey might be nearing an end."

Undismayed, the youth began his chores with a distinct bounce in his step. Leaving Melchior, his lighthearted whistling could be heard as he went about his regular tasks to set up the campsite.

Later, as Gaspar was finishing his portion of their meal of figs, pomegranates, and hard bread, he brought up the star's position in the early morning sky. "Our star is not so distant, I would say."

Balthazar easily added, "For the past several days, it has been almost directly overhead as we have ridden. It also is managing to guide us to civilization. Namon, am I correct that Jerusalem is about fifty leagues from here?"

"Yes, sire, the capital of the Jewish kingdom lies in the mountains ahead of us. I estimate it to be at least a sennight away. Climbing through these low hills and then riding up into the mountains will slow our progress."

"The City of David—Jerusalem ... in Judea," Melchior slowly added, knowing his own thoughts were spinning in everyone's head. Out of nowhere, and somewhat startling even himself, he continued, "Judea has been ruled for almost four decades by King Herod, who holds his authority from Augustus Caesar himself."

"The might of Rome mixed with the ancient religion of Abraham," Kateb commented dryly.

Melchior picked up on the instant fear that Kateb's

words caused in Bijak, who as usual was near him when the camp had settled in and the conversation began each morning. Seeking to ease the youth's concern, Melchior lightly said, "I actually have met Herod—though it was many years ago in Rome."

All eyes turned to him in interested speculation, waiting for him to continue.

"I was a young man, and almost forty years have passed. But even then, Herod was a man recognized by Rome as a capable leader—as he has proven himself to be in several ways. My father had traveled to Rome to try to launch our country of Assyria as a trading partner within the empire. My brother and I were a part of the entourage. I met Herod during a reception in his honor after Roman authorities had crowned him king of Judea, Galilee, and Perea. Today, his kingship extends even farther, as I have been aware over the years. Herod's allegiance to Rome remains firm. His loyalty to that empire can be seen in his building of the port town of Caesarea a few years ago to honor Augustus Caesar."

"I have been to Caesarea," put in Balthazar. "It is a beautiful modern city built in the Greek tradition. I found it interesting that a city built to honor the Roman emperor had been constructed by an Idumean Jewish king in Palestine. There he also built a temple dedicated to Roman gods, where the emperor is worshipped as a deity himself."

Gaspar observed, "This has to have made Herod somewhat unpopular among the Jews' leadership, as well as with the general population in the lands he rules."

Balthazar responded, "True. But his reputation as an astute statesman has helped stabilize the region's economy. Herod's allegiance is unquestionably to Rome, and this protects the region as well. However, along with his Roman and Greek leanings, his ruthless ruling style has alienated many. His history includes dealing brutally with those who offend him—including family members. It is well known that he deliberately set aside his first wife, Doris. Later, he murdered his second wife, Mariamne, as well as most of her family, including their sons and her brother."

The group digested this unwelcome news about the leader of the lands they were entering.

Melchior tried to ease the tension by telling more of his own personal acquaintance with the Roman-appointed king. "Herod and my father found common ground in that they both enjoyed architecture. This link created a mutual interest and established a foundation for later economic ties, which was responsible for a great growth of trade in my land. Of course, it did not hurt that Octavian basically told Herod that he expected his new Palestinian king to trade with my country."

"Who is Octavian?" asked Bijak.

Gaspar answered for Melchior. "The great Roman leader Augustus Caesar was called Octavian when he was younger—a little older than you are now, I should imagine." Turning to Melchior, he inquired, "So you have personally met and know the Roman leader well?"

Somewhat embarrassed, Melchior replied, "Yes and no, and certainly, I do not know him *well*." Explaining further, he added, "We were both about the same age, and he treated me kindly."

"And your father?" Balthazar companionably urged.

"King Aralius of Assyria."

Gaspar grinned at the others. "If we wind up in trouble, Melchior, here, will be able to smooth the way for us with his many personal contacts."

Balthazar spoke with a no-nonsense attitude. "The stories of Herod's cruelty are legion. He has ruled by terror, and Rome has looked the other way, allowing this client king of theirs to become a savage tyrant."

Back into the frying pan, Melchior thought as he sensed the renewed tenseness in Bijak. "Herod is not the ideal leader, it is true, but he has kept the Roman peace in the region."

Namon spoke from experience. "In earlier times, travelers like us had to constantly fear bands of cutthroats, but Herod's methods of handling such groups—which were brutal, indeed, if even half the stories are true—have made the roads much safer for trade to flourish. The result is that both Judea and Herod have been greatly enriched."

"It is my understanding that taxes in the lands Herod rules are higher than anywhere else in the world," Melchior again contributed. "He pays for his building projects, including the historic and prolonged rebuilding of Solomon's Temple, via levies and taxes, which are as high as ten percent of a merchant's profits."

Gaspar asserted, "I think we can all agree that we should avoid contact with Herod."

Later, while Bijak was alone with Melchior, the youth asked a series of disjointed yet fearful questions. "If the star has stopped over Jerusalem, does not that mean that we have to enter that city? Because it is taking us there? Where Herod is the king?"

His mentor calmly yet honestly tried to ease the youth's concerns. "We will have to determine that as time goes by."

During the next several nights' march, the star steadily shone straight above them. It barely moved its position as they rode through the lower hill country and then up into the Judean mountains. A noticeable chill in the air made them all want to move faster, as it was clear the weather was changing. Winter in this region was relatively mild, but it also indicated to the travelers how long they had been on the road from their separate homelands.

At last the time came when Namon, who almost always was ahead of them in the distance, halted his camel and waited for them to join him on a high overlook. The star, as they all were calling the light they had been following for months, shone directly above them. Its brightness was somewhat dimmer as the morning dawned, but that was usually the case when the sun rose. In addition, there was a seasonal change coming, and no one considered that there was anything different about their steady beacon.

"Behold, Jerusalem!" Namon proclaimed.

Below them, but still quite distant, travel-wise, lay the walled city of Jerusalem. They could see two impressive structures. The early morning sun glinted off the white stone of a large raised structure, which no one doubted was the fabled Temple of the Jews. It captured the eye to the exclusion of all other buildings, even as far away as they were.

Namon pointed to the city. "As we are looking down toward the plateau where Jerusalem is located, the rebuilt Temple of Solomon is to the right. Herod's palace is slightly nearer to us on the left—the one that looks like a fort."

Each of the travelers surveyed the walled-in city, still many leagues off, and each of them felt that the next several days would be fateful ones. Melchior declared in a more serious tone than usual, "We will stop near here and rest. Our star has led us to the City of David."

The three magi uneasily stared upward and outward.

But it was to no avail. Their guiding light was not present in the evening sky.

They had not been worried at first because the skies had been cloudy during the day. As the camels stomped their feet and snorted at this unusual delay in their schedule, the travelers considered the possibilities of their loneliness and even vulnerability.

Melchior started to speak but had to clear his throat first. Taking a deep breath, he quietly said, "I believe we all know what this means."

Balthazar weighed in. "We have no choice."

Gaspar reluctantly spurred them onward. "We have just this one night's travel to reach Jerusalem, if that is where we are to proceed. The temperature is continuing to drop, and we will be warmer as we travel."

Melchior stated the thought they were all considering. "Will we be safer inside or outside the walls of Jerusalem?"

The question hung in the air until a cold blast of wind blew it away as they shivered on their mounts. Kicking his camel, Namon moved forward, and the others fell in line as they began the descent to the city.

The next day, as they were approaching what Namon said were the flatlands of the Mount of Olives, Jerusalem rose under a sky of dark gray clouds. A trail of brown dust ahead of them, however, indicated a fast-moving group of horses, headed in a straight line toward them. Uneasily, they looked at one another.

Namon signaled they should stop and gather close.

Too soon for comfort, a troop of soldiers slowed and drew rein, essentially blocking further movement, had they been so inclined. At the head of the group of ten horsemen was a grizzled soldier who advanced to meet them.

"I am Decanus Hausler of the Germanic cohort attached to the Roman guards of King Herod." Following this fiercely delivered introduction, the muscular man curtly added, "Welcome to Jerusalem."

Their leader calmly answered, "Thank you for your greeting, Decanus Hausler. I am Melchior, erstwhile magus to the Assyrian royal court, the brother and son of Assyrian kings. I am traveling only for personal reasons."

Not to be distracted from his duty or admitting to being overwhelmed by the stature of the traveler, the soldier slightly nodded his head before turning to the man immediately to the right of Melchior. Obviously, he was waiting for the others to identify themselves.

"I am Balthazar, of the royal Arabian family—traveling for personal reasons as well." He used Melchior's specific words without looking at the old man.

"I am Gaspar, king of lands far from here, and also on personal business," the young ruler responded quietly.

The Roman soldier acknowledged the additional two royals with the same slight nod, and as his mounted soldiers surrounded the magi, he commanded, "We will escort you into Jerusalem where King Herod will wish to greet you and to welcome you to Judea, as befits your status." With that, he spurred his horse forward, imperatively shouting, "Make haste—the weather is about to change."

Clearly, the magi had no alternative. Although they were weary from their recent descent of the mountain and the last miles to Jerusalem, which had seemed interminable without their guiding light, each man began to mentally prepare for the unwanted meeting that lay ahead—and that all had wanted to avoid.

After traveling a short distance, the Germanic soldier's warning about the weather came sooner than he had hoped, and in a manner unexpected to the Eastern travelers. From the sky above, they were surrounded by cold white flakes that melted as soon as the white stuff touched their garments.

Bijak excitedly shouted, "What is this?"

Decanus Hausler had slowed their pace, and it was he who responded to the joyful surprise in the youth's voice. Gruffly, he stated, "It is called snow, and is a rare sight in this region. Actually, not long ago it snowed also—that was one of the biggest snowfalls anyone could remember. At least seven inches blanketed the land."

"What does it do?"

"Changes the world around you," the soldier commented in a quieter tone. "In my country of Germania, it snows almost every day of winter..." He stopped, not as if he had said too much, but as if the memories of the past were emotional.

All too soon for most of the group, including the soldiers, they found themselves passing under the opening of the Horse Gate that guarded the closest entrance to Jerusalem. As their various mounts clattered through the sleepy town, few people were out and about this early in the morning. However, as they loudly rode through the city, and the white flakes continued to fall, more and more people came outside to stand and gaze in wonder at the rare phenomenon.

Moving through the ancient city, Melchior speculated if their soldier guide was deliberately taking them past what appeared to be a prison tower on their left. Soon they were led through groves of trees and ponds with multiple semi-frozen, bronze fountains already covered in a white blanket of snow. Their armed escort finally halted in front of an immense platformed structure, clearly on the palace grounds, where a guard passed them through to a wide ramp that rose in front of them. That ramp led to others, but finally they climbed to the top of the last one. An open courtyard area steered them to an ornate columned front and to the main entrance of Herod's fortified palace. As all dismounted, with Melchior noticeably slower and stiffer than the others—although he did try to hide his fatigue—the door majestically and silently opened. Decanus Hausler entered and spoke to the attendant.

In less than a minute, a black-garbed man joined the soldier. After a few brief words were exchanged, the man moved forward and bowed deferentially to the three Eastern royals. "Welcome to the palace of King Herod. I am Seir, major domo. The king is being informed of your arrival. Custom demands, as you have come in peace and from afar, that you be given time to rest and to refresh yourselves before you meet with King Herod. Come, please, and follow me."

A Promised Messiah

Hours later, the three royals, who had not spoken together after being brought to the palace and then taken to separate opulent chambers, found themselves traversing silent hallways surrounded by alert guards. Finally, they were led into the presence of King Herod, ruler of the Judean lands under Roman authority.

This was the first time Melchior had seen Herod since the day they had met when Octavian had introduced them, all those years ago. Melchior was unsure if the man in front of him would remember that long-ago meeting. He carefully scanned the lined face to see if he could interpret the notably mercurial leader's intentions toward them. It was soon made clear to him that Herod was quite eager to meet and greet his visitors, who had been identified to him as royals from three different Eastern lands.

Dressed in a flowing scarlet garment with a jeweled diadem on his head, Herod rose from his ornate throne, where he was flanked by a bevy of others in his court. He moved forward, extending his arms in a benevolent gesture as he greeted them. "Noble visitors, welcome to my lands."

Behind Herod, the court came forward also—it was a tribute to Herod's dominating personality, thought

Melchior, that only now had he become aware of the others behind the Palestinian leader.

"I am Melchior, son of King Aralius and brother to King Aschalius of Assyria."

Herod immediately looked closer and exclaimed, "But I know you. We met in Rome. Augustus made sure I was introduced to you and to your father at the banquet for my ascension to the throne."

Melchior acknowledged the greeting with a slight nod of his head. "Your memory is as sharp as your reign has been long. However, my companions and I are not here in any official capacity. Allow me to introduce my friends to you: Balthazar of Arabia and Gaspar of distant Harawatzia."

In turn, Herod introduced the main members of his royal court, including several of his sons, among whom was Herod Antipater, nicknamed Antipas. At the conclusion of the myriad introductions, the travelers, when asked, assured their host that their initial comfort and needs had been met. At this point, Herod invited them to join him for more elaborate refreshments.

Later, after Herod finished washing his hands after all had partaken of the fairly extravagant meal, he smiled at Melchior as he probed in a firm voice, asking the crucial question that the three magi had been expecting. "To what do I owe the honor of three royal visitors venturing so far from the East?"

Melchior answered as had previously been decided among themselves when they were traveling. Ambiguously, he replied, "We are on an eternal quest for knowledge to which we have devoted our lives."

Herod barely hesitated at this rather unexpected response. Immediately, he countered. "Here in my capital,

Jerusalem is a city filled with scholars. You have certainly come to the right place. Many cultures intersect here in this grand city, whether Roman, Greek, Hebrew, Samaritan, or others."

"At this time, we are most particularly interested in learning more about the long history of the Jews."

Though Herod ruled as the designated king of the Jews, the magi were counting on his rocky and unorthodox relationship with the religious leaders due to his Roman and Greek leanings, as well as his Idumean heritage, to lessen his interest in them. As was hoped, their proclaimed request for information on Jewish history caused Herod to almost visibly dismiss them. "Certainly, I will do all that I can to assist your studies. As you have noted, the history of the Jews goes back to antiquity. You are welcome to stay here in Jerusalem for as long as you choose. Please consider this palace as your home. I will instruct Lieb, the highest ranking rabbi residing here in my palace, to assist you in this quest for the information you are so actively pursuing."

Calling Lieb to him, Herod directed the scholar to do all in his power to assist the travelers. It was soon decided that within the hour the three magi would join Lieb in the palace library, along with a few select rabbis of his choosing. In effect, Herod was rapidly turning his attention elsewhere. However, he did remain in their company for a while longer. For his part, Lieb excused himself and went to contact the other scholars who would assist in the research. Shortly, Herod suggested they might enjoy going to the library sooner rather than later. Before giving them into the care of a palace escort, he led them himself to the wide doors of the magnificent audience chamber.

As they moved through the expansive palace, the kingly trio shared private looks with each other that indicated their elation at how the meeting with Herod had progressed. As they walked through the palace, their guide's voice, discussing a particularly large statue, apparently alerted Lieb that they were nearing the library, where he was waiting. Joining them from inside the massive chamber, he dismissed their designated guide. His pride in their surroundings was revealed as he escorted the three scholars into the lavish room, flanked on each side by Greek statues. Inside, the library was filled with more statues, marble columns, large tables and chairs, and a manuscript collection that was the envy of most who came there.

In deference to the three visitors, two other men stood at the largest table in the room. Respectfully, Lieb introduced them as the Levite priests, Aharon and Ezra. Lieb announced, "Bearing in mind your desire to learn more of the history of the Jews, I felt these two rabbis would be most able to assist. As you might be aware, the tribe of Levi is descended from Moses' brother, Aaron. In addition to being a Levite, Rabbi Ezra is also a direct descendant of the Ezra who was instrumental in rebuilding the holy temple after our people returned from exile in Babylon over five hundred years ago."

In turn, the three of them were introduced. As all were settling into their seats, the library door opened, and another individual entered. It was not lost on the travelers that the interruption was unwelcome to Lieb, as a quick glance at his now impassive face showed.

The newcomer came forward, speaking confidently. "Forgive this intrusion, but King Herod himself ordered me to join you, believing that I might be able to help your research. I am honored to be in the presence of royalty and scholars. I am Dov."

Lieb addressed him somewhat coldly. "I did not think you would be joining us because King Herod always has so many tasks for you to do."

"In truth, our king does keep me busy. And this is another of the ways he wants me to serve him. Do not let me interrupt you further. Please proceed. I will add any small bit I can to your discussion."

Lieb had no choice except to include Dov in the gathering, but he did not add any further credentials for the newcomer, as he had for Aharon and Ezra. Slightly clearing his throat, Lieb addressed the visitors, and it was obvious he acknowledged that Melchior was their leader. "As King Herod bid us, we are at your service. You have complete access to any materials in our extensive library. How may we assist you? So that we can narrow our efforts and save time, if possible, is there any particular period of our centuries-old Jewish history that you are more interested in than others?"

Glancing at his fellow travelers, Melchior came to the point. "We are interested in learning more about the promised Messiah of the Jews."

Melchior's statement drew no facial response from any of the scholars, and Dov even seemed to withdraw from the discussion, as if the word *Messiah* meant nothing to him. Lieb, almost too casually, nodded to Aharon. "Perhaps you can best address this issue."

Accepting Lieb's invitation, the Levite priest calmly declared, "A messiah, in general, can be either a person or a thing, and does not even have to pertain to Judaism." As if his previous remark was of no major significance, he added, "A person can be consecrated with oil, and even an object, like unleavened bread, can ritually be made holy. Priests, prophets, a Jewish king—all could be declared to be a messiah."

Ezra added, "As a matter of fact, Isaiah wrote that the Persian leader King Cyrus, commonly called the Great and who was a non-Jewish king, was declared by Yahweh to be "his anointed,"[21] a messiah, therefore. Cyrus had set our people free, with the only instruction being to return to our old homeland and to worship Yahweh, whom he had come to revere himself."

Melchior bowed his head gently to the two men who had spoken, before observing, "It is our understanding that your God promised to send a specific Messiah who would lead your people to greatness."

Aharon answered, "There is a Jewish tradition that a Messiah will someday come. However, past scholars have determined that when or where this will happen is a mystery. Is this the person you are hoping to find information about at this time?"

Speculating to himself on why Aharon was not more forthcoming, even appearing to be evasive, Melchior replied, "Yes, this is the individual we are seeking ... to learn more about." He hoped that his brief pause had not been discerned.

Balthazar decided to speak up. "He is to come from the royal line of David."

The reference to a kingly Messiah did provoke a measured look from Dov. He scanned Balthazar's face, then looked at both Gaspar and Melchior, as if to determine—*Well, what is his intent?* Melchior wondered to himself.

At this point, Dov did interject. "As I understand it,

this Messiah will be a great political leader who will come in a time of need. However, with King Herod on his throne for almost half a century, and who is known to be a friend of Augustus Caesar, Emperor of Rome, it is unlikely that there is a need at this time for any Messiah to show himself. Indeed, going along with the comments of Aharon and Ezra, some would say that Herod himself could very well be the Messiah."

Seeing the startled looks on the faces of the rabbis, Dov downplayed his last remark. "Not that our King Herod would ever accept that this is his role in our history." Dov then excused himself. "With your research being religious in nature and about an event probably centuries away, if it has not already happened, I believe King Herod would feel that my spending more time with you would not serve him best. For my part, I fear my further presence might slow your efforts." Addressing Lieb, Dov finished with apparent deference. "If you will allow it, I will leave our visitors to you, who can help them the most. Do call on me if needed."

With that comment, he looked regretful to leave, as if sad that he could not be of more assistance. After general thanks and goodbyes had been given, Dov's departure definitely seemed to lighten the mood.

The three seekers of knowledge might not have felt quite so relieved if they had been aware that Dov straightaway made his way to Herod to give a report of the more specific reason that they had come to Judea—to learn about the Messiah. Herod thoughtfully heard the news before proceeding on to a meeting with his chief tax revenue collector. This stalwart individual, for his part, deemed his king must be mightily disturbed about something. He attributed the king's unusually preoccupied mood to be about matters in the kingdom that were far beyond the fact that taxes were being slowly collected, as in the rebellious past, due to the people's renewed resistance to paying the tribute.

Hours later, the three scholars were disappointed. Their session with Lieb, Aharon, and Ezra had merely served to confirm what they each had found earlier in their own research—and that had prompted each of them to begin their travels. Only a few new bits of information had been garnered. However, since they were to meet again on the morrow, hopes were still high that they could learn more in their messianic quest. Their additional hope was to leave the palace as soon as possible.

During the next days, a pattern was set that each morning following the early meal to break their nightly fast, that the scholars would convene together. Each evening, Herod would honor them with a sumptuous feast and entertainment. He always expressed his hope that their work was going well. They, in turn, vaguely responded that they were discovering much of the Hebrews' glorious heritage. Curiously, Herod never asked for specifics about their findings, though not one of the magi doubted he knew their daily results.

As they began another day of scholarly pursuit in the library, it was obvious to Melchior that his fellow travelers were as discouraged as he was. It had become clear to them that although they had free rein in the library, they were never left alone to talk among themselves. Housed in separate areas, the magi were always officially escorted to and from their quarters for any and all movements outside their rooms by efficient servants—actually guards, for all intents and purposes. Melchior continually asked himself:

Are we among friends or foes? All of them had wanted to avoid Herod. None of them had wanted to enter Herod's palace. Now, it seemed, they were virtual prisoners—at all times watched and monitored by both seen and unseen eyes.

Entering the library this day, Melchior was struck by the looks of dismay he encountered from his colleagues. They must find a way to end the present state of affairs. He determined that this day or possibly the next would be their last in Herod's palace. Unfortunately, and much to their dismay, on each of the mornings of their stay, Namon had reported briefly to Melchior that the skies continued to be overcast. This meant that no stars could be seen in the night or early morning sky. Namon, too, was aware of spying eyes and ears, and he would phrase his words vaguely. This morning he had greeted Melchior by simply saying, "I rode out early this morning to exercise the camels, which were restless. There is no other news to report."

Was this to be the end of their quest? Their studies were yielding little to guide them forward, and their beacon had deserted them.

Lieb greeted Melchior and the others in a subdued manner, as if he too felt the ominous surroundings, which he should surely have been used to in the volatile leader's palace. "Today, I thought we would look at parts of the book of Daniel," Lieb began as they moved to the center table where an old manuscript had been placed. "This prophet lived during the reign of Cyrus, and his story is entwined with that famous leader of the Persians. Rabbi Ezra, our resident expert on this time period, will lead us."

As the three kings turned their attention toward Ezra, Melchior clearly remembered the night when he and Bijak had been reading this prophet—the night Balthazar and Gaspar had ridden into their camp. He silently approved that neither of the other two magi had indicated that they knew anything of consequence about this prophet.

Ezra briefly gathered his thoughts, and then began talking fluently of the period of the Jews' continued captivity under the Babylonian Empire. Bowing to Melchior, he said, "Some of what I will be addressing today is historically known to you and the others, but especially to you, Magus Melchior, since Assyria and Babylon were neighbors geographically and shared some cultural ties. I believe that old Assyria was to the north of Babylon in the valley of the Tigris River?"

Melchior nodded agreement to Ezra's somewhat rhetorical question that apparently was meant to invite his input if he wanted to join in and share with the group. Ezra interpreted Melchior's silence as an indication that he should continue his presentation. Knowledgeably he presented the facts. "King Cyrus, by then already being acclaimed as Cyrus the Great, was a Mede who emerged over five hundred years ago as the leader of the Medes and the Persians. About twenty years into his reign, he somewhat peacefully captured Babylon by damming the nearby waters of the Euphrates River and practically walking into the city. With the capture of Babylon, Cyrus became the new earthly master of the Israelites. At this point, he controlled western Asia, making him the most powerful ruler in the world at that time.

"When Cyrus conquered a new land and its people, his treatment of the newly-occupied regions included a policy of allowing the people to continue to govern themselves and to keep their religions. This method of ruling helped him to maintain his mastery over the fallen people, and also made them so loyal to him that his reign over them was generally a peaceful one. Dare I say that the Romans have followed the precedent set by Cyrus. This current world-dominating empire is generally lenient in allowing conquered countries to govern as they did prior to falling to Rome and to practice their past religions. Thus, we have been allowed to continue our ancient Judaic faith.

"Returning to Cyrus's reign—our God once more was generous to his people, keeping his covenant with the descendants of Abraham and specifically with the people of Judah. In time, King Cyrus became close to the Judean Daniel and called him friend. Over the years, Cyrus and other kings valued him as an adviser, a magus ..." At this point, he bowed slightly to each of the three royal scholars listening to him, then continued. "As I just noted, this Israelite prophet influenced a number of kings during the Babylonian exile of our people. First, in his youth, he interpreted two dreams of King Nebuchadnezzar, which came true." Ezra halted again, as if he wanted to say something more, but was holding back.

Melchior urged, "Please tell us what you are thinking. Maybe it will be a key to enlighten us."

Ezra looked searchingly at the three magi and then spoke in a reverent tone. "Daniel foretold that Nebuchadnezzar would go insane, but would regain his sanity when he acknowledged the power of our God. In the fourth chapter of his book, Daniel recorded this king's newfound belief, following his time of insanity and then the regaining of his senses. Nebuchadnezzar's words were that he would 'praise and extol and glorify the King of heaven.'"[22]

The opening of the library door caused Ezra to halt

at this dramatic point of his presentation, as Dov entered the room. Civilly, the newcomer addressed those present. "Forgive my intrusion, but I had heard that Daniel was going to be discussed today. He is a fascinating person in our history, and I wanted to be present."

Lieb responded to Dov's unexpected entrance. "Of course you are always welcome. Pray, be seated. Ezra, please continue."

Ezra seemed to be reshuffling his thoughts, and it was clear to the magi that he had become slightly rattled by Dov's arrival. Melchior wondered why Herod's special adviser wanted to hear the discussion on this particular writer and, additionally, why Ezra was so obviously uneasy.

Finally, the rabbi cleared his throat and took up his narrative. "Thereafter, Daniel was revered. Twenty-five years later, after Cyrus conquered Babylon and appointed King Darius to rule that land, Daniel's influence remained a force. His advice was valued over that of other counselors."

Melchior was aware that Ezra was choosing his words with care and that, at the least, something of importance had been left out. With his audience extended to Herod's personal—*well,* spy *is the word that seems most appropriate,* Melchior thought—Ezra was speaking slower, as if he were measuring, even guarding his words. Or was he only trying to keep the history clear for his audience, with the many kings who were in the narrative. The story of the prophet had moved onto Darius' famous reign. Melchior's attention was recaptured when Ezra mentioned that at this time, the king was sixty-two years old[23]—*several years younger than I am now,* Melchior thought.

"Darius appointed Daniel as one of three presidents in charge of over one hundred twenty satraps—governors—that he appointed in various parts of the realm. When the king revealed that he was considering an even higher position for the Jewish prophet, the governors determined they had to act. They decided that using Daniel's faith in his God would help them to discredit him, and thus they could be rid of him once and for all. As a group, they went to the king and urged him to issue a decree that, on the surface, would prove the people's loyalty to the king. In reality, however, it would be a trap for the influential Daniel. For one month, no person in the land would be allowed to pray to anyone except to Darius. Any offender to the order would be thrown into a den of lions to be devoured.[24]

"The king almost immediately signed the edict, which they urged, 'as befits the laws of the Medes and the Persians, which cannot be revoked.'[25] Daniel, learning of the signed document, left the palace and returned to his home so that he could continue his own personal habit of praying three times daily to the Lord. Confident that Daniel would not follow the decree, selected satraps followed him to his home. After hearing him pray aloud to his God, they brought him to Darius, who had no choice except to throw him into the pit, where the animals had not been fed for several days. The den was sealed; Daniel's fate seemed a given. King Darius, however, was so concerned for his friend Daniel that he could not sleep that night. He even rejected any of his concubines who sought to distract him and fasted through the long hours until dawn.[26]

"In the morning, Darius went to the lions' den. Even as he approached it, he called aloud to see if Daniel's God had somehow saved him. To the king's astonishment, Daniel responded that the lions had done him no harm because he himself had not harmed the king. Immediately, he was ordered to be released, but his accusers with their wives and children were thrown into the pit. All were attacked and eaten alive by the raging lions. King Darius then proclaimed to all the nations of the world that every kingdom in the empire should tremble before the God of the Israelites."[27]

Ezra, made stronger by the telling of the prophet's trials, quoted from memory the words of the new decree: "He is the living God, he endures forever, his sovereignty will never be destroyed, and his kingship never end."[28]

The solemn silence that had taken over the room was broken by a seemingly guileless question thrown out by Dov. "Did I miss your telling our guests about Daniel killing the dragon and disgracing the priests of Bel?" Dov's words immediately changed—even chilled—the atmosphere around the table. "I am always amazed that this man could slay a live dragon with no sword, simply by feeding it a mixture of pitch, fat, and hair rolled into a ball and that this concoction made it burst apart."[29]

The strength of Daniel's faith did not appear to be strong enough in Ezra for him to chastise Dov, more than to weakly say, "Not yet."

Dov commented almost carelessly, "I have been told that when people read this book, that their assessment is that someone else wrote parts of it. Have you told them of this so-called prophet writing that he had received visions of four mythic beasts rising from the sea? A reader gets the impression that he is almost obsessed with lions, inasmuch as the first such beast that rose from the water was a lion that, incredibly, had eagle's wings.[30] Will you be sharing your judgment on these things as well, Ezra?"

To the three scholars, it was clear that Herod's personal

adviser had the focused objective to cast doubt on the prophet's authenticity.

Melchior felt certain that this session would move forward in a new direction if Dov stayed. They would waste the next precious hours if that occurred. He decided to intervene. "Thank you for honoring us with this prophet's deeds, Ezra. I would like to study Daniel's book." Noting the inquiring looks of the others, he added, "I always find if I have had the chance to read something myself, that I am then able to understand the events better—especially if they can be confusing, as Dov is indicating."

Taking their cue from Melchior, the other two magi spoke up, with Balthazar speaking first—and truthfully. "I, too, would appreciate reading this original text."

"My colleagues have spoken my own desire," Gaspar added. Rather forcefully, he stated, "You can all feel free to leave us. Shall we gather later today?"

Lieb agreed to the delay, but cautioned, "Daniel's book is small, but in writing of the Babylonian kings with whom he interacted, the stories can be quite confusing to newcomers of our history."

Willing to cater to the royals, Dov still said that Aharon ought to stay in case they had questions on the complicated writings. On the surface, Dov appeared delighted at their request, even as he said his schedule would not permit him to return later in the day. No one doubted that he would be reporting to Herod within minutes of his leaving the library.

A few hours later, when the group reconvened to listen to Ezra's discontinued presentation, the magi had a new respect for Daniel. Each was almost grateful for Dov's initial interference because this had contributed to the unexpected opportunity to personally study the original manuscript in Aramaic.

Melchior had studied Daniel with the perspective of his own purpose in traveling to this region foremost in his thinking. Carefully scanning the faces of his colleagues, he was certain that Balthazar and Gaspar had found new insights, as he had. The prophet of old had much to tell those willing to dig beyond the surface of the words and the events in the history of Judah. He was more than eager to continue the session with the Jewish scholars.

Ezra began with a semi-apology for the morning's interruption. However, after hearing the rabbi's first words, Melchior had to wonder if the man might not have spent some time in Herod's presence during the intervening hours. With a slight nervous nod, Ezra spoke, "I must beg your forgiveness, my most esteemed and learned audience. It was not my intent to delay your seeking information about events in the history of the Israelites. Their many times in captivity is important to understanding who they are—who we are—and my intent was to inform you of Daniel's place in that history. However, it has been called to my attention that as you are especially interested in the Messiah, I should skip most of Daniel as a waste of your time. I propose that we move on to other prophets since this writer has little to say about the possible coming of the Messiah."

Melchior dared a look at his companions, and saw that each was trying to come to terms with this change of events. Ezra was stating a bald-faced lie, according to what they had read. And in the tenth chapter, who could the man dressed in linen[31] possibly be except for a messiah-like person? Melchior was extremely disappointed at what he had to conclude was Herod's direct command to Ezra. He gave a fleeting thought to the fact that Ezra knew that the three magi had just had the opportunity to read all of the ancient manuscript. To people of their intellect, it would be obvious that references were made by the prophet to events that could be related only to a future presence far beyond mortals. In other words—and most probably—to the future-promised Messiah.

Gaspar was the first to speak, as he dryly urged, "Will you not touch on the dragon that Dov so earnestly wanted to hear you discuss?"

Ezra did not catch Gaspar's patent sarcasm. Eager to latch onto anything that would keep them from asking more about the Messiah, he eagerly responded, "Yes, we can certainly spend time on the dragon's tale. In actuality, the creature was one of the gods of their Babylonian captors." With that, he was off and running in a direction that extolled Daniel's talents of being able to prove the falseness of the priests of Bel, along with conquering the dragon that was also worshipped.

As the tale from the past spun out, the wintery sun slowly moved its rays across the room. Ezra concluded his remarks. "I am happy that Gaspar and Balthazar kept asking such astute questions about the rather awesome events in parts of this book. Daniel is truly a man of God and a hero to the Israelites, as he survived the ordeal in the den of lions and the dragon perils. He showed us how to live in godless times among unbelievers."

Suddenly, as Lieb rose to end their long day, Melchior let out a cry of pain and sagged in his chair as if he were having severe chest pains. All eyes were on the older man as Balthazar, nearest him at the edge of the table, rose in concern to help. Farther away, Gaspar grabbed a clean goblet and filled it with water as he too hurried to their leader's side.

Only Balthazar saw the wink from Melchior as he came to the aid of the apparently stricken man. Rising to the occasion, Balthazar urged the others, "I state my right to care for Melchior. Please help me to immediately take him to his room. I am hopeful that this long day is all that has led to his current situation."

Lieb offered the medical skills of Herod's personal physician to attend Melchior. But Balthazar quickly yet courteously replied that he felt the sick man would be more comfortable among his friends. Then he directed his next words to Gaspar. "I need your assistance to care for our colleague."

CHAPTER 8

Bethlehem

The door to Melchior's chambers closed behind the servants who had carried him from the library on a stretcher. Balthazar took a seat and wryly inquired, "What is this all about, my friend?"

Melchior threw off the bedcovers but did not rise right away. He looked to the closed door in anticipation that Lieb might call the royal physician anyway. "Thank you, Balthazar, for your quick thinking to help me pull off my plan for us to finally have some private time together. In truth, I am not that good an actor. My cry of pain was because my bad left knee did buckle awkwardly when I rose up after sitting for so long."

Balthazar's eyes twinkled as he glanced at their youngest companion, who still appeared shaken over Melchior's distress. "Gaspar, I could not let you see that Melchior was not ill. Please forgive me."

Gaspar quickly dismissed the apology. "It is apparent that we have wasted our time here. Herod controls everything and everyone in this palace. We are hearing and learning only what he wants us to know." Almost sadly, he said, "We will never hear what Ezra might have told us about Daniel's visions."

Solemnly, Balthazar agreed. "As I have told you both,

my belief is that the words about a son of man rising to dominion and kingship is almost certainly a reference to the Messiah we seek, even if Ezra claims there are no messianic observations in what we all read today."

"I am agreed with you," Melchior strongly responded. "We have no recourse—we must find a way to escape what has become a prison."

In a distant part of the palace, Herod was listening to Ezra's report. Dov was nearby to offer advice, if needed. Ezra was completing his account of how the afternoon session had progressed. "As you directed me today, my liege, I was successful in diverting attention from Daniel's writings that some might interpret as relating to the supposed Messiah."

Herod seemed to gaze off in the distance as he sat, but the drumming of the fingers of his right hand on the throne indicated his frustration. Finally, he mused quietly, as if merely reflecting aloud, "Yet you say that each of them was given the time to read the book in its entirety?"

Glancing guardedly at Dov, the now-worried rabbi confessed this was the case. "It was a direct request of Melchior. The other two kings wanted to read it as well." Seeking to escape the wrath of his proverbially short-tempered monarch, he hedged, "Dov brought up that others might have written parts of the book. Knowing that this book is confusing to the uninitiated—and since at that time I had not spoken with you—well, as I said, I felt it was a natural request and that they would learn little."

Slowly, Herod's dark eyes moved to Ezra's face before he voiced his displeasure. "Three scholars—coming to Jerusalem to discover more of the history of the Jews— and you do not think that at least one of them might have detected some reference to the Messiah in your Daniel's writings?"

Inwardly cringing that Herod once more was separating himself from his Jewish ancestry, Ezra tried to defend himself again. He began this attempt to acquit himself of perfidy by saying, "None of them indicated they had learned anything from the short time they had to read. In fact, their youngest member, Gaspar, only wanted to hear more about the dragon that Dov mentioned earlier."

Savagely skewering him, Herod demanded, "Did you *enlighten* him on this vital point?"

"Yes, yes, I did." The glare from both Herod and his henchman Dov finally pierced Ezra's consciousness.

"Enough!" Herod roared. "Did you not then allow them to go off together? This was something you knew I had put in measures to prevent—successfully—until you allowed them to be closeted together."

Desperate, Ezra defended himself. "Lieb allowed it as well. What does it matter? The old king is probably dying. All of us present felt he was having a heart attack. Few people of his obvious age recover from such a shock."

Herod motioned to an attendant by the door to come near and rapidly instructed: "Send my physician to Melchior. Tell him to report back to me immediately."

Turning to Dov, Herod jabbed at him. "So much for your plan to disillusion them about Daniel. You all have foolishly let them read this so-called prophet, who clearly was misguided based on his own garbled account of events."

Dov took the reprimand in stride; he had been in this position on more than one occasion. He waited for Herod's anger to cool, and hoped that Ezra was right that Melchior was deathly ill. He could see that Herod's ever-fertile mind was already plotting a new strategy related to the visitors from afar. Knowing when to keep quiet and thus avoid calling attention to himself, Dov did not try to defend himself as Ezra had. It was his experience that Herod rarely allowed others to influence him once he had made up his mind about something. The best way to stay alive was to let Herod believe he was always right and to let him weave his own complex plans for survival.

Within a matter of minutes, the outside guard opened the door to admit Qoheleth, the king's personal physician. Hurrying forward, the newcomer bowed and waited for Herod to give him leave to speak.

"Have you already examined King Melchior?" Herod demanded.

Noting the heightened color in Herod's face, along with his slightly quickened breathing, the man of medicine wondered to himself if Herod might not be the sicker man of the two older men. Fairly calm, Qoheleth reported, "My way was barred by the youngest." As Herod's eyes tightened in anger, the doctor added, "I was told that Melchior is resting quietly and appears slightly improved. I was also told that if my skills were needed, they would ask for me. I tried to be admitted, but Melchior himself called from inside the room, in a fairly strong voice, that he felt he merely needed to rest. With that, I could hardly impose myself further."

Herod's exasperation was clear. He dismissed Qoheleth with the words, "If you are called to his chamber, inform me immediately."

As the door closed on the exiting physician, Herod spewed angrily, "They have had time to make a plan. Gather the chief priests and scribes in the palace."

In almost a frenzy, he screamed, "*Now!*"

The following day, the king's private scribe sent an engraved invitation to each of the magi requesting them to join Herod in a gathering of his counselors that same evening. There was little doubt it was an ultimatum, but the three kings eagerly read it. One way or the other, both sides were eager to meet and to part. In the interim since their last meal with King Herod, they had been able to remain together following Melchior's supposed health scare. Their plans were made—as Herod obviously had made his.

In traveling attire, the wayfarers joined Herod in his private chamber. The ruler was regally dressed in his usual red. Gathered with the powerful leader of Judea were the three scholars, Lieb, Aharon, and Ezra, as well as the ubiquitous Dov. The magi correctly assumed that this meeting was not to be shared with the vast array of court followers and attendants, as had always been the case at their regular festive evenings with Herod. Because of the scholarly gathering, they did not fear for their safety, but each wondered why the seemingly secretive meeting was being held.

A meal had been laid out, which was welcomed by Melchior, Balthazar, and Gaspar, who meant to be on the road this very night. The unpredictable Roman-Judean ruler was a benign host, welcoming them and urging them to dine with him. After being assured that Melchior was well and strong after a day of resting, Herod graciously displayed the wealth of his kingdom. Exotic foods from across the breadth of his lands, including citrus leaves for their pleasure from Eastern lands, were brought to the table.

Conversation was general—and generally evasive—until the food was cleared away. With only the eight of them in the room, Herod opened up as to his reasons for this private gathering. Addressing Melchior, he graciously inquired, "Have my rabbis been able to help you to the degree you had hoped in your research on the history of the Jews?"

Not appearing to be aware of any other issue than the impartial question, Melchior replied. "Lieb, as you bid him, has always made us welcome to the extensive library of materials accumulated here. Many ancient and original documents have proved to be interesting and helpful resources. Having now been able to confer together, we three feel we have imposed on your hospitality long enough. We must be about our business in our extended travels." Graciously, Melchior added, "Unfortunately, this requires our leaving your most welcoming presence and palatial residence here in Jerusalem."

Giving nothing of his thoughts away, Herod appeared regretful that they would be leaving. "Melchior, you appear to have made a rapid recovery, but you are entirely welcome to stay as long as you desire. You must be aware this is not fit weather for travel. It has snowed or been exceedingly cold almost every day of your stay—a unique weather pattern not often seen in this region."

"We believe that it is better for us to leave than to remain here longer."

"Where will you go from here? I will gladly send men to accompany you."

"That is a generous offer, but having traveled in safety for many months, we do not fear the unknown."

"Do not be offended, Magus Melchior, but it has come to my attention that your studies have been concentrated on the coming of a messiah among my people, the Jews. A liberator, if you will—a Moses, for example?"

Melchior's eyes fleetingly met those of Balthazar and Gaspar before he again turned to face Herod and firmly stated their position. "We seek not simply a messiah, but *the Messiah.*" Then, and as if compelled, Melchior forthrightly queried, "Where is the infant king of the Jews? We saw his star in the East and have come to do him homage."[32]

Herod narrowed his eyes as if facing a previously undiscovered foe. Visibly, he grew threatening while looking at his stunned phalanx of scholars. "An infant king of the Jews, you say?" Exerting supremacy, Herod asserted. "*I* am the king of the Jews. And though I have sired many children in my life, I have no infant children at this time."

Making an effort to mask his anger, Herod turned to Lieb and commanded, "Please do enlighten our magi here as to what you told me earlier."

Lieb clearly was hesitant to respond after Melchior's dramatic declaration followed by Herod's authoritative rebuttal. "Sire, you mean about no clear reference to the coming of a Messiah?"

"Yes, Rabbi Lieb, as you told me was your conclusion earlier this morning."

"Well … as you directed me yesterday, King Herod, my fellow scholars, Aharon and Ezra, and I, along with other scholars in differing fields, have diligently reviewed our knowledge of any messianic figure. In our writings, we have had many 'anointed ones'—but as to a clear reference to a specific person who might be called 'the Messiah'—er, we found no such person ever mentioned."

"Sire, if you will pardon me?" Dov interjected himself into Lieb's fairly weak performance. At Herod's nod of approval, he addressed the visitors. "Days ago, when I was in our great king's library and first heard of your interest in a messiah, your pursuit intrigued me to learn more. I had thought—and still have reason to assume—this future and possibly mythic person will be a public figure, possibly with a religious agenda, but that will not necessarily be the case. Overall, my intent was to speedily further your quest."

Glibly, he began to present extenuating circumstances. "Never has there been less need in our history for the appearance of either a political or spiritual messiah. King Herod has the reins of his kingdom well in hand, politically. Spiritually, he has spent several decades of his life rebuilding the Temple of Solomon. Indeed, all Jews are grateful for his dedication to his faith. Let me now address the question you have just specifically asked. Unfortunately, my recent research definitely does not indicate any probability of a newborn king of the Jews. Our king is too modest about his own progeny. He is, of course, the loving father of almost twenty children, but the youngest of them is well into manhood."

Herod stopped Dov with a hand gesture. Appearing to be in a good mood, he said, "Dov always believes I can do no wrong."

Turning to the magi, he tried to sound cordial; however, his agitation was clear in his rigid posture. "But beyond your seeking a child—what is this about a star that you have been following? I am in the dark about this. I do not recall any of you three mentioning a star previously."

Balthazar entered the arena of discourse. "Pardon, Highness, we meant no disrespect. You have been gracious and hospitable throughout our stay. We will let the world know the kind of leader you are." He bowed his head slightly in Herod's direction, hoping his satire would not be apparent.

Authoritatively, he continued. "As to a star, my own personal awareness of the activity of the planets caused me to take action and to travel afar. We who are astrologers study the skies to interpret news and events about our world. The universe has much to tell mortals if we can find the way to interpret the signs given to us. Several months ago, the largest object known to man in the solar system, Jupiter, had an unusual visitor in the realms above us. As you assuredly know, this planet is named after the mightiest god in Roman mythology. Astrologers commonly refer to it as the king's star. The planet Saturn, designated as the shield of Palestine, among its other names, was on a path to pass by Jupiter. It did more than come near. My studies, which I would not dream of boring you with any further, led me to believe that a great leader had been born or would be born soon. Immersing myself in research, I felt I had to personally follow through on what the universe was telling me. My story is similar to Melchior's and Gaspar's own reasons for traveling."

"Quite an original quest," Herod acknowledged. Somewhat accusingly, he peered at his own counselors. "None of my advisers made me aware of any significant events in the skies. Uninformed as I am about celestial occurrences, however, and no matter how it is that you each arrived in my kingdom, I do have some information for you three Eastern travelers."

Glancing briefly at Lieb, Herod moved forward his own agenda. "Forgive me for not speaking with you first, Lieb, but mere minutes before our three honored guests arrived, Ezra brought my attention to a very minor prophet, Micah. Since you three magi are determined to continue your journey, maybe this will help to guide you along your chosen path. Prior to Ezra speaking, I feel I must warn you that this Micah lived eight hundred years ago. His relevance to your quest might not be as helpful as it first appears."

Ezra rose and bowed to each royal personage, starting with Herod. "My own personal priest brought this to me, as our king has told you, just a little while ere we were to gather here tonight. Therefore, I have had little time to assess what it might mean. As King Herod stated, I too must caution you not to be hopeful about this very minor prophet's few words. Micah was a Judean, and in all likelihood, he was merely trying to give his oppressed people hope for the future since the times had been dismally bleak for them for such a long period of time."

Lifting an ancient piece of papyrus, he then read to the assembly in a clear voice:

> "But you,…Ephrathah,
> the least of the clans of Judah,
> out of you will be born for me
> the one who is to rule over Israel;
> his origin goes back to the distant past,
> to the days of old."[33]

Finished with the brief words, Ezra then deprecatingly shrugged his shoulders as if validating the patent vagueness of Micah's ancient verse.

Melchior asked for the obvious clarification. "Ephrathah?"

Rolling up the parchment, Ezra answered, "It is a reference to Bethlehem—the little town of Bethlehem."

"This is wonderful!" Melchior responded, as if totally enthusiastic. "We now have a new piece of the puzzle we are trying to decipher. In truth, we must consider what this means."

Herod spoke up, as if a new idea had occurred to him. "I am wondering suddenly if Micah was really making a bold prediction. After all, King David was born in Bethlehem. A descendant of his was likely to come to the forefront again from this same area. Also, there is no clear time reference to when this might happen. His prediction probably was fulfilled many hundreds of years ago. In all likelihood, this is possibly only a reference to the shepherd David, since he did become the ruler of Israel. If that is the case, then these words are not a prophecy but a statement about the past."

As if nothing was rehearsed, Dov commented, "The people of Bethlehem are frequently called Ephrathites to this day. During the recent census of Emperor Augustus Caesar, the town was crowded with people returning to their homeland who had scattered to other areas over the years. The alehouses were filled with jovial travelers all claiming kinship to their royal ancestor David. Because of how hard it had begun to snow, I stopped there myself on the way from returning from my own registration in Masada. The inns were full to capacity, but somehow, a place was found for me to stay. I have to say it—and mean no offense to anyone present here—but some of the pseudo 'royals' were disgustingly drunk and offensive."

The Judean ruler then took over and jovially responded, "One cannot be responsible for all of one's relatives, be they distant or close. I try to honor my heritage, and I have been assured by others that my deeds will live on long after I am gone. The rebuilding of the Temple of Solomon will be my greatest legacy—of that, I am certain. However, since my days are limited, I too am eager to learn if a future ruler may have been born. No one really knows what the future holds, does one?"

Herod then said to the magi, "Go and find out all about the child ... and when you have found him, return here to me and let me know, so that I too may go and do him homage."[34]

Acknowledging his words, the magi swiftly left Jerusalem. Their immediate concern, once they had escaped, was if their star would ever return to guide them.

And there in front of them was the star they had seen rising.[35]

AUTHOR'S NOTES
FOR MELCHIOR

The opening event in Melchior's book of the meeting between Augustus Caesar and the Tiburtine Sibyl, as she is known in history, is considered to have happened. On that fateful day, Augustus asked her whether anyone would ever be greater than he, and would he be worshipped as a god. She initially told him that he would be ... "Until a virgin gives birth to a child and yet remains a virgin." Almost immediately, she then saw a magnificent celestial object soaring above, and prophesied to Caesar that a child of humble birth had just been born to a virgin, whose divinity would later be revealed. Further, he would change the world, be victorious in the end over death, and would reunite all nations. Any number of versions of this legendary event have been recorded over the centuries.

The idea of a virgin birth was probably scoffed at by Emperor Augustus Caesar, as well as, seemingly, an incredulous young Bijak who queried his wise mentor, Melchior, to explain it to him—much to Melchior's dismay. Later in life, the emperor did build the *Ara Primogeniti Dei*, "Altar to the Firstborn of God," to commemorate portions of the sibyl's prophecy. I should also mention that Augustus Caesar is generally ranked as the greatest Roman emperor in that empire's more than one-thousand-year reign.

The historical dilemma posed by the monk Dionysius Exiguus, when he reordered the calendar about AD 525—or CE, as we are encouraged to write today—created critical dating problems as I waded into Herod's dates. In the restructured dating system, Herod the Great had his date of death changed to 4 BC (or BCE). Although not a mathematical genius, even I recognized that I could not write about Herod meeting the magi a few months after AD 1 if he had already succumbed to the syphilis that supposedly killed him. If there are errors of dating throughout this book, then it is either my fault or the fault of historians—'nuff noted on this!

As for the lovely event of the star of Bethlehem leading the Eastern magi to the birthplace of the infant Jesus, it has been dealt with for centuries by both religious and nonreligious historians—not to mention myriad artists—along with astrologers and scientific astronomers for a little over two thousand years. Was it a true star, a supernova, a comet, a once-ever conjunction of the planets, a meteor, or a miracle? Note that the brilliance of a supernova can be seen sometimes for up to two years.

Most scientists who study the stars in reference to past celestial events use data collected since ancient times by the Chinese. According to China's astronomical records, three supernovas occurred in 4 and 5 BC—putting those events in the running for the "star" of Bethlehem that spurred the magi to travel afar. It is also true that several planetary conjunctions occurred during that time frame, putting those phenomena into the mix for the magi's star.

According to the gospel writer Matthew, the magi asked Herod, "Where is the newborn king of the Jews?" Two different translations of their next statement refer to the star itself and their purpose. One version is that they then stated to Herod, "We saw his star as it rose and have come to do him homage." A second translation is, "We saw his star in the east and have come to do him homage."[36] Whether there is scientific evidence for the star or not—and there does seem to be sufficient data—I accept that the magi responded to a message from afar that an astonishing event had occurred, the Messiah had been born, and that they followed a luminous celestial object—a star—to the birthplace of Jesus Christ.

Several years have passed since I wrote *A King's Story*, my first book on the magi. That most special literary endeavor has been the spiritual joy of my life. However, an unbelievable number of people asked me over the years when I was going to write the story of the other two kings who followed the star of Bethlehem to the birthplace of the Christ Child. My immediate response to them was always something along the lines of, "This was all that came to me."

How foolish we mortals are.

As I finally realized that each of these people was pushing and shoving me toward my future destiny with Melchior and Balthazar, I began to see the signs from God that were (almost literally) hammering me over the head. For example, it was in late spring, *the day after* I had finally decided I would write about Melchior and Balthazar—and nowhere near the January sixth date of the Epiphany, the time celebrated as the three kings' arrival in Bethlehem—that a small church about a mile from my home had posted this sign: "Wise men still seek Him."

Imagine, my delight in seeing those words.

Again, as I was stalling, out of the blue, Anna from my church prodded me, "You have so much more to give." I could go on and on and on! At one of my book signings at Fort Leonard Wood in Missouri for *A King's Story*, a man gave me an extra twenty-dollar bill after purchasing my book, saying that I should use it for my mission. I told him I had no mission, but he said I did.

I will end these comments on God's plans for me with several events that occurred at a Sunday Mass on July 15, 2018, at St. Gabriel the Archangel Catholic Church, where I sometimes attend. On this occasion, I was seeking more than my usual request for encouragement from God that I was doing acceptable work for him, and was using the talents he has given me in an appropriate manner. I was almost immediately reassured as the choir began to sing: "Be not afraid, I am with you always ..." Then, in the sermon, the priest stated, out of nowhere, "In Christ there is no east or west." His words directly related to my many directional problems of the magi coming from the east, meaning that they were heading west. This was always a scenario for me regarding directions to and in the Holy Land. Please accept that I was continually trying to map-check these "foreign" lands and travelers.

The true reassurance for me, however, came as the following intercession was later read aloud from the altar: "For all who spread the Word of God, for preachers, teachers, parents and *writers:* that they may announce God's loving compassion faithfully and convincingly so that others may encounter the living God ... let us pray to the

Lord." I know these are the exact words of the intercession because I stayed after the service to request permission to take a picture of it since it had touched me so deeply. I will always be grateful that one of the Mass celebrants allowed me to do this. *Never before nor since have I heard this same intercession—which was for everyone, but most especially for me on that day.* As an FYI, I do feel that all the "areas" apply to me in some way—preacher, teacher, parent, and writer.

As you read the next two stories of this trilogy, please remember that they were written to stand alone for each of the magi's separate experiences. Also be aware that stories from the Bible have frequently been woven into events in the lives of Melchior, Balthazar, and Gaspar, and that some of those words were spelled and phrased differently from how we write today. I deliberately chose to keep original texts as often as possible, so please do not think those words are in error. One example would be "for ever"; today, it would be written as one word.

Interested readers might want to now read the "Author's Notes" after Gaspar's book, the last one of this magi trilogy (but the first book written and published) to learn how the story of the youngest king first came to me.

BALTHAZAR'S
BOOK

PROLOGUE

Prisoners

Circa AD 20

The canopy of stars shining above was still glorious as the wandering Balthazar and his companion, Kateb, settled comfortably into their camp routine. Conversation was minimal as the two men tethered the camels, which also were ready for rest after traveling in the cool of the night for almost five hours. Now, the animals, like their two-legged masters, would enjoy extended leisure until a decision was made to move on to a new location.

Suddenly, tremors in the desert sand underfoot alerted all to the fast approach of horsemen from the south. The camels rumbled their concern as they awkwardly rose to their feet. Acting quickly, Kateb grabbed the ropes hanging from their halters. Balthazar assessed the riders who had daringly moved into their campsite.

An outrider of the band of Bedouins that encircled the camp edged his mount forward, then challenged the man standing calmly in front of him. "We seek a royal of Arabia, one called Balthazar. Are you this man?"

"Well, I am Balthazar, and I am from lands in Arabia." Ignoring the rider's blunt words, he requested, "May I ask who I am addressing?"

Relaxing somewhat at the polite response to their abrupt entrance into the camp and the rudeness of his question, the rider answered in a less abrasive tone that yet did not give away the reason for their unexpected appearance and demand. "All will be explained by my lord and master. I must request that you accompany me to our leader's camp."

CHAPTER 1

The Past Returns

The rugged Bedouin leader looked admiringly at Balthazar, who had just been brought into his presence. Not speaking at first, he then intoned in an appraising yet compassionate voice. "Ah ... the man who does no wrong." The eloquent words hung in the air until he shrugged his shoulders. "However, I am powerless to alter your fate. I am bound by honor and a pledge given to Herod Antipater that the favor he did for me long ago would one day be returned. You are my prisoner. My debt to him is paid." There was a finality to his words that indicated the Bedouin would not be altering his decision.

Seeming to accept the inevitable, Balthazar's deep bass voice resonated for all in the camp to hear. "I thank you for your first courteous words and for the fact that your capture of Kateb and me brought us no harm."

"As to courtesy, I am remorseful in not introducing myself to you earlier. I am Nazim Tariq Umarah abu Sharif. But you may call me Nazim."

Both men bowed formally, after which the prisoner returned the honor, saying simply, "And you may call me Balthazar. This is Kateb who has been my companion and friend for many a decade."

Nazim acknowledged Kateb, who submissively bowed

slightly to their captor. Immediately, Nazim's focus returned to Balthazar. "Do you have any questions I may answer for you?"

"About our stay with you?"

"Ah, yes, let us call it a 'stay'—a long-term visit, if you will." He smiled beneficently.

"We may come and go as we wish?" Balthazar inquired.

"Within reason—in our camp. Of course."

The unspoken words were that they should not press their privileges and that only in camp were they free to—well, be free.

"You mentioned Herod Antipater. May I ask why our time with you is related to the present tetrarch of Galilee?"

"It is a long ago story. But come, let us be comfortable. The night is upon us and the desert winds have brought their evening chill. A fire and food will lift your spirits." So saying, he led his prisoners to where others had begun to gather.

After they had settled in, Nazim answered Balthazar's question. "My debt to Herod of Galilee, known to you as Herod Antipater but whom I personally call Antipas, was incurred long ago. Suffice it to say that I owe my life to him. I pledged to repay that debt with whatever he required me to do. Years later, he informed me that my vow would be redeemed when I had taken you, Balthazar, prisoner. I have done so."

Balthazar and Kateb exchanged glances that shared an awareness of events beyond this moment in time.

Acknowledging Nazim's words, Balthazar asked, "You have tried more than once to capture me, I believe?"

"I have."

"Once was about three years ago, when we were leaving the city of Susa and a sandstorm blew in?"

"It is true. Somehow, you escaped. It was as if you had

vanished off the face of the earth. There was no explaining your disappearance, or even how you survived the storm— as we discovered a few months ago that you had."

Kateb and Balthazar unrepentantly smiled to one another but offered no comment.

Nazim urged, "You look as if you both know something I do not know, and maybe should have known—or should know now."

"Let me simply say that since you have finally captured us, there is a reason higher and mightier than you can know as to why you have succeeded this time when you failed to do so at other times."

"You speak in riddles, but it is an intriguing enigma, I am certain. I implore you to share it with us." He smiled deprecatingly. "Speak, please. We do have plenty of time."

Balthazar considered his words carefully. "My life took a different path over two decades ago—even more, if the previous years of study are counted." He looked up at the clear night sky before turning toward Kateb who purposely had been seated across the fire from Balthazar by their captors.

"My friend Kateb and I were witnesses to an extraordinary event with two other magi who were similarly drawn to our destination by a star."

"Magi—wise men? A star?" prodded Nazim.

Balthazar looked directly at Nazim and then to the others around the campfire, who respectfully listened to his story.

"Yes, to start with, a star." He waited a moment. "Or a merging of planets. Or a still unexplainable phenomenon. In the time before I began my travels to follow this inexplicable light, I determined that the planets Jupiter and Saturn were on a trajectory to cross paths. As one who studies the movements of the stars and planets," he explained to the group at large, "this was a significant event. When these two planets—or whatever portent it was—finally met, a unique event occurred. A vivid light emerged which, as time passed, moved steadily across the night skies in a westerly direction from my home. Those who study such phenomena believe that uncommon occurrences in the world above us herald extraordinary events on this earth. I was compelled to follow this new starlike object to where it chose to lead me. It is a decision I have never regretted. It changed my life.

"I will tell you further, Nazim, that the events surrounding my decision to follow that guiding light continue to be paramount in my life. It is possible that you will become part of the story as well."

Nazim replied, "Your words are now more than intriguing." He shared his broader view. "My people believe in destiny and that our fate was decreed before we ever were born. I have lived by that creed. Indeed, your presence here at our shared campfire is proof of this very fact. It was decided by powers greater than mine that I was to be saved by Herod Antipas, that I told him my debt would be repaid by whatever he asked of me, and that he redeemed my bond by requesting you to be captured. These things are done, and we must both move forward."

He bowed his head in prayerful acceptance before continuing. "But I beseech you to tell us more of the story related to your own star of destiny."

Balthazar gazed at Nazim and then looked searchingly at the others in the glow of the firelight. His eyes made contact with most of those in the circle—hardened men of the desert—his captors. What could or should he say to them? Briefly, he caught Kateb's seemingly calm look, borne of his own part in the story that would now be shared with these rugged men. Finding the inner peace that he always experienced when he related selected events of the star, their journey to Bethlehem, and the child they had found, Balthazar began his narrative.

"The story I am about to share with you can be confirmed by others. Kateb was with me, as were my fellow magi—Melchior, our leader, and Gaspar, the youngest of our trio. I have told you of the convergence of the mightiest of the planets, but this story is one that seemingly has no ending. Indeed, from my further studies, I am confident that this was not the beginning of the story, nor has the story ended—although it took place almost two decades ago. There is much in my heart I cannot share with you, but what you will hear is a story of both vile hate and supreme love. Some or all of it you may question—that is only fair—but every word I speak happened and is true."

Although Balthazar had spent countless hours in the past twenty years considering the significance of the events of his own life, it was not a story he had shared often. His reasons for following the star and what followed the decision of all three magi to leave the palace of Herod the Great as soon as they possibly could were thoughts not readily spoken. In addition, he had to consider that this Bedouin leader felt indebted to the present Herod, who, if rumors were true, had been involved in his own father's death. The long arm of the ruling Judean family had once more proved a potent enemy.

Making the decision of what he would initially share, Balthazar added. "It is, as you have noted, Nazim, a truth that our fates are in the hands of greater powers than we can conceive. What will be will be."

CHAPTER 2

Beginnings

"Let me begin at the beginning—a very long time ago."

So saying, Balthazar settled in to share his story, and with a smile and a hand gesture, he urged those around the fire to do the same.

"My father and his father's father, back to antiquity, have led a kingdom by the sea that rivaled many. For centuries, my people traded with the great lands of this world. Our influence was mighty in days past and remains so today. Great Rome comes to trade, just as in earlier times, the world sailed to and from our shores. My ancestors include the mighty Phoenicians, who later sailed from new lands of power on the Eastern Mediterranean.

"I can claim both kinship and regal authority to my homeland."

The quiet assertion of royalty stirred his listeners. Aware that he had their full attention, he lowered his voice and continued. "But my heart and my quest for knowledge took me from the sea and led me toward a different destiny. Some would say I was a disappointment to my heritage; others would disagree."

He ruefully laughed, encouraging them to share in the unwitting irony of this remark.

"The sea is in my blood, but the stars have directed my

life's course. When my father and uncles took me out on the Erythraean Sea to teach me their craft, I spent more hours of the night studying the heavens than I did learning the skills vital to a seafaring kingdom. I was never so happy as when I was drifting on darkened waters under a glowing night sky. The scenes I envisioned in those youthful days, however, are as nothing compared to where my life on land has taken me.

"Eventually my father gave in to the inevitable and allowed me to be my own person. With his blessing, I found new kinship among scholars in Egypt. For many years, I studied there. It became one of my great joys almost daily to go to the magnificent Library of Alexandria in that country. I read the works of the ancient Greeks in original texts, but to my total delight, I was also able to explore other disciplines of study as well.

"The Greek culture seeks to develop the whole person, and so I was not limited to studying literary sources, but expanded my horizons. I studied great religions, and found both comfort and challenges in reading texts of ancient prophets. Nevertheless, my greatest joy came from learning more of the universe, which had so intrigued me as a child. While studying in this great center of learning, Kateb and I met. We soon found ourselves to be kindred spirits. To this day, we share a continued love of learning. Since those early days of our youth, we have traveled the world together."

Here, Balthazar paused and beckoned across the low-burning fire, urging Kateb to join him. At the look of warning from his captors, Kateb stoically remained where his guards had placed him. Noting the reaction from his own men, Nazim motioned them to stand down. This also subtly signaled a change in the demeanor of all. The group of hardy tribesmen generally relaxed their guard, and Kateb gestured that he was fine to stay where he was. His guards grinned in good humor. One reached across to Kateb and handed him a skewer of meat to show he was now one of them.

Balthazar continued his tale.

"Eventually, I returned to my father's kingdom, but always there was a wanderlust in me to seek I knew not what. When my father died, my twin brother ascended the throne. Since he has fathered many children, I no longer felt that one day I would have to assume the kingship of my country. Dare I say I was grateful for his faithfulness to his wife and to our land."

Some ribald talk and laughter followed this comment. Soon, Nazim brought his men to order and with a hand gesture indicated his guest should continue.

"I became known in my land as one who charted the stars and their portent. When a phenomenon occurred in the skies, my people turned to me to interpret the meaning. It is my belief that higher powers than we recognize rule our lives. Messages are all around us—if we but become aware of them."

At this point, his audience fidgeted a bit, and some looked fearfully skyward. With the sun rising in its seemingly preordained daily ritual, however, they did not give in to fears that might have alarmed them if Balthazar's words had been spoken in the dead of night. Smoothly, Balthazar continued as if he had not noticed his audience's concern at his words.

"As I delved into the past and studied and corresponded with scholars around the world, the universe spoke to me across the ages. Signs of wonder often have appeared first in the skies. It is up to us mortals to try to interpret them. I should add that Kateb and I regularly correspond with astronomers in other lands. From ancient times, astronomers—some call us astrologers or stargazers—have observed and recorded celestial events.

"Over four thousand years ago, in distant lands to the east, people began to chart events in the skies. About four centuries ago, in the lands of the Qin dynasty, they began keeping even more detailed records of star patterns and phenomena that were outside the normal nightly display. The present Han leadership of those far-flung lands has encouraged these studies to continue—which are different from our traditional astronomy in what I call our Western world. Their long-term observations intrigued me as soon as I learned of the existence of such ancient records. Therefore, I focused not only on what my cohorts were studying and writing about, but I also made use of the wealth of information available to me from near and far.

"It is the tradition in these lands that their leaders and emperors must receive a mandate from the heavens for them to come into authority. Similarly, to continue ruling, signs must be favorable. This emphasis on the events in the skies and the affairs of this world cause them to pay close attention to spectacles and occurrences in the skies above us, such as meteors and comets."

Seeing the quizzical look on the faces around him, Balthazar said, "Falling or shooting stars, basically."

Nazim spoke now. "Whereas our desert lands are fiery during the day, we spend much time in the cooler hours of the evening, traveling and doing tasks. My people have often seen these shooting stars, as you call them, rapidly crossing the skies. We consider them good luck for the first person who sees one. I have an older cousin who says his firstborn child is destined for greatness because at the very moment of his birth a tremendously bright star blazed across the skies outside the birth tent."

Laughter again burst out among the men, and Nazim's shoulders shook with his own merriment. Quizzically, Balthazar and Kateb looked to him for an explanation. Nazim shared the cause of the laughter. "My cousin's son is over sixty years old, and my men wonder when he will fulfill his father's expectations."

Quickly doing his own mental math, Balthazar gently said, "Ah, possibly that event is the comet the Roman world refers to as 'Caesar's comet.' It heralded great changes in the Roman Empire, including being used as an indicator that the just-assassinated Julius Caesar had been deified."

As Nazim and his men looked at Balthazar, he could not help grinning himself as he kindly added, "Your cousin's son could still be a person of destiny."

While the friendly laughter subsided, Balthazar glanced to Kateb, who encouraged him with a confidential look that he should proceed on the path he had chosen as he spoke to their captors. "I said earlier that I would begin at the beginning, and this concludes my early adventures—or misadventures, depending upon who is telling the story. Now, I will tell you of the beginning of the journey that so changed my life."

CHAPTER 3

The Journey from the East

"For some time, Kateb and I had been studying a particular area of the skies that had become intriguing. Jupiter, the largest object in the skies, was once again making its appearance. We delighted, of course, in searching the canopy above to try to understand its mysteries. Suffice it to say that this region of the sky held myriad stars that had long interested me.

"On this particular night, as I viewed the clear heavens, there was no doubt that an extraordinary event was happening. Whereas on previous nights, there had been only the known—suddenly the unknown appeared as I gazed westward. Never had I seen such a glowing sight in the night skies. Its pure whiteness shimmered steadily, and it was many times the size of the other objects in the sky. Luminescent in the depths of the night, a star glowed with an unearthly light such as I had never beheld before—nor since."

Balthazar paused, as if the memory still left him searching for words. His audience was spellbound at the wonder in his voice and the beauty his words evoked. Some waited in anticipation of his next words. Others gazed skyward. Those who looked up seemed to seek some proof of his story, though it was evident from his words that the event had occurred many years previously. The storyteller looked to his friend Kateb, and they shared their usual joy that was no longer disbelief: Long ago, it had become a bond of faith in the future.

Nazim courteously waited for Balthazar to continue, but it was obvious that the Bedouin leader was eager to hear more.

Balthazar took up his story after glancing at his listeners. "Try, if you can, to imagine how startled I was. Shooting stars and comets and meteors streak through the sky—some faster than others. As I looked precisely in the area of the sky I had been studying for weeks, this blazing star simply and suddenly appeared. This is not a frequent occurrence, I assure you. Plus, this phenomenal object did not move as I gazed and measured and took notes throughout that long night. There was no moon and, therefore, its powerful beams shone even brighter than it might have if the moon had been full. When morning dawned, it remained glowing as it had during the night.

"By the way, as we continue to talk, I will regularly call this marvel in the sky a *star*, if that is acceptable."

Nods of somewhat puzzled agreement greeted Balthazar's last remark, but he continued with no further explanation.

"As the heat of the day rose with the sun, the star finally was gone. All that day, I could not wait for evening to arrive so I could find out if this was a once-only event or if it would be aglow again. Unfortunately for me, Kateb was away visiting his family, and I had no one else with whom I cared to share this remarkable sighting.

"That evening, hours before the star could have appeared, I was in place. Would it be there in the western sky? Would it burst forth from the surrounding stars, as it had before? If it came, how long would it remain? What could it mean for us here on earth? As you can imagine, my mind was engaged with the where, when, and why of the starlike object's appearance.

"This night things were the same yet different."

Balthazar's words stirred his listeners once again. Some even appeared to be on edge with his last comment. Most seemed as eager as their leader to hear more. After all, their "guests" showed no inclination to escape, and here was a rare opportunity for a new tale to be told that just might be worthy of a retelling in other times and places.

Taking up his story, Balthazar said with a tone of triumph, "And, lo, the bright beacon was there among the other stars as soon as the night darkened. As before, it roused my never-ending thirst for knowledge. But it also spoke to my heart. The star awakened something deep in my soul. Somehow, I knew that my destiny was tied to this glowing orb.

"I took no notes that night although that had been my sole purpose in being in place so early. Undoubtedly, I dozed, but always it was there, shining brilliantly—beckoning me to what—I did not know. What I did determine was that if it was present on the next night—with no apparent lessening of its brilliance or size—then I would send a message for Kateb to join me immediately on the site of a high mountain where we frequently found ourselves seemingly able to touch the sky. He and I had spent many a night stargazing on this height, and I wanted him to share in the glorious experience of this phenomenon. I wondered if my blood brother would feel any of the sensations the luminous light evoked in me.

"On the third night, I had my supplies packed. As soon

as it appeared, I dispatched a messenger to where Kateb was staying. As I traveled, I urged my camel forward with all speed. This was when I discovered a new dimension to this celestial visitor. While riding the leagues to our mountain vista, the star never came closer. Indeed, it seemed to move as I moved—but ever farther away—and ever westward. After traveling through the early morning, and as I climbed to the heights, its beams disappeared, as on the first two nights. By the late afternoon, Kateb had joined me. He, too, had traveled quickly, spurred on by the urgency and mystery of my missive to him.

"After rejoicing in each other's safety, all conversation turned to the star. Kateb had similar questions to the ones I had posed to myself. Was he too late? Would the bright orb appear? When I told him of the singular impression I had experienced—that the star was moving as I rode forward— he suggested some theories as to what this could mean. Kateb had enough faith in me that he did not consider me addled—as some of you may."

Most of his audience quickly denied any such thoughts. But he knew there had to be skeptics, and that only good manners kept them from admitting their doubts.

Unfortunately, in the silence that followed Balthazar's last words, the remarks of a weathered nomad on the far side of the fire could be heard. "I'll listen a while longer, but ..." The man realized his remark had been too loud, and his next words died on his lips. Apologetically, he bowed his head as his fingers touched his forehead, seeking forgiveness of the speaker.

Balthazar smiled his acceptance. Gesturing to the now-frowning Nazim that the remarks had given no offense, he continued his narrative.

"To Kateb's joy, the star appeared as on the previous nights. He was astounded because while he was visiting his family, he too had continued to view that same area of the sky that we had been studying together. I remember well his words: 'How could I not have seen this wonder in the sky?'"

Eyes swiveled to Kateb, and he confirmed with a vigorous nod to the listeners that those were his exact words. Balthazar asked across the campfire space, "Do you want to tell them more?"

Kateb responded pacifically, "No, the story is yours, my friend."

Accepting the encouragement from his fellow prisoner, Balthazar spoke once more.

"As long-time friends and colleagues, it is not necessary for us always to speak our thoughts or to linger long over decisions. Acceding to what I had told him previously about the light in general and its westward progression, our gear was shortly repacked. And just that quickly, our attempt to determine if the star moved as we did was in motion. Although our camels had settled down for the night, they were used to our nighttime adventures, and within minutes, we were lumbering down the west side of the mountain.

"For days and nights, we proceeded across the lands. Mainly, we traveled by night." He quizzed the gathering, "How else to follow our guide?" Receiving nods of agreement and encouragement, Balthazar summarized their trek across the unknown lands those many years ago.

"Our needs were few, and our determination never wavered as the leagues passed into the distance. South and west, the star never faltered. What if it never stopped? What if it moved out over the sea in the middle of the earth? This, of course, was of no concern to me with my seafaring background, but still, the question was an open one—*where* were we being led? And equally as important, *why* were we being led to an unknown destination?"

From the low murmurs following Balthazar's questions, it was obvious the camp agreed that these were significant answers to learn. Quickly, their attention returned to hear more. Nazim spoke for all as he courteously asked, "So where did your star lead you?"

"To a new beginning."

Kateb assertively answered Nazim. The confidence in his tone spread a silence of speculation through the gathering. One man suddenly felt the need to add a new piece of fuel to the dying fire, though the rising sun was already beginning to lighten the darkness. As the sparks flew upward in the dawn, eyes followed the live embers as if in a mystic pursuit of the truth.

Balthazar knew Kateb would say no more, so he smoothly echoed his friend's words. "We were indeed led to a new beginning. In our travels, we had singularly believed we were alone. In addition, the star was ours—no others we had met seemed to be aware of its existence. In towns or villages where we entered, casual inquiries left us with the decided idea that only we were seeing this star of wonder. This, however, proved not to be the case."

Looking around at the camp, Balthazar noted weariness on some of the faces in the group. He was aware that in their seeking to capture him, the men had been engaged in hard riding for any number of days. Courteously, he said to Nazim, "The day is dawning. Mayhap I should wait for another time to tell of further events?"

Nazim seemed almost startled that Balthazar was offering to stop speaking. Quickly, he negated that idea.

"Unless you yourself are tired. I know I am anxious to hear of who else is important in your story."

The men, too, were roused, and the nomad who previously had suggested he might leave soon, urgently called out. "Please, you and Kateb have both just spoken of intriguing events. A new beginning, and other travelers, does not sound like the place to end your story. We wish to hear more. Yes?" He looked to the other men, urging them to also encourage Balthazar.

Nazim put forth the command that was a subtle apology. "Bring our guest water. We have been remiss. May the gods forgive us."

After quenching his thirst and hearing the change of tone from Nazim that he was a "guest," Balthazar looked carefully at his audience. If the life he and Kateb had been leading had come to an end—as would seem to be the case, now that they were captives—how should he regard his future with these rugged Bedouins? He certainly had firsthand awareness that out of adversity comes opportunity. Briefly, he recalled what King Solomon had written about wisdom in the book of Proverbs. This was a book he had taken to heart after returning from the town of Bethlehem in Judea. In addition, the Israelites' book of Daniel had served him well in leading him to the events he had decided to share with his captors. Since that long-ago time, he had studied many of their other holy books. There was indeed much to tell his captors.

Centuries before Daniel lived, Solomon had written that submission to the will of the Israelite's God was the beginning of wisdom.[37] Acceptance and submission to a destiny he had not chosen, but nonetheless had embraced, had served him well over the years. He would not question why he was here. He would not fear for his life. Instead, he would equally embrace this opportunity to share the mystery of the star and of the infant born so humbly under its luminous light.

These strangers—his captors—wanted more from him and wanted it now. Gladly would he share the momentous events of his life, and they could believe or disbelieve as they chose.

CHAPTER 4

The Others

"Then one night, as our camels plodded in the vastness of the desert sands, we became aware of others coming from the east, as we were. Kateb and I were approaching a small oasis, where we planned to briefly refresh ourselves, when the sound and vibrations of other travelers carried across the distance. We felt it was safer to remain where we were since an oasis is considered neutral territory, even by marauders. We dismounted, refreshed our camels, and waited for the strangers to arrive.

"Shortly, three men approached. They, too, had obviously traveled from afar but were much better equipped than we were. The regal appearance of their leader, though he seemed young, struck me immediately. He was accompanied by a veteran of desert life, who was evidently sizing us up for what type of threat we might pose. The third man was the oldest of the newcomers, and he was the man who spoke first. After thanking us for sharing the life-saving water, he introduced himself as Raheeb. He stated simply that the younger man was Gaspar, without giving him a title. The man named Gaspar and I had already exchanged welcoming looks. His clear gaze made me feel at ease that he and the other two men posed no danger to us.

"The third man, whom we later would know as Namon,

seemed relaxed on the surface, but I was certain he did not want them to remain long. Meanwhile, Gaspar and I were already sharing information. When he seemed to offhandedly say he enjoyed studying the stars, this instantly confirmed that my first instincts were correct—we need not fear him or his companions. Almost casually, he glanced at the heavens, and I knew that he knew that we were on the same quest. His next words justified my thinking as he commented, 'The stars are particularly clear tonight to the west in the Pisces constellation.'"

Murmurs of pleasure reached Balthazar, and he felt that most, if not all, had caught the message delivered so succinctly those many years ago. "Yes, this Gaspar and I had both made the discovery of the star. He, too, was on the same mission to follow the bright beacon to wherever it chose to lead him. Excitedly, we exchanged ideas until, simultaneously, all remounted and became as one.

"Several nights later, our numbers grew larger again. This time, a very old man and his very young companion were sitting near a fire. Rather amazingly, they were studying together in the middle of nowhere. And, as previously with Gaspar, there was an instantaneous recognition by all that our meeting was meant to be. This older man, Melchior, became our leader by virtue of his age and wise nature. Gaspar immediately united us as one, saying we would be stronger together than separately. Though we each came from different areas of the Eastern world, we were as one from the beginning. Stargazers and astrologers, our backgrounds were diverse yet similar, and we three magi, as we were oft called in our lands, had left our safe homes to become desert wanderers in search of we knew not what.

"We assuredly each knew that just as we had been

compelled to travel west, so too were we destined to meet and to merge our separate skills, strengths, and knowledge. Further, as we learned more of what each of us could provide about the star, we discovered an incredible parallel in our lives. At some point in our telling of the separate events we had experienced in finding the star, we learned that we each had found information—even inspiration—in the writings of the Israelites. Melchior had studied, among others, the prophet Yeshayah—I have also heard him referred to as Isaiah. Gaspar's search for knowledge and enlightenment included studying many of the old Hebraic writings. He continually asserted that those works pointed to a Messiah being born who would be a great king and who would come from the lineage of David, their shepherd king."

At the mention of a king and the ancient writings of the Israelites and a Messiah—whatever that personage might be—his audience stirred anew. Many looked to Nazim to see his reaction. Their leader, having known Herod Antipas, as well as having heard from the son about his father's brutality and the cruelty of one of the older sons, was not inclined to be too impressed that the Jews might have been awaiting a Messiah to lead them to glory. *Yes,* Nazim thought to himself, *the Jews certainly needed better leadership than the Herod family provided.*

Antipas had personally once told Nazim—admittedly, when they had both been indulging in a night of drinking and carousing after a hard-fought battle—that his father, King Herod, a mere four days before his death, had changed his will to make another son, Archelaus, the heir to the Judean kingdom instead of Antipas. This Herod, however, had ruled so poorly for two years that the Roman emperor Augustus Caesar, who had been urged by the

Judean population to dethrone Archelaus, eventually took the kingship from the Herodian leaders. Augustus had appointed Quirinius to oversee the Palestinian lands. Judea then had been demoted to a mere province—although an imperial province—of the mighty Roman Empire.

Nazim was aware that the entire area had been divided into thirds, with three of the remaining sons of Herod, now called the Great, being named tetrarchs instead of kings. It was Nazim's understanding that the Israelites had rather consistently been lowered in prestige over their long history—not to mention having oft been enslaved. He had gathered that they were supposed to be the chosen people of their God. However, he was not sure he would want that honor if he were a member of the twelve tribes of Abraham and had endured what had happened to them over the centuries.

Therefore, he smiled indulgently at both his men and Balthazar and contented himself by saying, "Kings are only as good as their deeds."

This struck Balthazar, who also knew of the Herodian legacy, that Nazim was more astute than he had at first seemed. Returning to the night the three magi had met, he thought it politic not to add that his new companions had royal bloodlines, as did he.

"I will tell you all that from that moment forward, we three were bound together—as were our companions—by the light of that distant object, which might have been anything from a new formation to a merging of planets. Again, our individual studies had found nothing in history to indicate such a powerful light had ever been seen before. In the days that followed, and as we rode or camped, we put our collective knowledge of the stars together.

"The largest planet known to man, mighty Jupiter—named by the Romans for the greatest of their gods—was in the western skies. Saturn, another planet and called their shield by the Israelites, was set to pass nearby. And then Venus, the morning and evening star, extraordinarily also was making an appearance, as was Mars. Could this be the 'star' we saw? Was the light from this rare planetary alignment in the western skies enough to be the star that guided us?

"We humans like to have answers. Was this occurrence in the heavens simply a random event? Or had it possibly been destined from the beginning of time? We debated these questions and more, not just to pass the time, but to find a reason to explain our finding each other as we had.

"As I just said, we humans like answers. Furthermore, astrologers like we three magi believe the heavens have messages for us if we are open-minded and care to gaze upward. We believe that comets and meteors, as I mentioned before, have implications for mere mortals. Remember our earlier discussion of Nazim and his cousin's son, which I said might have been what the Romans call the Julius Caesar comet? Not everyone seeing it had the potential to change the world, but perhaps just observing such a sight might inspire greater deeds than might have been done otherwise."

As Balthazar paused, Nazim spoke his thoughts. "You are right, Balthazar. How many people viewed that blazing sight and considered its potential—what it meant for their own lives? Was it meant for only one person? Why couldn't many people have been receiving a message from the gods? My cousin happily felt it was a symbol of the promise of his son. Perhaps we should rethink if the sign was simply meant as a blessing to him of long life and happiness. Of a certainty, my older cousin did have a good and happy life, and his son is fulfilled as well—maybe that is enough. If the Romans deified their recently assassinated leader, that was their interpretation. Assuredly, great and glorious things occurred in the lives of many of those who saw the comet, as you call it. And as you kindly said—time yet remains for my cousin to become a person of destiny."

Nazim's thoughtful words brought silent nods of agreement from his men. Balthazar realized that he felt calm and peaceful in the midst of his captors. These were good people—although capturing him might normally have put them in a vastly different category. Briefly, he had the thought that this inner peace might, hopefully, survive his next words. If he were to tell the magi's story to this particular audience, he could not leave out the vital encounter so important to what happened in the weeks and months that had followed.

Before plunging back into the tale, he singularly addressed the Bedouin leader. "You have spoken wise words tonight, Nazim. On the matter of interpretations of enlightenment from the stars, this is an important, thought-provoking comment. Many see the events, but how many of them can be affected? Surely not just the mighty are the recipients of messages from above. Also of importance is your earlier statement that our actions and deeds do matter—especially when they impact others. This is true of all people."

Balthazar's words were not simply praise of Nazim who, as his captor, literally held the power of life or death over him. He had truly meant his words of commendation. But, then again, he also was desperately trying to fend off a possibly hostile scene—either in the next few moments or in the future—by finding common ground of agreement for the two of them.

Stalling no further, he spoke in a calm voice. "At this point in my chronicle of this extraordinary time in my life, I believe that the totality of several events of those days is the reason why Kateb and I are here as prisoners in your camp."

With this telling remark, Balthazar plunged ahead.

"For weeks on end, we travelers trudged across the leagues through unfamiliar regions. Finally, we entered the Hamad Desert and proceeded through it, as in the other deserts that my companions and I had traversed, together and separately. We trekked up and down sand dunes and through the gorges of the Syrian Steppes. The star never wavered leading us steadily westward toward the Judean foothills, and then up into the Judean Mountains.

"As time passed, we began to note that our star was no longer as distant. Indeed, as we climbed that Judean mountain range, it was almost directly overhead—as if we were nearing our final destination. Then one evening, after we had navigated up a particularly steep height, Gaspar's guide, Namon, indicated that the Israelites' Holy City of Jerusalem could be seen in the distance. At that moment, I wondered anew that if our search was indeed for a king— and possibly a king of the Jews—was it not appropriate that we were nearing the City of David? Since the region had been conquered by the Romans seven decades earlier, was not a mighty warrior-king, like their King David had become, exactly what the Israelites needed? Their promised land being ruled by others, together with their own inferior position, was not what most would envision as success.

"As the leagues brought us nearer to Jerusalem, Melchior confided in us some of his past history. He was aware that for almost forty years a man he had met in Rome when he was a young man currently ruled as the Judean king, Herod I, as he was known in those days." Looking apologetically yet firmly at Nazim, Balthazar continued.

"We all knew Herod's renown as a great builder, including his accomplishments in constructing the modern city of Caesarea—named for the Caesars. In addition, we were aware of his early reputation as a fearless leader in battle. If great Rome had confidence in him, who were we to question his abilities? However, there had been rumors for years, heard even in my own distant lands, that to defy him or to stand in the way of his continual rise in the political world was possibly to sign a person's own death warrant."

Stolidly, Nazim returned Balthazar's gaze but made no attempt to stop him from speaking.

Content that the subject of the Herods had finally been broached—and for the moment, at least, was an acceptable topic—Balthazar briefly stated that the preference of the three magi was to avoid encountering Herod. Yet this had proven impossible for several reasons including specifically that, after their descent, they were met by an armed cavalcade of the Judean king's Germanic mercenaries, and had been escorted under guard to Herod's fortress-like palace. To the Eastern travelers, he noted to his rapt audience, this was a major difficulty, but Balthazar then added that an even more significant scenario had occurred.

"The day before we would have had to make a decision on whether or not to enter Jerusalem or to bypass it entirely, our star disappeared."

Aware of his listeners' startled reaction to this disclosure, Balthazar rushed forward to tell of the subsequent events.

"Since it was unexpectedly beginning to snow—a definite rarity in those lands—being given regal protection from the elements and increasingly lower temperatures should have been a boon. Unfortunately, it was immediately made clear to us, after being greeted by Herod, that he had been aware of our travels through his vast lands. He also seemed to know about our pointed inquiries for information in various places in his realm.

"We felt we were fortunate that Herod recognized Melchior as an acquaintance from their time in Rome all those years earlier. Melchior told Herod that we were not traveling in any official capacity but merely were wanderers continuously seeking knowledge. He said that we had come to Jerusalem because of the many scholars known to live there. This was our previously agreed upon story, to which we planned to adhere, if possible, when talking to him of our quest. We stated truthfully that we were particularly interested in learning more of the long history of the Hebrews. Herod apparently accepted this as a reason for our asking specific questions, during our travels through Palestinian lands, about the Jews' religious history.

"As a result, in no time at all, Herod had given us the freedom of his palace library. He even instructed his personal magus, Lieb, to assist us in whatever we wanted or needed. This was both good news to us and bad news as well. Our hope was to stay as short a time as possible in the vicinity of Herod, but as men with a thirst for knowledge—any knowledge—having this magnificent library opened to us for our exclusive use was a gift we could not forgo. Dare I say we were like little children let loose in a honey shop.

"However—and I did not mean to make light of the dire position we felt we were in—the most important issue to all of us was what to make of the star's disappearance. Personally, I was astounded at the sequence of events that found us in Herod's palace. With our guiding light having vanished, did this mean our journey had been completed? Were we wrong to consider Herod a foe when even now he was helping us? The thought had to have occurred to the others, as it did to me, that the potential for the Messiah to already be in the City of David was too obvious to be ignored. Our quest seemed over as far as traveling was concerned. How, then, to find this personage in a city as large as that one was another problem to be discussed. But this was not to be.

"A factor leading to our further discomfort was that we three ... er, companions had effectively been separated from one another. It was soon clear to me that orders had been given not to allow us to have any private conversation together. Within the library, a scholar-rabbi had been assigned to each of us, with the stated intention that this person would be at our beck and call for whatever we needed and whatever access we desired to the precious books and manuscripts.

"Outside of the library, guides—in reality, guards—met us each morning as we left our separate quarters, which were notably quite distant from each other. These individuals escorted us to and from our rooms, to the library, and everywhere else in the palace. During lavish dinners with Herod, we were always seated apart. The pattern that was emerging was making us eager, after a few days of such treatment, to leave the Herod Palace at the first opportunity we could reasonably do so.

"In addition, we were particularly aware that a man named Dov seemed to be too closely attached to our mercurial host for our well-being. We felt that he was regularly informing Herod of our research. We easily determined that Lieb, a rabbi, and the other Levite scholars whom Herod had provided us, definitely did not have a comfort level with this man either. At times, Dov deliberately seemed to be thwarting our efforts, as he encouraged the Levite priests to downplay the role of a messiah. I remember well an occasion when he agreed with the Levites as they indicated that messiah-like individuals were common throughout Judaic history. After their comments, he said that Herod's deeds might make *him* worthy to be the long-awaited Messiah. Several of the rabbinic priests became almost apoplectic at that statement.

"The situation was becoming intolerable, and it was our earnest desire to end our protracted stay. On the same eventful day that we planned to put a stratagem in operation to leave, Herod seemed to have had a similar idea. It was mutual that it was time to part ways. Our persistent research, especially after Lieb and another rabbi, Ezra, had unwittingly helped us to find additional material on the prophet Daniel, must have annoyed the changeable king. Undoubtedly, Dov had brought word of our findings to Herod, putting him on the alert to our seeking knowledge of the Messiah and what this might mean to his reign. Herod feigned a willingness to provide an armed bodyguard for us. He even stated that if and when our mission was accomplished, he would come to witness to the presence of the Messiah—to do him homage.[38]

"Melchior added fuel to the fire that eventually enraged Herod when he finally put forward our belief that the

Messiah would be an infant who would, in time, lead the nation of Israel to glory. Inasmuch as we had planned our own departure for that very night, Melchior was not only seeking any further information that Herod might have, but also was using this as a method to spur our exodus from the palace. It was evident that Herod had become furious with us. However, he did give us intelligence, supposedly just provided to him, that an ancient Hebrew text written by a minor prophet named Micah might help us.

"At first, we were clueless to what the words in the almost-millennium-old manuscript meant because Micah had referred to a place call Ephrathah,[39] and not one of us was familiar with that name. Ezra informed us it was a reference to the little town of Bethlehem. It was not much—along with the fact that the prophecy was almost one thousand years old! Nevertheless, it was more than we had learned during our controlled studies in the palace. Seizing the moment, we declared it our intention to include it in our continued search. Herod was almost gleeful. From his point of view, the long-outdated text had little power to hurt him. As I told you, his last words to us were in the form of an order—that when we found the child, we should return to let him know so that he could go and do homage."

Balthazar's voice had slowly become hoarse, as he had been speaking almost nonstop for quite some time.

Observing that their "guest" looked exhausted, and that his age was showing, Nazim decided to end the session. Rising from where he had been sitting for the same length of time, Nazim acted as if he needed to stretch his back. "A good place to end, Balthazar. We thank you for an entertaining and interesting evening. Assuredly, you and

your fellow ki—er, companions"—here, he grinned good-
naturedly at Balthazar—"were happy to be on the road
again. I insist that you save the rest of your story for another
day. We will have many more together."

CHAPTER 5

Renewed Hope

That evening, after the sun's blazing rays had finally faded and lessened the broiling heat of the day, it was rewarding to Balthazar that most in the camp seemed to have congregated in the general area where he had spoken through the early morning hours. Because they had stayed in one place, the evening meal was a bit more elaborate than the usual nomadic travel fare. During the day, a large young lizard had ventured near and had been killed. Probing scouts had found a nest nearby, and the lizards made a delicious meal when roasted over an open fire. The prisoners were given knives—indicating their altered status in the camp—to cut the meat off the shared food as it was passed from person to person. In addition, regag bread was baked in the sand—a treat for all. Between the basic staple of dates, the plentiful well-roasted meat, and the fresh bread, everyone felt replete as the evening hours approached.

Nazim courteously waited for the necessary camp activities of cleanup and the tethering of the animals to be finished before inviting Balthazar to resume his story, if he so chose. "Did you both enjoy the meal?" he queried as a starter.

The magus responded first. "It was most pleasant to eat food prepared by others. Although I am fond of Kateb, and we routinely share cooking duties, neither one of us is a particularly good cook. Would you agree, my friend?"

Kateb wryly responded, "If I do say so myself, the meals I prepare are better than yours, but no one here would be impressed by my skills." A ripple of laughter followed this self-effacing remark.

Nazim then graciously inquired, "Balthazar, would it be too much to ask that, if you feel able, you might tell us more of the intriguing story you were sharing with us a few hours earlier? Do not hesitate to say if you prefer not to do so at this time."

"I would be honored to tell you of what happened next."

Balthazar waited for the others to settle in as they preferred—some nearer, some farther. Without giving too much significance to it, he noted that the jeerer at the start of his story was sitting closer, seeming to indicate he wanted to hear better.

"As we urged our camels forward, fears and questions surged anew for each of us. Would Herod keep his word that we would be safe in his lands? Without having conferred together, we later talked and confirmed that we each felt a need to be continually on guard from that time forward. We would be absolutely foolish not to consider the ruler's past record of dealing with others over the years. After all, if the rumors were true—and there were too many instances to ignore—Herod had murdered family members, from wives to sons, and had brutally slain all who opposed him as he sought to first win and then to strengthen his hold on the Judean crown. A king's power is not to be taken lightly."

An ironic look passed between Kateb and Balthazar, who intentionally did not look at Nazim.

"A second concern was how we would proceed without

the star to guide us. We had been given directions to Bethlehem, which is in a generally southern course from Jerusalem. However, that was merely a formality on our part. As much as anything, accepting the ancient words about the little town of Bethlehem was only a ploy to leave the dangerous confines of Herod's palace. Months ago, and separately, each of us had found our way ever westward by gazing to the heavens and following the beacon of light that had continuously moved forward. Individually, we had been prepared to follow wherever it led. After joining forces, our separate goals became threefold stronger.

"But now we were cast astray. The heavenly light was no longer there to guide us. We wondered if our leaving Jerusalem was the reason the star had not reappeared. Was the person we were searching for, the Jews' Messiah, already living in the city of David, his regal ancestor? Were we foolishly leaving the place where the star had led us? Was it possible that we were actually aiding Herod in leaving his center of power?

"Personally, I felt rudderless. It was as if everything was amiss in the world. As I speak to you today, it is still difficult to describe my mental state that night. Suffice it to say that if a sandstorm had buffeted me for days and I had lost all sense of direction, I could not have felt more adrift.

"Bearing in mind that our apparent destination was Bethlehem, we left Jerusalem through the southwestern Fountain Gate and prepared to descend from the city's heights into the Hinnom Valley. Within a few paces, however, a foul odor came to us—it was the stench from the city's sewage dump near where we were riding. Symbolically, it seemed appropriate that our state of anxiety was matched by this foulness.

"In the Jewish leader's desire to be rid of us, he had not offered to let us stay another night. Further, he did not probe why we would choose to leave as the sun was setting. We were prepared, of course, to say that travel by night was preferable. Since he knew that we were dedicated to the study of the stars and that this was clearly vital to us, it would have been an easy enough way to cover our real reason for departing at sunset. As we left, the skies had been overcast, light snow was falling, and what little hope we had of sighting our star was vastly diminished."

Lowering his voice, Balthazar glanced at the men gathered near him. He realized that the time of night that he now was speaking was similar to when he and the other magi had ridden away from Jerusalem those many years ago. Some of the wonder of that realization must have shone on his face, as he noticed the men's obvious attention to his strained words. Several faces in the crowd reflected the stress that Balthazar and the other magi had felt.

"Those next hours were some of the longest I have ever spent. As we rode, the ever-darkening night sky made travel slow as we maneuvered down the long, winding road that took us ever farther from Jerusalem. The low-lying Judean foothills on our mountain pathway gave us unsure footing on the icy road, and when the night darkened as the time went past midnight, we finally decided that the going was too treacherous to continue. Nonetheless, in some attempt to cover our tracks if a pursuit were to be mounted, we went off the main way, such as it was, and turned southeastward for a number of miles."

Balthazar's deep voice rolled across the campsite, reflecting his past anxiety. "Talking together as we rode, we decided that we would continue our trek by always moving away from Bethlehem, just as we were doing. After all, if we never went there, then we could further our effort to avoid Herod tracking us.

"It was certainly in my mind that if the star had left the skies, then its message was no longer pertinent to us. We might as well turn homeward. It was a lowering thought, but what alternative was there? Melchior and Gaspar had left their lands months before, as had I, and much time had been invested by each of us. Yet of what earthly value was there in continuing on this quest? Any sensible, pragmatic person would abandon the mission— of course, this same person might never have ventured forth in the first place.

"After finally deciding on a site to stop as morning neared, we discussed the events that had happened in Herod's palace. Remember that this was actually our first time alone outside the stringent confines of Herod's palace in the days after we were purposely separated. With the inevitability that the star had vanished—after all, we had not sighted it for several weeks—our future was uncertain. We knew it had not reappeared because while we were in Herod's palace, Namon was given the freedom to care for the animals. He had generally insisted on leaving the palace in the early evening to exercise them. In our brief contacts with him, he reported that in his various excursions, the skies had been overcast because of the continued snow; therefore, no stars at all could be seen.

"In our discussions that morning, we agonized what should be our next step. Though we had bonded as one, remaining together seemed useless. Our separately defined reasons for leaving our lands had been to follow the beacon in the sky, which moved as no star ever had. But clearly, we wise men, as we were all purported to be, had been wrong. We had mistaken the light for something it was not.

"Gaspar, as the youngest, was the most loath to let the quest end. Melchior had the wisdom of old age to guide him. However, he did not want his young companion, Bijak, to be saddened by the end of what the youth might see as a now-purposeless journey. Therefore, our leader's response was an attempt to be even-keeled. Of course, he, too, recognized the fruitlessness of waiting for the light to reappear. As learned men who had studied the heavens all our lives, we knew these things simply did not happen in the skies above us. A phenomenon like the star might appear once, but then its reappearance—if ever—might take centuries. And remember, in all our research, none of us had found any evidence of its appearance before. Additionally, it had been sighted by us for many a month. The chance of its reappearance was fairly impossible.

"Again, as I have told you, I was devastated. To have traveled so far and endured the rigors of the journey, and then to have escaped the dangers posed by Herod—for my quest to end so ignominiously was like a mortal wound to my psyche. Calling myself every kind of a fool, I was the first to state that I would leave that very night to return home. Kateb spoke to me privately and tried to dissuade me. However, as quickly as I had once decided to follow the star, I determined just as rapidly that I would abandon the quest.

"Could I sleep that day? To say that I tossed and turned would be an understatement. I have told you that I felt rudderless. Lost? Definitely. Despairing? Totally. Rarely had I failed at anything in my life. It was not just my arrogance and pride that were affected by this decision

I had so quickly made to return home. Always seeking answers, I had none for why this journey was ending so poorly. I tried to rationalize why I was so full of despair.

"What matter was it to me if the Judaic Messiah had been born or not? I was not a Jew. This was not my faith. Why should I worry that these people would have to wait longer—they had waited seemingly forever after all.

"I finally had to tell myself this was simply not meant to be. Several times I told myself: Accept that you misinterpreted the star's meaning. I counseled myself that there was a more rational explanation why the heavenly body had appeared in the first place. But then, immediately, came the tumbling thoughts of how Melchior and Gaspar could have come to the same findings, set out as I had, and been wrong, as I was. I respected them as men of great intelligence—and so, again, *how* and *why* roiled through my consciousness.

"When sunset arrived, the camp came to life. Lying in my tent, I listlessly asked myself where I would go from here. What purpose would I have? What goals would challenge me? I am sure it is clear to you that my thoughts were low indeed."

Having shared his dark thoughts of that stressful time, Balthazar simply ceased talking.

The men looked their surprise that he was no longer speaking. Enthralled by his remorseless questioning of the ineffectiveness of his quest, they too mourned its apparent end. Some could be said to share the apathy he had felt so long ago.

Nazim could not summon the energy to speak—to console. Truly, he knew not what to say. He too had faltered at times in the past, made poor decisions, even lived to regret them. But always, he had persevered and staggered forward. The thought hit him that this was a time for decision-making himself. He had captured Balthazar, as requested—nay, ordered—by Herod Antipas. What was he to do now? Could he turn this peaceful old stargazer over to the Jewish leader? What plan did Herod have for the man?

Nazim shook off his brief reverie and asked, "So, Balthazar, where did you go from there?"

"I went out from my tent, joined Gaspar, Melchior and the others. We said our farewells, mounted our camels, and as we looked to the west—there was our star."[40]

CHAPTER 6

The Quest Continues

The men went wild with exclamations of delight. Kateb laughed mightily at the genuine pleasure and enjoyment that these bold warriors so openly expressed at this new turn of events. He and Balthazar exchanged good-humored looks that also conveyed their usual awe of the various events of their journey.

"Yea, the star shone steadily high in the sky. In fact, we had to look almost straight overhead. Imagine our joy—our ecstasy—as we sighted our guiding light. I can still hear Gaspar's cry of elation, along with the youthful cheering of young Bijak, who was giddily rising up and down in his saddle, knowing we had sighted the star."

Balthazar's voice lowered several octaves as he continued.

"Melchior stated reverently, 'We are near. Consider the star's height. It is directly overhead.'

"Gaspar breathed his relief—'We were not wrong.'

"Excitedly, I expressed my incredible joy: 'Let us be off!'

"With that, the camels bounded forward, as if they, too, sensed our unbridled wonder. We marveled anew as we rode west once more and descended from the mountainous way onto the moor that, just as we had traversed the deserts and lands to this place of destiny, the star had been a faithful beam from afar. As it now shone on high—seemingly brighter than ever since its reappearance—it had to herald significant news.

"My doubts of the previous days were erased forever. Our westward-leading, luminescent light was undoubtedly a sign from a higher power. What other explanation could there be? The significance of its disappearance as we had entered Jerusalem came to have an even greater meaning. If the personage we were being led to—and again, the research seemed to indicate it would be a child—was to be a Messiah, a great leader, then would he not have a great impact on the present king of Judea? It was almost a certainty that as the child grew older he inevitably would usurp the Herodian family's legacy. In light of this singular scenario, the star's disappearance was an extremely telling event."

As on the previous times when Herod was mentioned, Balthazar recognized that he was on thin ground. Knowing what he knew, and having come to this point in his chronicle, he looked at Nazim. His own manner was matter-of-fact. There was no challenge to Nazim's authority. And this time, there was no cringing over consequences. As he experienced it anew, the power of the past gave him the courage that he had not felt strongly enough earlier.

Rather surprisingly, however, Nazim seemed untroubled by the narrative. There was no change in his demeanor. Clearly, he was at least awake to the consequences as he asked, "Your thinking was that a child of destiny would be a threat to the Herod dynasty?"

"Yes. Assuredly one or the other would have to be diminished—nay, possibly eliminated."

"Not necessarily. I can certainly think of powers that

coexist. Are not the Jews a religious group, rather than a tribal power? Would not this Messiah be a religious leader? Herod certainly had rabbis in his palace who helped you in your research. This seems to indicate they were not in disfavor with him. Was he not a Jew himself? I am certain I have heard that he was called the king of the Jews."

"You are correct about his religion, Nazim. Herod's family background, however, was that he was an Arab, as you are. *Only* about two centuries ago, his ancestors were forcibly converted. Because of the ancient lineage of the Jews, to staunch members of the tribes of Abraham, this meant he was barely a member of their faith. An Idumean by birth, Herod was seemingly a practicing Jew, but few would have called him a religious man.

"It is also important to recall that the Romans were regarded as the rulers of the Western world—as they remain today. Herod's appointment to the throne of Judea came from them. The term is that he ruled as a 'client king.' In effect, this means that he himself was subject to the Romans. His first allegiance, therefore, seemed to be to the Roman Empire.

"Adding to the many issues was that Herod's own father had become a Roman citizen. Many wondered if the son was simply a Jew in name only. After all, when he built that port town of Caesarea, he did name it to honor Augustus Caesar, who had been acclaimed by the Roman Senate as a direct ancestor of their Roman gods. Herod also built a number of non-Jewish temples in that important coastal town, including a major one to the goddess Roma. It could be argued that being a Jew was merely a means to power for him and possibly had been so even for his own forefathers.

"His religion always seemed to be a distant second to

Herod's public desire to show allegiance to Rome and to Augustus Caesar. Rarely did he appear to honor Judaic traditions. For example, he had golden eagles—a powerful symbol of Roman authority—erected outside the Temple of Solomon. This was an outrage to the Jews because it reeked of idolatry. Furious, many Jews in Jerusalem rioted to tear down the offensive and idolatrous images. Unfortunately, during the aftermath of that violent event, Herod executed many of the youths who had torn down the eagles."

Namon queried further after Balthazar paused in his recitation. "But was not Herod's most famous building project the fabled temple in Jerusalem?"

"You are correct again. He spent nearly forty years enlarging the Jerusalem Temple of Solomon, always seeking to enhance the original structure. That building was certainly considered by the Jews—and by Herod himself—to be his mightiest architectural endeavor. It seems to be a common thought that not only he, but others, considered it his greatest legacy—what he would be most remembered for doing.

"Over the years, I have learned much of the faith of the Jewish people. Herod also expanded and restored the Tomb of the Patriarchs in Hebron, where the great men and women of the Jewish faith are buried. Abraham is the father or founder of Judaism, and he is buried in Hebron with his wife, Sarah, as well as their son Isaac and his wife, Rebecca. This couple's son, Jacob, lies there also, with Leah, his wife.

"But to go back to your original question, it is probably true that many Jews consider their heritage to be that of a religion, rather than a nation. Most Jews, however, would say they are both a religion and a nation."

Nazim sought further clarification for his people. "Was

I not also correct that the Romans called Herod the king of the Jews?"

Balthazar agreed. "That was a designation of his by the Romans." He then asked a significant question of his captor. "So now I ask you, Nazim, knowing what you know of Herod's son and their history, do you find it conceivable that this family would easily give up their power?"

Unable to control an abrupt bark of laughter, Nazim acknowledged the verbal hit. "Balthazar, I have to admit that you are correct. Another point I would make, of seeming relevance, is that the events you describe took place, as you have said, about two decades ago—yet Herod Antipas rules still in Jerusalem. Of course, he is not a king as his father was, but as the tetrarch of Jerusalem, he has power over one-third of his father's extensive kingdom."

More seriously, Nazim prodded, "Therefore, a question I would pose to you, Balthazar—and it is possibly unanswerable—is why this person of fate is not known today. So, continue please, if you would, to tell us what you three magi found."

Bowing to Nazim, Balthazar took up his tale once more. "Shining brightly in the night sky, the star beckoned us on, and we rode steadily that night. As morning approached, we camped as usual. Together, we conferred with Namon, who had learned more about the area while we stayed at the palace. And so, as always, he was our authority on where we might be heading. Among other places, there was a group of small almond-growing villages in the area, including Beit Safafa and Artas, as well as Bethlehem. This little town, as you know from our previous talks, was the birthplace of David, their royal king of old. It was also the town the prophet Micah wrote about, and was the place to which Herod believed he had misdirected us regarding the eight-hundred-year-old prophecy.

"And so, once again, Bethlehem was in the picture. With distances being shorter between settled areas, and because it was still quite cold with snow that continued to fall off and on, we traveled both at night by our star's light and then during the warmer parts of the day. When we took up our travels, we came first to Beit Sahour, but inquiries led us nowhere. Days passed, and we rode to Artas—to no avail. In both towns, our carefully worded inquiries met with no news. When we did receive information, it proved to be another false lead, taking us elsewhere. And so it continued. We finally became conscious that Bethlehem had to be the destination to which we were being led—and so it was."

Murmurs from his listeners let Balthazar know he had their attention still.

"Bethlehem rests in the lowland hills of Judea and is a moderately sized small town. With its importance in being the birthplace of David and his father, Jesse, it had become a place for faithful Jews to visit. Travelers frequently stop there during the three visits the Hebraic law requires of all faithful male Jews.

"You might be wondering what questions you should ask of people as you search. Where do you look first? How will you know you have found *the* child? Obviously, we knew by this time that mentioning the possible birth of the Jewish Messiah was not the thing to do. Herod was too near and too interested. We were agreed that whatever we did, heard, and learned could affect the destiny of many people.

"Having met with no answers in other places, I will tell you that we were not exactly losing hope, but neither were we certain of the future. We had found no recent clues, and our resolve was somewhat shaken as the miles mounted, along with the villages we passed through.

"As usual when we entered a town, the size of our group drew attention. The people of Bethlehem were no different. Men, women, and children gathered to lead us to water, to sell us their wares, and to dispense free advice as to where we should eat and stay. Our camels received water first, and we suitably dispensed money for services.

"I had dismounted and walked a little away from the others when a woman simply stated to me, 'You seek the child.'

"My first reaction was amazement, followed by elation. I responded, 'He is here?'

"'Down past the last inn to your left—there you will find him.'

"She then moved away, as if nothing else needed to be said. I quickly indicated to the others—without words—that I had news. When we remounted, I confidently told them, 'Our journey is ended.'"

CHAPTER 7

The Arrival

"Following the woman's words, we came to a home near a cave. A carpenter was working outside on a piece of wood where we halted. As if it were the most natural thing in the world for us to be there, he put down the plank and inclined his head in greeting. Dismounting, we followed him to the wide entrance of their humble abode. A woman, veiled in blue, was holding a young child, and gentle animals were gathered nearby. Instinctively, we knelt. My heart was ablaze with love—yea, adoration. There was no doubt for any of us that the star had led us to this child of destiny.

"'You are welcome.' The lady in blue—Mary, by name—graciously spoke in a youthful, melodious voice. There was no question of why we were there. And she continued calmly, 'This is Jesus.'

"Ah, the steady look from the child—not an infant—a personage, even so young. His brown eyes looked at us with a world of wisdom. He regarded each of us separately, and when he met my eyes, I was humbled and astonished and beggared. Yea, beggared! Royalty looked upon me with kindness and empathy. I, who had power over others, willingly ceded authority to this righteous child."

As at other times, Balthazar was overcome by the emotions and memories of the past. He lowered his head— possibly in prayer.

No one spoke.

When Balthazar seemed to recover sufficiently, Nazim gently urged, "We would hear more."

"The father—his name was Joseph—joined us and protectively went to his wife and child. We were certainly a crowd in that small space. Melchior addressed them first, telling our tale that we had seen his star and had followed it. He introduced us each in turn and our companions as well."

Eyes turned to Kateb, and he nodded his head in acknowledgment that he had indeed been present. No longer were Kateb and Balthazar looked upon as prisoners nor even as guests—now, they were persons to be esteemed. Most in the crowd did not understand the significance of this talk of a visit, decades ago, to a family living in a faraway town called Bethlehem, but if a star had led these men to a special child and his parents, then something more was bound to come. With no place else to be and no tasks to do, their attention was riveted on this curious yet fascinating story.

"After Melchior told more of our journey and our joining together as one, he indicated we had brought gifts. With that, we each presented our offerings. Melchior brought forth his magnificent gift of gold, a worthy tribute to royalty. Gaspar's gift of rare myrrh was reverently presented. My gift was precious frankincense."[41]

The listeners clearly approved of the gifts—based on the talk that immediately began—and recognized the quality of the offerings from the oriental royals. Gold was always valued, of course, not to mention needed. Myrrh was a priceless gift, used for healing and prized above an ingot. Balthazar's gift of frankincense was costly and had great value for religious purposes. The stunning presents were superb largesse, and only a mighty king would have been worthy of three such gifts.

"Joseph spoke for the family as he graciously thanked us. Mary said that, in time, the gifts for their baby would be put to good use.

"At that point, I found the courage to inquire if others knew of their child.

"With a benevolent smile, Mary answered, 'A few. You have certainly traveled the farthest. On the night of his birth, shepherds came.' It seemed as if she would have said more, but then did not.

"Joseph compellingly added, 'Animals were there too and warmed the cave.'

"Melchior immediately questioned, 'A cave?'

"Joseph explained. 'The inns here in Bethlehem were all filled with travelers like us, and midnight was nearing on that cold winter night as snow fell. A kindly innkeeper directed us to the cave you just passed. My wife's time was upon us, and there was nowhere else to stay.'[42]

"Mary told us simply, 'I gave birth to our child right over there. We laid him in the manger[43] filled with hay for the animals to eat.'

"Gaspar breathed the words, 'My God,' and Joseph responded, 'Amen.'

"As we looked at the father, he smiled his pride in the child. His eyes crinkled humorously as he asked, 'Would you like to hold him?'

"I blurted out yes, before the others, and so I was the first to be given the honor. I had rarely held a baby in my arms, but it seemed to be the most natural thing in the world for me to take him and hold him close. My eyes were riveted on his face, and I took in the goodwill coming from this small bit of humanity. As I rocked him, he calmly closed his eyes and slept. Looking up toward Melchior and Gaspar, who had come near on either side, we three broke into broad grins of joy. Tranquility and silence filled this home of peace and love.

"How long we stayed that first visit is uncertain, but it was lengthy. Mary and Joseph warmly encouraged us to stay and eat with them—which we did. Because of our numbers and the unexpectedness of our arrival, we said we would leave, but that was out of the question we were told. The least we could do was to provide food for the meal, we urged, and our offer was accepted. Gaspar's companion, Raheeb, and young Bijak went to the bazaar and brought back a veritable feast, which was enjoyed by all.

"Babies supposedly sleep a great deal, but this child of grace did not. His nap in my arms seemed to refresh him, and he slept no more while we were there that first day. Always tending to their baby's needs, the couple was still interested in all the details of our research and travels. With so much to tell, conversation never lagged, and there was always another aspect of our journey to discuss.

"I will tell you also that, as if by mutual consent, our stay at Herod's palace was glossed over.

"Instead, we spoke of the writings in the books of the Tanakh that had helped us piece together our final conclusion that we searched for a religious figure. Nay—I will say it—the promised Messiah of the Jews. Melchior referred to his extended searches in their religious writings that had been spearheaded by his friend Seth. He spoke of diligently combing through the first five books of the Torah, and later of finding a significant passage in Isaiah that led him to think a child would be born to a pure woman.[44] Humbly, he had bowed to Mary, and she lowered her head, accepting his homage.

"Gaspar then spoke of his studies that indicated the child would come from the line of David. When he mentioned this, Mary and Joseph looked at one another. Gaspar saw the glance and took courage to ask of Joseph, 'Are you of the House of David?'

"'I am,' Joseph responded. 'Mary also is from David's line. It is our tradition that a man should seek a wife from his own people. We are from the tribe of Judah, which was David's tribe as well. I had admired and loved Mary from afar, and when it became my honor to be her husband and to be the father of this child, I was overjoyed. Our coming from the House of David was the reason we were here in Bethlehem for the birth.[45] If you recall, Augustus Caesar had issued a decree for a census of the world to be conducted.[46] It was the first time, ever, that such a census was ordered throughout the Roman Empire. Everyone had to go to his own town to register—that is our Jewish way— and the Romans approved that it could be so done. This meant that we had to travel to our original tribal town, rather than register where we currently were living. Mary and I went up from the town of Nazareth in Galilee, where we lived. Entering into Judea, we eventually arrived here in Bethlehem, known as the home of David, because of our belonging to that house and line.[47]

"'Although Mary was far along, we thought there was enough time for us to travel there and then back to Nazareth for the birth of the child. We had to travel slowly because of her condition. I dared take no chances in safeguarding her and our baby. But as we entered Bethlehem, Mary's childbearing pangs began. The town was crowded that night. There seemed to be no place for us to stay. Being only human, I panicked! Frightened for Mary and our child, I rushed from inn to inn and pounded on unknown house doors. I begged strangers for help, but I need not have worried. At last, a kindly innkeeper allowed us to stay in the cave near his inn where animals sheltered. When the time came for her to have her child, she gave birth to a son. We wrapped him in swaddling clothes and laid him in the manger.'"[48]

Balthazar continued to repeat Joseph's simple words from memory.

"'While there in the cave, an extraordinary event happened. In the nearby countryside, there were shepherds who lived in the fields. At night, they took turns guarding their flock from danger.[49] I will only say to you that a message from the heavens came to them on the night our son was born. Although the shepherds were terrified, the heavenly messenger said they should not be afraid, and that in the town of David, a Savior had been born to them. They were told they would find him in swaddling clothes— those same coverings we had wrapped our child in at his birth. The shepherds later told us that they quickly made the decision to come to Bethlehem. There was no doubt in their minds that the angel's words came from our God. So they hurried and found us with our baby, who was lying in the manger.[50]

"'When they saw the child, they repeated to his mother and me what they had been told by the angel. Both Mary and I were astonished at what these men said. When the shepherds left, we could hear them glorifying and praising God because what they had been told had occurred exactly as the heavenly messenger had said it would.'"[51]

Balthazar continued his tale. "Joseph, definitely a man of few words, as we later learned, now stopped speaking. Of course we had questions we wanted to ask him, but we respected his unwillingness to tell us more of their astounding story. We had just met these two visibly holy people; who were we to press for more details at that point in our relationship?

"Gaspar then told them of his study of the planets and that the alignment of Jupiter, Saturn, and Mars signaled to him that a great ruler would soon appear. They expressed their interest in knowing more—it makes a fascinating tale, if I do say so myself.

"As for my own contribution, I spoke of readings in the book of Daniel that I had found, some of which had confused me. That prophet had written of a person coming on clouds from heaven, who would be sovereign over all men and for all eternity."[52]

As Balthazar spoke these words, a low murmur broke out among some of the men. At least one voice was raised, querying the events.

Nazim quickly took charge. "You have given us much to consider, friend Balthazar. It is not our intent to tire you excessively. Let us be done for today."

CHAPTER 8

Newcomers

When next they gathered to speak, Nazim asked Balthazar if he would mind if others joined in hearing his words. Several wives had come into the camp, including Nazim's wife, Haleema. Some of the men had told their wives about the story Balthazar was weaving. Now, the women wanted to hear for themselves. Somewhat sheepishly, Nazim said there might be children with them as well. Unhesitatingly, Balthazar agreed to speak to a larger gathering.

Nazim noted that with the expanded group, Balthazar would have to speak louder. "I hope that will not be offensive."

Balthazar's deep laughter boomed forth as he declared, "No one has ever found it hard to hear my voice. It is probable that you will have to tell me if I speak too loudly!"

With this convivial announcement, he prepared to speak once more of his experiences with the other magi. Considering his new audience of women, he felt that what he was going to say on this occasion would carry even more significance.

Reverently, Balthazar began with this same thought. "Nazim, I thank you for the opportunity to tell of our time in Bethlehem. I find it amazing that what I had planned to tell you men today now also will be heard by your families and most especially your wives. I presume that the newcomers, including the children, are here because they are aware of what happened to us three magi and to the shepherds as well?"

The nodding of covered heads and a general agreement that this was the case confirmed his thinking.

Then Balthazar held up a yellowed sheaf of parchment, obviously written long ago. He told the group that years earlier he had recorded what he was about to tell them so that the events and words would not be lost. As he spoke, it was clear that he did not need the writing on the paper to jog his memory. The story he told was engraved in his mind and on his heart.

"We were invited by this most welcoming family to stay longer. All of us had found ourselves to be in such harmony that it was easy to accept their gesture of hospitality. Truth to tell, it turned out to be one of the most special times in my life—in all of our lives. After we had told Mary and Joseph of how we had found them by following the star, we let them know our eagerness to learn more of their lives. The couple seemed to take it for granted that the power of God had brought us to them in Bethlehem. We believed that this made them most agreeable to tell their story.

"Mary and Joseph told us of events that happened on the eighth day of Jesus' life, when, according to the Law of Moses, they took their child to be circumcised, and he was officially given the name of Jesus. When that day came, they took him to the Jerusalem Temple of Solomon observing the tradition that every firstborn male must be consecrated to the Lord. A part of the purification ceremony is the sacrifice of an offering, which for them was either a pair of turtledoves or two young pigeons.[53]

"On this special day, they met a devout man named Simeon. He had yearned for Israel to be saved and comforted for all the centuries of servitude it had endured. It was felt by all that the Holy Spirit had especially blessed this man because this same spiritual being had revealed to Simeon that he would not die until 'he had set eyes on the Christ of the Lord.'[54]

"Mary shared the extraordinary words that this holy man told them when they brought their child inside the temple that day. Simeon immediately took the infant into his arms and blessed God, saying: 'Now, Master, you can let your servant go in peace, just as you promised; because my eyes have seen the salvation which you have prepared for all the nations to see, a light to enlighten the pagans and the glory of your people Israel.'[55]

"As the father and mother stood in wonder at what Simeon was saying, he blessed them and said to Mary, 'You see this child: he is destined for the fall and for the rising of many in Israel, destined to be a sign that is rejected—and a sword will pierce your own soul too.'"[56]

Balthazar would have said more, but the almost united intake of breath, mostly from the women, caused him to pause. Cognizant of the pain his words must have created in the mothers, he felt that he somehow had to acknowledge their distress. However, he was not certain what he could or should say. His own heart writhed as he remembered Mary saying those words to him. He recalled how she had held her child closer, as some of the women were doing with the infants in their arms. Her face had been drawn in concern—not for herself he had been certain—but for what the words foretold about her son and his future rejection. He could see her in memory as she had rocked her child

—seemingly to ward off the painful words of destiny. Balthazar remembered other words Mary had spoken: She treasured all these things and would remember them all the days of her life.[57]

Finally, deciding that he might well make matters worse and that it was best to simply continue telling the holy family's story, Balthazar told of another event that had occurred in their lives. He hoped it would prove a distraction as he began anew, trying for a somewhat lighter tone of voice.

"Let me tell you of another holy person Mary and Joseph met on that same day of their child's circumcision. She was a widowed prophetess, Anna, then eighty-four years of age. She had dedicated herself to serving God and never left the temple where she fasted and prayed. Now she found this holy family, and to all those looking forward to Jerusalem's deliverance, she immediately began to praise God about this child.[58]

"The next day, when we returned to visit again and Joseph was busy with his carpentry work, Mary told us of other significant events related to her child, Jesus. Bear with me, please, as I tell you about her cousin Elizabeth, who was married to a priest named Zachariah. Their stories will unite in a wondrous way, as you will shortly hear.

"Zachariah belonged to the Abijah section of the Jewish priesthood. This loving and religious couple had been married for many years, but were childless. With both husband and wife getting on in years, it had long been accepted that Elizabeth would never conceive a child,[59] though this did not keep them from hoping and praying.

"Months before Mary was with child, Zachariah was exercising a special priestly office. It was his time to be the only priest who would perform a ritual custom to enter the sanctuary of the Lord and to burn incense there. By tradition, the whole congregation remained outside while the priest tended the brazier in front of their most holy place.[60]

"At the hour of incense, on this extraordinary occasion, an angel of the Lord—a messenger, if you will—appeared to him. The angel stood on the right side of the altar. Understandably, Zachariah was overcome with fear.[61] The angel, however, said to him, 'Zachariah, do not be afraid, your prayer has been heard. Your wife Elizabeth is to bear you a son and you must name him John. He will be your joy and delight and many will rejoice at his birth, for he will be great in the sight of the Lord.'[62]

"The angel told more good news: 'Even from his mother's womb he will be filled with the Holy Spirit, and he will bring back many of the sons of Israel to the Lord their God. With the spirit and power of Elijah, he will go before him *to turn the hearts of fathers toward their children* and the disobedient back to the wisdom that the virtuous have, preparing for the Lord a people fit for him.'[63]

"When the heavenly being ceased talking, Zachariah daringly said to the angel, *'How can I be sure of this?* I am an old man and my wife is getting on in years.'[64]

"The angel initially replied, 'I am Gabriel who stands in God's presence, and I have been sent to you and bring you this good news.'[65] Then his posture changed, along with his voice, as he righteously declared, 'Listen! Since you have not believed my words, which will be true at their appointed time, you will be silenced and have no power of speech until this has happened.'[66]

"Outside, meanwhile, the people were waiting and were

surprised that Zachariah had been inside the sanctuary for so long a time. Their amazement grew when Zachariah finally came out and no longer could speak. Quickly they concluded that he had received a vision in the sanctuary of the Lord. He could only make signs to them and remained speechless. Although now mute, he continued his priestly tasks until his time of service was finished, and then he returned home.[67]

"Later, Elizabeth his wife did conceive a child, as the angel had said she would. For five months, she kept to herself. Mary told us that her cousin gave all homage to God for her being with child, saying, 'The Lord has done this for me.'[68]

"This story now turns to young Mary. In the sixth month of Elizabeth's pregnancy, that same angel Gabriel was sent by God to a town in Galilee called Nazareth. Mary lived there with her parents. She was still a youthful virgin, although she had long been betrothed to a man named Joseph, who was from the House of David also[69]—yes, this same couple, Mary and Joseph!

"Gabriel's greeting to Mary was profound: 'Rejoice, so highly favored! The Lord is with you.'[70]

"As you might imagine, she became deeply anxious hearing these words and asked herself what this greeting could possibly mean.[71] But the angel then said to her, 'Mary, do not be afraid; you have won God's favor. Listen! You are to conceive and bear a son, and you must name him Jesus. He will be great and will be called the Son of the Most High. The Lord God will give him the throne of his ancestor David; he will rule over the House of Jacob for ever and his reign will have no end.'[72]

"Mary said to the angel, 'But how can this be, since I am a virgin?'[73]

"'The Holy Spirit will come upon you,' the angel answered, 'and the power of the Most High will cover you with its shadow. And so the child will be holy and will be called Son of God.'[74]

"After this, the angel Gabriel told her, 'Know this too: your kinswoman Elizabeth has, in her old age, herself conceived a son, and she whom people called barren is now in her sixth month, *for nothing is impossible with God.*'[75]

"'I am the handmaid of the Lord,' said Mary, 'let what you have said be done to me.'[76]

"With those words of acceptance, the angel left her."[77]

Clearly, the men, women, and even the children who were able to comprehend some of what Balthazar had just told them were mesmerized by his words. Seeing no reason to explain the unexplainable—and grateful for that—Balthazar testified further. "Soon after these events, Mary set out and traveled as quickly as she could to the town in the hill country of Judah, where Elizabeth and Zachariah lived."[78]

Slowly taking a deep breath, he continued with what Mary told him next had occurred so extraordinarily.

"As Mary greeted her cousin, Elizabeth was overjoyed as the child in her womb leaped, and Elizabeth, too, felt the power of the Holy Spirit. She exclaimed aloud in a prayerful voice to Mary. 'Of all women you are the most blessed, and blessed is the fruit of your womb. Why should I be honored with a visit from the mother of my Lord? For the moment your greeting reached my ears, the child in my womb leaped for joy. Yes, blessed is she who believed that the promise made her by the Lord would be fulfilled.'[79]

"And Mary said:

> My soul proclaims the greatness of the Lord
> and my spirit *exults in God my Savior;*
> because *he has looked upon his lowly handmaid.*
> Yes, from this day forward all generations
>   will call me blessed,
> for the Almighty has done great things for me.
> *Holy is his name...*"[80]

As Balthazar finished saying from memory the stirring words of Mary's response, he wondered what his audience's reaction would be. Reverently, he finished, but no one spoke as they continued to gaze at him, clearly wanting him to share more about Mary. Accepting their respectful silence, Balthazar continued the young girl's story. "Mary stayed with Elizabeth several months and then went back home,[81] since she herself had concerns to deal with about her own pregnancy."

Low murmurs and nods from the crowd briefly interrupted his thoughts and words, but the reactions let him know they understood his meaning about the situation for the unwed mother-to-be, Mary.

"The time eventually came for Elizabeth's child to be born. In due time, she gave birth to a son[82]—just as the angel Gabriel had told her husband, Zachariah, would be the case. As had also happened, during the entire length of the pregnancy, Zachariah had been mute. Though other relatives and neighbors heard about the future birth of their child, they did not hear it from him because he had not been able to speak from the exact time when he had questioned the angel how he and Elizabeth could have a child at their great age.

"Then, on the eighth day, Zachariah and Elizabeth brought their child to the temple to be circumcised. Those in charge assumed the parents were going to name their newborn son after his elderly father, but Elizabeth firmly stated, 'No, he is to be called John.'[83]

"Those present, including family and friends protested. One official challenged her. 'But no one in your family has that name.'[84] Many tried to find out from the still-speechless father what he wanted his only child—and, therefore, his heir—to be called. Zachariah signaled that he wanted a tablet or paper to be brought. When this was done, Zachariah wrote in a bold hand: 'His name is John.'[85]

"Their initial astonishment at the father's written words grew tenfold because at that instant his power of speech returned.[86] Zachariah immediately praised God for the first time in almost a year. Then he proclaimed these and other prophetic words:

> *Blessed be the Lord, the God of Israel,*
> for he has visited his people, he has come to
>   their rescue
> and he has raised up for us a power for
>   salvation
> in the House of his servant David …
> thus *he remembers his* holy *covenant,*
> the oath he swore
> to our father Abraham.[87]

"To his son John, he proclaimed,

> And you, little child,
> you shall be called Prophet of the Most High,

for you will go before the Lord
to prepare the way for him ...
and to guide our feet
into the way of peace.[88]

"All their neighbors were filled with awe as they listened to Zachariah's words of faith and hope. The whole affair was talked about throughout the hill country of Judea. Indeed, many wondered aloud, 'What will this child turn out to be?'"[89]

Balthazar put away the notes that he had been holding—but had not needed. While he had repeated Mary's, Elizabeth's, and then Zachariah's words, his voice had emphasized various phrases, but not once had he looked at the paper in his hands.

No one stirred in the crowd until a young voice was heard. "Mama, I'm hungry."

The young child's words broke the spell of Balthazar's surprising story that had included the warm, astonishing, faith-filled meeting between the two women, and which had ended with the powerful, prophetic words eventually spoken by Zachariah to his son John.

Nazim's face bore a thoughtful look, but he said nothing, except to announce firmly that the children needed to be fed, while also expressing his regular concern that he did not want to tire Balthazar. With that, the assembly broke up to tend to their earthly needs.

CHAPTER 9

How Jesus Came
to Be Born

Balthazar was most pleased the next time they all met. Somehow, the group seemed to have almost doubled in size. He was aware that new people came to the semi-permanent camp on a daily basis. Both familiar and unfamiliar faces met his gaze—men, women, and children, all were gathered near him. Eager but deferential, they waited for him to begin. Clearly, they wanted to hear more—some for the first time, of course. The obvious place to start on this day was with Mary's return to Nazareth. As he stood up to speak, the crowd grew silent.

"This is how Jesus came to be born. His mother, Mary, confirmed this to us. Joseph also told of the events that led to his becoming the earthly father of the child Jesus. Mary's parents, Anne and Joachim, had betrothed their daughter to the carpenter Joseph. For his part, Joseph, a most righteous and holy man, had come to love Mary as she grew in grace and beauty in their village of Nazareth. A betrothal in the Jewish faith is regarded as the time when the woman becomes legally married. The formal marriage ceremony can occur anytime from months to years later— mostly dependent on the age of the bride. She is considered to be married when the betrothal is announced, and later cannot belong to another man, unless she is divorced from her betrothed. This pledge is made between a couple and is an unbreakable vow. Only extraordinary events can break the betrothal.

"Therefore, when Mary set off to visit Elizabeth, she was betrothed to Joseph, but had not had relations with him because she still lived in her father's house since she was so young yet. Because she had stayed with her older cousin for nearly three months, when she returned to Nazareth, it was observable to others that she was with child—a scandal was in the making.

"Joseph's first reaction was astonishment that the young girl he had practically revered as being perfect could have had relations with another man. He felt he had been betrayed by his betrothed, whom he had previously thought was the most chaste and virtuous girl in all of Nazareth. Legally, he could divorce her for the infidelity she had shown him. Being a man of honor and because of his love for Mary, Joseph weighed his decision so as not to act rashly. Aggrieved by her apparent treachery and bolstered by others in the village, his pride was on the line.

"Finally, he made the decision to divorce Mary quietly. He had not spoken to either Mary or her parents, but he felt he had no alternative. Still, he wanted to spare her public shaming and determined he would divorce her informally,[90] for her sake more than for his.

"On the night he had made up his mind to do this, the angel of the Lord appeared to him in a dream and said, 'Joseph, son of David, do not be afraid to take Mary home as your wife, because she has conceived what is in her by the Holy Spirit. She will give birth to a son and you must name him Jesus, because he is the one who is to save his people from their sins.'[91]

"Now all this took place to fulfill the words spoken by the Lord through their prophet Isaiah:

> *The virgin will conceive and give birth to a son*
> *and they will call him Immanuel.*[92]

"When Joseph woke up, you will not be surprised to hear that he was amazed at what had happened to him during the night. As a faith-filled man, he did not hesitate to do what the angel of the Lord had told him that he should do. He immediately took Mary, his wife, into his home. Although he had not had intercourse with his virginal wife, in time as I have told you, Mary did give birth to a son. As the angel also had instructed him to do, Joseph named the child Jesus, which is a name meaning 'God-is-with-us—Immanuel.'"[93]

With these words, Balthazar felt there was little more to tell them about this holy family whom the magi had found by following the star. He was satisfied with what he had shared until he looked at the faces still peering intently at him. Instinctively, he knew they wanted more, but was not sure what else he should say. With a smile, he simply asked, "Is there more you would know?"

The floodgates seemed to open among them, but no one had the temerity to put forth a direct question. Finally, Nazim spoke up. "My wife, Haleema, and I talked last night. She and the women wonder about these angels you have brought up several times, including just now, when you said one came to Joseph. Where do they come from?

How do they appear from nowhere and, apparently, exactly when most needed?"

Suddenly, a child asked what all really wanted answered: "Who sends them?"

Balthazar considered what he might answer. He felt that not just the women and children but the men, too, probably had similar questions about what or who angels might be, as well as, ultimately, from where they came.

Gathering his thoughts, he said, "Our wise leader, Melchior, was a Zoroastrian priest both before and after he was an adviser at the court of his brother. Much of what I know about angels comes from Melchior talking to us of these not-of-this-earth creatures. In the Zoroastrian religion, their great god Ahura Mazda has similar beings, who seem to be powerful, though lesser beings. I know little more than this. However, if one thinks about it, our leaders here on earth accomplish tasks in much the same manner. One person cannot do it all, and so duties must be given to others so that work can be accomplished. We humans are grounded to the earth, but our beliefs in higher powers generally attribute supernatural powers to them. I, myself, have no trouble understanding such a chain of command."

Nazim spoke for his people. "This Gabriel—he is in personal contact with what you say is the Jews' one God?"

"I believe that would be an accurate way to state the relationship. Also, even among the angels, there seems to be a hierarchy. Gabriel is an archangel. In their book of Daniel, this same Gabriel was ordered to explain to the prophet the meaning of dreams he was having."[94]

"Ah, you spoke of Daniel the other day."

"Yes, Daniel wrote several centuries ago, and the information I found in his writings encouraged me that the star was leading us to a supernatural being who would rule for all eternity."

Nazim probed further. "Then you believe that this child, born so humbly in a cave, is the supernatural being you say will rule for all eternity?" Somewhat suspiciously, he added, "Over whom will he rule?"

All in the crowd waited for Balthazar to reply to this query.

"Nazim, I am certain that the questions you have raised will be the subject of debates for centuries to come. As for me, based on the extraordinary circumstances that led me to this child and what I feel in my heart, I believe Jesus is—as you have said—the true supernatural being who, in time, will rule for all eternity."

Nazim doggedly pursued his thoughts. "Then I would ask, as before, *why* has he not come forth?" The camp listened intently to their leader and nodded in agreement— this was truly a question of great merit. "He would be a young man now, providing he survived, something not guaranteed to all, as we know. Where is he now? What is he doing? There has been no radical changing of the political powers that rule this earth. Rome is as powerful as ever in the lands where you say this child was born. If anything, the Roman Empire has exerted even more of its power over the conquered lands of the Jews as shown by the dethroning of the Herodian family and then the partitioning into thirds of those lands that Herod once ruled. Certainly nothing has changed in the land of my birth. Life goes on as it always did. What say you?"

Over the years, Balthazar, too, had thought about the concerns Nazim was raising. When would this child of destiny make his presence known to the world? Looking to Kateb, with whom this and similar conversations had been held over the years, he wondered what to say. His voice reflected his indecisiveness on how to respond, but he told the crowd the truth as he knew it.

"My friend Kateb and I have spent many a day and night considering these same questions—more so of late than in earlier times. As the child was an infant and later as he grew of age, we spoke mainly of the past and the miraculous events that had brought us to his birthplace in Bethlehem. Obviously, we did not expect that a babe in arms would have any impact on the world, nor even as a youth. But as time has passed, and in recent years, we have wondered where he is and what is he doing. Nazim ... I have no answer. This divine child—a young man, as I am speaking to you today—has yet to reveal his presence, as far as we can tell."

"So in all these years—and even to the present—you have not tried to learn more of his doings, possibly even to aid him, since his family would seem to have only a carpenter's earning power?"

"Nazim, there is more to tell that you do not know."

"Well, we are listening, as always."

Kateb's Tale

A new voice interjected Kateb's presence for the first time in the days since his initial words expressing his personal strong belief. Almost hesitantly, he asked both Nazim and Balthazar if he might speak. Balthazar, eager for his friend to share what he had personally learned, beamed his assent. Nazim graciously indicated that they would welcome his words. Kateb remained seated as all eyes turned to him.

"Before Balthazar addresses why we have not sought the child over the years, I would first speak more of these angels, Nazim, that you and your people were wondering about previously. Balthazar said that he knew little more of them than what Melchior told the magi, but this is not totally the situation. Angels played another role on the actual night the child was born."

Balthazar briefly commented, "Kateb is right—as usual."

Quietly, Kateb resumed speaking. "You have heard a little of this story already, but I would have you listen anew. I can certainly understand how these angels' sudden appearance and disappearance might make you wonder who and what they are. Here is more truth—and hopefully it will be helpful." Almost matter-of-factly, he then added,

"Of course, it is possible you may have even more questions after I speak.

"In the countryside outside of Bethlehem, there were shepherds who tended their flocks nearby.[95] After Jesus was born—that very night, in fact, when Mary carefully was tending her newborn infant and had placed him in the manger where the animals fed—another manifestation of his greatness occurred. On that cold night, once again an angel spoke to mankind. The shepherds' flocks had long been bedded down for the evening. Midnight was close. At night, possibly even more than during the day, a shepherd is ready to defend his sheep from predators and other harm. Thus, several shepherds were in the field, guarding the animals entrusted to their care.

"On this night of all nights, an angel of the Lord descended from on high, and the glory of the Lord shone around this messenger and on all below. The dark night was lit by a light such that none of them had ever seen before. Soon, other angels filled the night skies. To put it mildly, the shepherds were terrified.[96] We know of these events because, as Balthazar has indicated, in the time we spent with Mary and Joseph, they freely told of us of many of the events surrounding the birth of their child.

"I decided to find these shepherds and, if possible, to learn more of their story. While the magi were with this holy family and were learning more of Mary and Joseph's experiences, I trekked to the nearby hills where the shepherds lived and tended their flocks. When eventually I found them, they eagerly shared their wondrous story related to the infant Jesus."

Here, Kateb posed a scenario to his intrigued listeners. "I want you to think of the coldest night imaginable. At night in the desert, we regularly experience temperatures dropping, but I want you to think colder than that, and then colder still. I want you to imagine a cold so brutal that rain—if it were to fall at that time—would change into white flakes as it falls from the skies. These flakes also would be cold, unlike warm rain from above. Then these snowflakes would gather—one on top of another in untold numbers—until a blanket of white would cover the land."

Kateb picked up a handful of grainy sand and let it drizzle through his fingers as he then said that the snowflakes that fell from the sky that night were as many as the grains of sand falling from his hand. He picked up more sand, in both his hands this time, and let the new infinitesimal bits fall in the same place as his first handful so that they could better picture how the snow would accumulate and grow in depth.

He then dramatically concluded his visual demonstration by announcing in a firm tone, "This is how the world was changing on the night this child of glory was born. The snow, silver-white in the darkness, falling from the heavenly skies, was another reflection of the child and his family. For me, its beauty and purity signified the nature of this newborn baby."

At his first words and gestures, the children had giggled and squirmed as they pictured such a scene. A white blanket from above changing the world into a playground of frozen sand—what a wonder. Although some of the adults grimaced at the thought of such cold, they too embraced the scene Kateb was picturing for them. The imagery that the whiteness of the snow was symbolic of the purity of the child made a strong impression on many of them.

Kateb continued his narrative in an affirming voice that heralded the truth of his words and contributed to a mounting inspiration among his listeners. "The shepherds told me that the snow began to fall just as nighttime came. They could do nothing more than huddle together with their sheep and hope for better weather. The night itself was dark except for one lone star that glimmered high in the sky. Surprisingly, from their vantage point in the hills, this star gave a great light. However, they paid no heed to its presence high above them because all their energies were focused on the cold and their flocks.

"Here are more of the events of that special holy night that they shared with me. It was the middle of the night when, from above, the messenger angel of the Lord appeared to them, and with this being came a wondrous stream of light that lit the field and all creatures in it. As I told you, more of these beings filled the sky, and these simple shepherds were terrified. They became even more fearful when the largest winged creature in the sky above them began to speak to them. However, the words from this extraordinary visitor from on high brought such a message of wonder that their fear soon left them. They, too, were faithful Jews, and they tended their flocks as Abraham of old and Moses' wife's family also had done, ages earlier. As with all Jews, they had long waited for the promised Messiah to be their new King of Israel.

"The angel's words were seemingly beyond belief. 'Do not be afraid. Listen, I bring you news of great joy, a joy to be shared by the whole people. Today in the town of David a savior has been born to you; he is Christ the Lord. And here is a sign for you: you will find a baby wrapped in swaddling clothes and lying in a manger.'[97]

"When the angel finished speaking, a great throng of other angels—more of these heavenly messengers from above—appeared from out of nowhere and began praising God, singing these words:

'Glory to God in the highest heaven,
and peace to men who enjoy his favor.'[98]

"The wonder of these messages was as awesome as the beauteous winged messengers from on high. When the angel chorus and messenger left, the shepherds' faith was ignited. They said to one another, 'Let us go to Bethlehem and see this thing that has happened which the Lord has made known to us.'[99]

"There was no question in their hearts and minds but that this messenger spoke words of truth. No harm had come to them, and they decided that they must quickly do as the angel of the Lord had told them to do. Still conscious of the need to care for their flock, the shepherds selflessly determined that those who had been on guard in the fields that night should be the ones to go first into Bethlehem. Those fortunate ones hurried away to find the baby the angel had said would be the Savior of the world. As they were told, they found Mary and Joseph, with the couple's newborn infant, awake in the manger. Coming nearer to this blessed family, they worried that their humble clothing and trade would be offensive. Speaking not a word, they did not put themselves forward.

"Becoming aware of the shepherds, Mary and Joseph beckoned the visitors to come nearer to the manger. With encouragement from both parents, the shepherds told the story of the appearance of the angels and the specific words that the angel of the Lord had said. They remained until morning, and then left so that the other shepherds could come to the birthplace in Bethlehem. Heeding the words of the heavenly messenger that they should share their story with others, they had no hesitation in talking with me. They told of a stable and how the animals helped to keep the small family warm on that cold winter night."

Kateb looked at the gathering around Balthazar and him. As if compelled, he spoke more of his interpretation of events.

"What I want to say to each of you is that the manner of the birth of this child has a significance for the world. The star that Balthazar first sighted in our land, and Gaspar in his, and Melchior as well in his faraway land, was a signal to men of learning that an extraordinary event was occurring. From time long past, the heavens have held mysteries far beyond the ken of men, and it has also been, we believe, a way that the powers above have communicated with us mortals below.

"These three magi and those of us who accompanied them were from different cultures and areas of the world. Yet somehow—in the vastness of the lands where we all were traveling—we found each other. How could this happen except that an all-powerful personage controlled our destinies, even though we felt we were in charge of our own fortunes and deeds. Only a majestic master planner from on high could have guided the magi to find one another. When our groups all joined together, we became more than our separate parts. Our backgrounds were dissimilar—from the magi themselves to us, their companions. I do assure you, however, that it was not mere coincidence that we became as one.

"Was this enough for such an almighty somebody or something to have made happen? No—more people had to know of this child's birth, especially those living in Judea. The three magi from different lands were not enough for this powerful being to be satisfied that the birth of the child—the Messiah—would be made known to others. You probably have an awareness that the magi came from wealth and nobility and, as I just emphasized, from separate and distant lands.

"But this child of destiny has assuredly come for all mankind—from the highborn to the lowborn. Shepherds are often considered to be among the lowliest of beings, although in past times, this was not the case. In Egypt, however, where the Jews had been held in captivity for centuries, shepherds were despised as the least of the slaves. In the Hebrew's book of Genesis, it was indicated that shepherds were detestable to their Egyptian captors.[100] While in the lands called Palestine, where the Jews finally settled, shepherds have come to be considered on par with dung sweepers.

"The point I am trying to make is that by having these shepherds to be the first to learn of the actual birth of the child, it is apparent that this Jesus has come to earth for all mankind. It is possible that his mission and message, when he comes into his own, will be strongest among people who have seemed powerless in the past. The angel emissary from on high appeared to the shepherds—out of all the peoples of the earth—and to them alone he told of the birth of this special child. This being was not born just for the Jews. He was born to be the *Savior to the world*.

"These lowly men were gifted with a very significant message from higher beings than we humans. In addition, they knew of Jesus's birth on the very night he was born— and before we travelers from the East learned of the infant's mortal existence. It is not too much to stress the momentous nature of the angel's clear-cut statement that the joyous words and message were to be shared with all people.

"Balthazar and I have spent much time thinking and delving into the importance of these words. In the past, we have been reluctant to share the story of the child Jesus for the reasons we have made known to you already—that is, to keep the holy family safe. The words to the shepherds obviously were not spoken directly to us. Nevertheless, we concluded years ago that the words do mean sharing with not just some of the people on this earth, but all the people."

Kateb smiled to the gathering around him as he gently said, "You are obviously among these people."

Silence reigned in the camp at these words.

Days earlier when Balthazar had begun to tell the story of the magi and their following a star, the men were noticeably respectful of his words. In the beginning, the listeners were prepared to be entertained by the extraordinary events he was narrating. And, after all, what else did they do themselves daily as they rested from the heat of the day? It was their tradition to talk among themselves, play desultory games, and possibly bicker at times but, all in all, to take their rest and live their lives from day to day.

When Balthazar and Kateb had been captured, the prisoners had provided an interesting change from the usual camp routine. Their leader, Nazim, clearly felt a degree of admiration for the captives. This had led to the eventual breaking down of the barriers between them and the newcomers—who, in fact, were no longer considered captives but were being treated more like royal guests.

Therefore, as the days and nights passed, a change had slowly become evident among the men. When they told their wives, sisters, and daughters—who had subsequently joined the regular sessions when Balthazar was speaking—the women were as intrigued as their husbands and brothers had become. Why would the men share the words of Balthazar if not because there was more to the stories than simple entertainment? Something was stirring in the hearts of these desert men and their family members, from the wives down to the children.

With Kateb having told the story of the shepherds, they found even more to relate to since this was no longer a story of high-born travelers following a mystical star but of others similar to them. It had become a tale of men who had to work for a living and who might never be sure where their next meal was coming from—or if it would be enough to tide them over until they could eat again.

Nazim looked at his men and their women and children, along with his own family. The capture of Balthazar had been a thorn in his side for years, as he felt under obligation to Herod Antipas. His driving purpose in finding Balthazar had been to pay back the debt he owed to his erstwhile ally. The plan had been to capture Balthazar and then to take him to Jerusalem. There, he would have turned his captive over to the Judean ruler, and probably would have been given fetes in his honor and even a monetary reward. Whatever form Herod's gratitude would take would be secondary to the release Nazim would have felt in upholding his honor for this long overdue debt. The fulfillment of that burden would have been enough.

However, in the numerous days of being in Balthazar's company, several new factors were causing additional soul-searching for Nazim. Knowing full well the Herodian family's reputation for reprisals against their enemies, he had to wonder what would happen to Balthazar and Kateb once they were handed over to Herod Antipas. These two old men had done nothing to the son of Herod the Great. It was common knowledge that Antipas felt no great love for his father, but the son had wanted Balthazar captured for some reason, and it was probably not a righteous one. Even if he allowed his men to take Balthazar and Kateb to Antipas in Jerusalem without his going as well, the onus for their probable deaths would still be on him. Could he allow this to happen?

Furthermore, another new element in this situation was the developing dynamic that Balthazar and now Kateb appeared to be hinting at—that he and his people were becoming a part of this greater story about the infant and the star that had led them all to Bethlehem. This child—grown to a man—seemingly was here on earth for some greater purpose than was the norm for a person born in such a lowly manner. Hearing Balthazar's and Kateb's words, Nazim found himself thinking of his own role in the magi narration.

As the leader of his people—the guardian of them, in fact—he had to consider more than his own personal desires. Were his captives merely two old men who long ago had angered Herod? Or were they blessed by the one God of the Jews and were indeed people to be heeded? If this were so, how could he bring harm to them?

On the other hand, did the ancient religion of the Jews have anything to do with his own Arab ancestry?

The most plaguing thought for Nazim was whether he was leading his own people astray by elevating Balthazar and the other two magi as veritable prophets.

He needed answers, but the path he should take would not be clear until more questions were asked.

CHAPTER 11

What Now?

Nazim broke the long silence since Kateb's last words. "Both of you have made a number of interesting, even intriguing, statements. However, there are still other points that are unclear to me. If one were to accept your evidence that this star led you and others to a person of destiny, is this same person a military leader or a religious leader? You have spoken of a messiah—this would seem to mean a religious leader.

"If this child—now a young man, according to the years that have passed—is to be a religious leader, why were not the rabbis made aware of the birth of this person you seem to believe is their long-awaited Messiah? Why make his presence known to foreigners? To lowly shepherds? Why not announce his birth to the hierarchy of religious leaders?"

Balthazar and Kateb's usual nonverbal communication was in play as each looked at the other. However, to the men and women awaiting a response, the silence spoke volumes. The tribe looked at one another acknowledging Nazim's point, and respect for their leader notched up a little higher. He had brought up an important point for which neither of their learned guests apparently had a ready answer.

Finally, Balthazar replied, "Nazim, your points are valid. Kateb and I have oft debated these questions over the years. And the answer to all of them is that we do not know."

The words hung in the quiet of the night. Whether young or old, male or female, no one said a word.

Balthazar's next words were spoken in a reflective tone. "We are only human beings, just as you are. We can pose question after question and ponder the answers we think are correct, but if there is a higher authority causing these events to happen, his reasons are beyond our limited understanding. Who am I—who are any of us—to question his authority or reasons for doing anything, much less for sending an infant to be the Savior of the world?"

These words were greeted by looks of empathy from the men and women gathered close. Most of the onlookers rarely thought deeply about events around them, and certainly not of events they could not control. They woke up each day, did whatever tasks were required of them, and were grateful for the food they found and the water so scarce in these parts. The fact that the sun rose each day and set at night were simply markers of the passing of one day into the next.

However, as with most people who live outdoors almost all of the seasons of the year, they recognized there was a certain order to the occurrence of natural things. The sun rose and set daily. There were times of heat and others when it was hotter still. There was a pattern to life and to the lives of human beings. In their hearts and souls, they were aware of a higher power who, at some point in the greater order of things, had brought life to the world. This greater being, therefore, must oversee the cycle of life and death for all beings—humans as well as animals. This was probably the limit of most of their thoughts about how their world moved along from day to day.

But now, spurred on by Balthazar and Kateb's words, they found themselves seeking and wanting more.

In due course, Balthazar took up the all-important issue of whether the Messiah would be a religious or a political leader. He began to delve deeper. "As to the destiny of this child and his reason for coming to earth, there is much to consider. In truth, their almighty being might seem to have made a mistake, not to have made the birth known to the elders and faith leaders of the Jews. If the rabbis had knowledge of such a person, they almost certainly would have taken him under their wing, and tutored him as he grew into a youth and toward his destiny. What an honor it would have been for them to mentor him. Such a person's presence in a synagogue, from infancy on, would have given credibility to his leadership when he—and presumably they—finally chose to let the world know that the yearned-for Messiah had actually been living among them for many years.

"But think further, my friends. On this same point, was he not made known to the rabbis in some limited form by both of the separate prophetic words and actions of Simeon and Anna? Surely rabbis knew of this holy man Simeon, who had been in the synagogue on a regular basis for years. As for Anna, she was said to be a prophetess who never left the Temple—what of her words to those around her? I can only suggest that the rabbis chose not to listen.

"Again, why let the Messiah be born in such a lowly place and to a carpenter and his inexperienced young wife? What in the world was this almighty being thinking? And again, I say I have no answer. But I tell you that he must have had a deep and profound reason for allowing events to proceed as they have—both then and now."

Reverently, Balthazar spoke his own deep faith. "For me, I know that my own life has been guided by this greater force on high. Kateb and I have told you much of what occurred during this special time in our lives. I have decided that I will tell you of another event that we three magi—Melchior, Gaspar, and I—experienced.

"Nazim, before Kateb told you of the events that happened to the shepherds on the night the child Jesus was born, you asked me why, in all these years, we magi did not try to follow the child's progress or to aid him in some way. Yes, we could have assisted this carpenter family with our wealth. Maybe our collective power, even wisdom, might have helped them and their special child in some small way. I have told you several times to prepare yourself to be amazed. I say this again regarding what I am about to tell you.

"However, as we have talked long this day, maybe it would be better to continue tomorrow?"

Almost as one, the camp broke into speech.

"No, continue."

"Please—tell us more."

"You cannot stop now!"

Nazim was among those urging him to continue, and Balthazar accepted their eagerness to hear more.

"As you wish. I have told you that we visited with the family for a number of days. Soon we began to talk among ourselves and decided that it was time to leave. Having come to know this holy family and experiencing their openness in sharing many of the extraordinary events in their lives, we were all deeply conscious of Herod's departing words. We felt he had given a command that when we found the child that we should return to Jerusalem and bring him information of the baby's existence. Herod said it would be his intent to go then and give homage to this person.

"For many an hour, we three discussed the ramifications for this special family if we were to return to Herod with the news that not far from Jerusalem the Messiah had been born and was living in humble circumstances. We had great concerns if Herod was indeed sincere. The stronger possibility was that he would view this innocent babe and both the parents as potential threats to his throne and to his dynasty. The evidence cannot be denied that over the four decades of his rule, Herod ruthlessly and consistently eliminated dangers to himself. Melchior had shared several stories of Herod's cruelty and of his reputation to let nothing—and no one—stand in his way. I, too, had heard of his dark deeds.

"As we conferred on what to do about returning to Herod with news of the child's birth, Melchior told us many additional events that had occurred during Herod's reign. I believe I have told you that when Melchior was young, he had met Herod in Rome when the Idumean was crowned king of Judea. Melchior's country had trading ties with the Judean leader until it could no longer justify keeping trade relations with him, due to the many treacherous acts he had commanded or even did himself. Now, Melchior revealed even more acts of treachery that Herod had committed.

"Nazim, in view of your relationship with Herod Antipas, I feel it is important—the honest thing that I must do—to let your people hear some of the facts related to

Herod the Great's ruthlessness, even with his own family members."

Balthazar looked straight at Nazim to gauge his mood about how much should be revealed about the older Herod's past actions when he had menaced and harmed others to ensure his remaining on the throne.

For his part, Nazim was already aware of many of Herod's destructive acts. He had spent time with Antipas, after all, and learned of other vile deeds over the years. The facts were the facts, however, and his people had a right to hear some of those evil actions—they could be called nothing less. It was obvious that Balthazar was waiting for Nazim's consent before speaking of the many indefensible acts during Herod's four decades on the throne.

He spoke now in response to the questioning tone in Balthazar's voice. "I know some of what you are about to tell my people. Speak freely and fear no retribution from me."

Balthazar mutely nodded his thanks and then told some of the specific atrocities Herod the Great had committed. "Herod had several wives over the years; among them was his beautiful second wife, a Hasmonean princess named Mariamne. He seems to have loved her, although the marriage was first made, in part, to solidify his ties with the Judean nation's former ruling family. Previous to Herod, that dynasty had ruled Judea for almost a century. After the Roman leader Mark Antony deposed and executed the last Judean-Hasmonean king, Herod came to power, taking that leader's place. However, he was never truly popular with the majority of the Jews he ruled because of his Idumean birth and because his own father was an Edomite. The generations-old conversion to Judaism, rather than an ancestral history going back to Abraham, contributed to the general rift in his relations with the Judaic people. By wedding Mariamne, Herod hoped to curry public favor.

"Intrigue surrounded this marriage from the start, as well as jealousy. There is evidence of Herod's love for Mariamne inasmuch as he had given orders that if he were to die before she did, that she was to be killed so that they might not be separated even by death. This strange act of love became unnecessary, however, when Herod became convinced that she was being unfaithful to him. Herod's sister apparently told him that Mariamne was planning to poison him, and he stopped any such plan by having his wife executed."

This story of love and murder had Balthazar's audience in its grip. "Obviously, Herod's sons by Mariamne did not take kindly to their mother's murder. Whether it was true or not—and it probably was true—her two sons, Alexander and Aristobulus, were later accused of plotting to dethrone Herod. Wielding the power of a tyrant, Herod rid himself of the threat from the children of his own blood by bringing charges of treason against them to Augustus Caesar. Their deaths would not disturb him greatly since he had many other sons among his numerous offspring.

"Eventually, Augustus decreed that Herod could put these two sons on trial in court. They were both found guilty and ordered to be put to death by strangulation—a particularly slow death. They were executed just a few years before our arrival. And in fact, Nazim, these two sons' deaths paved the way eventually for your Herod—Antipas—to become one of the three ruling sons in the triad that Rome put in place in the Palestinian lands after Herod the Great's death.

"Melchior informed us of other close family deaths that occurred over the years—Herod had a brother-in-law ruthlessly executed, along with other wives of his." With more to tell, Balthazar pressed on. "Outside of the family, inevitably, Herod brooked no challenge to his authority. During his reign, as I have told you, many faithful Jews did not regard him as one of them. Rumors constantly surrounded his past, including that his grandfather had only converted to Judaism for political reasons—unforgiveable to a true Israelite. When he came to power, Herod developed a spy system to learn of any people who might be suspected of plotting his downfall. Once he became concerned about an intrigue, he swiftly eliminated the person or groups involved. Over the years, he harshly dealt with protests, and those who opposed him had a way of disappearing or having untimely deaths.

"I mentioned earlier about the golden eagles—basically, a Roman effigy—that Herod had erected outside the Temple of Solomon. I also said that this was particularly offensive to the Jews because the worship of idols is forbidden in their religion. This, then, was at the root of the Jews' intense opposition to the placement of the eagles above a gate of the temple that Solomon had built ten centuries earlier. Additionally, the eagles represented the hated Roman authority over the hapless Hebrews and were considered another Herodian insult directed at them. Soon after the eagles were put in place, religious protestors pulled them down and cut them into pieces. Over thirty of these men were captured by Roman soldiers. Herod had the leaders burned alive to prove that he held total authority over Jewish lives and actions.

"Think on this, please. Perhaps such stricture as he took against these protesters was another reason that the child's birth was not made known to leaders of the Jewish faith. Herod's spy system and desire to halt any and all opposition would have meant that if he became alerted that a young child of promise was in the care of the rabbis, he would have taken action to protect his kingship. Over time, it would have been impossible to conceal that this child was believed to be the hoped-for Messiah who would lead the nation to victory over oppressors. The child would never have been safe in such an environment. We three magi believed it was infinitely better that the infant was born to an obscure family with no political leanings.

"However, I tell you now that this child *did not need our help* to survive."

These dramatic words were followed by a question from Balthazar which he himself then answered, or at least responded to quickly. "How do I know this? Listen to what occurred on the night before our planned return to Jerusalem to tell King Herod of the child's existence, as he had requested. You know, of course, that we three considered his words as an order that we would ignore at our peril."

Following these words, Balthazar simply looked at Nazim and shrugged briefly yet eloquently. Nazim correctly interpreted this to mean that Balthazar and Kateb's presence, nay their capture after all these many years had passed, was directly related to the magi's decision— for whatever reason it had been made—not to return to Herod. In his turn, Nazim's own slight smile, possibly of remorse, was poignantly expressive.

The powerful portent of Balthazar's words effectively forestalled the slim chance that those in the crowd were no longer willing to listen further at this time. They eagerly waited for his next disclosure.

CHAPTER 12

The Warning

"I will begin with what happened to me." Balthazar's words rang out with faith-filled conviction as well as the truthfulness of the events that he was about to share with them.

"Having said good night to all, I went to my room at the Bethlehem inn where we were staying. I was full of misgivings if the decision we had jointly made that day—to report back to Herod—was what we should really do. Bearing in mind his history and his almost direct orders to us to inform him of finding the child, I definitely knew we were in a dangerous situation. If we should incur Herod's wrath by his later becoming aware that we had not only found the child but had stayed a length of time with this family, he would have felt little compunction to take revenge—his usual method of operating.

"We did feel that the danger to our own persons was something we could handle at this stage of our lives. Death frightened not one of us, I can assure you. Our status in our lands was an additional factor that protected us. The death of one or all of us would have been avenged by our families and our separate countries. Together, we had power and thus a degree of safety to defy Herod.

"However, the peril for Jesus and his parents was another

situation entirely. Once we left—or fled, as Herod would have perceived it—they would have been at the mercy of the merciless king of the Jews. The dilemma was staggering. The crux of the alternative was that in giving Herod details of the defenseless child's whereabouts, we would be putting Jesus, Mary, and Joseph in the danger we would be avoiding ourselves. These were factors that weighed heavily on us.

"There were other aspects to our final decision to report back to Herod. As an influential trio, we had decided that we would put pressure on him that this child was to be protected at all costs. We would tell Herod—diplomatically, yet firmly—that we would hold him personally responsible for the child's ultimate safety. We also would tell Herod that we would provide for the child and his family whatever they needed. We would make it clear that this would include a bodyguard of sorts. Furthermore, that person or group would be in contact with us over the years to keep us informed of this holy family's safety. Our hope was that such safeguards would be sufficient to preserve the child's well-being.

"Nevertheless, it was long before I fell asleep. And in fact, I was then plagued with nightmares that reflected the chaos in my mind and heart. In the midst of my tumultuous dreams, however, suddenly, there was a calmness. I believe that I was awake yet asleep as a vision came to me. This experience was somewhat similar to what we learned had happened to Joseph during his nighttime angelic visit. You will recall that an angel appeared to him and told him that he should not divorce Mary, but should instead take her into his home and protect the child she carried.

"To this day, the clarity of my own herald's words has never left me. The message was a strongly worded warning that we three magi should not go back to Herod. I was told to depart to my own kingdom, using a different route from the one I had taken when following the star. Melchior and Gaspar were to do the same. We were all to return to our separate homelands without informing Herod[101] of our finding the child we believed was the long-awaited Savior of the Israelite nation.

"I then fell into a calm, deep sleep and did not stir till morning. When I awoke, I remembered the entire message I had been given. Oftentimes, when we dream and then awake, we can recall only brief bits of dreams and sometimes nothing at all. This was not the case for me. Every aspect of what had been told me was phenomenally clear—as it is even now, as I tell you of what occurred.

"I quickly rose to convey to my fellow travelers what had transpired in the night. I was hopeful—nay, positive—that the other magi would be willing to follow the directive I had been given. I felt certain that when they learned of my dream, they would abide by the message. I could hardly wait to tell them. Dressing hurriedly, I left my room and almost crashed into Gaspar, who seemed in as much of a hurry as I was. We hastily smiled and greeted one another as we moved swiftly to the gathering area, where we found Melchior already waiting for us.

"'My friends, listen closely.'" Melchior immediately began.

"As was usual, Gaspar and I deferred to Melchior, letting him speak first. His words were astounding to hear, and if I had not been courteously sitting, I tell you truly, I might have fallen down. He began by saying he had a dream that involved all three of us. He then described the identical vision I had received. Looking at Gaspar, who was on the edge of his chair, staring intently at Melchior, I knew without his saying it, that he also had been visited by the spiritual messenger.

"Yes, incredible as it may seem to you, we three each received exactly the same significant warning during the night! The messenger's definitive words to leave immediately, to not report back to Herod, and to return to our separate lands by different routes were the same for each of us.[102]

"What Melchior spoke was the totality of my own dream. Clearly, Gaspar's rushing into the hallway alongside me that morning was his excited effort to quickly tell us of his own dream.

"Were we amazed? Of course, we were."

Balthazar let the crowd murmur among themselves and consider what his words meant. When he began to speak again, they came to attention immediately.

"As interpreters of dreams, we each had vast experience with nighttime events. But not one of us was aware that any three people had ever had precisely the same dream as another person had experienced—down to the least particular and even at the same time of night—which was what had happened to each of us.

"Since this was to have been the day of our departure, it was a simple matter to quickly follow the warning we had been given. Our goodbyes to the child's family had been made the day before. Within minutes of our sharing with each other the phenomenal message, we were striding to our camels, along with our individual companions. Heeding the words not to return to Herod, we traveled farther southward at first and then by entirely different routes, as the heavenly messenger had told us, we left Judea separately.

"As we bid our final farewells to one another, we talked

of reuniting in the distant future. To ensure the safety of the child, our decision was that we would not meet for many a year. However, we did arrange a system whereby we would be able to communicate with each other so that we could take action if Herod ever tried to take revenge on any of us.

"Regarding the infant, we felt that cutting ties completely with him and his family would be to his benefit. As influential as we were, our power was as nothing to the protection that this child so obviously had. He needed nothing from us. Wholeheartedly, we felt that whoever or whatever his guardian was, this personage had the power to govern the universe."

Balthazar had planned to end his comments with those words—what more could be said, after all? Yet having shared so much with these people, he discovered that he could not simply stop here. Thus, he spoke anew. This time, there was a difference in his tone of voice from the narrative storytelling manner he had been using. "Nay, I cannot end here with so strong yet so vague a statement. I must follow my heart in speaking to you further."

As at other times, he began by posing questions to the group of men, women, and children in front of him. His first inquiry was an intense one. Afterward, he paused to allow its impact to be felt: "Who can tell at what point we three magi came to realize that the supreme being of all life, as we know it, was the entity responsible for this God child's appearance on earth?"

Balthazar's question hung in the air. Then he asked another one.

"After all, had we not had the extraordinary experience that a never-before-seen star had led us, individually yet together, to his birthplace in Bethlehem? The reality that our luminous light had disappeared when we approached Herod's palace in Jerusalem was further proof that the child would be protected until his mission on this earth was fulfilled. Years later, I am still amazed about the initial disappearance of the star as we neared Herod's Jerusalem center of power. Similarly, the star's reappearance as we left that city staggers me to this very day.

"After listening to the virgin, Mary, tell of the incarnation of her child, we had to conclude that an amazing event had taken place in her life, and that her child was meant to have an almighty influence on this world at some time in the future. The simple carpenter Joseph had been visited by an angel who told him to take Mary into his home and to safeguard the child she carried. We magi, similarly, were separately warned by a messenger from above not to return to Herod, and that we must depart by different routes from the ones that had brought us to the little town of Bethlehem.

"As men who always seek greater knowledge, we had always sought answers and facts in our various studies. But it is also a fact that when scholarly research cannot be advanced further, and there are still unanswered questions, then other explanations are needed. The spiritual world does not always go hand in hand with what our senses tell us. Yet for each of us three magi, the only possible conclusion we could draw was that our lives on this earth were—and are—governed by a being far beyond our comprehension."

In a thoughtful voice, as he looked individually at as many of them as possible, Balthazar seemed to wonder aloud. "An additional query for you gathered here today is to ask yourselves if your lives are also in the care of this same higher being?"

Balthazar waited a moment or two for them to assess his last remark and then continued. "Now, I would turn to a question that we magi posed to each other. You might have wondered about this as well. *Why us*? Why were we three men from three different kingdoms and even different religions brought hundreds of leagues—guided by a star, no less—to the lowly birthplace of a Jewish child?

"We also had to consider what further role did we have in this wonderful—well, to speak boldly, this miraculous—event? Surely following the star to its final destination and then finding the child was *not* the end-all for us. There had to be more. Of a certainty, there had to be more required of us. Like the shepherds, we were witnesses to an unprecedented event in the history of the world. Were we to do something or nothing?

"The intensity of our feelings as we traveled from Bethlehem was extraordinary. We had separately been blessed with unbelievable nighttime messages. The significance of those dreams—nay, those *warnings*—was that we were to quietly leave Judea and to have nothing more to do with the child or his family. Telling others and proclaiming what had happened to us was what we most wanted to do. But we were agreed that in speaking of these events that we surely would call attention to this child which, in time and in all likelihood, would put him and his parents in jeopardy.

"We could only conclude that if Herod was not to know of the birth of Jesus, then seemingly the rest of the world was not to know of his birth either—at least not from us."

CHAPTER 13

Why Us?

The voice of a child was heard. "Then why are you telling us?"

The innocent inquiry seemed to freeze everyone.

Eventually, Balthazar responded. "Ah, indeed, why? Why you? Why now?" Balthazar smiled at the child, and then he looked long and searchingly at Kateb before speaking. "My dear little one, that is another answer, I do not know. What I do know, however, is that in the ancient Judaic collection of books, there is a unique one called Psalms. In it—I believe it is the eighth psalm—there is a passage that says that out of the mouths of children and babes comes wisdom."[103]

To the larger group, he shared, "This child has asked a question that has been a nagging one in my mind and heart for almost the entire time I have been speaking with you. Why am I telling you this story of my life as it relates to this child of destiny? Mayhap I should not have spoken to you of these momentous times in my life, as well as in the lives of Kateb, here, and my fellow travelers, Melchior and Gaspar. Perhaps it was unwise—but I think not. I feel your good intentions toward Kateb and me—though I do not forget that we are your prisoners."

The crowd as one, through negative head shakes and

palms raised outward—meaning they had no intent of harm—indicated its current goodwill toward Balthazar and Kateb. Nazim looked at his people, and a small smile crossed his face, but he uttered no comment. He did, however, appear to hold his youngest son, who had snuggled onto his lap, a tad closer. A nearby onlooker might have seen a kiss planted on the child's head.

Balthazar had not looked at Nazim because he was extremely interested in the reaction of the assemblage to his last remark. Satisfied with his quick assessment, he too had a slight smile on his face.

When the gathering finally settled in once again to hear more, Balthazar continued. "We magi had agreed that never purposely would we do any future actions that would cause harm to the child. Therefore, I tell you that not one of us has ever returned to Bethlehem or to Jerusalem in Judea to try to find this child of mystery. Do we wonder about him? Constantly! Do we yearn for news—good news, of course—about what has become of him and his family? Absolutely! Dare we return? Try to make contact? Send emissaries? Never!"

Spellbound, his listeners awaited Balthazar's explanation.

"In so doing, we might cause an unintended chain of events that would bring catastrophe not only on Jesus, Mary, and Joseph, but possibly on others. I will tell you, however, that as the years have passed, not a day goes by that I don't consider what Jesus might be doing. When he was twelve years of age, I know that he went to Solomon's Temple, and an important event occurred.[104] I cannot tell you any details of that time in his life, but my heart glowed as my thoughts were centered on him for days on end.

"How has he spent the years of his life? What has he done to fulfill his seeming destiny here on this earth? As has been noted, he would be about twenty years of age now. Joseph probably taught him the carpentry trade. Did he have any formal education? Has he left his parents' home? Are they still alive? Joseph was a number of years older than Mary, but younger than me, and I am certainly in good health still. As was my own habit when Jesus was younger, I imagined him playing as a child, then becoming older each day. I picture him daily now as a young man.

"When will he make his presence known to others? To the world? Will we learn of his teachings through caravan traders bringing word of a youthful preacher who speaks to the crowds and exhorts them to … well—to do what? I have no knowledge of the message he will bring, but I am confident it will be one of peace and harmony. I cannot conceive that he was brought into this world to do harm to others. My faith is strong that he is here on this earth to do good things for mankind."

Breaking the silence that followed Balthazar's answer to the child, Nazim asked, "Do you believe you still have a role, as you phrase it, to play?"

Looking at the Bedouin leader, Balthazar responded. "If I had any doubts that more was required of me, my presence among you right now is the answer."

Noting the quizzical look of many in the gathering, Balthazar added his pensive thoughts in a voice that gained momentum as he spoke. "Here are my thoughts…Why did it take so long for the Herod family to capture at least one of us? Somehow, the powerful Judean king, Herod the Great, could not track us. Had *we* been so wily as to outmaneuver forces such as he commanded? I think not. For us not to be captured—even killed for revenge in all these years—we surely were protected beyond those meager measures we took. Always, our guiding principle was to try to ensure the safety of this holy family. I truly believe that the supreme being who cared for the child must have covered us and our tracks in an infinite veil of secrecy.

"It is important for me to tell you that never have I felt compelled to share the myriad stories I have told you over these past days to any group of people. Yea, I have shared some of these events with family members and close friends, but never to strangers—and never to the extent of what I have told all of you.

"After the child, here, asked why was I telling my story to you, I asked you to ask yourselves why indeed was it you—and why now? Obviously, the second question is answered easier. Or is it? One answer would be that Nazim ordered us to be captured, and this was carried out by your skilled trackers. Therefore, I, and thus my companion, Kateb, are here as prisoners awaiting our fate.

"But I would have you think deeper and further.

"Your leader, Nazim, played a role in this story years ago when he and Herod Antipas fought on the same side. He would have died, except for the intervention of this son of Herod the Great. The debt of his life was to be redeemed at some time in the future. If Antipas had immediately requested, or ordered, our capture by Nazim as fulfillment of the debt, how would that have affected the child Jesus and his family? Was he more vulnerable then, than now? Or is the reverse true—that he is safer now, and therefore my capture will not harm him as it might have in his earlier years?

"Can I say this as fact? Of course not, but it is a possibility that we must consider. This is almost like a "what-if" game. What if this had or had not happened, then what are the consequences of this, that, or another event? Here, let me give you an example. What if I had not decided, as a young man, to study the stars? What if my father had made me follow in his footsteps rather than letting me forge my own path? What if I had not chosen to study the particular area of the sky where the blazing star appeared? Similarly, this what-if game could be applied to Melchior and Gaspar. What if each of them had ignored the star's call? Had missed its presence in the sky?

"And again—let us consider *what if* Nazim and Herod Antipas had never met? Would we all be present here and now wondering *why* I chose to tell you my story?

"I hope my words and the tale of our following the star are causing you to consider deeply and to wonder about these what-ifs of the past that so impact the present. I think you would have to agree that we would almost certainly not be sitting here now, and you would not be considering what role you have. Please notice that I did not say, *what role you might have*. I deliberately said, *what role you have*.

"And now, I hope you are wondering *what* happens next."

CHAPTER 14

The Crisis of Faith

When he began to tell his story, Balthazar had observed how the men, women, and children regularly deferred to Nazim. However, as he asked his last question, he was aware that more than one in the gathering either gazed steadily at him or put his or her head down, as if in silent contemplation. He chose to keep his silence.

Suddenly, the man who had expressed cynical criticism at the beginning of their sessions asked, "What would you have us do?"

Almost as one, the others looked to the new voice, then toward Balthazar, as if their companion spoke for them.

Startled by the sudden weight of the responsibility he felt at the question—that was almost a plea—Balthazar marshaled his thoughts as he searched for an answer. Eventually, he responded, "I cannot tell any of you what to do. After all, I am your prisoner and hold no power over myself, much less you."

This response shifted their attention to Nazim, almost in an accusatory manner.

As if Nazim had been awaiting this turn of events, he looked carefully at his people, almost on an individual basis. In a contemplative voice, he spoke engagingly to all. "There would seem to be some issue as to who is the prisoner and who is in charge. As I have listened these several days, I have felt the power of Balthazar's words and the faith he has exhibited, apparently for many years since following that long-ago star. I believe that what began as a way to entertain you, my people, through a story or two, has turned into something more.

"On the one hand, an observer might say that there is no way that these events could have occurred. That person would deem you, Balthazar, either an excellent storyteller, at best, or a liar at worst. The middle-ground observer would offer the thought that you are a person who is under an illusion and that, therefore, you are possibly not even in your right mind. The things you have told us, of a star leading you blindly across deserts—and not just you but others—speaks of a mind not in touch with reality. Then you spoke of angels bearing messages to a young maiden, and then again to her intended husband not to cast her aside.

"Furthermore, Kateb—probably your paid companion—claims that hordes of angels appeared to shepherds telling them that their long-awaited Messiah had been born in a lowly stable. You, as I recall, spoke of a cave. Kateb told us the angels were gloriously singing in the sky above. Beyond belief, I say!"

His people seemingly held their breath at these brazen words.

"Yet you then added more. You likewise expect us to believe you when you tell of the great God of the Jews—nay, even of the universe—causing this virgin to be with child, yet she remained a virgin. More fantastic still. An intelligent person would question several, if not most, of the stories you have told us."

What had begun as Nazim's mere recital of what Balthazar had told them seemed to have become a criticism of the truth of their prisoner's words. "You invoked the names of several of the Jews' ancient writers as you imply that they were prophesying events that you say you witnessed, or that were fulfilled in the little town of Bethlehem."

Looking at Balthazar, Nazim asked, "Have I spoken truly of what you told us?"

"Yea, those are among the words I spoke." As if compelled, Balthazar added, "You did speak truthfully of what Kateb said too."

The Bedouin skeptic chimed in. "Balthazar also told us of a relative of Mary's being struck dumb by questioning what an angel said to him."

Another man spoke up. "Then the power of speech returned when the old father said his name was to be John."

A timid feminine voice was heard. "A cousin of the holy Mary had her baby jump inside her when Mary came to visit."

A third man added. "Don't forget how all three of you magi had the same dream on the same night—and probably at the same time—warning you not to return to King ... er, to Jerusalem." Many realized that the man had not wanted to offend Nazim by saying the name of Herod as the villain in the tale.

Nazim eyed his people. "You have all listened well. These things I heard as you did, and like you, I have spent time considering the truth of these wild and extraordinary claims. I am sure I could skewer our Balthazar with questions and scenarios and might find several holes in his story that do not seem to fit." The Bedouin leader directly looked at Balthazar as he made this remark, but then held up a hand as if to ward off protests from the camp. "But that is not my intention."

Here, he winked at his son, who grinned joyfully, although probably not fully comprehending his father's remarks. Others smiled to each other and at both Balthazar and Kateb when they heard their leader's last remark and saw the interaction with his young child.

"If—and I do have to stress *if*—this story is true, then I must consider, as Balthazar has told us that he and his fellow royals did in the past, what repercussions there might be if I take him back to Herod Antipas. Why does the tetrarch of Judea so badly want Balthazar to be captured? When our prisoner is brought to him, should I not tell Herod Antipas what Balthazar has revealed to us during his time here?"

As if speaking to himself, Nazim pondered aloud. "Two factors, if not more, must be considered. What will happen to Balthazar—and to Kateb, as well. He, of course, is free to go, but I have a feeling he will insist on remaining with Balthazar."

Nazim looked across the way to where Kateb inclined his head, acknowledging that indeed that would be the case. Loyally, he would go wherever Balthazar was taken and share his fate—whatever that might be.

"Other factors to consider involve the ramifications on the young man Jesus. Would Antipas feel he had to find him? Would this Jesus be considered a threat? Is there danger for Mary, his mother, and for Joseph, his father? Maybe time is on their side. With the passage of the decades and no evidence of wrongdoing on the part of Jesus and his family, the present Herod might deem the three of them as no harm to him."

Conscious of the interest his words were garnering, Nazim continued to speak his thoughts aloud. "However, knowing the history of the Herodian family as I do, I think this will not be the case. If Herod Antipas ordered Balthazar to be captured as payment of my debt, then the past is not past, but is pertinent to the present and to the future. Therefore, I—nay, we—must consider that in returning Balthazar and Kateb to Jerusalem—as prisoners—that we would bring harm to the family that has so captivated us these several days."

At this juncture, Nazim's voice lowered, then came to a complete halt. A look close to agony crossed his face. Long seconds passed before he slowly began speaking, but this time, it was in a harshly grating voice, full of pain. "Balthazar ... my people ..." Nazim faltered again.

Burdened beyond bearing, and then in a voice tinged with compassion and sadness, he tried again, "...I must tell you a vile story, told to me by Antipas on a long-ago night in the distant past. The event has only now come back to me—just now."

Sorrowfully, he spoke to all. "Mayhap we should send the children away, for this will be terrible to hear. But I say they should remain because although this has seemed a special time for all, our children need to know what other people are capable of and that bad things can happen to innocent people."

Settling the matter that the children should remain, Nazim began to tell of that long-ago night when Herod Antipas had shared a tale of horror that his father, Herod the Great, had initiated.

Relentlessly, he revealed the event. "Antipas and I had fought in a vicious battle one day, with much blood spilled—most of it from our enemies. Cold corpses were, even then, being dragged away under cover of darkness. We had been victorious, and as the wine and liquid spirits were liberally drunk, we boasted of deeds that day and in times past.

"Suddenly, Antipas said to me, 'Today's spilled blood was as nothing compared to what my father did on this very night years ago.'

"As I repeat to you today what he told me, I can hear the distress in his voice. When he spoke of the past that night, I now remember almost seeing his memories returning to that distant time, as his voice dropped chillingly, and he told me, 'My father—the *great* King Herod—slew innocent babes to keep his kingdom and so that, one day, I could rule in his place and do similar bloody acts, just as I did today.'

"Herod's son told me of the orders that went out to kill all children under two years of age in a certain area of the realm.

"Why such a specific age—and so young, you must be asking yourself."

Mercilessly, Nazim told details of yet another treacherous Herodian act. "It was because, previously, travelers from afar had arrived in Jerusalem and had brought deeply disturbing news to King Herod. Antipas told me that the men were stargazers, who said they had followed a light in the skies for months and leagues on end. These travelers believed the star was to lead them to the newborn Messiah of the Jews."

Horrified at what he was hearing, Balthazar uttered a sound of protest.

Kateb put out a hand and lowered his head, as if to ward off what was to follow.

Nazim looked at the old magus. "Balthazar, a thousand pardons. But now that you have told your story, I have become aware that I already knew of you and possibly know something that you do not. When Antipas demanded I capture you, I did not know that you were one of the stargazers he had told me about on that terrible night when he revealed the lengths his father was willing to go to preserve his throne for himself.

"Listen further to what I was told. Antipas said that his father pretended to these men—kings and magi from the East, he called them at one point in the retelling of the atrocity—that they were to continue their search for what they believed was an infant, who was likely to be the long-awaited Messiah of the Jews. The key, however, was that they were to return to him when they found this child so that Herod could, as Antipas phrased it, 'pay homage to the child.'"

To Balthazar, he then grimly asked, "Were not those your same words: Herod wanted to do homage before the child?"

Mutely, Balthazar nodded his affirmation; those were the words he had said.

Stoically now, Nazim finished his story. "When these three men failed to return to him, Herod dismissed their fantastic story as rubbish. But as time passed, doubts tormented him. Herod found himself always conscious that if their quest was a true one, that somewhere in his kingdom an infant had been born who would eventually pose a threat to him or to his family's reign. In addition, the arrogant Herod had become furious at having been outwitted by the wise men.[105] Having told the Eastern travelers of a certain ancient passage in an almost one-thousand-year-old book of the Jews, he cast his eyes and spies to a small town called ... Bethlehem."

Brutally and swiftly, Nazim said, "Soldiers were dispatched. The number of children murdered that night grew to about forty babes, all males, who were in or around Bethlehem on that fateful night."[106]

Mothers sobbed, children clung to them, and grown men hung their heads. Kateb swiftly moved to Balthazar's side and held his old friend as they both shed tears of agony at the dreadful words they had just heard.

CHAPTER 15

I Believe He Lives

Several days passed. The mood in the camp was somber. Even the children played quietly. In the first hours of that first day, few spoke, and when they did, their voices seemed lifeless.

On the third morning, a gentle yet firm voice called to Balthazar, seeking to speak to him. Haleema, Nazim's wife, had taken courage in hand and come to him. Courteously, he joined her outside his tent. Unable to help herself, she drew back at how he appeared to have aged since her husband had revealed the story of the forty innocents who had been slain.

Not waiting for Balthazar to speak, Haleema declared, *"I believe he lives."*

When her faith-filled words entered his consciousness, Balthazar could only stare at the woman who was seemingly risking much to come to him.

"Others believe too," she added confidently.

The old man straightened his slumping shoulders as the impact of her words brought him hope for the first time in days. It was as if he were coming alive after being buried in pain for the past three days. However, he could only utter, "Why? How?"

"Why do I believe—and the others as well? Who can

say? What I do know is that from the first words Nazim told me about you, my heart has felt lighter. That is the reason I begged my husband to let me hear more of your words when you spoke next. In turn, I told the other women—many of their husbands, brothers, and fathers also talked of the story you were revealing. Your words have touched us."

Balthazar gravely requested of Haleema, "What do you believe?"

Hesitantly at first, she began to voice the thoughts she had come to tell him. "For myself—I believe your story to be true. I believe the star you followed led you to the one you have called a child of destiny. I believe he lives."

"How can you believe he lives after what Nazim told us?"

She gently chided him. "How can you *not* believe that his father in heaven did not foresee what was to happen? Did not protect him?"

Balthazar confessed his anguish. "I have tried to tell myself these things too. But again and again, I have faltered these past few days. The slaughter of the male children in Bethlehem has to be the explanation of why we have not heard, in all these years, of his taking up his mission as the Messiah. My part in his death seems to be an inescapable fact."

"Ah, but I beg you to consider this, please. His family was not from Bethlehem. You told us they came from another town—you said it was called Nazareth. Surely, for one reason or another, they left before the slayings occurred."

His eyes slowly shed their sorrow as Balthazar listened to Haleema state the case for the infant Jesus having escaped death from Herod the Great.

In a lilting voice that rang with intelligence, she added,

"Surely, the child's God father warned the family to flee. It does not matter where they went. No personage as powerful as the one you have told us about would have failed to keep his child safe, along with the earthly parents to whom he had entrusted that child."

At this point, Kateb came from inside the tent where he had been trying to get Balthazar to eat some food. Smiling a sincere greeting of joy, he approached and knelt before Haleema, honoring her strength and wisdom. Kateb's open gesture startled the woman, and she quickly urged him to rise.

Balthazar stated the obvious. "You heard?"

Addressing their visitor, Kateb said, "Haleema, your words of faith have rejuvenated not just Balthazar, but myself as well. During the days that have passed from the time Nazim told of the tragedy of the infants, we have tried to bolster each other's faith. However, too much pointed to the reality that surely the babe Jesus had not escaped the wrath of Herod. This was the only definite fact we could conclude as to why, in all these years, no whisper of the works of the Messiah of the Jews has come to us. As Balthazar told you all, we dared not make inquiries as to his activities, but it was so incredibly unlikely that word of his existence had never come to us. With the son of Herod the Great telling the story to Nazim, we had to believe that our Jesus had not survived."

Balthazar sighed and then spoke in a voice still racked with sorrow. "But what about those forty innocent children, Haleema? I had thought—had hoped—as did Melchior and Gaspar, that this child's purpose was to bring peace and hope to the world. I bear responsibility for their deaths. Dare I say it? The killing of all those innocent babies is not just on my shoulders but is the responsibility of Jesus' father as well."

Haleema sighed too at his words of grief and blame. She then attempted to ease his pain. "I have considered also this terrible loss. I ache even now for the mothers and families of those little boys. But as you said earlier, it is beyond our human ability to comprehend why things occur—in this case, why such an atrocious act was allowed to happen. But, Balthazar, I do know that you should feel no blame for their deaths. Herod the Great is responsible. He gave the orders in a greedy act to keep his kingdom. Do consider this also, please. I truly believe that those forty children's lives were given to protect Jesus. They did not die in vain."

Balthazar and Kateb looked searchingly at Haleema, trying to follow her reasoning.

She explained her thinking. "Herod must have believed that among those children killed was the child you were seeking. Thus, he would have no longer felt threatened. His search for the child would have ended with this terrible, murderous act. I have already asked my husband if Antipas told him of any other such killings, and he answered that no other mass slayings of children occurred."

Haleema continued. "If Jesus is indeed the son of the supreme being of all things, then I believe that he has come to earth to do good for multitudes of people. I also firmly believe that my people are among those numbers."

Then, Haleema urged, "Come."

Mutely, they followed as she led the way.

In astonishment, they soon realized that the members of the camp had gathered in the area where they had listened so respectfully to Balthazar. As the trio approached, a murmur of satisfaction came from the throng. Walking a pathway that opened before them, Balthazar and Kateb moved forward to where Nazim was standing to greet them. Nazim acknowledged his wife's part in bringing the two men to the group. She graciously nodded her head and went to where her children stood.

Nazim spoke. "Ah, Balthazar, it is good to see you, and Kateb as well. I see that Haleema has worked her magic on you. I do not know how I could lead without her. I tell you both that she strongly berated me for telling you of the terrible deaths of the innocents. In her wisdom, she told me how she has concluded that your Jesus lives. Were those her words to you this morning?"

Balthazar bowed to Haleema before responding to Nazim. "Yes, she rebuked me too. My offense was for doubting that Jesus survived—and lives to this day." Confidently, he added, "I am certain that she and Mary would be great friends, should they ever meet."

Nazim acknowledged the compliment given to Haleema and then took charge once more. "Balthazar, Kateb, last night I met in council with my people. It is their decision that you are to be set free. As of this moment, you are no longer our prisoners."

"But what about Herod Antipas and your—" Balthazar began, but was cut short by the Bedouin leader.

"It concerns me not at all. In point of fact, I was required only to take you prisoner. I did that."

His people nodded at the cleverness of their leader.

Nazim looked carefully at Balthazar. "My concern is for you, at this point in time. I hope you will consider your stay with us to have been well spent. As I said, you are free to go. We have provisioned your camels with food and water."

Balthazar and Kateb looked at one another. As always,

no words were necessary between them. Tentatively, Balthazar inquired, "Must we leave? I mean—do we have to leave right now?"

Smiles broke out on every person's face in the camp. Nazim opened his arms wide as he exclaimed, "You would honor us greatly by remaining with us. There is much we would know still."

Balthazar spoke from his heart. "I told you truthfully that you have become a part of this story. A few days ago, when I thought I had finished telling you our story, I asked a question meant for each of you. Since then, both Haleema and you have given me the gift of hope, while I had thought that I was giving you something. Yours is a mighty gift.

"So, now, I ask it again: I hope *you* are wondering what happens next? Undoubtedly, it will be a wonderful new story for all of us."

AUTHOR'S NOTES
FOR BALTHAZAR

In many ways, Balthazar's book was the easiest of the magi trilogy to write. Since the other two books on Melchior and Gaspar had been completed previously, I finally was able, during those writing stints, to reconcile the issues that I related at the end of Melchior's book. Specifically, one concerned the geographical difficulties of which kingdoms the royal magi were from, and at what point they were traveling north, south, east, and west in their celebrated travels. Also, the star of Bethlehem's origin was a conundrum. As a person of faith, I had no problem accepting that the star appeared to each of these royals in their separate distant lands and then led them to the little town of Bethlehem—that had been accepted from my earliest childhood days. However, as a teacher who was always interested in astronomy, I had to resolve to the best of my ability—if possible—the practical as well as scientific aspects of that wondrous "star."

With those issues in the past, Balthazar's book took on its own identity. Gaspar's book, *A King's Story,* which came to me in such a glorious manner, was written first. As the youngest, he returned to discover "if the man had fulfilled the child's destiny." Melchior's book, placed first in this trilogy, tells of the magi's initial extraordinary journey to Bethlehem and of how they escaped Herod the Great's palace. Therefore, Balthazar's story became the vehicle to tell of the magi's final arrival in Bethlehem, while it fills in religious and historical gaps by having Mary and Joseph tell their personal faith experiences.

Inasmuch as Balthazar's story takes place in a void of time when there had been no news for two decades of the person they found as an infant: Jesus, son of Mary and his earthly father the carpenter Joseph, this magus' faith is possibly the most tested. Balthazar had never faltered after their finding the babe, until he learned from Nazim of the slaughter of the innocent children of Bethlehem.

Biblically, the magi had been warned in separate dreams to depart Bethlehem, and not to return to Herod in Jerusalem, as the mercurial king had urged them to do. In defying Herod, the magi had been concerned that their deception might have caused harm to the holy family the star led them to—as Balthazar indicates. With Nazim's revelation, suddenly Balthazar seemed to finally know why they had heard no news of the child or the young man of destiny they assumed Jesus would grow to become. He had to have been killed around the age of two with the other innocent baby boys. It took a woman to help him find faith and hope once more, just as it took the young woman Mary to answer the call of God and to share her son with the world.

What sustained my faith to finish this second book, which actually completes the magi trilogy, and to move events forward to the next step? Here and there, far and near, signs were once again given to me. Christmas cards of the magi adoring the Christ Child in manger scenes in July spurred me along. Past and present voices, new and old, regularly reminded me that my procrastination must end and that there was more I should write. Tasks assigned to me by leaders at St. Anthony of Padua Church in St. Louis, Missouri, my hometown, raised me up on eagles' wings.

Here's one that happened the weekend I finished the final rough draft. I have been a member of St. Anthony's parish, off and on, since I was in the eighth grade. Our dear St. Anthony is known as the saint who can find things that are lost—if only he is asked. I have morphed over the years into being able to stretch my prayers, and his tasks, to ask for more than physical lost items. For example, I might pray, "St. Anthony, please help me find a way out of this, that, or the other...jam/problem/situation that I am facing." He comes through like a champ!

So on that significant Sunday morning, I had suddenly realized that the key to having my magi trilogy successfully published could be unlocked by St. Anthony! I sent up a most fervent prayer. *Then,* within three hours, I was standing in a hallway at the St. Anthony Friary—a place I might have walked through, at the most, once in my life. I was waiting to see a nun—Sister Delores—who was working with the RCIA candidates I had been guiding along for about ten months. Completely unaware of what I would find, I looked to my left. Extraordinarily, hanging on the wall, probably for decades (after all, the parish is 150 years young) were amazing and powerful scenes from the life of St. Anthony, along with written commentary of the circumstances of some of the various miracles he had performed both during and after his lifetime. If he could perform those inexplicable miracles, then he could perform the "miracle" of publication!

Just as Balthazar questioned the Bedouins, I will inquire of you, Dear Reader: "And now, I hope *you* are wondering what happens next. Undoubtedly, it will be a wonderful new story for all of us because wise men—and women—and youths, still seek him."

I hope you will enjoy Gaspar's story, which ends my *Trilogy of the Magi* and was actually, as I just commented, the first book I wrote on the three kings of Christmas lore. The Author's Notes for that book is an absolute must-read as well—some inquiring readers might even want to read it first, as I suggested to you after Melchior's story. Or you could simply begin *A King's Story...*

GASPAR'S BOOK

A King's Story

*There were many other signs that Jesus worked
…but, they are not recorded in this book.*

John 20:30[107]

Two Thieves

Egypt – Circa 2 A.D.

As dawn neared, moments before the Egyptian sun would cross the El Quisiya horizon, two thieves intently watched a small family's campsite they had just stumbled across in their prolonged trek north toward Cairo. A man, garbed in brown, was adjusting a donkey's harness. Nearby, a woman was playfully tousling her young child's dark hair as they shared a slight jest. The mother, dressed in dyed wool, with a blue mantle covering her dark hair, glanced up at the man. "Joseph, are we ready to leave?"

In a quiet, measured voice, he responded, "Yes, Mary, almost ready. My dear, I have been thinking about what we discussed last night—that maybe enough time has passed, and we have traveled long enough." Loving eyes followed his son's movements. "We have been blest these past years, and I think you are right—we have come far enough to be safe. We should settle here."

The woman's answer reflected an obvious longing to put down roots. "It would be wonderful to stay in one place instead of moving from village to town, and then on again weeks or months later. Son, did you hear your father? We are going to live here."

Her son, however, was looking at the exact spot where the two thieves were hidden.

With the element of surprise rapidly vanishing, Hemar, abruptly and with little thought, charged forward drawing his short knife. "The kid's seen us, Dismas!" In a surly, rasping challenge to the family, he ordered, "Your money or we kill the boy!"

Moving as only a mother can when her child is in danger, the young woman grabbed her son and drew him to her protectively.

Swearing aloud, Dismas followed his partner from their hiding spot, while directing his movements toward the muscular father who had quickly moved toward his wife and child. "Halt—"

Unaccountably, his command trailed into silence. Breaking into a sweat, Dismas stopped in total dismay as a wave of remorse overwhelmed him. Attempting to physically shake off the unfamiliar feeling, he menacingly moved his knife at the seemingly helpless family. The feeling of regret intensified as he locked gazes with the beautiful woman safely enveloping the child in her arms. Her calm acceptance of his presence rattled the robber as her screams never would have. She spoke no word and neither did Dismas, who was tongue-tied for possibly the first time in his life. Hemar, too, was mute now as he looked to Dismas for help.

Moments passed—Mary simply held his gaze with the most compassionate look he had ever received. Backing up one step at a time, Dismas wanted to stay in her presence, but felt his intrusion was the blackest deed of his life.

Grabbing Hemar by the sleeve, Dismas skulked away into the vastness of the land.

CHAPTER 1

The Child's Destiny

An Eastern Kingdom – Circa 33 A.D.

"Raheeb, faithful friend, I plan to journey afar again."

"Yes, my king, I know."

Gaspar chuckled at his servant's matter-of-fact response, "You know?"

"Why else have you prepared your kingdom and your son for your absence?"

Instead of answering, the monarch moved toward the open balcony and gazed west into the night sky as if seeking an answer among the gleaming stars above. Raheeb silently followed and, as raptly as the other, stared intently westward.

Quietly, Gaspar continued. "I must be a poor ruler to leave my people a second time. But indeed, I have weighed this decision for decades, Raheeb."

"As you decreed, your son has been governing our lands for almost two years. Long ago the people accepted your order that he begin to take over the reins of ruling in your place—though I am certain they cannot fathom what possessed you to give him your regal authority."

"Can you?"

Scanning the starlit expanse, Raheeb stated, "You must return to see if the man has fulfilled the child's destiny."

With surprising passion, Gaspar declared. "Years before you and I began our extraordinary quest which ended in Bethlehem, I charted the stars. I have wondered and conjectured all these thirty years and more, since those incredible days and nights, what became of the child and his family. Continuing to study the ancient writings, I am torn to pieces! My love for my country—my son—my need to seek again the child—now a man, whom the star drew us to so long ago..."[108]

The words hung in the air between the two men. Raheeb finally spoke in a low voice, "Jesus is thirty-three years old.[109] Time enough for those writings to be accomplished."

"Yes, yes, my point exactly! A man—ready to come into his kingdom if the stars and scripts have foretold correctly. My continued studies of the skies, the prophesies, the evidence of my own eyes, the experiences of the journey to Palestine with the later warnings about Herod—the source still so unfathomable after all these years—all point compellingly to a master of men!"

Raheeb finished his king's thinking. "The portentous events proclaimed by the stars would seem to be near at hand—if not fulfilled already."

Gripping the balcony railing, Gaspar enthusiastically went on, "Let us consider what we have previously verified, Raheeb. To start with, he was born in a Roman province, and according to their astrological signs, his birth was a phenomenon."

Gaspar paused to rationally present the highlights of the historical and astrological evidence. His confidant, smiling in the dark, prepared again to hear Gaspar's defense of the hypothesis that was also an affirmation of the scholar's life-long search for knowledge—the hallmark of all magi.

"Jupiter and Saturn aligned together, then Mars the next year—surely when the skies bring such signs, we lowly humans must consider what they foretell. Almighty Jupiter—to the Romans, their god who rules over all other gods and mankind as well! Saturn—tradition among the Latins associates it with justice! Mighty Mars—the Roman god of war!"

Raheeb responded. "In truth, what else can be interpreted, but that the greatest ruler of all times—powerful yet just—is near at hand!"

"These signs were apparent only in the constellation Pisces. *Pisces*—the writings relate it to the Hebrews. Raheeb, the *Hebrews!*"

"Yes, Sire. Our journey indeed did end at the birth site of a Hebrew child."

As if this pronouncement ended the one-sided defense, he halted. Both men raptly gazed outward. Each was remembering the wondrous triumph of starlit sights that had stirred their younger selves and changed each forever.

Neither man was aware of the passage of time while their memories traveled back through the years. As the crescent moon edged slowly westward, Gaspar broke the companionable silence, and Raheeb respectfully listened anew. "Does the world need such a king? Who but a powerful ruler could ever hope to overthrow the Roman Empire? Its talons ensnare the earth, grasping everything and everyone. That empire covets the world!"

Raheeb interjected. "Visitors to our land tell of a Rome descending into debauchery as Emperor Tiberius broods in suspicion that all are his enemies save a select few."

"Consider also that this same empire arrogantly rules the Hebrews as it does the rest of its lands, demanding obedience and holding its crushed victims in contempt. The Hebrews, as you know, Raheeb, are a people whose religion for untold centuries has held that a great king will arise from their midst—not just a messiah, but *the* Messiah. My studies of the Hebraic writings continually point to this figure, and to the Jewish prediction of his birth from the line of David."

Raheeb took up the well-known story. "The child's parents, Mary and Joseph, were in Bethlehem for the Emperor Augustus Caesar's census, registering in the town of their ancestor King David.[110] Is this not further proof that the stars led us truly to the birth of a person who will undoubtedly change the world, and who could overthrow the now-corrupt Roman Empire?"

Gaspar's steadfast look of triumph prefaced his next words. "Let us look to our own writings. Zoroaster, our Eastern teacher and prophet, five hundred years ago, predicted a new religion and a Messiah. It was thought for a time that the rise of the Macedonian, Alexander, three centuries ago, might have been the person Zoroaster preached about; however, though Alexander's rise was wondrous, and he brought significant changes to the world, no new religion evolved.

"So why now, after all these years, do I feel the need to return to the land of the Hebrews? Dear friend, I have not simply been rambling. Zoroaster was thirty-three when he completed his predictions. Alexander was thirty-three when he died. My thirty-third birthday occurred while we traveled. The Hebrew child, now a man as you stated, is thirty-three years old. His time to rule is near, I am certain."

Gaspar paused before continuing. "This talk of ages brings me to my own. I have been blessed with good health, past sixty though I am. Of we three magi, who each individually studied the heavenly messages and felt compelled to learn the reasons for such wonders, I was the youngest. When we parted those many years ago, we all agreed to maintain contact over the years."

Raheeb broke his respectful silence. "I myself carried messages through the intervening years between you three seekers of knowledge. Melchior was already old at the child's birth, while Balthazar, your wonderful friend, has not been heard from in years. The last information we had of him is that more than a decade ago marauding Bedouins attacked his camp near Petra."

Gaspar spoke with a new urgency. "Only I am able, of the three, to bear witness that the child's birth was foretold in the skies. There were others who came, of course, and knew of his greatness even though he was born in a lowly stable. Shepherds were given a glorious gift the night he was born."[111]

"Sire, you and I have often discussed our wonder that even the animals seemed to adore and honor him!"

"But enough of dwelling in the past! As this thirty-third year of his life is upon us, I have made plans for this journey, and today I have decided that the time to return is now. I informed my son after we supped." Gaspar put his arm around his comrade's shoulder and confided, "He, like you, seemed unsurprised. More to the point, he encouraged me. My plans are to leave before the next full moon wanes. I will travel lightly, knowing the land of my destination on this trip. I plan to take only two others, including Zaphta, son of our old tracker Namon."

Abruptly, Gaspar felt the physical and emotional withdrawal of his companion. He continued, however, on what he had known would be one of the most difficult aspects of his decision.

"You must not be offended, Raheeb, I beg you. This is not easy for me. Your health has not been good for several years; this we both know. Last winter, it took all of our physicians' skills to keep you alive. My love for you is as strong as if you were my own brother! Was it not I who spooned your medicines to you when no one else could reach you in the darkness of your near-death? You have recovered, but have reached your seventh decade. As I plan to travel quickly, and the trip is not an easy one, for your sake, I must venture forth without you. Stay and be as astute an advisor to my son as you have been to me."

Raheeb, Gaspar's confidante, advisor, friend and servant, had known full well of the regent's activities and private preparations. He had realized that his enfeebled health would be a factor, and was prepared to convince his ruler to allow him to return also.

"Oh wise one, master of these lands beyond what the eye can see, I beg leave to question your decision and to put forth my own humble plea."

"You will not change my mind, as I do this for your own good, rather than my own. I do not wish to leave these lands without you. It is my deep love for you which makes me want to see you alive and well upon my return."

Raheeb now spoke with deliberateness. "Master, you have noted well as we conversed this evening that I was with you on that long ago journey. I served you in my youth as I do in our old age. I have obeyed your commands since before memory can recall." His voice gained vigor. "As

I reminded you before, I served as a messenger between you, Melchior, and Balthazar as you corresponded and continued your studies. Wanting always to assist you, I have made it my life's work to serve your needs. When you turned the kingdom over to your son, the prince, I knew the time was nearing when you would want to go west again.

"How could you wonder that your beloved son and I know of your restlessness and desire to learn the destiny of the Hebrew child when always your first questions of travelers center on the lands where the star led us. In my hope of shortening our search, I sent Zaphta to find news of the whereabouts of Mary, Joseph, and their child Jesus."

Now it was Gaspar's turn to interrupt. "Ah, ever-practical Raheeb! As I searched the skies and the parchments, you searched the lands." Eagerly, he begged, "You found them?"

"Sire, if we had searched in the early years, the trail might not have been so hard to follow. Treachery followed their path and we undoubtedly hold great responsibility for it."

Horrified, Gaspar queried. "How could this be?"

"It concerns Herod the Great, King of Judea, in those days."

"That creature—Herod was all sincerity on the surface, but true to none, with the heart of a viper!"

"Each of you three wise men, through what device none of you could fathom, received the same dream to return home by a different route and to have no further contact with Herod."[112]

"They call us magi, learned men, but not one of us could satisfactorily explain the incredible occurrence of a night vision the same for each of us. Melchior told of his experience first. Balthazar and I were amazed to hear our own dream told by another. We thought if the child was protected by such a powerful force that could make three men have the same dream, then the child would not need our protection and would be safe from harm."

"Remember the old rumors coming out of Palestine of the murders of innocent children, especially boys?"

"Yes, but they were so monstrous it was difficult to believe it could be true."

"Zaphta confirmed the atrocity. Herod, enraged at our not returning with news as he had requested, and fearful over our direct questions about a newborn king of the Jews, ordered his men to execute all male children up to two years of age who were in Bethlehem."[113]

Gaspar's immediate exclamation of horror signaled his dismay of Herod's despicable command. However, he immediately and unequivocally stated, "Our Jesus could not have met such an end. He yet lives!"

"I, too, do not think he died then at Herod's hands. I instructed Zaphta to search until he found this special family. Eventually, he discovered details of their joining a Jewish settlement in Egypt.[114] The father was a carpenter; they had a son of the right age; and no one ever spoke ill of the family.

"Zaphta even heard a story about thieves who were near an Egyptian village named El Quisiya. The robbers had the region terrorized. The story is told that the thieves left the area on the very day that the family came to the village. The robbers left behind all they had stolen from the people living there. Unaccountably, the credit for this was given to the family of the child Jesus.

"Further, Zaphta learned that one day the family simply left,[115] and were not heard from again. He returned to me with no other news to report. All further attempts to find them failed, although he searched many other regions in Egypt."

At the look of disappointment on Gaspar's face, Raheeb continued. "Zaphta came to me a few moons ago with news of a strange tale from the caravan drivers of a young rabbi from Nazareth who has been stirring up the crowds in and around Capernaum."[116]

"Did he learn the man's name?"

"Jesus—and an Aramean driver joked that he was said to be the son of a carpenter."

In the silence following his words, Raheeb drew erect and with great dignity addressed Gaspar. "You spoke of your need, your mission almost, to bear witness once more to the truth that you three kings followed the stars to the birthplace of a new ruler. Think you, that only you of royal birth, were witnesses? I, too, was present! It was I who brought your gift of myrrh safely over the many leagues of our travels. The babe gazed upon me as he did upon you of higher lineage. Never have I spoken to you of my feelings and other events of that first night, but I will tell you now so that you may understand.

"In the early morning hours before you and the others awoke, I went back to where we found them. His mother bade me bring the child to her. He looked into my eyes, but it was not an infant who gazed at me. Words are beyond me to describe that look or how I felt. But know this: As much as I love you, honor you, and have served you faithfully, if you would release me from your service, I would return to find Jesus and would serve him to the end of my strength and all my days."

At the conclusion of this speech, Raheeb began to kneel.

Kathryn Muehlheausler

Stung by the words and humbled beyond measure, Gaspar bent to raise his old servant. "How selfish my thoughts to keep you safe here at home suddenly seem. Raheeb, this day I release you from my service!"

At Raheeb's involuntary gasp, the regent spoke from his heart, "But now I beg you—as my friend—accompany me to where the stars led us before."

CHAPTER 2

A Master and Magician

The crowd was a bubbling cauldron of emotion and noise and color as it surged the last miles toward Jerusalem's gates.[117] Gaspar and Raheeb had become separated in the melee as the dirt road twisted up the hillside. Progress had been slow for several days as they had been caught in a great throng, which was mostly composed of Jews traveling to the Holy City for the celebration of Passover. Yesterday had been the only day of recent progress because, although they usually did not travel on the Jewish Sabbath—the holy day when faithful Jews did little—they had suddenly both felt a compelling motivation to reach Jerusalem as soon as possible.

Their trek across the mountains and sands, guided by Zaphta, had been uneventful. Now they were enjoying the present cacophony and kaleidoscope of excitement that surrounded them. Camel harness bells and the trill of children's laughter mingled with the no-less-jubilant voices of the adults eager to end their travels at the Jews' crown city. The enthusiasm of their fellow travelers on the road, together with the inevitably slower pace, had helped make the final stage of their own entry into Jerusalem somewhat enjoyable since they could go no faster than the crowd itself. With Palestine abloom in vivid spring colors, they felt refreshed and eager to continue their search.

Astride his camel, Gaspar easily viewed what was the Valley of the Kedron, miles ahead, that would take them directly into the Israelite's ancient capital city. Turning in his saddle, he sighted Raheeb about a hundred paces back, deeply engaged in conversation with a wayfarer also riding a dromedary. Gaspar smiled as his mount loudly protested his request to allow Raheeb to catch up. He had little to do except guide the slow-moving camel and listen to the crowd's multitude of languages—many of which he understood. Two Greek men on donkeys close by were discussing a strange incident.

"I tell, you, I was there; never have I seen such events. Over five thousand of us had spent three days with The Master. We had followed him from the Sea of Galilee, and during these days he made the crippled walk, cured the deformed, the blind, the mute![118] He did, truly! Daily he preached, telling us to live better, to avoid hypocrisy, to share our wealth. His voice, without effort, reached to the farthest edges of the crowd. The people seemed to hear his words without straining. By the third day, towards the late afternoon, people were hungry—I know I was! The children, especially, needed to be fed.

"Now this is exactly what happened, Euripides! A small boy came forward with a basket of loaves and a few fish and silently offered them to The Master for him to eat. One of the men nearby told the boy to feed his friends with the little that was there.

"Instead, our Master took the small basket, said a prayer and looked upward. Then he told his close followers, his apostles, to pass the food among the people. All were fed and there were baskets—*baskets,* I say—of leftovers!"[119]

Euripides' voice expressed his friendly skepticism. "A strange story; unbelievable, to say the least."

"I swear by mighty Zeus that it happened as I have said!"

Greatly intrigued by the incredible tale and the person the Greek had referred to as "The Master," Gaspar wanted to hear more, but Raheeb was almost abreast and calling for his attention. Clearly eager to make introductions, Raheeb brought his own camel and his companion's up beside Gaspar and spoke urgently. "My Liege, this is Sahran, an Edomite trader. I have learned much from him that I believe is important to our search."

"It will be an honor for me to tell you, King Gaspar, but as I told Raheeb, I heard the tale from my sister who is known both for her exaggeration and her religious fervor."

"Let him hear what she said and judge for himself."

"Well, Your Majesty, in my travels I regularly stop at the home of my half-sister, Sarah, near Bethany, which is where I am planning to stay this night. The last time I visited, she had an entertaining tale of horror or wonder—you decide which—after the tale is told." The Edomite continued, patently relishing his tale. "Dwelling in Bethany is a family of one brother and two sisters. Mary and Martha, the sisters, are as different as day from night. Well, to move us forward, the brother Lazarus[120] is really the most important person."

Here Sahran paused, "Of course, *if* it is true, the most important person is the magician. By the way, as we have leagues to go in this accursed heat and traffic, do you want the long or short version?"

Raheeb interrupted. "Please tell my master the magician's name."

"It's one that the chief priests up there in Jerusalem don't want to hear any more about, I can tell you that!"

Lowering his voice conspiratorially, he added, "The word is that they're out to get him. There's a reward for anyone who brings them evidence of whatever new blasphemy he utters. He's got them jittery up in old Solomon's Temple! I guess they're worried about the shekels I hear he's costing them."

"But his name please, Sahran."

"Oh, sure, didn't I say it yet? His name is Jesus."

Raheeb had been awaiting the look of excitement that Gaspar shot him. "Listen, My Lord," he advised.

Feeling rushed to tell the story, the Edomite was offended, but Gaspar mollified him by urging, "Could you describe this Jesus to me?"

"Well, as to that, I've never seen him myself, but he is young, I hear. Or at least young compared to the graybeards in the synagogues who hate how he's raising the common folks' hopes."

"What hopes would those be?"

"He's all the talk from up by the Sea of Galilee to farther south than Beer-sheba. From your dress and voice, you seem to be Easterners, so you probably don't know much of the Jewish religion. You need to know that for thousands of years, the Hebrews—we call ourselves the Chosen of God—who, for the same thousands of years, have been overcome and enslaved by whoever happens to be conquering the world at that particular time—well, we— those who believe strongly, that is—think that the Jews will be saved by a Messiah who will deliver all from bondage. Though I ask, what bondage? I'm doing okay.

"So, here comes this upstart Galilean, comes right into the synagogues, mind you, and tells all the elders and chief priests that the Scriptures are going to be fulfilled. Now this is hearsay again—heresy to them, of course. But they say, he said, when it was all said and done, that he was the one who had come to fulfill them![121] That is some of the blasphemy old Caiaphas wants to catch this Jesus saying!"

The throng of people had been creeping along at a veritable standstill. Their ebullient, conversationalist Sahran digressed. "Are they singing up ahead?"

Straining to hear, Raheeb started to answer that he wasn't sure, when Sahran began speaking again. "I guess they may as well sing! I'll be lucky to be near my sister's home by nightfall if this pace doesn't pick up soon. Which brings me back to the story Raheeb wanted me to tell in the first place.

"Lazarus, he's the brother, remember, had just died. The family sent word to Jesus, who was supposedly their friend, but he had other things to do, or didn't get the message. For whatever reason, he didn't come for two days.[122] When he finally did arrive, Martha, the boisterous sister, runs to meet him. The story I got from my sister was that Martha gave him a tongue thrashing. But then she said to Jesus that she knew he could ask his father for anything, and that if he'd been there, Lazarus wouldn't have died.[123] Most of this does not make sense to me—what could Jesus or his Father do anyway? Lazarus had been dead for days by that time!

"Right after that, Mary, the quiet sister, came along with other mourners. Jesus was crying along with them, but then wanted to be taken to the cave where Lazarus had been buried. People in the crowd were getting mad at Jesus—probably for not coming sooner.[124] Now this is where the story gets real creepy—the magic part.

"Jesus tells them to roll back the stone.[125]

"Martha chews him out saying her brother would be smelling since he had been dead four days."[126]

Sahran paused and started rummaging in his saddlebag. Pulling out a tattered rag, he sheepishly continued. "The whole story is so absurd that I wrote down what my sister swears he said. It makes the whole story better, I think, to hear the exact words: 'Have I not told you that if you believe, you will see the glory of God?'[127]

"After these magic words, that's when my sister said the people did what Jesus had said and pulled back the stone."[128]

The storyteller paused for effect, knowing from previous tellings that his listeners would soon ask, "What happened then?"

Raheeb quietly pressed, "Continue, Sahran."

"Jesus loudly said, 'Lazarus, here! Come out!' The dead man, with his feet and hands still bound in linen and a cloth around his face, came out from the cave where he had been buried for four days. Jesus said to them, 'Unbind him, let him go free.'"[129]

Gaspar made no comment, simply staring to his left.

Nettled, Sahran finally muttered, "What's he staring at? The only thing out that way is Bethlehem."

Roused by the name of the little town, and as if there had been no pause, Gaspar probed, "Do you believe the story?"

"Bringing a dead man back to life? It was trickery—magic—a clever sham! I told you that all along." Sahran laughed at the apparent gullibility of his listeners. "It was deception, of course. The followers of this Jesus had to have set up the whole affair to make him seem to have extraordinary powers beyond what any human being can have."

"Did your sister believe it?"

"Didn't I say she's unreliable? She's a religious fanatic! Actually, she did believe it at first, but when I explained how it was probably a practical joke, or that these particular Jews were in cahoots to make this Jesus person really seem like he might be the Messiah, and have such powers, she saw the sense of what I was saying."

"Why did you write the words down?"

Uncomfortable with Gaspar's piercing eyes and questions, Sahran sought to end their meeting. "That means nothing. I told you—it makes a good story! The back way to Bethany is to the left up ahead. I can't make any money moving at this pace! May your journey be a success and your burdens light." With these words, Sahran whipped his camel forward.

As the curtain of people closed around the disappearing Edomite, the two men were united in their silence. Gaspar finally queried in a despairing voice, "Have we come all this way for a magician?"

Raheeb somewhat desperately responded. "There have to be more than two people named Jesus—it is the Greek version of the common enough Hebrew name, Joshua." Seeking a diversion, he noted. "Our garrulous friend at least seems to be right in that there is singing going on up ahead. Can you not hear it?"

"Only faintly, my hearing is not so good as it once was. I am happy that someone feels like singing today." Gaspar's words were in the querulous voice of an old man facing his diminishing capacities and the possibility of defeat. For the first time on this trip, the aged regent was feeling the immensity of the task he had undertaken.

"Do not despair! We were advised to make our way to the Jerusalem Temple to seek answers about the Messiah.

On the morrow, we will have reached our destination. Zaphta already has our lodgings arranged for tonight. All will be well."

Needing to further express reassurance for both of them, Raheeb encouraged. "That Edomite is an undoubted cynic and talker. We did expect great deeds of the child—the signs in the skies were for no common mortal."

"Raheeb, Raheeb! My thanks for your efforts, but think further. No mortal could bring a man back to life! If Sahran was right about the magic, we know that magicians are merely sleight-of-hand tricksters. Some are better than others, and this man must have been very good indeed. But a magician was not the person we have come such a distance to find. A great hoax by the sisters, brother, and this Jesus is certainly more believable. Power is a poisonous serpent. A child born into poverty would have little chance of overcoming a common background. How shameful it would be for all, if this man has become someone's pawn."

"My Lord, we have no evidence that this man is the same person the star brought us to so long ago. The man and woman, Mary and Joseph, were kind beyond measure. The infant I held—so—never can I find the right words. He seemed to be almost—filled with goodness. Never will I believe such a thing could happen."

"He was a babe, Raheeb! We do not know what happened to him. Even if Zaphta was right that the family went to Egypt, he could find no further trace of them. Both parents might have died—maybe he was then raised by others who discovered his powers and took advantage of his youth."

"The person we seek is not a charlatan."

"Your words do give me hope, my friend. Well, listen

to another tale of wonder I heard. Two Greeks near me were speaking about a person one of them referred to as 'The Master.'[130] This man was said to be curing people of all manner of illnesses. He even fed a crowd larger than the one we are in here from a child's small basket of food. The Greek telling the tale vehemently claimed that he had seen all this happen with his own eyes. Now who knows if he was telling the truth, but at least these were acts of compassion. If we are only to find a magician, may he be someone with such goodness in his heart."

Faith in their mission somewhat restored, both men became aware of the words of a song that had spread from the travelers up ahead. The Aramaic words were a continuous chant: "Blessed is he who comes as king in the name of the Lord! Peace in heaven and glory in the highest."

The crowd's demeanor was undergoing a change as well. Those not singing were in a frenzy. Some were shouting, "The Messiah! The Messiah!" Others expressed their faith differently.

"He rides in triumph to Jerusalem!"

"'Hosanna to the Son of David!'"[131]

"'Hosanna! Blessings on the King of Israel, who comes in the name of the Lord.'"[132]

"Deliver us!"

Palm trees along the side of the road were stripped and the fronds passed among the travelers and singers. A procession of sorts seemed to have formed. One man, his face alive with excitement, reached high to thrust stalks into their hands shouting, "The King—he goes to the Holy City! He leads us to glory!"

CHAPTER 3

Solomon's Temple

One thousand years earlier, Solomon's reign had been the glory of Israel. His choice of Jerusalem as the site for the construction of the Temple elevated her above all other cities. Consisting of pylons, courts and a naos leading to the Holy of Holies that housed the Ark of the Covenant, the Temple of Solomon was a monumental structure of the ancient, often nomadic, Hebrews.

During the forty-year reign of Herod the Great, Jerusalem architecturally was rejuvenated and enhanced as she had not been since the time of King David's son, Solomon. In another city, not Jerusalem, the magnificent Herod Palace in the northern part of the town would have been the focal point of all eyes. In this city, it was one of several splendid structures that included three great towers known as Phasael, Hippicus and Mariamne. There was a great fortress, Antonia, at the Temple enclosure. The greatest ornament to the city, however, was recognized to be the temple itself, which was still being improved by Herod Antipater, the son of Herod the Great.

The ornate temple was the heart of the Holy City. For Jews to remain in a state of holiness, the Law required that a ritual blood sacrifice be offered in the Jerusalem Temple of Solomon at least once during his life. A thriving industry had emerged out of the ancient holy practices of Abraham, Isaac and Moses. Within the sacred portals, faithful families paid homage and supported their priests and religion. Turtledoves, spotless kid goats, downy sheep and burly oxen loudly awaited their fates. Coos, squawks, bleats, and baas raucously blended with sellers' chants. Clinking coins, dearly earned, purchased passage to a higher life as sestertius and denarii increased the Temple treasury and monies from distant lands were converted into Judean coinage.

The overt sights, sounds, and smells of the Hebraic religion were not readily apparent to the three Easterners staring upward at the massive stone, timber, and metal structure.

Gaspar voiced his thoughts. "Only once before have I felt this overwhelmed."

"It rises to the clouds," breathed Raheeb.

Zaphta said, "It is a fitting tribute to a great religion."

"Come, let us ascend," urged Gaspar.

Several hundred steps later, the trio stood outside the main Temple pylon. Before they entered, they paused to view the Holy City below.

An obsequious bystander, noting their foreign attire, inched forward, first looking around as if someone might be watching. "For a shekel, I will tell you of the rich history of Jerusalem and will graciously point out the grandeur surrounding our Holy City. Do you know which height is Mt. Tabor?" Glibly, he purred, "For a few coins more, you can hear of the many miracles performed here. I can take you to the Sheep Pool where recently a man who hadn't walked for almost forty years was healed!"[133] Lowering his voice, and as before scanning the area, he bartered, "Have you heard yet of the scandal which just took place in the Temple?"

Raheeb, wiping the sheen of sweat shining on his forehead from the labored climb, ordered the schemer: "Be off! This is King Gaspar you are insulting."

"A King! Generous High One! It would be my most special pleasure to inform you of the outrageous acts of the upstart Galilean."

Again, Raheeb had been about to warn off the man, but the latter's groveling words caused him to probe, "What Galilean?"[134]

Sensing the chance for income, but careful not to offend the man referred to as a king, the tale-bearer sought a middle course. "The desecration happened in the inner Temple."

"Tell us," Zaphta urged.

Tossing a coin to the man as he moved forward, Gaspar took over. "Inside someone of authority will assist us."

The contrast between the brilliant Palestinian sun and the darkened recess of the interior chambers of the temple temporarily blinded the visitors. As their eyes adjusted to the dimness, they were aware of the approach of a silent black-garbed figure. Slightly past middle age, his robes proclaimed him to be a high-ranking dignitary. Bowing low before Gaspar, he spoke. "Welcome, King Gaspar, to the Temple of Solomon. I am Jeroboam, a servant of Yahweh. If you will permit, it would be my great honor to attend you today."

Rather than question how a secluded rabbinical priest would know his name, Gaspar graciously acknowledged the introduction. "We arrived in your city yesterday at sunset. My friend Raheeb and I are not as young as Zaphta, our guide, so we retired early and arose late. We have made this magnificent temple our first stop."

A slight inclination of Jeroboam's body indicated the merit of this remark. "I hope your night's rest at the Black Grape and Bed was pleasant," he stated, more than inquired. Gaspar stiffened at this obvious second remark concerning his party's activities. Aware that his objective had been achieved that the religious leaders were powers in the city, Jeroboam made a surface apology. "Visitors of Your Highness' status usually stay at the Black Grape and Bed. Word of an Eastern king visiting our city was brought to us by those who know that we would wish to honor you."

"I wanted no fanfare on this journey and, therefore, have chosen to travel in relative anonymity. My search is for knowledge rather than recognition."

"How may we enlighten you?"

Considering the rabbi's earlier comments, Gaspar could not help but feel that the temple leaders had known of his mission and whereabouts for weeks. He and his companions had not attempted to disguise their reason for traveling. They openly questioned others on their journey about information on the Messiah, specifically, and anyone proclaiming such a destiny to be theirs. Recalling Sahran's words from yesterday that the elders of the Temple were seeking evidence against the Galilean, whom they had learned last night was the person in whose procession they had entered the city, Gaspar wondered if they were in a place of peace or enmity.

Testing Jeroboam, Gaspar ventured. "We arrived with a festive group of travelers yesterday."

"Ah, yes. As you probably know this is the season of Passover when Jews purify themselves. Although a time of great solemnity, it also is a time when families and friends who might see each other at no other time of the year gather and celebrate together."

"Apparently, it was more than this. We were a part of a procession for one the people refer to as the Galilean, Jesus of Nazareth. We were unaware of his presence ahead of us as we traveled, but he must be an interesting person. We would like to know more of him."

Seeming to accept Gaspar's comments at face value, Jeroboam warned. "You do yourself no good to seek news of this imposter. The common people certainly have embraced him for the moment. In a few days, they will undoubtedly turn from him and give their adoration to another."

"Why do you say this?"

"People are fickle. Today, your friend; tomorrow, your enemy—rejected."

"Why is this Galilean so popular?"

"He is no longer popular, I can assure you, King Gaspar. But let us not dwell on this disreputable false teacher. Allow me to escort you through the temple. Then our High Priest Caiaphas would like to meet you. Presently, he is involved in an important matter."

Moving with their guide to the edge of one of several pools in the vicinity, Gaspar said, "Yes, I am anxious to see your great temple. Even as far away as my home, we know of its wonder. But you have intrigued me, Rabbi Jeroboam. You say this Galilean is no longer popular? What could have occurred between today and yesterday, when a leagues-long procession praised him in song?"

Gaspar had been aware for some minutes of activity in adjacent areas to where they stood. There was even the possibility that Jeroboam was deliberately trying to keep

Gaspar from viewing what seemed to be the remnants of a major cleanup.

Realizing Gaspar would not be satisfied until he was told, minimally, some of the Galilean's story, the rabbi gave in to the inevitable. "The crowds have been swayed by his words. He has been fortunate to be in the right place at the right time and cures have been credited to him. People see what they want to see; hope needs little enough to build on it seems. Rumors have been flying for months. They attribute all manner of feats to him. Indeed, it would be entertaining if not for the seriousness of his offenses."

"What offenses?"

"Inciting the mob for one."

"An unofficial procession?"

"Oh, there is more to this than that."

Deciding that Gaspar knew little to nothing about the Galilean, Jeroboam spoke of the concerns the rabbis felt at the words and actions of the Jewish upstart. "He entered Jerusalem yesterday afternoon, hours before your arrival. He really had few followers since most were innocent travelers, like your party, simply sharing the road with him and traveling at the same time."

His confidence building, as if he were convincing himself, Jeroboam built a strong case that the upstart Galilean was a threat. "Several years ago we welcomed him to our midst when he first began his ministry.[135] Anyone who seeks truth is encouraged to preach, to enlighten, and in turn to be enlightened. His views were radical, however, and turned many against him through careless interpretations of the Scriptures. The son of a carpenter, he keeps low company associating with sinners and tax collectors." [136] Becoming impassioned with his diatribe, Jeroboam failed to note the visual exchange between the three visitors. "He has probably destroyed any credibility he had!"

"What did he do that was so terrible?"

"Arriving with a crowd of his followers, he decided to impress them with theatrics such as this temple has never seen. He upset the tables of the moneychangers, ranted and raved, and shouted words of pure blasphemy: *'My house will be called a house of prayer,* but you have turned it into *a robbers' den.'*[137]

"The chief priests are meeting, even as we speak, to discuss his fate. At the least, he will probably be banned from the Temple."

"Aiee..." the low, half-strangled cry from Raheeb caught everyone's attention and halted the diatribe against Jesus. Gaspar, previously intent on Jeroboam's words, had failed to notice Raheeb's reaction to the harsh utterances. Grasping his old comrade, he feared the worst. Raheeb was bathed in sweat and holding his left arm as if in pain. Conscience-stricken as he assisted his faithful friend to a nearby bench, Gaspar recalled Raheeb's labored ascent to the Temple.

Having found a cloth and dipping it in a nearby pool of water, Zaphta bathed Raheeb's face while admonishing, "Be still."

When Raheeb showed little signs of recovery, Jeroboam offered. "We can let him rest in a room down this corridor where it will be quiet for him. I will have some acolytes assist you in making him comfortable."

After several hours of obvious distress, with no discernable improvement, Raheeb was to be conveyed to their hostel. His labored breathing at least indicated that he lived. Zaphta was out making the arrangements and the sick man was asleep. Gaspar had spent a short time in the permitted temple areas, where he was introduced to some of the Sanhedrin Council. One member, Joseph of Arimathaea, offered to look at Raheeb, and then had given advice for treatment. Now, Gaspar was waiting outside the room for Zaphta's imminent return so that Raheeb would not be disturbed any more than necessary. The acolytes assigned to help were talking with two newcomers. Their conversation was so intense that it attracted Gaspar's attention.

"For my part, I think the Nazarene carried the day. His arguments left me dumbfounded that a man from such a lowly background could have such a grasp of Holy Scripture and be so logical."

Responding to this firm statement, another acolyte queried the initial speaker, "Mark, you heard more than we did since we were back here all afternoon. Why did they even let him speak after his desecration of the Temple?"

"With so many people here for the Passover, and many of them seeming to support the teachings of the rabbi, Jesus, I think Caiaphas is listening to his father-in-law, Annas, and is taking a wait-and-see attitude."

"More likely, Caiaphas wants to let the man condemn himself with his own words. Those were devilish questions the Council posed today."

"True, but he infuriated them when they asked him by whose authority he speaks and acts as he does."[138]

"That is an answer I would like to have heard! What did he say?"

"He was clever. He said something like he would ask them a question, and if they answered it, then he would answer their questions."[139]

"He dared to say that to them?"

"Yes, and incredibly, they went along with it."

"What was his question?"

"You would have loved it. Am I correct that you went out to the desert to hear John, the prophet, speak once or twice?"

"I did. He had some interesting ideas and if our times, as decadent as they are, could produce a prophet, I agree he was one. But what does John have to do with the question Jesus asked?"

"He asked if John's baptism came from heaven or from man.[140] The scribes and chief priests gathered together to argue it out. He had them on that because if they said from heaven, then he could have asked why they refused to believe John. If they said from man, then the people would have turned on them because just like you, they hold John in esteem. Many also feel he was a real prophet. Finally, the elders replied that they, 'did not know where it came from.'"[141]

"They'll hate him even more for having to say that in front of a crowd!"

"I have heard that John the Baptizer was related to Jesus."

"Yes, I believe that is true. My Uncle Mark told me that John is Jesus' cousin."

Another acolyte exclaimed, "Listen to what I heard when I brought a blanket for the sick man. The Nazarene was calling the scribes and the Pharisees corrupt and hypocrites!"

"That has to have sealed his fate!"

"It was almost as if he wanted to anger them. His words showed little temperance, although when I heard him speak once in Capernaum—when I was visiting my mother—that was certainly what he preached then."

"They also had tried to trap him on the issue of paying taxes to Caesar."

"Then they could have had the Romans put him in jail. Well, did he get us out of paying taxes?"

"You said he was clever. Did he outwit them on that one?"

"That was one of the times he called them hypocrites. It was as if he was aware of their malice, but was toying with them. Now these were his words, not mine: 'You hypocrites! Why do you set this trap for me? Let me see the money you pay the tax with.'[142] One of them handed him a denarius, and he said, 'Whose head is this? Whose name?'[143]

"They replied, 'Caesar's.'[144] He finished them off then by saying, 'Very well, give back to Caesar what belongs to Caesar—and to God what belongs to God.'" [145]

"I bet they didn't like that answer."

"It surprised them, I think, because they backed off. Then Jesus went after them using parables. The words were a thin disguise. There was no doubt that he was aiming his barbs at the Pharisees, scribes and even the chief priests. But some of the things he said troubled me."

"Why should any of it bother you, Mark?"

"Don't laugh at me, but if he is telling the elders they are not going to be saved and that they are hypocrites, does not that mean that he would think the same about us?"

"Why should you care what he thinks?"

"I do not, of course! But—when I heard him speak before, and even here today—well, his voice has such quiet authority. His eyes are so kind, so honest. He looks right at you when he speaks, almost as if he could see into..."

"See into what, Mark?"

After a moment's hesitation, Mark ruefully continued, "Pay no attention to me."

Jesting, one of the rabbinical students said, "We will not ever again—if you start to think this Jesus is the Messiah."

"Tell us a story that bothered you, Mark," one of the younger students seriously requested.

Mark looked into the young man's eyes and seeing his own troubled concerns mirrored there, responded. "Jesus said a landowner planted a vineyard, leased it to tenants, then went abroad. At vintage time, he sent his servants to collect the produce due him. The tenants seized the servants and beat them mercilessly. Another servant was sent, but was treated in the same manner. The landowner finally sent his own son. The tenants actually killed the son. Jesus questioned the group what the owner would do when he comes? Then he immediately answered his own question, indicating that the owner would judge them and treat them as they had treated his servants, and then would take the vineyard. Those listening in the temple protested the servants' harsh end. But Jesus finished this parable by asking, 'Then what does this text in the scriptures mean: It was the stone rejected by the builders that became the keystone?'"[146]

When none of the students spoke, Mark thoughtfully continued. "In another parable, Jesus actually compared the kingdom of heaven to a wedding feast to which a king had invited special guests. Some chose not to come, going about other business, which they thought more important. Furious, the king told his servants to go and invite everyone they could find to the wedding—good and bad alike. However, one of the guests did not have on a wedding garment and when the king came, he said the man should be thrown into the dark where there would be 'weeping and grinding of teeth.'"[147]

Mark finished his story in a sorrowing voice. "Jesus' ending words to that parable bother me still: 'For many are called, but few are chosen.'"[148]

Gaspar desperately wanted to speak to the young men, especially the one named Mark, who seemed almost convinced that Jesus from Nazareth in Galilee might be his people's long-awaited Messiah. The old king believed that his search must have ended. As he started to move toward them, however, he heard a moan of pain. Needing to attend Raheeb, Gaspar agonized over the low-voiced statements coming from the group.

"I saw one of his followers stay here in the Temple after he left today. He seemed secretive."

"They are going to arrest Jesus."

"They will do more than arrest him if Caiaphas has his way."

CHAPTER 4

The Arrest

The innkeeper lumbered over to where Gaspar sat in exhaustion. Abram smiled sympathetically as he poured more wine. "How is Raheeb today?" he inquired.

"His pain seems less since he was bled again. He is not moving as much; overall, he is listless. Your good wife, Judith, insisted that she wanted me to leave the room, and eat here while he is sleeping."

"It is good to see you downstairs. If you don't take better care of yourself, you'll be lying on the pallet beside your friend."

"You are right, Abram. I appreciate your concern."

Attempting to mask his feelings, Abram bluffly responded. "One sick person in the inn is enough! None of us are as young as we once were! By the way, did Zaphta find the herbs you wanted for Raheeb?"

"Not yet—we fear they are not to be found in these lands."

"What will you do?"

"Zaphta continues to search. If he is unsuccessful, he will leave to find and bring back the plants and dried herbs we need. Raheeb and I will stay here in your excellent hostel until either he is stronger, or Zaphta returns with the medicines."

"Good King Gaspar, we will be honored by your patronage. Whatever my wife and staff can do to make your continued stay more comfortable will be done as soon as we know of your needs."

"Many thanks, Abram. It seems an eternity already since Raheeb became ill."

"Not so long. It was three days ago. Today begins our feast of Passover."

"Then I must return to relieve your wife. She will have many preparations to make."

"No, stay. This is the day of Unleavened Bread. All will be ready at the time it is needed. Our ceremonial evening meals, called Seders, which we will celebrate tonight and tomorrow—the first two days of the festival—have special foods, most of which she has prepared. The Paschal Lamb is being readied even now."

"Actually, Abram, there is something you could possibly find out for me."

"What do you need done?"

"When we were in the temple the day Raheeb fell ill, a young rabbi named Jesus was causing quite a stir. He was debating some issues with the chief priests. I have a special interest in finding him. I was wondering if there is any news of him?"

Abram's friendliness underwent an abrupt change. "I know nothing of the Galilean."

Perceiving the landlord's closed features, Gaspar gently prodded. "I did not say he was from Galilee, Abram."

Flustered, the man muttered. "You would do well to avoid contact with this man. He is dangerous."

"To whom is he dangerous?"

"He has many enemies."

Gaspar encouraged his reluctant host. "Tell me what is happening. What have you heard?"

"The rabbis have been talking—actually, arguing, for days. Messengers are constantly coming and going. There are rumors."

"What are the rumors, Abram?"

"It is not healthy to meddle in Temple matters."

"What do they fear about this man?"

"Their world would end if his words were to come true."

"I do not understand."

"Everything he preaches is an affront to them. He challenges their authority, their teachings. He quotes the Scriptures often, and they do not like to hear what he says."

"Have you heard him yourself?"

"Once I heard him speak, but he talks in riddles and I could not understand all that he was saying. He said, 'If anyone has ears to hear, let him listen!'[149] Now I ask you this—he was speaking to hundreds. We all had ears. How could we hear without ears? So, who was he speaking to, if not to us?"

As tired as he was, Gaspar could not help but laugh. Abram's good spirits revived with Gaspar's smile. "I heard that someone once asked him why he speaks to the people as he does. He answered, 'The reason I talk to them in parables is that they look without seeing and listen without hearing or understanding.'"[150]

"Strange words, indeed."

"Well, I have been a stranger to my kitchen long enough."

Gaspar rose, while saying, "It is past time for me to attend to Raheeb. Abram, if you hear any further news on these matters, please inform me immediately."

"I haven't changed your mind, I can see. Yes, I'll let you

know anything I hear. You probably won't like the news if I read the signs of the times right."

"Majesty, wake up!"

"Abram?" The demanding voice of the landlord broke through Gaspar's restless sleep.

"My wife said I should wake you—there is news you will want to hear."

"Is it Raheeb?"

"No. It is about the Galilean we spoke of yesterday."

Alert at these words, Gaspar listened in total incredulity to Abram's startling words. "Last night at Gethsemane on the Mount of Olives, Jesus was arrested. [151] It was late, past midnight. He was taken to the home of the High Priest, Annas."[152]

"Do you know the charges? How could this happen?"

"I'm not sure exactly what they are holding him for, but the general charges concern blasphemy. His disciples tried to stop the soldiers. There was blood shed. The one they call the Big Fisherman grabbed a sword and struck off a soldier's ear. The veterans who broke their fast here had a wild tale that Jesus healed their comrade on the spot.[153] They also said that one of his own followers betrayed him."

"Who would have done such a thing?"

"Judas Iscariot is the name they gave. He was given thirty silver pieces[154] according to other things they said."

"I must go and see what I can do."

"Majesty, you must not!"

"Nonsense, they can do me no harm. I am a king."

"I tell you it is not safe—your Jesus claims to be a king and look what they are doing to him."

"Will you watch Raheeb for me? Have your nephew come and help. I will pay him well to assist you and Judith while I am gone."

"We will take care of Raheeb, but it is foolish to make such powerful enemies."

"While I prepare, find someone who can take me to where Jesus is being held."

Within the hour, Gaspar had entered the courtyard at Annas' house. It was obvious that exceptional events had transpired even this early. Requesting to speak to Annas, Gaspar was told that he was not there. At Gaspar's insistence, the servant told him that Annas had gone to the palace of his son-in-law, the high priest Caiaphas.[155] The distance between the two places was not far, but Gaspar, feeling that time was of the essence, regretted the loss of even these few minutes.

Arriving, he urged that he be immediately announced to Caiaphas. He had to wait to hear the answer to his request, however, because the piercing crows of a nearby cock kept him from hearing. When all was quiet, the servant again repeated, "High Priest Caiaphas is not available."

"I must speak to him."

"He is presiding over a meeting of the Sanhedrin."[156]

"So early in the morning? What is the purpose of the session? Speak, man!"

The authority in the king's voice drew forth the reluctant answer, "The elders are questioning a false prophet."

"Tell them that King Gaspar requests to speak to the Sanhedrin immediately."

"No Gentile may speak when the council meets, Highness."

"I will wait here, then. I must have the opportunity to speak to Caiaphas."

"As you wish."

Almost an hour went by before Gaspar was finally admitted into Caiaphas' chambers. Peering intently at the powerful man, Gaspar recognized immediately that the rabbi would be implacable. Despairing inwardly, the old man fell back on his own regal influence knowing he was fighting for another man's life.

Caiaphas' demeanor made Gaspar uneasy, although his words were gentle enough. "King Gaspar, my sincere apologies that you have had to come here for us to have the opportunity to meet. I was concerned when I learned of your servant's sudden illness in our temple. Although I had hoped to meet you, I felt you would not want me to disturb the efforts to revive your servant."

"Thank you for remembering—Raheeb is recovering still. My business with you so early, however, is because I have heard disturbing talk of the arrest of the man known as Jesus of Galilee, sometimes also called simply the Nazarene."

"A matter of little import, Your Majesty."

"The circumstances seem to indicate that this Jesus is of great importance."

Haughtily, Caiaphas responded. "These matters are religious in nature. But to satisfy your request for information, I will tell you that the Sanhedrin Council questioned him about his disciples and his teachings."

"What problem could there be? It is my understanding that he openly spoke to the crowds. Did he not speak regularly in your Temple? Is he not considered to be a rabbi?"

"The matter is out of my jurisdiction."

"What do you mean?"

"The Romans are handling the case now."

"What? What have you done?"

At the alert movement of a guard who had been standing inside the door, Caiaphas signaled that there was no need for action. Addressing his unwanted visitor, he demanded, "King Gaspar, why such interest in this man?"

Unintimidated, Gaspar proclaimed. "I have known him from the time he was a babe. I am certain there is no criminal action that he could have committed. Long have I waited to speak to you on this matter, and now you tell me he is not even here?"

"Your pardon, King Gaspar. But how could I have known of your interest in this low-born person?"

Not deigning to answer, Gaspar demanded, "Where have you taken him?"

"The Sanhedrin recommended that he be sent for justice to Pontius Pilate, Roman Procurator of this Imperial Province of Judea. The Governor will decide his fate."[157]

Abruptly, Gaspar turned his back on Caiaphas and left immediately.

During the trip to the Praetorium, Gaspar actually felt his hopes rise. He knew little of Pontius Pilate, but the charges were vague. He felt that the Roman Governor would probably try to appease the Jews, but without doing excessive harm to Jesus himself. Too, the problem was a religious one, and the Romans rarely interfered in the religious matters of their conquered nations. With the Jews apparently not wanting to punish Jesus themselves, preferring for some reason to use the Romans as some sort of scapegoat, the plan would surely backfire.

The litter-bearers lowered him to the ground at the Praetorium. Advancing to the impressive door, he eagerly requested to see Pilate. Told he would have to wait, he admonished that his business was supremely important. After an interminable wait, he was ushered into Pilate's presence. The august representative of the Roman Emperor was seated as Gaspar was ushered into the room and formally announced.

Rising as his visitor advanced into the room, Pontius Pilate welcomed his royal guest. "King Gaspar, I extend greetings and salutations on behalf of Emperor Tiberius. Welcome to Palestine!"

"Your gracious words, Governor Pilate, and the urgency of my coming to you this morning, encourage me to quickly come to the point of my business."

"What can we do for you?"

"I have just been told by High Priest Caiaphas that the Sanhedrin has asked you to intercede in a dispute they have with the man known as Jesus of Nazareth. He is a person I have long taken an interest in, and I would take it as a personal favor to me, if you would recommend that he be released."

"I would not attempt to question why an Eastern ruler would have a long-time interest in a person I had thought was a carpenter's son. However, your desire to have him released coincides with my own humor to set him free; therefore, I will speedily send you on your way. Since he is from Galilee, and as both a Jew and a Galilean falls under Herod's authority, who is here in the city for the Passover, I sent him to Herod Antipater."[158]

At the name Herod, Gaspar expelled a horrified cry. Pilate responded immediately. "What have I said to so disturb you?"

"Herod—that man, his family!"

"Yes, the Herods have been in power for years. As tetrarch of Judea, his justice is applicable here."

"Justice—the children, so long ago!"

"Pardon, King Gaspar, but I do not understand your meaning."

"I ramble to no purpose. May I impose on you to give me quick passage to Herod?"

"Of course!" Raising his voice, he issued orders to immediately provide an escort. Pilate himself walked Gaspar out of the chamber. Their passage was interrupted, however, by an imperative message from Pilate's wife. The woman bringing the request was dismissed with the reply that he would attend his wife when he could. Pilate continued walking, but remarked off-handedly, "My wife has become greatly disturbed about a dream which has frightened her excessively.[159] You are married, I presume, King Gaspar?"

"I have had no wife for many years."

Sighing, Pilate said, "Well, having been married, you know that wives must be placated, or life does not always run smoothly. Your escort awaits you already, and hopefully your mission will have success. I leave you to attend to this new crisis in my life."

Gaspar dreaded the confrontation with the vicious weakling Herod, who had beheaded Jesus' cousin, John. That story, as related by his landlord Abram and recalled in all its horror, was that Herod's audacious stepdaughter Salome had pleased the salacious ruler with an exotic dance.

He had promised her anything—up to half his kingdom—as a reward for dancing for him and his guests. Salome's request for the head of the Baptist on a platter was granted in part because he had made the promise in front of so many of the leaders of Judea.[160]

Upon arrival at Herod's current pleasure palace, Pilate's written introduction admitted Gaspar immediately. Assuming his most regal manner, he hoped it masked his horror at his first sight of Jesus since infancy.

With Herod's wife and stepdaughter Salome out shopping the Jerusalem bazaars, the Judean ruler had welcomed the opportunity to interrogate Jesus who stood, hands bound, in the center of the room. Herod had been enjoying the entertainment afforded by the chief priests and scribes violently pressing their accusations and awaiting his pleasure. Hoping to see a miracle—or at the least, an amusing magic trick from the pretender—Herod's cup overflowed with an Eastern monarch requesting a boon of him!

Having no compunction about interrupting the proceedings, Herod greeted his royal guest effusively. "Your presence, King Gaspar, both honors and delights us." Gesturing toward Jesus, he added, "Pilate's personal note informs us that you have an interest in this man?"

Proceeding cautiously with the Palestinian ruler, Gaspar humbled himself in hopes of elevating Herod's ego and thus helping save the life he sought. "Your reputation, Mighty Ruler, is well known. Being in the company of royalty is exhilarating, King Herod. Surely it is a rare pleasure for us both."

Gaspar knew that Herod Antipater was only the tetrarch, rather than the king of Judea, as his father had been. However, the younger Herod's preening at Gaspar's remarks indicated he was on the right path by flattering the Judean. Unhesitatingly, he continued. "The fame of your court, the buildings you have constructed here in Jerusalem and in other cities—all are recognized throughout the lands. I had to pay my respects to such a fabled ruler."

Redirecting Herod's attention to the prisoner still standing bound, but now unblindfolded and with downcast head, Gaspar pretended indifference to Jesus' plight, seeming to align his interest as one king to another. "So the rabbis have come to try to get you to see things their way regarding this man from your district of Galilee?"

With a regal personage seeking his company, Herod's interest in the prisoner was waning rapidly. At no time did he see eye-to-eye with the synagogue leaders, who generally deplored his worldly and lascivious conduct. Furthermore, the prisoner had refused to utter a word in his defense. Replacing his earlier delight in the proceedings, Herod was becoming heartily sick and tired of the whole business. "I have questioned him at length. He refuses to say anything, and appears to be no threat."

Gaspar slyly commented, "For a man who is said to be a king, he certainly does not play the part well."

Having read Pilate's note, Herod looked slightly suspicious at this comment from a man who might have seemed more sympathetic to the prisoner's situation. Unable to determine precisely what was meant, he decided to see where the conversation would lead, and therefore simply agreed. "No, there is nothing regal about him."

"He doesn't appear threatening as either you or I might appear in similar circumstances."

"He has been a bore actually—harmless in the extreme."

Sulkily he added, "I had hoped to see some miracle from him.[161] Obviously, he is incapable of the magic some say he has done."

Seizing the opening, Gaspar commented, "Perhaps if he could use his hands, he might be able to perform for you."

"Excellent idea! Unbind his hands." An idea having occurred, Herod ordered, "My purple cloak[162]—have it brought immediately. Any magician—any king—needs to dress for the occasion!"

Immeasurably relieved at the less dangerous direction the proceedings were taking, Gaspar struggled inwardly at the humiliation Jesus would undergo in this assembly of his enemies. His sense of outrage and pain were so strong that he almost forgot the character he had adopted in Herod's presence. "Give him some water. Please, someone!"

Herod laughed childishly, mistaking Gaspar's meaning. "Yes, yes! Magicians frequently use water for their tricks. Splendid idea, King Gaspar."

The elders of the temple were frowning at Herod's change of heart and seeming dismissal of their attempt to punish Jesus. Jeroboam, the only one of the temple contingent to have spoken previously to Gaspar, stepped forward. "This man has dared to call himself the Son of God today before the Sanhedrin."

"Nonsense!" Herod interrupted.

"Gracious Herod," Jeroboam continued, "Listen to the blasphemy. The words are written here exactly as he proclaimed when we asked him to tell us if he was the Christ: 'If I tell you, you will not believe me, and if I question you, you will not answer. But from now on, the Son of Man will be seated at the right hand of the Power of God.'[163]

"We followed up his own words by specifically asking,

'So you are the Son of God then?' He answered thus: 'It is you who say I am.'"[164]

Jeroboam stated, "We needed no other witnesses at this point. We had heard it from his own lips![165] The assembly then brought him before Pilate who has sent us on to you for justice!"

Petulant at the implied criticism in front of a royal, Herod sought a way to escape making a decision in the matter. Gaspar, feeling that Pilate was the more sympathetic of the two officials, inferred to Herod that he could send Jesus back to Pilate.

Eager to escape possible humiliation, Herod thoroughly enjoyed this unlooked for opportunity to reprimand the temple leaders. "This affair is not worth our effort. You make a mockery of my authority by bringing such a case to us. Be careful in future that you do not waste our time again. Free him or take him back to Pilate[166] as you wish." Dismissing the temple leaders along with the prisoner, Herod turned to Gaspar and cordially invited him to share a late morning repast.

Gaspar felt his continued presence would keep Herod from changing his mind. Also, there was a legitimate concern that if the women returned, they might yet influence Herod. Gaspar accepted Herod's invitation believing that if the Hebrew hierarchy did not immediately release Jesus, then Pilate would order it when Jesus was returned to him. Forcing himself to endure Herod's company, he fervently hoped he could conceal his antipathy to Antipater throughout the meal.

Later than he would have liked, and finally having used Raheeb as an excuse, Gaspar was on his way back to Pilate to find out if Jesus had been released when the litter abruptly came to a standstill. Shouts of rage interrupted his thoughts. He could see that the Praetorium was still up ahead, and he worried about the halt and the crowd's noticeable anger. Calling to his litter bearers to put him down, Gaspar wanted to assess the best way to proceed. Standing amid the crowd, he realized the bearers had thought they were dismissed, and his calls for them to return went unheard among the other voices. Now, as he tried to push his way through the maddened throng, fear surged anew in him as the shouts of the crowd revealed its dangerous mood.

"The true Messiah wouldn't let them arrest him."

"The chief priests must be right."

"Crucify him!"[167]

The hate in the last man's voice impelled Gaspar to continue to force his way through the crowd that had assembled outside the Praetorium. All of Palestine seemingly knew of the arrest and imprisonment of the man from Galilee.

A gasp from the crowd and pointing hands drew Gaspar's eyes upward. The balcony scene pierced his soul and his eyes locked on the man he had spent his life following. His aged eyes could not really see the face, but clearly Jesus had been abused. The regal cloak was torn at places and dusty, as if he had fallen or been shoved to the ground. His hands were disgracefully tied in front again. Exhaustion hung on the weakened body.

Pilate apparently wanted an audience for his final decision while people in the crowd were demanding silence to hear the proceedings. The Roman's voice carried out to those gathered below as he demanded, "'What charge do you bring against this man?'"[168]

"'If he were not a criminal, we should not be handing him over to you,'"[169] a spokesperson for the Jewish officials responded.

"'Take him yourselves, and try him by your own law.'"[170]

"'We are not allowed to put a man to death.'"[171]

The crowd responded with cheers, jeers or pleas.

A reverent voice near Gaspar lamented. "He said he would die according to the Scriptures."[172] The man closed his eyes in pain at his own words.

Pilate raised his hand for silence. His challenge to the prisoner rang out: "'Are you the king of the Jews?'"[173]

"'It is you who say it.'"[174]

To the Governor's amazement, Jesus offered no further reply to the charges. Pilate felt that jealousy and concern over the growing influence of the upstart Galilean were responsible for the mockery of a court he was being asked to oversee. The man's innocence was apparent, and he had no desire to condemn the prisoner. Hoping to provide a solution where all could save face and the Jewish hierarchy could have effectively chastised and warned Jesus, Pilate decided to fall back on a tradition at festival time.

After ordering that the notorious prisoner, Barabbas, be brought from his cell. Pilate addressed the people below him. "It is our tradition to release a prisoner for you, the people, during your Passover feast. Anyone you choose!" Pilate finished with the offer. "'Which do you want me to release for you: Barabbas, or Jesus who is called Christ?'"[175]

The chief priests and elders had worked the crowd well.[176] Their followers were in amongst the mass of people persuading them to call for the release of Barabbas and the execution of Jesus. At Pilate's words, they out-shouted the few friends of Jesus who dared to give public support for him.

"'Barabbas.'"[177]

"'Let him be crucified!'"[178]

Horrified, Pilate tried to lessen the frenzy calling for Jesus' crucifixion. "'Why? What harm has he done?'"[179]

The crowd became even more frenzied shouting their choice louder still. "Barabbas! Barabbas!"

Fearing a riot, Pilate held his hands out for silence. His wife's frightening dream to have nothing to do with the Nazarene suddenly being recalled, he ordered that a nearby bowl of water be brought forward. Deliberately, he washed his hands in front of the mob saying, "'I am innocent of this man's blood. It is your concern.'"[180]

Barabbas, as his shackles were taken off, stared in disbelief at the figure being taken away on the Roman Governor's orders to be scourged and crucified for him. The intense dark brown eyes of the man Pilate had called the Christ would haunt him all the rest of the days, and particularly the nights, of his life.

CHAPTER 5

A Criminal

Insignificantly crushed in the crowd, Gaspar could not believe that Pilate had ordered the crucifixion of an innocent person. Visions of the barbarism to come brutalized the remembered tenderness of the birth he had witnessed at Bethlehem. The baby, the child, the man—destined to be nailed to the cross from birth! Who could stop this farce? Pilate would not; Herod was impotent. The chief priests seemed the manipulative power behind the whole of it. His eyes, rising to the vacant balcony where the injustice had been perpetrated, were drawn to the rapidly darkening skies. To his overwrought senses, it appeared even the heavens above were distraught at the events that had just transpired.

Wildly, the old king looked for succor and support. Where were the thousands who had hung on Jesus' words? The miracles performed had undoubtedly been witnessed by many of the same people who had made up the mob today. Where were those he had cured? His followers— those men referred to as apostles—could they not mount support? He knew none of their names. The one called the Big Fisherman—where could he be found? What could a follower of Jesus with such a common street name do to gain support and sway officials who had determined their stance? More than likely, those apostles were fearful they would be imprisoned and even put to death, if they attempted to intervene.

Not willing to concede defeat, although feeling powerless, Gaspar tried to fight his way forward through the milling throng. His strength, however, was nothing compared to the numbers pushing him back. Giving in, he let himself be moved as the rabble willed.

The crack of a whip in an interior courtyard stilled the crowd. The scourging had begun.[181] Again and again, the harsh slash of leather tore bare flesh. Monotonously the whip ripped and shredded. Most in the crowd were silent, but somebody was calling aloud the count: "...nineteen, twenty...." The whip could be heard in an unholy syncopation of swish-slash/swish-slash. At thirty-nine, the relentless count and the whip ceased—forty, less one, the allotted punishment for one not of Roman citizenship.

Body limp with sweat and his spirit weakened, as if he had endured the strokes himself, Gaspar was shoved back into a wall. Spent, he remained there, despairing of the will to live. Suddenly, someone shouted. "He comes!"

Soldiers unceremoniously shoved the spectators aside clearing a wide swath for the condemned man to tread toward Calvary. The old man was glad his position against the wall kept away the terrible sight of his beloved Jesus struggling to his death. The sounds alone were almost more than he could endure.

"Make way, or we'll have you carrying the crossbar as well."

"He's covered in blood!"

"A crown of thorns[182] for a king—that's rich!"

Slowly, the crowd dispersed. Some followed the weary

way to Golgotha,[183] also known as Calvary. Others exulted. Some wanted only to slink away from the horror they had helped perpetrate. Many wept. The paradox for the faithful: Had God deserted them?

Gaspar, too, was torn. Could he endure witnessing the death of the gentle man bearing his cross up the hills of Jerusalem? He was with the babe at the beginning, must he not finish what he had seen begun? Or could Pilate yet be influenced to stay the sentence?

Deciding on the latter course, Gaspar moved toward the inner Praetorium, but found his clothes caught on a large thorn bush. Attempting to disentangle himself, his right hand was gouged by a steely barb. Instinctively reacting, he jerked, but then impaled the back of his hand on another of the nail-length thorns. The intense pain staggered him; he almost fainted as he drew the thorn out half the width of his pierced hand. The deep wounds bled profusely, but he ignored them except to bind his hand with material torn from his clothing.

The courtyard was now completely empty. Gaspar staggered forward in weariness and pain to attempt once more to persuade Pilate to halt the proceedings. His worn and bloody appearance, however, caused the Roman guard to contemptuously dismiss his request for admittance. The soldier barred the way stating that Pilate had given orders not to be disturbed, and that no further official business would be conducted this day.

Realizing the uselessness of pursuing this course, Gaspar sorrowfully plodded in the wake of the last of those moving toward Golgotha. Mental and physical pain a part of him, he trudged toward the notorious place of the skull.[184] At its base, he halted and looked upward.

Three crosses etched against the skyline forced him to his knees. Dropping his head, he doubted he had the strength to continue. Despondently, he reflected: I will die here with the man I sought; maybe this is the fate destined for me.

"Old man, this is no place for you."

Startled from his stupor, Gaspar stared into the hardened eyes of a young man crouched nearby under the shade of a date palm tree. There was no compassion in the other's eyes, and Gaspar instinctively knew that the man, who was hardly more than a youth, had been watching his slow, painful movements toward the hill of Golgotha and his fall of despair. His only concern being Jesus, Gaspar had no energy to spare for the cruel jesting of one who had probably been in the mob calling for the crucifixion.

Neither man moved nor directed a comment to the other for several minutes.

Shrewdly, the younger man bided his time.

At length, the enfeebled man attempted to rise. Forgetful of his bandaged hand, he pushed upward with it. Pain shot through him anew, and fresh blood oozed from the makeshift bandage as he collapsed back on the ground. Glancing swiftly up to the height, the man lounging in the shade waited, but offered no assistance. Gaspar brought a leonine look to bear on the younger man.

Insolently, the seemingly relaxed stranger shredded a leaf frond while eyeing the injured man. Nodding toward the height above them, he finally asked, "Want to get to the top?"

Humiliated and feeling at the end of his strength, Gaspar felt every year of his age. With his blood dripping onto the dusty road, and no other aid in sight, he guardedly said, "My strength will return momentarily."

Eyeing again the crosses upon the hilltop, the lounger exhibited a sense of urgency he had masked before. Harshly he queried, "Why else would you be here if you didn't want to gawk at the condemned men?"

With years of experience in judging others, Gaspar felt that the young man must need his help as much as Gaspar needed aid. Some urgency required the younger to want to climb the height, but he was obviously reluctant to go alone. Assessing the man's question about condemned men, Gaspar realized he was probably in the company of a criminal. He felt no fear for his personal safety, however, because as nonchalant as the man wanted to appear, Gaspar sensed that they shared a similar pain.

It was evident his evaluation was close to the mark, when the other broke the silence, "Well, do you want to go up before they die or not?"

Noting again the second reference to more than one person being executed, Gaspar quietly spoke. "Your assistance would be appreciated."

Betraying his background, the other questioned, "What's in it for me?"

"Getting to the top."

Startled that the old, injured target was apparently sharper than he looked, the youth eyed him closer, then rose and strode over to Gaspar. None too gently, he assisted Gaspar to rise. Although exhausted and in pain, Gaspar was aware that the young man walked with a slight stiffness as if he was in physical pain also. Even though both men were impeded, initially they made progress. Gaspar, however, began to move slower and slower as Golgotha's steepness overwhelmed him, and his hand throbbed and continued oozing. Finally, in exasperation, his comrade growled, "You're bleeding like a stuck goat!"

"Please, let me rest. You go ahead; we are almost near the top."

Eyes ahead where the three crosses pierced the skyline, the youth began to move away, but hesitated and returned. "Do you have something to re-bandage your hand?"

"Here, tear this more."

Roughly, the desperate man ripped off a new strip of cloth from Gaspar's clothing and wound it over the first bloody bandage. When done, he urgently ordered, "On your feet, old man!"

Nearing the zenith, Gaspar staggered as his anguished eyes looked upon Jesus, the Christ, in the last stages of his mortal life. His comrade hesitated also and uttered a snarl of ineffective rage, as he too took in the scene of horror.

Grotesquely outlined against a near-black sky, the three wooden crosses bore suffering men. Two unknown criminals hung strapped to crosses—how long they had been there, Gaspar could not have determined. Upon the central cross[185] hung the limp body of the man who had claimed to be the Son of God. Hands and feet had been nailed to the boards unlike the other two men. Rivulets of blood seeped from the circlet of thorns pressed into his head. The sides and shoulders of his body gave graphic evidence of the scourging he had endured. Gaspar prayed to he knew not whom that the closed eyes indicated death.

A number of people occupied the grim hilltop. Soldiers diced[186] at the foot of the middle cross—regretfully, Gaspar realized it was for Jesus' clothing. Mourners were mostly alone except for one group of weeping women and a young man hardly older than the youth whose body trembled by Gaspar's side. Most of the those who had taunted Jesus the Christ had previously slunk away from the scene of horror.

Observing the direction of his companion's haunted eyes, Gaspar quietly asked, "Who is he?"

"My brother...Dismas."

Gaspar offered his sympathy. "I am sorry."

His words, however, roused the wrath of the other. "Don't be! This life is nothing to be sorry about leaving!" Angered beyond reason, he drew away from Gaspar as if the other man represented all the people and the events in his life that had conspired to place him here to view his dying brother. Wanting to say more, Gaspar waited as the enraged younger brother walked slowly toward the far cross.

Gaspar then was distracted as several of the temple rabbis who had previously climbed the hill, angrily challenged the soldiers. "The inscription! Who authorized that sign? Take it down immediately!"

The soldiers ceased their dicing, and the leader addressed the irate speaker. "We were told to hang this sign."

"It is wrong! Change it at once!"

"'King of the Jews,'"[187] the soldier read in a perplexed voice. "What is wrong?"

The chief priests protested that the sign was to read, "'This man said: I am King of the Jews.'"[188]

"He'll be dead in no time. It will come down then."

Furious, the rabbis moved away still gesturing and talking angrily about the inscription. As a group, they began to hurry back down the hill.

Humbly, Gaspar recalled the words Raheeb and he had spoken before they undertook their journey—they would be witnesses that the star of Bethlehem had led them to a child of destiny. The sign proclaimed him to be the King of the Jews just as the star had heralded a royal birth. He and Melchior and Balthazar had not been led astray! The comfort was fleeting, however, as he slowly found the courage to look again upon the pain-wracked body above him. That an innocent human being should have to endure this intense anguish! How could men do this to one another? Sorrowfully, he heard the taunts of others.

"'If you are God's son, come down from the cross!'"[189]

"'He is the king of Israel! Let him come down from the cross now, and we will believe in him.'"[190]

"Let the man he calls God, his father, rescue him!"

Sorrowing, an onlooker turned to leave muttering, "He turned water into wine. Now he refuses vinegar and is mocked."

As if Gaspar's thoughts about the cruelty he was witnessing were known, Jesus spoke from the cross. "'Father, forgive them; they do not know what they are doing.'"[191]

One of the criminals hanging on a cross joined in the abuse, jeering—yet maybe pleading. "'Are you not the Christ? Save yourself and us as well.'"[192]

The criminal that Gaspar had learned was named Dismas rebuked the other. "'Have you no fear of God at all? You got the same sentence as he did, but in our case, we deserved it: we are paying for what we did. But this man has done nothing wrong.'"[193] Dismas quietly begged the man nailed to the middle cross, "'Jesus, remember me when you come into your kingdom.'"[194]

"'Indeed, I promise you,'" Jesus told him, "'today you will be with me in paradise.'"[195]

Gaspar wondered what the angry young brother would think of these words from the dying man's lips. Looking around in the unexpectedly dim light, however, Gaspar could not see Dismas' brother. For himself, the wonder of the moment was that, given Jesus' own agony, he was still concerned with others.

The soft sobs of several women drew Gaspar's attention. Peering closer, he realized one of them was Mary, the mother of Jesus. Though she was racked with misery, the purity and beauty that was both physical and spiritual had not palled through the years. The young man he had glimpsed earlier at the foot of the cross held her close in comfort.

Jesus finally spoke to them as they mourned. "'Woman, this is your son.'"[196] Then to the man, "'This is your mother.'"[197]

The atrocities done to her son appeared to have almost literally pierced her heart. At the words from Jesus, the young man held her even more tenderly. Gaspar backed away, feeling he could not intrude on her sorrow.

Darkness seemed to have overcome the day, as the sun was eclipsed. The tortured, gaunt man cried out in a loud voice. "'Eloi, Eloi, lama sabachthani?'"[198]

One of those still there questioned why he called upon the Old Testament prophet, Elijah.[199]

Another despairingly interpreted, he has called out: "*'My God, my God, why have you deserted me?'*"[200]

Breathing his last, Jesus proclaimed. "'Father, into your hands I commit my spirit.'"[201]

At the moment of death, the heavens poured forth thunder and lightning. Torrents of rain pummeled the earth. Lightning, bright as day, flashed across the macabre scene. Gaspar, although drenched, remained with the others. Even through his terrible grief, he was aware of the elemental display in the distance, as thunder and lightning centered over Jerusalem itself. A loud thunderbolt sounded as if it had hit a building in the city.[202] Those on Calvary heard and felt a reverberating shudder.

Gaspar bowed his head dispiritedly as the rain pelted him. Jesus was dead. Agonizing, he tried to fathom why this had been allowed to happen. This man had suffered so intensely because he had told men to live better and to love one another. Some great entity had apparently granted Jesus special powers to heal the sick and to bring joy. It made no sense to the distraught man that a god who could control the heavens, and bring people back to life, would then let his own son die so cruelly by the hands of men. Abjectly, he grieved.

Since it was Preparation Day, the day before the solemn Sabbath, the Jews wanted the body of Jesus taken off the cross and buried. Wanting to have the grisly proceedings of the entire day over, the soldiers broke the legs of both criminals to hasten death. Although Jesus had already died, as a final precaution, one of the soldiers pierced his side with a lance. Immediately, the last of his blood and water flowed forth.[203]

Thunder and lightning flashed across the skies while rain drenched the remaining mourners and soldiers. A centurion, standing near, spoke from the heart as others cringed in fear at the elemental display of the heavens. "In truth this was a son of God."[204]

Wanting to believe in the man whom he had followed so loyally, Gaspar could only watch in resignation and defeat as the lifeless body was lowered into the mother's waiting arms. Her renewed tears, as she held her child's mutilated body, and rocked him in death as before she had rocked him in life, were poignant reminders of the atrocities of the day. Gaspar felt overwhelmed, but moved forward to assist in any small way he could.

He stiffened in alarm as a man whom he recognized from the Temple as Joseph of Arimathaea,[205] a member of the Sanhedrin Council approached. Mary, however, appeared to accept his presence. Devoutly attending upon the dead man, Joseph laid out a shroud, and comforted Mary. "Pilate has given me permission to bury the body."[206]

With no intention other than to be present at the hurried burial, Gaspar followed respectfully in the wake of those who sorrowed. Jesus was laid in linen wrappings in a tomb hewn from stone in which no one had yet been buried.[207] Soldiers, who for reasons unknown to Gaspar, had been assigned to guard the tomb, began to shove a gigantic stone in place to enclose the body in its final resting place.

Racked in mental and physical anguish, Gaspar turned to leave, when the young man who had been at the foot of the cross, approached. "Sir, I am John, a follower—a friend—nay, a brother of Jesus. His mother has requested to speak to you. Will you come to her?"

The rain was lessening in intensity as Gaspar moved to speak to Mary. The grieving woman spoke first. "Pardon, sir, I believe I know you, but am not certain. Are you not one of those who followed the star to my son?"

"Good Mother, that you should speak to me at such a time. Yes, I am Gaspar."

"How wonderful that you should have been here at the beginning and the end!"

"Mary, I tried to stop..." Gaspar's attempt to speak ended in a sob.

As if she were his mother, Mary enfolded Gaspar in her arms and comforted the older man. "It was always to have happened in this way."

"I do not understand."

"It was foretold in the Scriptures.[208] Indeed, my Son knew that he would suffer grievously at the hands of the elders, chief priests and scribes. He also spoke of other events to come as well."[209]

CHAPTER 6

The King of the Jews

It had been dark for several hours when Gaspar slowly approached the inn. Reaching to unlatch the door handle, he was met by an excited Abram. "You are safe! We worried when sundown came and went, and still you had not returned. Quickly, come! We know of the crucifixion, but see what has occurred!"

Ushered forward, Gaspar beheld his old servant and friend seated at a table. "Raheeb?" he incredulously questioned.

"My, Lord, I am well."

"How can this be?"

"At the height of the storm, when the thunder and lightning were at their greatest, I came fully awake and felt no pain. I have been awaiting your return here for hours. When you did not return, Abram and Judith invited me to eat the Seder with them."

"Raheeb, you have been very ill! You must return to your bed to rest!"

"My Lord, I feel no physical pain—only my great sorrow over the death of Jesus."

"Have you heard what else occurred during the storm?" Judith asked.

Gaspar, still stunned by Raheeb's recovery as well as by

the events of the horrifying day he had endured, could only look inquiringly at Judith, who was eager to speak. "The Temple veil was torn right down the middle! A monstrous bolt of lightning struck it at the beginning of the storm."[210]

Wonderingly, Gaspar responded, "I saw the lightning from Golgotha. It seemed to have hit in the city—but the Temple—and to destroy the veil!"

"You were there at Golgotha?"

"On Calvary at the crucifixion?"

In concern, Judith halted the men's questions as she drew their attention to Gaspar's bloodied hand that she had just noticed. "How did you hurt yourself? Let me cleanse it, and you can tell us of this exhausting day."

Later, speaking to everyone, and not attempting to mask the heartache he felt, Gaspar began to relate the events of the long day. Gathering his thoughts, he told of his efforts to stop the crucifixion. "I tried all morning to stop it. I went to both Annas and Caiaphas, Pilate—twice. I even went to Herod—that weakling!"

"The son of the man who slew the babies?" Raheeb asked in horror.

"Yes, and clearly he has inherited his father's brutal ways. As we now know, it was he who ordered the beheading of the cousin of Jesus, John the Baptizer. Once in Herod's presence, it took mere moments for me to realize that he could be influenced through his pride. Although I despised myself, I was momentarily effective in delaying the inevitable."

Judith inquired, "Why do you say the inevitable?"

"His mother told me herself."

This time Raheeb eagerly spoke. "Mary is still alive! And Joseph?"

"I did not ask, but he was much older than Mary as I recall, and he was not there. At the end, as Jesus was being buried, his mother noticed and remembered me."

"What a terrible day for any mother to endure!" Judith sympathized.

"It was dreadful. She was calm, yet her tears watered the earth."

At this point, Gaspar was not sure what to say in front of Judith and Abram, but they were obviously also disturbed by the events of the day. Judith's next question indicated her continued interest. "Good Gaspar, you said that his own mother told you it was inevitable that he was to die?"

"Perhaps I misunderstood her meaning. She seemed to be implying his death could not be stopped by any mortal."

"How could a mother know of her child's death—or any person know of another's? We all thought Raheeb would die any day, but here he sits saying he is well!"

His own thoughts uncertain, Gaspar found himself at a loss for words.

Suddenly, the abrupt interruption of two soldiers roughly opening the hostel door distracted them. The first soldier demanded. "Innkeeper, bread and drink! Quickly, man, it's been hours since we ate! Have you seen anyone skulking in this neighborhood tonight? Soldiers sighted a member of a criminal gang in this area at sundown."

"A criminal?" shrieked Judith.

"Two thieves were hung on crosses today on Calvary—there was at least one more in the gang. We believe he's the half-brother of the leader Dismas. When we cornered them last week, Dismas could have escaped, but instead he took us all on and fought like a tiger. After ordering the brother to quit fighting and escape, he blocked the door. We must have wounded the brother because we followed a trail of blood, but lost him somehow. The whole gang was wanted for crimes going back decades. They're wanted from here to Egypt."

After drinking half the tankard Abram had provided, the garrulous soldier continued. "He was seen on Calvary at his brother's execution. As soon as we recognized him, we went after him, but he escaped in the dark and rain."

Judith pressed. "What does he look like? What was he wearing?"

The second soldier answered. "He blends in with everyone else in Palestine—brown hair, average height, same clothing. He'll probably have a fresh wound, but we don't even know where it would be."

Gaspar quietly asked. "What will happen to him if he is caught?"

"Oh, we'll catch him all right! And if he's still alive after that, with all the trouble he's been to us, we'll put him up for show on Golgotha, just like we did with the other two."

Draining the last drops from the tankards, the soldiers left with one of them half-heartedly complaining to his comrade, "We'll be out chasing this thief all night, and tomorrow I've pulled guard duty at the tomb of the King of the Jews!" Their crude laughter could be heard through the open window as they took up the hunt again. Striding away, the man's last words drifted back, "Tribune Sextus is in charge of the tomb and he never cuts us any slack."

Abram bolted the door after the soldiers left. "If a thief is around, we had best take precautions." He reflected. "Free food and drink for protection—ah well. You do realize why they are guarding the tomb of your Jesus, don't you?"

As both men shook their head negatively, and Gaspar

encouraged him to go on, Abram answered while locking a window shutter. "The chief priests have urged that a special guard detail stand watch outside the grave. They fear his followers will steal his body."[211]

"Why would anyone do such a thing?" exclaimed Raheeb.

"There's a wild tale I heard from Isaac the tanner that Jesus said he would rise from the dead. Gives you the creeps, doesn't it?"

At the dumbfounded look of his listeners, he chuckled and continued. "The chief priests figure his followers will steal the body, and then say he rose from the dead as he claimed he would. By requesting the Romans to guard the tomb, they believe this will squelch any rumors and prevent it from happening altogether."

"Surely the Romans will not guard the body forever?"

"Actually, it is supposed to happen in three days' time."[212]

Gaspar suddenly said in amazement. "You are right! Scriptures proclaim it and the chief priests would definitely fear it! By plotting against Jesus and carrying out their cruelty, they may have created more problems for themselves than if he were alive."

"Are you saying you truly believe he will rise from the dead?" breathed Judith.

Pausing before answering, Gaspar answered thoughtfully. "I am not sure what I believe—although I always knew he was to be someone special. For this reason, Raheeb and I made the journey, again, here to Palestine to see if his destiny had been fulfilled. The heavens led us, and others from afar, to his birthplace in Bethlehem. Later, we three kings all had the same dream on the same night telling us to avoid Herod's treachery. He was surely protected then, and his birth happened as predicted of the Messiah. Stories are told throughout Palestine of his miracles. In our homeland, we recently heard of him through caravan drivers. He cured the sick; expelled demons. I imagine you have heard that in Bethany, just miles from here, he is said to have raised a man named Lazarus from the dead."

"*I believe!*" The confident words from Raheeb silenced the king and drew amazed gasps from Judith and Abram. "He will rise from the dead! I know it. My heart, which caused me so much pain and now does not, tells me it will be so."

"Think what you are saying," cautioned Abram.

Turning to Gaspar, Raheeb questioned. "When did Jesus die?"

"He was on the cross for hours."

"It stormed about three hours past midday. Did he die then?"

Quietly, Gaspar told what he had witnessed. "It had been dark since the middle of the day, with the threat of rain, but as soon as Jesus died, the skies above opened. At the very moment of his death, the storm struck with an intensity I have never experienced."

Raheeb spoke confidently. "How could you not believe that the wrath of their almighty being could cause such happenings if one whom it held dear was being innocently punished? The heavens foretold his birth! The same heavens would surely storm at his death." Firmly he added, "I was healed today because of Jesus."

Abram muttered. "To say such things is blasphemy."

Staunchly, Raheeb eyed the landlord. "Abram, think about the temple being damaged in the storm."

"No, no, that was purest chance."

"Not everything can be laid to chance," Raheeb said, smiling gently. "It was not chance that led us to his birth. It was not chance that allowed the miracles to occur— maybe one, maybe two, but not all. No mere magician in public places could fool thousands of people. The cures were performed on suffering people, who in many cases had been stricken for years. Much of his life was predicted in the ancient testaments and writings. King Gaspar has studied them for years, and often we discussed the possible interpretations. Now, in our lifetime, the Hebraic scriptures are fulfilled."

He lowered his eyes in humility. "We have been blessed."

Gaspar gently spoke to his friend, "Raheeb, your faith is inspiring. Would that I could share it entirely. But you were not present on Golgotha. He died in despair although earlier he forgave his tormentors as he hung in agony."

"Why do you say he despaired?"

"His last words ached with both physical and mental anguish. He cried out. 'My God, my God, why have you forsaken me?'"[213]

Abram seized the words. "If his father was God, why did he call out to his God rather than to his father? No, Raheeb, this was not the Son of God. This was a man who had been disillusioned in life, and even at the hour of his death, he could not face reality. He was just a man—not a god—and definitely not our Messiah."

"Gaspar, were those his last words?" Raheeb entreated.

"Yes." Hesitating, he then added. "No, he did say something else. Let me think." The two men waited expectantly hoping to hear words that supported each's separate stance. Finally, Gaspar admitted he had not heard the words clearly, but it seemed Jesus had said. "'Into your hands I commit my spirit.'"²¹⁴

Raheeb's face lit up with joy. "He did not lose his faith!"

Abram graciously admitted. "While it would seem he did not lose his faith, entirely, I cannot believe that faith was well-founded. The Sanhedrin was wise to post a guard. If his followers have the same beliefs as you, Raheeb, he will rise by faith alone!"

Judith spoke out, "I have to admit a liking for the man. I never saw him or heard him—this inn and the cooking keeps me busy day and night. He certainly was no coward; he could have catered to the chief priests at any time. Even this morning—before his last words, anyway—a strong reprimand or maybe even the flogging would have satisfied most of them. He took on the moneylenders in the Temple. Up against the High Priest, the Roman Governor—face to face. The nails in his hands and feet! I mean no disrespect for his sufferings; indeed, it is unbearable to think of them. To hang from his nailed hands for three hours! My heart goes out to him. It is difficult to even think of what he went through."

Undone by her own words, she sighed deeply, but then was compelled to add. "His last words—well, I've cried out myself at times wondering if we have been forsaken. I imagine most of us at one time or another have felt deserted. He had more cause than some. This has been a long, difficult day for all."

Abram slowly added his thoughts. "I cannot name the reason why, but a sadness has come upon me. It is as if this day is the end of something. Jewish chief priests and Romans united—the death of a person you say the heavens drew you to—mayhap our world will never be the same again."

Holding out his hand to Raheeb, Abram continued. "It was good to share the Seder with you. Let us shake hands and remain friends always." Here he paused, then looking into the other's eyes, stated, "If he rises from the dead, your faith will be a lesson for us all."

"Time will tell," and Raheeb grasped the other's outstretched hand in friendship.

The next day was the Sabbath and the Jewish community obeyed the Law of Moses as it was written: "These are the things Yahweh has ordered to be done: Work is to be done for six days, but the seventh is to be a holy day for you, a day of complete rest, consecrated to Yahweh. Whoever does any work on that day shall be put to death."[215]

Strict laws regulated activities including the amount of walking which might be done. In conquering Palestine, the Romans were forced, almost of necessity, to adhere to the same slow Sabbath regimen; therefore, the day was generally one of rest for everyone in Jerusalem. This particular Sabbath, being a part of the Passover festivities, as well as the day after the death of one whom many now remembered as being ever of gentle heart, seemed to take an eternity to pass.

Not wanting to offend their host, although they longed to go to the gravesite, Gaspar and Raheeb abided by the edict to limit walking. Instead, Gaspar confided to Raheeb all that he had seen and said and been saddened by during the previous day. The wounds were too new, too painful for them to think beyond the present. To wonder what the days to come would bring was to speculate about a new order, a new world. Each preferred to let it reside in the future, and so they talked mainly of the yesterdays in their life.

Some of their conversation concerned the young criminal still on the loose. Raheeb speculated the reason for his being seen in the neighborhood. "Could he have followed you?"

"It is possible. However, I lost sight of him almost as soon as we had climbed the hill. He became angered when I expressed sympathy to him. I would say he would not seek my company."

"He is a thief. We must take particular care since your robes would have indicated to a professional thief that you are a man of some wealth. For such a person, it would be easy enough for him to discover your whereabouts."

"The soldiers apparently spotted him on Calvary and immediately pursued him. I, of course, stayed until the end—until Jesus died. Then, I remained to honor him at his entombment. The brother would have been in hiding long before I returned, unless he was a fool, and he certainly did not seem one in the short time I spent with him."

"Well, we would be extremely foolish ourselves not to take extra precautions."

"Surely he would leave Jerusalem since the authorities are after him still."

"The gates are being especially well guarded. He will not be able to escape easily. I learned from Abram, who always has the latest news, that in addition to trying to capture the escaped thief, they are hoping to round up the followers of Jesus."

"For what reason?" Gaspar asked.

"I think it would only be to interrogate them. Probably

the plan is to frighten them and then release them—but who knows what the now-united Jewish leaders and Romans might decide to do."

"Hopefully you are right, Raheeb. I believe they are mostly fishermen from up north around the Sea of Galilee. The Romans will discourage any attempt to idolize Jesus. The Jews, too, will not want Jesus turned into a martyr. Both the Romans and Jews would probably be satisfied to warn the men to disband and to return to their nets."

The conversation edging too near the future, they dropped the topic and pursued another. And so they passed the Sabbath. Rejoicing over Raheeb's recovery, they chose not to probe too deeply into its timing. Significantly, they made no plans for the future although their fixed purpose in returning to Palestine had been to find Jesus.

CHAPTER 7

Raheeb

On the morning after the Sabbath, Raheeb awoke while darkness still reigned. Initially, he was thrilled to realize that he did not fear the day. It was a pleasure to breathe deeply, and not to be concerned that he would gasp for breath in doing so. Since his lingering illness the previous year, he had not had the strength of his youth or even middle years. During the last months, he had somehow mostly managed to hide his weakness from Gaspar and, thus, he had been able to accompany his king back to Palestine. Gaspar, of course, knew Raheeb was not completely well; this had been the main reason that Zaphta, each day, had gone ahead to secure lodgings and to prepare the way for the two older travelers.

What would this day bring? Would it be the most glorious day ever? Today, a man would rise from the dead. Had he really been blessed to see the son of God as an infant? To have held this child of destiny in his arms! Raheeb wondered when they would learn of the actual event. Perhaps it had happened already! Unable to sleep longer, he arose, dressed, and went downstairs. Others in the hostel still slept so he went out to the street where the sunrise was bathing the dawn in a halo of gold.

A sudden movement at the side of the inn caught his

attention. Someone seemed to be lurking in a storage area beside the building. "Who is there?" he challenged. Although no one replied, Raheeb felt certain that someone was nearby, rather than just some animal being startled. Knowing he should be more cautious, nonetheless he strode over to the side of the building where the noise had occurred. Investigating thoroughly, he could find no one. His thoughts turned to the thief known to be in the neighborhood. He had the feeling that the man had slept in the lean-to and that his own early rising had startled the sleeper. What would he be doing skulking here? Given what little Gaspar had learned of the man and of his crucified brother, Dismas, Raheeb wondered, as before, if he should fear for Gaspar's safety. Intuitively, though, he felt there was another reason than theft that the man was still in the area.

Dismissing the gang member from his mind, Raheeb considered what to do now. If Gaspar awoke and found him not there, he would be concerned. But it seemed ridiculous to wake him to say, "Go back to sleep, I am going to the gravesite. By the way, the thief might be near." Deciding it was still so early yet that he would not be missed, Raheeb turned west to where Gaspar had told him the grave was located.

Approaching the Gate of Ephraim in the northwestern sector of the city, a commotion drew his attention. Raheeb wondered who would be creating such a disturbance this early in the morning. Intent on seeking the tomb, he hoped he would not be kept from continuing his quest.

As if his own thoughts had forecast the scenario, Raheeb abruptly halted as soldiers dragged forward a young man, who was desperately struggling to escape. Two soldiers roughly clasped him, and Raheeb wondered at the panic in their voices.

"He's a thief!"

"This is your last crime for sure!"

"No, you're wrong! I spent the night in the city!" the young man shouted in vain.

"Someone took the body,[216] and you're a thief!"

The grizzled veteran growled, "You'll be hanging from a cross tomorrow—just like your brother!"

The words about someone taking a body compelled Raheeb to intervene; the threat of a brother on a cross spurred him to action. Even as he spoke, he wondered at his daring. "What are you doing with my servant?" he demanded.

All eyes stared at him in varying degrees of surprise, including those of his supposed servant. Hoping to keep the soldiers off guard, Raheeb knew that an authoritative tone would most impress them. "Unhand him, I say."

Seeming to ignore the soldiers, he then addressed the man he felt was surely a thief. "Young fool, running ahead of me. I should let these soldiers take you away, the little respect you show to me and to our king."

The mention of a king slightly unnerved the soldiers, but their natural Roman arrogance and training quickly reestablished itself. The leader angrily stated. "Your servant strangely resembles a thief we've been chasing for days!"

"Well, you will have to keep looking," Raheeb said firmly. "King Gaspar would be quite offended if you were to arrest one of his people."

Eyeing the captive's unkempt look, the soldier snorted in derision at this remark, but seemed less confident. One of the other soldiers spoke up. "We're wasting time here. The body snatchers are getting away as we stand here arguing."

Raheeb could not stop himself. "What body snatchers?"

Throwing a threatening look at his comrade, the first soldier said, "Grave diggers were looting this morning. Take your man. But be prepared to answer questions later about this affair. It's too early in the morning for honest people to be about!"

Although anxious to learn more about the grave diggers and the looting remark, and to find out why the soldiers were so obviously panicked, Raheeb thought it best to leave immediately. He realized that he would be subject to arrest himself if the soldiers found out how he had deceived them.

"Stay close this time," he harshly spoke to the released captive knowing the soldiers were still listening.

"Yes, master," the other responded, still dumbfounded at his luck.

Rapidly putting distance between themselves and the soldiers, neither man spoke. Raheeb felt that the youth was preparing to bolt as soon as he could. Without looking at the other, he ordered. "Don't be a fool, there are soldiers everywhere."

"Why did you do it?" the other prodded with no trace of gratitude.

"Do you know who I am?"

"You are with the other old man—probably his servant," the other snidely answered.

This confirmed for Raheeb that this was the thief who had helped Gaspar up Golgotha. "Why have you been hanging around my master? Do you seek to rob him?"

The youth threw him a murderous look, and angrily responded, "If I planned to rob him, it would have been done already."

"You will rue the day you harm my king."

"Do you think two old men scare me?"

"Does a cross on Calvary and an ending like your brother's scare *you*?" Satisfied that this effectively had impressed his brash companion, Raheeb sought the information he really wanted. "What was the talk about a body being stolen?"

"By all the gods, how would I know? All I care about at the moment is food." Noting Raheeb's stern look, he added, "I ran into those soldiers while trying to avoid three others. They're certainly in an uproar about something, that's for sure."

Raheeb looked upward and stated confidently: *"He has risen!"*

Wondering at the sanity of the man beside him, the other edged away, but considered it in his best interest to follow along for the time being.

Each wrapped in his own thoughts, they approached the inn in silence. Pausing before entering, Raheeb cautioned. "I warn you—harm no one in this place. I will seek counsel with King Gaspar as to what becomes of you."

"No man decides my fate!"

"If you choose to leave, do not plan to sleep where you did last night."

Startled and infuriated again, the younger man could find no words to respond as Raheeb opened the door and entered. With no better prospects and at least momentary safety, along with the possibility of food, he reluctantly followed.

Their entrance into the inn was met by several pairs of inquiring eyes. Gaspar, Abram, and Judith were in the common room, and Raheeb wondered what to say and where to begin. Recognizing the brother of the criminal

Dismas, Gaspar took the initiative. Not wanting to alarm Abram and his wife that a thief was in their midst, he greeted the newcomers. "Raheeb, who is your young friend?"

Having hoped to speak in private with Gaspar, and with no experience in fabricating the truth, Raheeb brought forth as honest a tale as he could. "I was out earlier and met this young man. After walking together, I asked him to break his fast here. I have brought you a customer, Abram."

The landlord looked askance at this opportunity and considered offering a bath rather than a meal to the disheveled newcomer. A customer was a customer, however, and if Raheeb vouched for him, he supposed it would be all right. He did doubt, however, if his establishment was safe with this man inside. Grudgingly, Abram offered. "Welcome, we have fresh fruit and bread."

Gaspar intently inquired. "What is your name, young man?"

Knowing that the old king had recognized him, he answered sullenly, "Daniel."

Judith's take on the whole matter was obvious with her next remark, "There is a known thief in the neighborhood. Raheeb, you were not wise to be walking alone so early."

Raheeb could wait no longer. "Sire, Abram, Judith, I have news—Jesus has risen!"

His words were greeted by degrees of incredulity.

"How can you know this?"

"What did you say?"

"Tell us what you have learned."

In his excitement, Raheeb forgot his efforts to shield the criminal. "Arising early, I decided to try to find Jesus' burial place since this would be the third day in the tomb.

When I arrived near the gates, soldiers had arrested Daniel, here, because they were seeking grave robbers."

Ignoring the remark about Daniel, Abram interrupted, "There is no proof in that!"

"I am certain it was Jesus whose body was missing!" Raheeb said excitedly.

Gaspar urged, "How can you be sure? Did they say his name?"

"No—they did not want me to learn what they were actually doing. But what other likely explanation could there be for the soldiers' panic? They spoke of a grave theft and were arresting Daniel."

Gaspar quietly addressed Daniel, "You were there first, please tell me what happened."

Daniel, who had been eating as soon as Judith placed the food in front of him, swallowed a large mouthful, and plainly preferred to take another bite of the loaf of bread clenched in his hand rather than to answer questions. All his life he had survived by his wits—half-truths or outright lies; now was no different. "I know nothing except that the soldiers were looking for a scapegoat and found me alone."

"They did not tell you why you were being arrested?"

"Raheeb told you already."

"Did they mention the name of Jesus?"

Gaspar noted the instant pain in the young man's eyes as the name apparently resurrected bitter memories of his brother dying with Jesus. Daniel looked down quickly, and as if the food in his mouth had turned to stone, muttered, "No."

Raheeb interjected, "The soldiers were shouting of someone taking a body. Grave looters do not take bodies; they take gold and other valuables. Soldiers on the day after the Sabbath are not out in numbers nor would they be panicked about grave robbers." He continued confidently. "Jesus' body was not in the tomb that the Roman soldiers had been assigned to guard. Jesus has arisen as he said. I believe it with all my heart."

His clear faith drew Daniel to let down his guard and say hopefully, "This Jesus died with my brother."

Judith, aghast at these words, shrieked, "I knew it! A thief at my table!"

"Silence, woman, we all know this," Abram commanded, though he had the grace to look sheepish at the exasperated look his wife threw him.

Gaspar intervened. "Dear Judith, please pardon this improper use of your establishment. Let us try to sort out what problems we might have brought you and decide on a course of action."

Judith sank into a nearby chair that King Gaspar drew out for her. She moaned aloud, "We'll all be arrested!"

Raheeb felt he had to make a clean breast of his part in this matter. "She might be right. I told them this man here was our servant, though they seemed to recognize him as part of Dismas' gang."

"Our gang was three people only and two died on Calvary."

Abram looked at his royal guest. "The soldiers will come sooner rather than later."

Gaspar instantly responded to the unspoken plea of his host. "We will depart immediately. Being uncertain ourselves of where we will go, you can truthfully tell the authorities that you were told nothing of our future plans."

Judith became an efficient force at this point. "Abram, go to my brother, he will find a way to help get them through the gates. Raheeb, why are you still sitting? Go—pack for your journey! King Gaspar, we must move quickly. You, there," she eyed Daniel who had started to rise, "do not move from where you sit!"

Each man instantly obeyed her commands and by mid-morning, the travelers were approaching the Water Gate of the city that was manned by three intent Roman soldiers. Gaspar and Raheeb exchanged worried looks as they slowed their camels.

"Halt!"

Raheeb responded. "King Gaspar and his two servants leave today for the Orient."

"No one leaves the city this day except by signed decree from the Governor."

"My good man, why?"

"I don't question orders. I just enforce them. Without papers, you won't leave."

"We could easily have obtained papers, but did not know of this requirement. Our business is urgent."

Arrogantly disregarding Raheeb, the guard impatiently demanded, "Why is that man's face covered? Show your face, *now*, or suffer Roman justice for your cowardice!"

Daniel, face and hands covered with linens, did not move.

Raheeb eased his camel forward to quietly address the guards. "Our companion is garbed such as he is so your eyes will not be offended. He has contracted the vilest of diseases—leprosy—while we have stayed in this miserable climate. Accept this offering, please, to use as you see fit to cleanse you or your city of his rotting flesh." Holding forth a bag weighted by coins, he shook it encouragingly.

Wanting the offered largesse, the soldier still knew

his duty. "First, he will have to show his face and speak." Crudely, he added, "We're seeking a dead man, and he qualifies it seems."

"His tongue has rotted, but your soldiers can undo the wrappings on his face. He has lost fingers, but can still ride with the reins wrapped around what is left of his hands."

"Raise your arms to show you still live," the guard ordered.

The specter slowly lifted hands and arms around which the reins were indeed wrapped. The camel snorted angrily when the reins tightened—whether by accident or design, no one could have known. As the animal viciously kicked out, the body swayed dangerously. None of the soldiers relished the task of looking beneath the wrappings. The coins were another story, however. Grabbing the hefty bag, the soldier curtly ordered. "Begone—before he falls off!"

As the travelers spurred their mounts through the gates of Jerusalem, one of the soldiers on duty spoke for all. "Dead men rising from the grave! Dead men riding camels! What's in that bag won't do any of us any good."

CHAPTER 8

A Brother's Fury

Wearily, the travelers halted the camels and prepared for the awkward moment of dismount. This was their eighth day of hard riding to put as many miles as possible between themselves and danger. Each evening, the two older men had collapsed with fatigue at the evening campsite. Daniel tended the animals and did the heavier camp duties. Fatigue left little desire for conversation except for brief directional comments. Theirs was an uneasy alliance, but all were interdependent upon one another.

Daniel was not in the least happy with the situation. Granted they had helped him escape, but as soon as he felt safe enough and had what he wanted from Gaspar, he planned to disappear. He could have traveled faster alone, but the safety represented by the king's power and money was not to be disregarded. Gaspar and Raheeb had left Jerusalem without having satisfactorily fulfilled their mission. Now, they were subject to arrest if Daniel's disguise was penetrated, and his identity became known. To have had to flee from justice in the company of a thief on the day when Jesus was to have proven himself to be the Son of God was bitter to both men.

Raheeb was totally dismayed to have placed his king in harm's way. Gaspar felt responsible for Raheeb since it had been his idea to return to Palestine in the first place. Their aching bones continuously reminding them they were no longer young, they depended more on Daniel as each hour passed. It was Daniel who decided where to pitch camp each night, and who tethered and fed the animals. Daniel was the one who put out the simple food that Judith had shared so liberally with them. He roused them each morning, and pushed them to their limits to distance themselves from Jerusalem.

Daniel was aware that Raheeb seemed particularly weary this evening, but he had decided that tonight would be his last with them. He was familiar with this area and the several caves in the surrounding hills that had harbored his brother and him in the past. It was a place favored by others who lived on the shady side of the law. These people would accept him, but not Gaspar and Raheeb. The fact that he would be on his own to fend for himself weighed heavily on him, but most of his regret was because his brother Dismas was dead. Now, he would have to depend on his own skills to survive. Clearly, he also needed to lay low for a time with the Romans actively seeking him.

He noticed Gaspar looking intently at him, and wondered if his uneasiness and plans to abandon them were that obvious. Not being one who spent time considering how others felt, he still realized it would be wrong to abandon the old men, particularly in this area of known ne'er-do-wells. Tonight, however, he was determined to succeed against Gaspar in what had turned into a quest for him.

In an effort to begin a conversation, Daniel inquired of Gaspar, "How does your hand feel?"

"If we did not have to ride each day, it would have healed quicker. Your leg seems to have improved."

"It was never much. A few more days ride north and east out of these hills, and you'll be safely on the road taking you to Damascus."

Gaspar leveled a look at Daniel and gently corrected. "Yes, we will all be safe then." As usual, Daniel was struck at the acuity displayed by the old king. He always seemed to be in control, and to know what Daniel was thinking even before he himself knew he was thinking it. For a person who made his living by outwitting others, this was a peculiar position to find himself in, day after day. He had even come to feel that the reason Gaspar went to bed so early each night was not just because he was exhausted, but also because it allowed him to avoid conversation. As if to again disconcert Daniel, Gaspar said, "You seem to know this area well, Daniel."

His natural instinct for self-preservation as usual coating his answer, Daniel vaguely responded. "Haven't been here for years."

"This area reminds me of the hill-country around Bethlehem with its caves."

"Yes, there are some in the area."

"A good place for such as we to rest in safety."

The irony of his phrasing was not lost on the young man who was beginning to enjoy the evening's sparring. "Safer for some than others." Raheeb, who was resting nearby, smiled at the exchange but had no desire to join in the verbal battle.

Gaspar asked, "Do you think you can abandon your disguise with our having ridden so far from Jerusalem?"

"We're not as far as you think. I'll keep it close in my robes in case a Roman patrol appears."

327

"It has been over a sennight, Daniel, with no pursuit. Can we assume that we are not being followed?"

"The closer you are to your kingdom, the safer you will be. Rome has a long arm. It would not do to disregard it. Keep moving."

Gaspar decided to challenge their young companion. "Your words this evening would seem to indicate the possibility that you are considering traveling alone."

"My way is not yours."

"Why must this be so?"

"Our paths go different ways."

Gently, Gaspar said, "Your brother's death could free you from those old ways."

Daniel shrugged while answering. "In our land there is an old saying, 'Once a thief, always a thief.'"

"Would your brother Dismas want you to die as he and your other comrade did?"

Rising abruptly, Daniel trod away into the night, growling his anger. "Leave it alone, old man!"

"How long did you stay with your brother that day?" Gaspar called out.

The words stopped Daniel in his tracks. Angrily, he wheeled toward Gaspar sneering his rage. "I stayed long enough to see him dying with your Jesus. Three criminals! One no better than the others!"

"I did not mean what you think I meant, Daniel," Gaspar said soothingly.

Refusing to be appeased, Daniel shouted and gestured wildly. "You don't know what I'm thinking or feeling or anything about me. My brother knew I was there for him. He knew that I would have sacrificed my life for him as he did for me."

"I was not faulting you for leaving. Daniel, I am sure your brother knew you loved him."

"You haven't any idea what kind of a man he was. He..." Daniel's emotions became too much for him, but he did not charge into the night again. Dropping to his knees, his shoulders slumped forward, and he hung his head.

"He...allowed you to escape while he fought the soldiers."

Attempting to stop the tears staining his cheeks, Daniel tightly closed his eyes. Trying to banish the scene that he had relived constantly since his brother's capture, he ground out. "I should have stayed and helped him. I was a coward. I ran—I let him be captured and he died to save me."

"You were injured. You would both have died. He wanted you to live."

Daniel stared blankly until Gaspar explained. "Soldiers eating at Abram's inn told us some of the details."

Halting at times, Daniel disjointedly spoke. "I had to see him one more time. I had to be there. It was the hardest thing I've ever done knowing what I'd see. I couldn't stay long—there were too few people and too many soldiers."

"Do you want me to tell you what happened?" Gaspar offered. "Is that why you followed me and have stayed with us?"

Daniel roughly responded. "I know what happened—he died miserably."

"Then what do you want from me?"

"He said something—I was too far away. Maybe—maybe you heard and might remember."

"I heard. I remember."

"Tell me."

"If I tell you, it will change you. It is nothing you might

think he would have said." Quietly, Gaspar added, "He did not speak of you."

Dejection apparent in every line of his body, Daniel seemed to seek further pain. "I must know. I have—had no one else."

Gaspar began to speak of Jesus, "The third person crucified that day..."

"Do not start about that man again! My brother is the important one to me!"

"He became important to your brother it seems."

Gaspar waited for any further reaction from Daniel. When none came, and Daniel's eyes remained downcast, Gaspar told of the words exchanged between Jesus and Dismas. After telling Daniel how Dismas had rebuked the third man, Gaspar ended, "Your brother came to believe in Jesus. His words carried deep conviction as he asked Jesus to remember him when he came into his kingdom. Jesus promised him more than remembrance, however. He proclaimed that both he and your brother would be that very day in paradise."[217]

Raheeb and Gaspar expected some immediate response, but none came. Daniel seemed to be made of stone until, at last, his shoulders heaved mightily as the two men respected his silence. After a few moments, Gaspar moved to give whatever consolation he might, but as he came near, Daniel startled him by harshly snarling. "No! I want none of your religious sympathy. Your Jesus caused the death of my brother!"

Raheeb cried out, "Daniel! How can you say such a thing?"

Violently, Daniel rose and shouted. "He would not have been on the cross if this Jesus had not filled his head with hope and lies." Angrily, he glared at Gaspar and Raheeb. "My brother was bewitched by your Jesus. Near the River Jordan, we had—a place where it was safe for us. A religious nut named John began to speak nearby and crowds came to hear him.[218] It was entertainment to see the people in their white robes being baptized. We used to while away the time joking about them in the heat of the day. Always he spoke of another who would come after him and whom the people should follow.[219] Dismas started to change. I told him he was a fool!

"I know now that we were in Jerusalem because Dismas was following Jesus. We would come across crowds in different towns where Jesus was—I thought we were trying to get rich off the religious fanatics! Dismas would disappear and then return later. I finally realized he was going out to hear the unbelievable words of this religious nut, just like he had listened to John." Daniel ranted on. "That is why he let me escape—he had become soft!"

Raheeb struggled to his feet and approached Daniel. "You are wrong. They were not lies, Daniel. Jesus promised those who believe in him everlasting life."[220]

"Who would want such a thing? Another life like this one?"

"No—a life of good deeds on earth—then the reward in the next."

"I never want to hear the name of Jesus again. I curse him, and you, and all that he said! Rising from the dead! What a trick—what a joke! My brother is dead! Do you hear me? Dead—because he listened to this man!"

Raheeb was searching for words to appease Daniel when suddenly he lurched forward. Slowly, he sank to the ground in obvious pain. Gaspar reached him first, although Daniel was closer.

"Raheeb, is this like before?"

Mutely, the older man nodded, and closed his eyes as another wave of pain shot through him.

"Daniel, help!" Gaspar pleaded.

CHAPTER 9

Revelations

In two weeks, much had changed. Summer's heat was upon the land. Gaspar daily worried if Raheeb would make it home. Daniel had reluctantly helped them find shelter in a cave where he had stayed in the past. He had clearly violated an unwritten code in bringing the two men to the isolated area where men on the other side of the law regularly sheltered. Gaspar had expected Daniel to abandon them once he had learned what his brother had said from the cross. With Raheeb stricken again, however, the young man had stayed on, although he openly desired to leave them.

As they sat in the coolness of twilight on this evening, Gaspar asked him why he had stayed. Daniel succinctly answered. "You helped me when you could have as easily let me fend for myself. Raheeb saved me when the soldiers had me under arrest. I pay my debts." Suddenly, he stopped speaking and strained to see in the faint light. Gaspar, alerted by Daniel placing his fingers to his lips ordering silence, waited in some alarm.

Out of the darkness, a voice called, "Can anyone hear me? I've lost my way—is anyone here?"

Deciding the voice was more alarmed than alarming, Gaspar ignored Daniel's hiss for further silence and called out, "Here, friend. Come, join us."

"Peace to you. My thanks for your words of welcome." The newcomer relieved his listeners by his mild greeting and pacific demeanor. Their visitor had a luxuriant head of pure white hair and a beard equally as white. His clothes were simple, and he carried nothing but a walking staff.

"Sit here," Gaspar welcomed. "Daniel, please bring the water gourd to refresh our fellow traveler."

His history betraying him, Daniel demanded. "Where do you hail from that you carry no water or other provisions? We're a long way from anywhere."

"What need is there to worry when people like you befriend me daily. I need no extra coat nor money. Possessions would only slow me."[221]

"What is your name?" inquired Gaspar.

"I am called Levi or Matthew, whichever you choose."

Trenchantly, Daniel almost threatened the traveler. "Why two names?"

"Formerly I was a tax collector and was known as Levi by most who knew me. My new friends call me Matthew."[222]

Before Daniel could throw out another insult, Gaspar said, "Well, we are new friends and shall call you Matthew. I am Gaspar and this is Daniel. Our companion, Raheeb, is resting over there."

"Again, my thanks. I was afraid I had become lost and had not followed the directions given to me."

Daniel eyed both Gaspar and Matthew mutinously as he returned to his interrogation. "Where are you bound?"

Calmly, Matthew answered. "After this stop, I am on my way to Galilee."

"You are certainly lost if it is Galilee you seek."

"I have a friend who I believe may be in this area. I

decided to come here first because of the good news[223] I bring him, although you are right, it is out of my way."

Daniel's abrupt tone conveyed his meaning. "Tomorrow you can be on your way."

"Matthew is welcome to rest here in our camp as long as he cares to do so, Daniel. Possibly you can help him find his friend when he is ready to resume his journey."

"Since you have welcomed me as you have, I gladly accept your offer. Blessings on you, Gaspar." Tentatively, Matthew continued, directing his words more to Gaspar than to Daniel. "Perhaps you might be interested in the good news I have brought?"

Daniel rudely interrupted. "By the gods, why would we be interested in news you have brought for someone else?"

"My words are for all people."

Daniel looked confused at Matthew's response. Gaspar stared intently at the newcomer, before he carefully said, "We would welcome the news. Have you been in Jerusalem?"

"I have been in Jerusalem for many days. Having been directed to go to Galilee, I felt the need to inform an old acquaintance of the great events which have recently occurred."

Daniel sneered. "This would be a friend who called you Levi?"

Unruffled, Matthew answered. "Yes, you are right, Daniel."

"You do know that the people in this area are cutthroats, thieves and other assorted ruffians?"

"Is that what you are?"

"Daniel, cease plaguing our guest. Matthew, please, do share the news with us. To what great events do you refer?"

Matthew suddenly seemed unsure of himself and of what to say.

Daniel shook his head in disgust, but Gaspar continued undeterred. "Is your news from Jerusalem concerning events around the time of the Passover?"

"Were you there then?"

"I witnessed a crucifixion."

"You were on Calvary?"

As Gaspar nodded, Matthew could not look him in the face. "We were...I should have been there, but I was afraid—we all were. All of us apostles—we were his chosen followers, but we failed him in his hour of need. All except John who was the youngest among us."[224]

"I knew him longer than you did," Gaspar replied gently.

Matthew leaned forward, eagerly asking, "How could this be?"

"Do you know the story of the birth of Jesus?"

"No, but how could you, if I do not?"

"I was there."

Incredulously, Matthew and Daniel stared at the old man. Gaspar said, "Raheeb was there too. We followed a star to his birthplace at Bethlehem in Galilee of Judea. Two other magi from Eastern countries also read the signs in the heavens. In our wonder at the phenomena in the skies, we each sought further enlightenment and knowledge. For months, we each individually, had followed the celestial omens. Eventually, we found one another. The star led us to a humble dwelling where Jesus, his mother, Mary, and Joseph were living.[225] But enough of the distant past, tell us your news."

Once more, Matthew hesitated, although it was clear that at least Gaspar and Raheeb yearned to hear they knew not what. Raheeb finally requested baldly. "Did Jesus rise from the dead?"

"Yes, he arose."[226]

"You—you have seen him?" Raheeb implored.

"I have both seen and spoken to him."[227]

"My God," Raheeb breathed in awe.

"Impossible!" Daniel roared out.

Gaspar urged, "Tell us everything."

"I caution you that the chief priests and elders refuse to acknowledge that Jesus rose. They say it is impossible— as Daniel thinks is the case. They accuse us of stealing his body.[228] We are the most obvious suspects, along with several others who associated with him. Even the Zealots, the fighting faction of the Jews, are suspected. The Romans have not yet realized what this miracle means. They are strictly concerned with keeping the peace."

Matthew continued. "As I told you, he rose from the dead. It was on the third day after his death, at dawn. Mary Magdalene, one whom Jesus saved from herself, and other holy women were bringing perfumed oils to properly anoint the body for burial.[229] They and the Roman soldiers found the huge stone rolled back in front of the place where Jesus had been buried. After the soldiers ran to report the theft, a man in dazzling snow-white garments addressed the women. 'There is no need for you to be afraid. I know you are looking for Jesus, who was crucified. He is not here, for he has risen, as he said he would. Come and see the place where he lay, then go quickly and tell his disciples.'[230]

"Overjoyed, yet fearful too, the women hurried to carry the same good news I have just shared with you. Jesus honored Mary Magdalene by appearing to her first. The other apostles and I had gathered together in fear in the same room where we had celebrated our last meal together with Jesus. We found Mary's story difficult to believe, but only Peter and John had the courage to run to the tomb.[231]

"Since he arose from the dead, he has appeared to many of us. He greets us with words of peace as I greeted you tonight. The first time he appeared, he showed us the wounds in his hands and his side."[232] Matthew paused at the powerful memory of the crucified, glorious Christ. Before continuing, he looked toward Gaspar and Raheeb then finally at Daniel. "He gave us a commission, 'As the Father sent me, so am I sending you.'"[233]

"What did he mean?" begged Gaspar.

"We are to spread his teachings. As he did while on earth, we have the power to forgive sins.[234] We preach and teach that love of neighbor and good deeds are the means to eternal life."

"You said he has come to you several times?"

"Yes, on the first occasion my good friend Thomas was not present. You have to know Thomas to appreciate what happened. He has a reputation for having to see things with his own eyes before believing. Anyway, after we told him Jesus had come while he was out shopping for food, he would not accept our story. I still cringe at what he dared to say. 'Unless I see the holes that the nails made in his hands and can put my finger into the holes they made, and unless I can put my hand into his side, I refuse to believe.'[235]

"Obviously, we were shocked that Thomas would say such a thing about The Master's wounds. About a week later, despite locked doors, Jesus came again. 'Peace be with you,' he said. Then he spoke to Thomas words that I will never forget: 'Put your finger here; look, here are my hands. Give me your hand; put it into my side. Doubt no longer but believe.' [236]

"'My Lord and my God!'[237] Thomas exclaimed.

"Jesus said to him. 'You believe because you can see me. Happy are those who have not seen and yet believe.'"[238]

Gaspar and Raheeb spoke in unison. *"I believe."*

Matthew smiled his approval. Daniel said nothing, but it was apparent that Matthew's words had made an impression on him. He found the courage to ask. "All the others believed, including you?"

"Well, the first time, I admit some of us thought he might be a ghost. That was when he calmed us, by offering, 'Touch me, and see for yourselves; a ghost has no flesh and bones as you can see I have.'[239] Joyfully, we shared our meal of grilled fish with him. Later we talked that a ghost would not have need of food."[240]

Daniel tried to convey disinterest. "What did you mean that he teaches forgiveness?"

Considering carefully before speaking, Matthew finally responded to Daniel's question. "Let me tell you the story of how I first met Jesus. One day, back when I was known as Levi—" Matthew paused to grin at Daniel. "I was sitting outside the Customs House collecting taxes for Herod Antipater. Jesus walked past and said, 'Follow me.'[241] I could not help myself, and so I left my work and followed him to hear his words.

"In his honor that evening, I held a reception in my house. I invited many friends and acquaintances. The Pharisees, becoming aware of this, were horrified and accused Jesus to the disciples, 'Why does your master eat with tax collectors and sinners?'[242]

"Jesus told the Pharisees, 'It is not the healthy who need

the doctor, but the sick. Go and learn the meaning of the words: *What I want is mercy, not sacrifice.* And indeed I did not come to call the virtuous, but sinners.'"[243]

Matthew directed his words to the young man. "Daniel, after his resurrection, Jesus met and spoke with us often and opened our minds to a new understanding. As the Messiah—the Savior of the world—he suffered and died for our sins. My sins….your sins….the sins of all peoples since the time of Abraham and Isaac. Indeed, since the beginning of time. His death upon the cross—the son of man and the son of God—opened the gates of heaven. Sincere sorrow for sins, penance, and then the remission of sins—we are to teach and to baptize those from all nations who choose to follow his way."

Gaspar eagerly spoke. "Matthew, will you come to my kingdom and teach my son and my people about Jesus and his words of healing, forgiveness, and mercy?"

The apostle responded without hesitation. "I will, Gaspar. I will come."

Through the night, Matthew, Raheeb and Gaspar exchanged stories about Jesus. Matthew told of the three years of public life, while Gaspar and Raheeb spoke of Jesus' birth and their later stay with his holy family. Gaspar shared many of the works that he and the other magi had studied before they followed the star to Bethlehem.

Matthew absorbed the details of that special journey. In discussing Herod the Great's motives, he told them of his own encounters with Herod's son, Antipas, for whom the taxes were collected and then delegated. "I became a tax collector because I could read and write and use the abacus. I was well paid, but became ostracized because of my job and relationship with Herod. Jesus did not shun me. He loved me for what I was.

"Gaspar, I will tell your people that Jesus lived as he taught. He told us to obey the Law of Moses, but also that the two greatest commandments were even above these. First, he said we are to love God, his Father, with our whole being. Second, we are to love our neighbor as ourselves.[244] During the years I spent with him, he taught of a loving, merciful, yet just God. He reviled no people except hypocrites and those who follow the laws so closely that they do not love their neighbors. I saw him lose his temper just once, and that was in the Temple when he chastised the moneylenders."

As the stars glimmered above on a gloriously clear night, Daniel listened to words that promised salvation. He looked at the three men and considered how unlike they were, yet each was united in a faith that the long-awaited Messiah had been in their presence. They talked openly of cures and events the likes of which the earth had never seen. A small but distinct part of him wanted to accept this offer of a new world and a new way of life, but his own entrenched experience to have faith and trust only in himself and his brother were too engrained.

When Daniel finally prepared to sleep, he expected to toss and turn, to dream erratically of angels and spirits walking on water. Instead, his dreams were sweet remembrances of his older brother Dismas and his childhood, and he lay wrapped in sleep well past the dawn. He awoke to find Matthew and Gaspar talking still and wondered if they had done so all night. It surprised him to feel disappointed that he might have missed something important.

Gaspar finally noticed that Daniel was awake and greeted him. "Good morning. Matthew has decided he must be on his way. He lingered to say farewell to you."

Matthew approached and warmly embraced Daniel who, feeling awkward, shrugged free quickly.

Taking no offense, the kind-hearted man took his leave of Daniel. "We will meet again when I fulfill my promise to Gaspar."

Reacting churlishly at this assumption, Daniel answered. "No. You will not see me. I'm only with these two for a few days more."

Matthew ignored his answer, instead responding, "Peace to you, Daniel." Turning to Gaspar and Raheeb, he bade them farewell. Individually, he addressed Gaspar before he strode out of sight. "You have the right of it, I should record the events of Jesus' life."

The Good Shepherd

After Matthew's departure, it had been decided that if Daniel could find one or two men to help with chores and assist in conveying Raheeb on a portable bed of sorts, then they could make better progress. They had traveled in this way for a number of days trying to keep the ill man as comfortable as possible. The previous evening, the men had demanded their pay. This morning, not too surprisingly, the three had awakened to find the men gone. With no other alternative, the decision had been made to return to their previous way of slowly moving with Raheeb.

Now, at midday and with little progress, they found themselves on the edge of a large flock of sheep. Shepherds in the distance were tending the animals. Rather than trek wide around the flock or cut through the center scattering the sheep, the travelers decided to call it a day and to make camp in this area of clear and sparkling waters. The frisking lambs provided amusement for the weary Raheeb, and he declared pleasantly, "How wonderful to live this way. I could remain here forever."

They heard anxious bleating in the hills to their left, and Daniel chuckled that one of the lambs had wandered too far. The calls became distant and Raheeb worried aloud that it would become lost. He gently urged Daniel to go after it, but the younger man countered. "A lost sheep is not my concern. It wouldn't come to me anyway. It would be too scared and would only run farther." Raheeb noticed one of the shepherds moving toward the hills. Alert that one of those in his care had wandered, he was apparently intent on finding it, and bringing it back to the flock. Watching the man until he was out of sight, Raheeb shared what he had seen. "Don't worry, one of the shepherds knows what has happened."

Daniel jested, with a newfound humor. "I'll stop getting ready to look."

Several hours later, while the flock had meandered south of them, the same shepherd appeared in the distance. He moved toward their camp, and they noticed a young lamb nestled in his arms.

Gaspar called a welcome. "Please, join us for a while. Take some refreshment."

As he entered the clearing, the shepherd soothed the young animal with a graceful gesture. Calmly, he spoke his thanks for the invitation, before announcing. "'My peace I give you.'"[245] Without any self-consciousness, he moved toward Raheeb first. Extending his hand, he placed it on Raheeb's arm so that the sick man would stop struggling to stand. "May my lamb rest with you?"

"Will he stay?"

"He brings my own special peace to you, my friend."

Raheeb settled back on his pallet and momentarily pondered the strange answer. His eyes remained riveted on the shepherd.

Daniel wondered why the man's beauty and gracious words appeared to leave the sick man awe-struck. When Daniel handed the shepherd a cup of water, he noticed that the man's beauty was marred by fresh scars. His hands had wounds that seemed still to be healing. In accepting the cup, the stranger briefly locked eyes with Daniel as if acknowledging a special bond between them.

As he turned from Daniel, the man went toward Gaspar, who had intended to speak. Instead, the shepherd addressed him. "You have traveled far, but your reward will be great." The words seemed to have a deeper meaning, and Gaspar wondered that the man—though a stranger—could seem to know him.

The shepherd sat on an elevated rock and drank deeply from the cup Daniel had given him. No one seemed inclined to break the silence although there was no awkwardness in the situation. The man exuded an indescribable presence that was nevertheless calming.

Eventually, it was Daniel who broke the stillness. "Your friends and the flock have moved on."

"We are old friends.[246] They can find me if there is need."

They seemed puzzled by his words, and he questioned them. "'What man among you with a hundred sheep, losing one, would not leave the ninety-nine in the wilderness and go after the missing one till he found it? And when he found it, would he not joyfully take it on his shoulders and then, when he got home, call together his friends and neighbors?'"[247] The man then finished his story. "If he succeeds in finding it, believe me, he is happier about this one than about the ninety-nine that did not wander away."[248]

While telling this story, the shepherd had seemed particularly to be focused on Daniel, although it was Gaspar who spoke up when he finished. "Yes, you are right. As a ruler—a leader—when I brought happiness or justice to one of my people who was disheartened or who needed my help, it always gave me greater happiness than when I was helping those who had more."

The shepherd addressed him. "Wise, Gaspar." The old king knew his name had not been told to the shepherd. He peered closer and recognition dawned on him in a spiritual awakening. Smiling gently, the shepherd made a request. "Have you any bread and wine that we might sup together?"

While noting, but not understanding Gaspar's stunned look, Daniel responded that they had some left. He brought what little they had, and apologized for the small amount.

"There will be plenty for all."

While the man took charge of the preparations, Daniel was surprised to note the broad smiles being exchanged by Raheeb and Gaspar.

Inexplicably, it seemed appropriate that the shepherd should bless the meal and then share it. Extending his hands over the bread and wine, he looked toward each of them. "'Do this as a memorial of me.'"[249]

Rising, he approached Raheeb. Holding out first the bread and then the cup of wine, he quietly spoke. Gaspar heard his final words and briefly closed his eyes. "Your pain will cease tonight, my faithful Raheeb."

To Daniel, he spoke only briefly. "You will labor long, but your work will be rewarded in heaven." He extended the bread and wine toward Daniel who reached for both, not taking his eyes from the shepherd's face.

Turning to Gaspar, the spiritual personage smiled deeply. "As you came to me in the beginning, and are here now, ever shall you be with me in a world without end."

At his words of limitless possibilities, their eyes closed to consider his message. When they looked again, he was no longer in the camp.

THE END

AUTHOR'S NOTES FOR
A KING'S STORY in
TRILOGY OF THE MAGI

Written 2008/Updated 2022

A King's Story has been a work of love for me. When I wondered at my temerity in writing such a book, became anxious over details, or worried about writer's block, again and again I felt the presence of God. As I wrote, whether I was riding in my car or sitting in church, I prayed for signs of spiritual support, and after several such times, I peacefully waited for them to occur—as I had begun to know would happen.

To be specific, let me share the first such occurrence. The initial plot came to me one January morning while driving to my teaching job in a public school. Four months later, as the school year was coming to a close—and I admit that I had completely forgotten about the idea—once again, out of the blue, the storyline came to me. This time, I thought to myself, summer is here, and I now have the time to write.

On that second drive, then and there, I decided that for research purposes, it would be necessary to immerse myself in Roman history as well as in biblical times. In addition, I would have to learn more about the ancient religion of the Jews. I felt I would probably need to get a second *Bible* because I might be turning pages quickly, and I would not want to risk the family heirloom. Then, I mentally cruised through possible books to read for research, and decided I would find a copy of *The Robe,* which I had never read—at that time I thought the events in it took place about 100 years after the crucifixion.

When I arrived at the public school where I worked, a note was in each teacher's mailbox that books would be available for the taking, due to the library's end-of-the-year giveaway of old or unused books. At 12:35 p.m., when my combined lunch and prep period began, I finally entered the library—not expecting that anything of value would be left by that time. Astoundingly, I walked straight to the end of the center table of discarded books, and there, side-by-side, lay <u>both</u> an old paperback *Bible* and the most dilapidated copy of *The Robe,* you could ever imagine. Both books, of course, are still in my possession.

My book is grounded in research by scholars before me, and in the words of the Evangelists. Words from Biblical passages were frequently used—as many readers surely noticed. Credit for the text and verses I used to reveal the events in the lives of Jesus, Mary and Joseph, goes to and is attributed, to that 1968 copy of *The Jerusalem Bible* left in the public school library. A major resource was the voluminous text *The Birth of the Messiah* by the scholar Raymond E. Brown, S.S. This book was recommended to me by Bill Shea, a parent of one of my older son's friends, who at that time was a professor at Saint Louis University. In Brown's book, I found a brief statement that the Holy Family was apparently robbed while in Egypt. An important portion of the plot thus fell into place, and became the Prologue of this last book of *Trilogy of the Magi.*

My then sixteen-year-old son, Bret, through his

education at St. Louis Priory, was my compadre on research, my helpful gopher, and initial proofreader. I would say, for instance, "Now I need the name of the well in the Jerusalem Temple." Within moments (and pre-Google) he usually had the requested information. I should note also that our family *Bible* was eventually used for study purposes—the most it had ever been used! Bret was invaluable in chatting with me about details of the men and women who lived two thousand years ago. A special thanks is due to Bret's teachers who imparted their knowledge to him. My thanks also to Bret for his perceptive words when he read the last chapter.

So that there will be no sibling rivalry, I am grateful as well to my younger son, Nick, who was in primary school when I originally wrote this book, and who supported me, hugged me, and made more than one meal for himself. I am certain that his months of cooperation came from his heart rather than my statement that we were going to Disney World after the book was completed.

I am grateful to all my family for their encouragement. Special thanks goes out to my Mom (still) and to my sister Marigold, both excellent proofreaders. My older sister, Philipa, gets a major thanks because she was the person who gave me pertinent background about Matthew, the Evangelist, for whom she had named her beloved son. This leads me to share with you another of those special spiritual moments I experienced in the initial writing of *A King's Story.*

Before I learned that *only in Matthew's Gospel can be found "The visit of the Magi,"* I told my sister that in honor of her stillborn child, whom she had named Matthew, that I had decided that I was going to use him (rather than Mark,

Kathryn Muehlheausler

Luke or John) to be the person who tells Gaspar, Raheeb, and Daniel about the events of Easter morning. She then told me she was fairly certain that Matthew was the Gospel writer who had gone to some of the lands of the wise men to do his work, and that he had died there.

Who invited Matthew to come to those distant lands? Was it actually King Gaspar himself? Why is the story of the three kings found only in the Gospel of Matthew? Could it have been Gaspar who first encouraged Matthew to write his Gospel?

With the above questions in mind, can it be doubted that at least one of the magi—those three kings of Christmas lore—would have wanted to discover what became of the baby boy whom the star of Bethlehem led them to decades earlier? Logically, the youngest would have been most able to live another thirty-three years, and to still be energetic enough to travel. Having Gaspar return to Jerusalem during what is known as Holy Week, and to unwittingly be a part of the Palm Sunday cavalcade, gave me the nucleus for *A King's Story*—and was the original idea that suddenly came to me that January morning.

Gaspar and Raheeb, together with the young gang member Daniel, and the hard-working Judith and Abram, represent all peoples whom Jesus the Christ, came to inspire and to save—high born, low born; Christian, non-Christian; male, female; scholar, scamp. In the opening chapters, the Greeks, Edomites and other wayfarers, along with the Jewish/Aramaic trader Sahran and his sister carry this same message that the Good News is for all people in all places.

Creating Daniel, the fictional ne'er-do-well brother of Dismas, the Good Thief, introduced the theme that Jesus

350

was born and died for all of us, and also provided a younger man to assist Gaspar when Raheeb became ill again. The Good Shepherd of the last chapter, who is visiting the shepherds of Christmas Eve, is concerned not only for the flock, but will go to any length to save the lost sheep, i.e. Daniel.

As for the title of this last book on the magi, I leave it up to you, the readers, to decide who the King may be.

My hope is that *A King's Story*—and now *Trilogy of the Magi*—will help spread the message that the Good News is for all times including the exciting early years of our newest millennium. Men and women of good will hopefully celebrate the past, and look to the future, as the world strives to live the words of the man humbly born in a stable at Bethlehem who desired all peoples to love his Father and their neighbor as themselves.

ENDNOTES

The Jerusalem Bible. Reader's Edition, United States of America, Doubleday & Company, Inc., 1968

Melchior's Book

1. Deuteronomy
2. Genesis 1:1
3. Exodus 3:14
4. Genesis 4:26
5. Genesis 4:26
6. Genesis 5:8
7. Genesis 5:31
8. Numbers 24:17
9. Genesis 5:27
10. Genesis 5:32
11. Isaiah 1:4-5
12. Isaiah 2:5-10
13. Isaiah 7:9
14. Isaiah 7:14
15. Isaiah 11:1-6
16. Daniel 6:17
17. Daniel 6:20
18. Daniel 6:22
19. Daniel 6:26-27
20. Daniel 7:13-14
21. Isaiah 45:1
22. Daniel 4:34
23. Daniel 5:31
24. Daniel 6:2-9
25. Daniel 6:9
26. Daniel 6:10-19
27. Daniel 6:20-26
28. Daniel 6:27
29. Daniel 14:27
30. Daniel 7:3-7
31. Daniel 10:5
32. Matthew 2:2
33. Micah 5:2
34. Matthew 2:8
35. Matthew 2:9
36. Matthew 2:2

Balthazar's Book

37. Proverbs 9:10
38. Matthew 2:8
39. Micah 5:2
40. Matthew 2:9
41. Matthew 2:11
42. Luke 2: 6

43 Luke 2:7
44 Isaiah 7:14
45 Luke 2:4
46 Luke 2:1
47 Luke 2:4
48 Luke 2:7
49 Luke 2:8
50 Luke 2:9-16
51 Luke 2:20
52 Daniel 7:13-14
53 Luke 2:21-24
54 Luke 2:25-26
55 Luke 2:27-32
56 Luke 2:33-35
57 Luke 2:51
58 Luke 2:36-38
59 Luke 1:5-7
60 Luke 1:8-10
61 Luke 1:11-12
62 Luke 1:13-14
63 Luke 1:15-17
64 Luke 1:18
65 Luke 1:19
66 Luke 1:20
67 Luke 1:21-23
68 Luke 1: 24-25
69 Luke 1:26-27
70 Luke 1:28
71 Luke 1:29
72 Luke 1:30-33
73 Luke 1:34
74 Luke 1:35

75 Luke 1:36-37
76 Luke 1:38
77 Luke 1:38
78 Luke 1:39-40
79 Luke 1:41-45
80 Luke 1:46-49
81 Luke 1:56
82 Luke 1:57
83 Luke 1:58-60
84 Luke 1:61
85 Luke 1:62-63
86 Luke 1:64
87 Luke 1:68-69, 72-73
88 Luke 1:76, 79
89 Luke 1:65-66
90 Matthew 1:19
91 Matthew 1:20-21
92 Matthew 1:22-23
93 Matthew 1:24-25
94 Daniel 8:16
95 Luke 2:8
96 Luke 2:9
97 Luke 2:10-12
98 Luke 2:13-14
99 Luke 2:15
100 Genesis 43:33
101 Matthew 2:12
102 Matthew 2:12
103 Psalms 8:2
104 Luke 2:42, 46-47
105 Matthew 2:16
106 Matthew 2:16

Gaspar's Story—*A King's Story*

107 John 20:30
108 Matthew 2:2
109 Luke 3:23

110 Luke 2:1, 4
111 Luke 2:9
112 Matthew 2:12

113 Matthew 2:16
114 Matthew 2:14
115 Matthew 2:19–20
116 Luke 4:31
117 John 12:12
118 John 6:2
119 John 6:9–12
120 John 11:1
121 Matthew 5:17
122 John 11:6
123 John 11:21–22
124 John 11:35, 37
125 John 11:39
126 John 11:39
127 John 11:40
128 John 11:41
129 John 11:43–44
130 Luke 9:49
131 Matthew 21:9
132 John 12:13
133 John 5:1, 8–9
134 Matthew 21:11
135 John 8:2
136 Matthew 9:10
137 Luke 19:45–46
138 Luke 20:2
139 Luke 20:3
140 Luke 20:4
141 Luke 20:5–7
142 Matthew 22:18–19
143 Matthew 22:19–20
144 Matthew 22:21
145 Matthew 22:21
146 Luke 20:9–17
147 Matthew 22:1–13
148 Matthew 22:14
149 Matthew 11:15
150 Matthew 13:13

151 Luke 22:47
152 John 18:12–13
153 John 18:10
154 Matthew 26:14–16
155 Matthew 26:57
156 Matthew 26:59
157 Matthew 27:2
158 Luke 23:7
159 Matthew 27:19
160 Matthew 14:3, 6–10
161 Luke 23:8
162 Luke 23:11
163 Luke 22:67–69
164 Luke 22:70
165 Luke 22:71
166 Luke 23:11
167 Mark 15:13
168 John 18:29
169 John 18:30
170 John 18:31
171 John 18:31
172 Matthew 26:24
173 John 18:22
174 Luke 23:3
175 Matthew 27:21
176 Matthew 27:20
177 Matthew 27:21
178 Matthew 27:22
179 Matthew 27:23
180 Matthew 27:24
181 Mark 15:15
182 Matthew 27:28
183 John 19:17
184 Luke 23:33
185 John 19:18
186 Mark 15:24
187 John 19:21
188 John 19:21

189 Matthew 27:40
190 Matthew 27:42
191 Luke 23:34
192 Luke 23:39
193 Luke 23:40–41
194 Luke 23:42
195 Luke 23:43
196 John 19:26
197 John 19:27
198 Mark 15:34
199 Matthew 27:47
200 Mark 15:34
201 Luke 23:46
202 Mark: 15:38
203 John 19:31–34
204 Mark 15:39
205 Mark 15:43
206 Matthew 27:58
207 John 19:41
208 Isaiah 53:5
209 Matthew 16:21
210 Mark 15:38
211 Matthew 27:62-65
212 Matthew 27:63
213 Matthew 27:46
214 Luke 23:46
215 Exodus 35:2–3
216 Matthew 28:13
217 Luke 23:43
218 Matthew 3:13
219 Matthew 3:11
220 Matthew 16:25
221 Luke 9:3
222 Luke 5:27
223 Mark 16:15
224 John 19:26
225 Matthew 2:9–11
226 Matthew 28:6

227 John 20:19–20
228 Matthew 28:13
229 Mark 16:1–2
230 Matthew 28:2–7
231 John 20:3
232 John 20:20
233 John 20:21
234 John 20:22–23
235 John 20:25
236 John 20:26–27
237 John 20:28
238 John 20:29
239 Luke 24:37–39
240 Luke 24:43
241 Matthew 9:9
242 Matthew 9:10–11
243 Matthew 9:12–13
244 Mark 12:29–31
245 John 14:27
246 Luke 2:16
247 Luke 15:4-5
248 Matthew 18:13
249 Luke 22:19

ABOUT THE AUTHOR

Kathryn Muehlheausler is a teacher and tutor, devoted Christian, and a mother to many over the years. *Trilogy of the Magi* is a passion project grounded in research by scholars and in the words of the evangelists. See kathiem. com for her other books including *Friar Tuck aka Friar Tuq*, and *A King's Story,* as well as surprising events of how the magi's story first came to her.

- To pronounce Muehlheausler, simply say mule-house-ler!